SIX MOONS, SEVEN GODS

THE LEGENDS OF BAELON

Robert A. Walker

Robert A. Walker

For my father, who taught me to write,
and my mother, who taught me to love.

Baelon

PROLOGUE

"Don't cry, my love, my little one. You shall never be alone."
Queen Isadora, age 22, to Princess Lewen on the day of her birth.

Sleep had never been so difficult to find. Not here. Not in this isolated haven where demons, real and imagined, dared not tread. The House at Dewhurst, nestled in the fringe of the Forgotten Lands and surrounded for as far as the eye could see by fields and woods, had long served as Queen Isadora's favorite retreat from the pressures of absolute rule. Yet something gnawed at her; something she could not name. Still restless, she rose from her bed to pad barefoot across the floor. A light breeze stirred her curtains as she opened the balcony door.

She assured herself she deserved this break. The rigors of planning the annual Lords and Ladies Feast had absorbed her the past moon. She regretted leaving the king to tie up loose ends, but she could no longer bear to work with the steward. Or to be in his company. Perhaps this was the root of her insomnia. When she returned to the castle, she would broach the subject with her husband.

But there was something else. She could sense it.

She stepped onto the balcony. It was the seventh moon of the almon. The morning air was crisp and cool, swept from the west by damp winds born over the Mersal Sea. Far to the east, the towering Lumax Mountain range lay like a giant serpent, separating the kingdoms of Aranox and Tegan. She wished it could be made to slither south and provide instead a barrier to the troubled Lawless Lands.

Hushed voices rose from below. An occasional clank of metal, a swish of cloth, the click of boot heel on stone—these were the only other sounds to greet her. *Back in Fostead, they would all be drowned by the village orchestra: carriages and carts rolling over cobblestones, street hawkers clamoring to be heard, the rhythmic clang of hammer on anvil...*

Louder voices, agitated and concerned, shook the queen from her reverie. Hands on the balcony railing, she leaned forward apprehensively, straining to hear more clearly.

"What do you make of it?" a deep voice asked.

"Still too distant," another replied.

Isadora could see nothing out of the ordinary. Scrub brush, rock-strewn dirt and patches of tall grass eventually surrendered to a forest of joining trees, its canopy of green, brown, and yellow hiding all beneath it.

More noise from below again caused the queen to shift her gaze. Four of the royal guard were now visible as they moved from beneath her balcony and across the courtyard. They walked at arm's length from each other, stopping simultaneously to stare into the distance. She noted with a hint of relief that none saw fit to draw a weapon.

"Do you see what I mean?" It was Rolft, the eldest and most trusted of her personal guards.

"I do." The unmistakable baritone of Fereliss.

"As do I," said Yurik, pointing to the east.

The queen looked again, and this time she saw it. A speck of moving dust had emerged from the distant woods. She stared at it intently until she was certain it was moving toward her rather than away. *Here it comes!*

"I see the horse, but are you certain of the rider? If so, your eyes are sharper than mine." It was Garth, the youngest and largest of her guards.

The rider? A wave of regret accompanied Isadora's sudden recollection of the previous evening's tense stand-off between Rolft and her daughter. The queen had put a quick end to it. *"You say 'cannot' Rolft, but the princess is of age now. If she desires to ride alone tomorrow, so be it. We shall not speak of this again."* Her heart began to race as she peered to the east. *Stay calm!* The speck was growing into a small dust cloud churning barren ground. *No, wait!* The flicker of long grey legs! It was a horse, but she could see no rider. And there was something awkward about the animal's gait.

"I'm sure of it now." Rolft's tone left little doubt as to his conviction or concern.

The queen resisted the impulse to scream aloud. *Sure of what!?* Regret was quickly turning to dread.

"It cannot be." Yurik glanced back at her with a furrowed brow, and then quickly looked away.

"Lewen," Fereliss said.

Isadora's mouth opened at the sound of her daughter's name, but no words escaped. *Lewen's horse...without a rider?* Her eyes were riveted on the galloping stallion, her heart pounding, blood coursing in her ears.

"Gods be merciful." Garth placed a hand on Fereliss' shoulder, perhaps as much to steady himself as to comfort his companion.

"It cannot be," repeated Yurik. Looking up at the queen, he cried in a pained voice, "Best go inside, m'lady!"

Isadora watched the horse as it drew closer, a part of her shrinking from it as though she could somehow keep what it represented at bay. She realized now what the guards had already deduced—that the rider was, in fact, not missing. The moving dust cloud had cleared into a steed, dragging its rider by one foot trapped in a stirrup, the body bobbing up and down as the horse galloped over rocks and around shrubs.

No one spoke as the stallion entered the fields surrounding the house, slowing its gait in recognition of its home. Isadora watched in disbelief, unable to look away as the scene unfolded before her. Tall grasses parted for the laboring animal. Periodic glimpses of a limp body—*please don't let that be my daughter*—in tattered, dusty garb. A twisted leg. Bones jutting from a mangled arm. A bloody head, its facial features no longer recognizable.

The horse came to a halt just before the stupefied guards. While there was little else to identify its rider, there was no mistaking the shock of yellow hair, or the jeweled necklace that had once adorned the queen. Isadora's trembling hand rose to her throat. *My doing!* She could not breathe, and all her senses dulled as the world collapsed around her. *I must go to her!*

Rolft was the first to move, knife in hand as he kneeled to free the princess from her stirrup. "See to the queen," he said.

His companions reacted quickly, turning just in time to watch the queen fall head-first in silence from her balcony. Rolft heard the sharp crack of her skull above the dull thud of her body as she met the courtyard stones behind him. Still kneeling by the princess, he closed his eyes and hung his head. There was no need to confirm what his heart already knew. This was a nightmare from which there would be no waking.

THE GUILD OF TAKERS

"In a world of give and take, we do our part." The Guild of Takers' credo.

Ruler Two

Ruler Two donned his ceremonial shabba, slipping his arms through its loose sleeves and cinching the robe around his waist with braided silk. He pulled the hood over his head until all but his face was hidden to the outside world and closed his eyes. He was a far cry from the frightened child that had first stepped inside The Guild's compound at age seven, was he not? No one who had looked upon him that day could have foreseen his many achievements: the soonest ever to graduate the School of Taking; one of very few to master every art taught there; the only overseer in Guild history to manage multiple territories simultaneously; the first student of the School of Taking to return as its headmaster; the youngest ever to become a member of the High Order. Most would consider his current position the pinnacle of success. But he did not.

He left his sanctum and proceeded down the hall until he reached the worm, a five-story spiral staircase in the center of The Hidor. Often, he would climb to the 'worm's head,' which extended well above The Hidor's roofline, allowing a clear view through its open wind catchers for as far as the eye could see. The desolate terrain of the Lawless Lands wasn't much to look at, but its vastness helped him think.

Today, however, he would exit the worm on the fourth floor and join his fellow rulers in the Chalice Room. He pictured the four of them: portly Ruler One with his bald head and saggy jowls, often seen waddling across the grounds to address the maintenance and upkeep of the GOT—The Guild's compound—or the needs of those who lived and worked there. Ruler Three always dressed in flowing gowns that hid her body's true shape. She was usually perched at her desk, her long gray hair pulled back from a scholarly visage marked by large round eyes that reminded him of an owl. It was a fitting look for one charged with managing The Guild's finances, including the supervision of all collectors and adjusters. Then there was Ruler Four, stone-faced leader of The Guild's small army. Impassive and aloof, and seldom seen without a fighting staff clenched tightly in his hand, he spent most days barking orders to those responsible for defending the GOT and protecting its underground wealth. And of course, Ruler Five, slinking around so quietly on his long legs that one rarely heard him until his swarthy complexion, thick black brows and gleaming white teeth, were inches from one's face. The way he smiled made one think he hadn't eaten in weeks. He, too, seemed well-suited to his tasks: the supervision of all watchers, the elimination of unsanctioned competition, the disposal of liabilities, and the maintenance of relations with those The Guild relied on, including The League of Assassins. He seldom stayed for any length of time at the GOT, and Ruler Two wasn't complaining. Something about Ruler Five reeked of evil.

Today, of course, they all would look quite similar, coequal members of the High Order, each heavily masked by their ceremonial garb. Their supreme leader, the magister, would join them, appearing as he always did, never seen outside his shabba. He probably slept in it. Only once had Ruler Two caught a glimpse of anything but the magister's wizened face, and that was when an unexpected gust of wind blew off the old man's hood. But even then, the swirl of dust that had accompanied the breeze made it impossible to see much. Ruler Two thought he might have glimpsed a deformed skull, but he could not be sure. And no one had dared stare.

The six of them were scheduled to spend the day together. Not a pleasant prospect. This was Reckoning Day, designed by the magister to determine each ruler's special tasks for the coming almon. It was the scarecrow's own remedy for "idle hands," based on his ludicrous assumption that routine operations left each ruler with spare time.

Ruler Two reviewed the basic framework of the reckoning: each ruler would present a list of proposed initiatives, briefly citing each project's purpose and benefit, the resources it required, and—perhaps most importantly—the name of the ruler expected to manage it. Proposed projects were limited only by one's imagination. Constructing a new wing to The Hidor, updating the Laws of Taking, adding to the school's curriculum, or building a new transport route—any such would do.

Following each presentation, rulers would be allowed to pose questions, advocate merits, point out drawbacks, and challenge estimated resources. After all, what did Ruler Five know about building bridges, or securing caches of ill-gotten gains in underground vaults? What business did Ruler Three have in recommending a new trade route?

When discussions concluded, each proposal would either be eliminated or added to the magister's list, which at day's end, the old man would prioritize and use to make assignments.

Ruler Two had found the best way to control his workload was to propose sensible projects within his own domain; otherwise, his spare time might be filled chasing after some other ruler's inane notion of what he should be doing. And none of them knew the first thing about the art of taking, or how it should be taught to others. He likened the reckoning to a strategic game of wits, really, each ruler trying their best to be the master of not only their own destiny, but that of their cohorts.

When all was said and done, he typically hoped to claim at least one of three informal symbols of reckoning success: inheriting the fewest projects proposed by others; foisting the most projects onto others' plates; or having proposed the largest number of projects prioritized by the magister, regardless of to whom they were assigned. If he could some-how manage all three, he could gloat for the next twelve moons.

This almon, however, his plan was even grander.

Ruler Two climbed the last of the worm's steps to the fourth floor slowly, allowing himself time to prepare, to practice the cleansing breaths and banish emotion. It was one of the first and most basic skills taught him by his mastertaker, Sarteeg, a maven not only of trickery, but of mindal, the ancient art of mind control. If the old man could only see him now, a member of the High Order, responsible for all aspects of The Guild's School of Taking and for the organization's succession planning.

One by one, Ruler Two's feelings slipped away, strongest to weakest, as though turned to liquid and drawn by wicking to some vessel outside his consciousness.

He stepped onto the fourth floor in stasis, the energy his excitement and trepidation had required now heightening his senses. He could hear the soft, rhythmic shuffling of the magister coming down the west wing's hall, a young nom with surer footing supporting him on either side.

Ruler Two slipped into the Chalice Room to find his equals already seated, silent and still. Ruler Five's eyes were closed beneath his bushy brows, his hands folded on the tabletop. Ruler Four sat rigid in his chair, no doubt eager to shed his shabba and don his military uniform as soon as possible. Ruler Three occupied herself in typical fashion, her fingers a blur as they played some mathematical game she had once tried to explain to him. Ruler One's eyes were easy to read. *You're anxious!* Ruler Two quickly surveyed the small room's preparations. If they were not to the magister's liking, Ruler One would start the reckoning at a distinct disadvantage. The room's walls were barren, save for a portrait of The Guild's founder. The narrow counter that ran the length of the back wall was draped with white linen and topped with an appealing presentation of fruit, bread, sweets and drink. He took his place between Rulers Three and Four, and across from Rulers One and Five just as the magister entered.

Two noms assisted the magister into his resting chair at the head of the table before leaving the room and shutting the door behind them. The magister appraised the room, his eyes settling on Ruler One. "General business," he said softly. "Truncated."

Ruler One used his hood to wipe his brow. "Nothing to report, Magister."

Ruler Two signaled the same.

Ruler Three rattled off a quick report. "Collections, normal. No adjustments warranted."

Can she never simply say, "Nothing to report?"

Ruler Four maintained his perfect posture.

Ruler Five waited, then cleared his voice. "Watchers report two uprisings in Tegan, both easily suppressed. One gatherer terminated in Aranox."

Ruler Two took note. Uprisings of unauthorized competitors were common enough, but a GOT gatherer executed by one of The Guild's own?

"Terminated?" asked the magister, seemingly reading Ruler Two's mind. "Which sector?"

"Waterford, m'lord. The Inland territory... managed by Overseer Rascall."

The magister's lips barely twitched. "General business is concluded. Let the reckoning begin. Ruler One."

As Ruler One filled his cavernous mouth with air, Ruler Two raised his left hand, two middle fingers curled beneath the tip of his thumb. It was the accepted way to request a break from normal proceedings.

"What do you proffer?" wheezed the magister.

"Moratorium," Ruler Two said. It was an immediate and unexpected threat to his cohorts' plans for the day. If granted, a moratorium would mean the postponement of the reckoning for a full almon, and the devotion of all The Guild's resources to a singular, monumental project. Ruler Three shifted uneasily in her seat.

"We have not honored moratorium since the last review of territorial boundaries, eight almons past," said the magister casually.

Ruler Two nodded. No one needed reminding about the last moratorium. It had been a colossal, tedious waste of everyone's time, resulting in very little substantive change. The magister was warning him.

"What do you advocate?" asked the magister.

Ruler Two did not hesitate. "Overthrow both kings, m'lord. Replace them with governance by the people. Self-governance."

Ruler One could not contain himself. A light scoff escaped his hood. The magister silenced him with a crooked finger pressed against a thumbpad.

"To what end?" asked the magister.

"To increase The Guild's control over all of Baelon, m'lord." *Keep it simple. To the point!*

"This has been tried before."

"Yes, m'lord. One hundred thirty-five almons ago." *I've done my homework!* "The landscape has changed."

"Indeed." The magister was silent for a long time. "Tell us how that change favors your proposal."

Gladly! "The last attempt was made when there existed a long line of respected heirs to each kingdom's throne, m'lord. The people of both realms took comfort in the promise of a familiar future. The GOT was not yet a century old and still wrestling with its own hierarchy. One hundred and thirty-five almons later, both realms remain in love with their kings, but the people worry. There is persistent talk about the future, and fear of the unknown. What shall come to pass when these kings are gone? Both monarchs are past their mid-life. Neither has a bloodline nor picked an heir, let alone identified possible candidates. But The Guild is stabilized, stronger now than it has ever been, its power and influence increased tenfold these past sixty almon." *Yes, Magister, a shameless compliment to you, but a complete answer to your question demands it!*

One of the supreme leader's yellow fingernails tapped the tabletop rhythmically. "A moratorium has been proffered." He made a sweeping gesture, allowing those around the table to view the dark openings of his shabba sleeves, into which his bony white arms disappeared. "Initial challenges are welcome."

Ruler Two knew the others' dilemma. Silence was tantamount to support. A proposal of this magnitude warranted a hundred questions, yet none wished to look foolish in front of the magister. He had caught them off guard. He waited, further entrenched in his position with each passing moment.

Ruler One was the first to be recognized. His jowls quivered as he spoke. "Self-governance as practiced in the Isles? I fail to see the appeal. We have trouble enough with two kings. Neither will bow to bribe or threat. In fact, they work against us at every opportunity. And you want to multiply that hardship? The Isles are subject to a dozen authorities, despite their tiny lands. How many do you think two realms would require? One hundred? Five hundred? Self-governance indeed!"

"It is not self-governance that has kept us from plundering the Isles," said Ruler Two. "We do not bother with them because the distance is too great, the journey too dangerous, the prize too paltry to warrant our efforts. The islanders are happy, but they are also wretched poor. It takes a quarter moon at best to reach the islands. A full crew to sail a ship there. I wouldn't waste the effort, let alone risk lives riding angry seas, not even were I certain to take everything of value from the Isles when I landed."

The owl sought recognition and received it, her well-preened feathers clearly ruffled. "That hardly meets the challenge posed by Ruler One. We all know the practical reasons for not operating in the Isles. Your recitation of them falls short of addressing the hardships we would face were both kingdoms to trade their monarchs for self-governance. Ruler One questions why we would choose to manage a hundred authorities when our hands are full with two. What about the numbers?"

"I thought you would be the first to make sense of them," said Ruler Two. "The reluctance of a king to dance with us is not inherent in his throne, but in his character. No two are quite alike. If I pick ten men off the street to rule Baelon, how many do you think will look the other way whilst we line their pockets? Three? Four? All we need is one! Think on it." He shot a glance at Ruler One. "How many did you say would be required to self-govern both the realms? How many of those hundreds will refuse our generous offers to assist? How many who might otherwise refuse us will have families to protect? You cannot help but see it now... The truth is quite the opposite of what Ruler One suggests. Increasing the number of authorities who govern will not complicate our work, but greatly simplify it. Even a small injection of our influence will spread like a disease until we are so embedded in Baelon's governance that we can never be removed. We struggle now to manage two self-righteous kings. Why, when self-governance will eventually manage our interests by itself? With leadership spread so thin that cracks in it cannot be avoided."

Ruler One sought to save face, but his request to be recognized was tentative. "You make it sound so easy. As though a snap of your fingers will make it so. The truth is that what you propose will be almons in the making. Why not wait and see who succeeds these kings? Perhaps it will be someone we can work with. Still far easier to manage two kings than two kingdoms, is it not?"

Ruler Two responded quickly. "How long would you wait? What are the odds that our self-righteous kings will choose successors they deem less virtuous? What if those they choose have heirs? No, of this we can be certain: with the monarchies in place, our future will always be *un*certain."

"Not true," said the owl, barely waiting to be recognized. "Not if we choose the kings. We need not wait. Why not kill the kings, as you suggest, and then replace them with our own puppets? So much simpler than messing with this nonsense of self-governance."

Ruler Two shook his head. "Perhaps Ruler Three is unfamiliar with the process that would commence were either of our reigning kings to meet their end today. It would take almons, be neither smooth nor orderly, and yet be overseen by layers of aristocracy sworn to uphold the interests of their departed kings. Trying to steer them toward your puppets would be like wishing a certain meal upon the table when you do not control the kitchen, the cooks, or the ingredients they are fond of. Ah, but what if instead, those struggling so hard were shown a better way to cook? A better way, as it were, to honor the interests of their late kings? A way to ensure the best interests of the people were always at the forefront of the minds of those who governed? What better time to suggest that better way than when the kitchen is in turmoil, the cooks fighting and confused? Self-governance will not be easy nor swift to achieve, but we will have almons, and once installed, it will be worth the effort a thousand times over. And its impact will last forever."

Rulers One and Three looked to Four and Five, impassive and in no rush to be recognized.

Already committed, Ruler Three took the initiative. The owl's talons danced in the air as she spoke. "Despite continued efforts to suppress us, both kingdoms now accept us as an unpleasant fact of life. By your own account, The Guild is stronger now than it has ever been. Our nets are cast over all of Baelon. No one dares to steal without The Guild's approval, or paying for the privilege. Our profits have never been higher.

"Yet *everything* is risked if your plan fails. We will be like some house pest having left the safety of the shadows, tempted by a morsel in the sunlight it did not really need. Though suffered in the shadows, we will not be tolerated in the light of day—not scurrying about the house whilst brazenly reminding all of Baelon why they hate us. The full wrath of both realms will be brought down upon our heads, like some giant boot heel intent on grinding us to dust!"

Ruler One nodded in agreement, his jowls jiggling, until she finished. Ruler Three looked from the magister to Ruler Five for some sign of support, but neither showed any reaction.

Ruler Two leaned slightly forward in his chair. "Part of what you say is true. Though they work against us, both realms are resigned to our existence. We are little more to them than an unpleasant fact of life. If we do nothing to further call attention to ourselves, our relationship will remain unchanged. But we can capture this prize, this 'morsel in the sunlight' as you call it, without leaving the safety of the shadows. If we act wisely, the kings' deaths will not be attributed to us. And we shall take no credit. Disposing of royalty is not my area of expertise, and it is decidedly no simple matter, but if Ruler Five cannot put two kings in the ground without leaving a trace of The Guild's involvement, then I have badly misjudged him. So far as the promotion of self-governance goes, our actions will be as innocent and commonplace as those of a farmer sowing seeds in troubled lands, for that is exactly what we shall be. Once planted, those seeds shall be nurtured by others with a desire so strong and so sincere to see them grow that they will come to believe they did the planting themselves. And we shall stand back and watch from the shadows as the fruits of our labor take shape."

Ruler Two sat back in his chair, satisfied with his defense. Ruler One would no longer meet his gaze. Ruler Three appeared unconvinced, but she was at a crossroads. Pushing past a certain point would not be in her best interests. She turned to Rulers Four and Five, her owl eyes imploring them to help her.

The magister flicked a bony finger in the air. "Ruler Four?"

"I see no major threat," said the veteran soldier. "If the kings are killed without attribution to The Guild, our reasons to defend The GOT will be no different than they are today. Even if the plot fails—if we are found out and the realms came after us—what will they do? Come here? I think not. Our predecessors knew what they were doing when they built this place. We are a full day's ride from Aranox, further from Tegan. A full day's ride across an open, hostile desert with no place to hide. If they do come, what will they do when dark falls and the prattlers emerge from their tunnels? What then? No. By the time the king's soldiers get here, they will need to turn around and scurry home, and they will be too late at that! If this were not the case, they would have been here long ago. No, if we are found out, I don't think they will come here. More likely, they will wage war on our takers in Aranox and Tegan...at which point our operations will go quiet for a spell, will they not? Until the kingdoms tire of chasing ghosts and declare false victory, and we resume our sport."

The magister sucked a breath of air into his failing lungs. "Ruler Five?"

The hint of a smile that had rested on Ruler Five's lips slowly spread into a full-fledged grin. His dark eyes stared at Ruler Two as though just beginning to recognize a long-lost friend. His snow-white teeth gleamed as he spoke. "No initial challenges, m'lord."

Overseer Reynard Rascall

Reynard Rascall knew precious little about The Guild of Takers for having been a member twenty almons. Not even his decade as an overseer had allowed him to see through the heavy shroud of mystery that enveloped The High Order. Perhaps, had he been raised in the GOT compound and schooled by grandmasters in the shadows of The Hidor, he would be more familiar. No matter. He knew what every thief knew: if you did not pay your dues, in full and on time, you would be made to wish you had. It was all The Guild needed you to know. All it wanted you to know.

They might be watching now. One could never be sure. A guild watcher could assume so many disguises. Reynard glanced out a window at the docks below. The Waterford Wharf was a manual laborer's paradise. Few places of business offered as many jobs to so many different trades. The number of dockworkers alone was impressive. During the day they were everywhere, from one end of the port to the other, lumbering up and down gangways, loading and unloading supplies, packing this, unpacking that, and forever washing down gangplanks for passengers and sailors alike. Fishermen mending their nets, shipwrights making repairs. All busy with their tasks, paying little attention to anyone not helping to ensure safety or success.

Now, at night, it was a different story. Most of those who toiled for a living had packed up at dusk and headed home.

The smell of fish remained. Outside on the docks, it was unbearable. Here on the second floor, it wasn't much better. How was that possible? Did the odor permeate the building, so that no matter where he moved, it surrounded him? Or had the stench on the wharf so attached itself to him that he now carried it wherever he went? Reynard sniffed the sleeve of his shirt.

Perhaps he would dispose of the furniture—one table, three desks, a few chairs he didn't really need—and see if that improved things. The room was spacious, with views of the seaport below. There were no interior walls, only several large wooden posts rising through the floor and extending to the roof above. There was shelving, a few stand-alone racks, and some pulleys with rope draped over ceiling rafters. All useless to Reynard. For almons the room had functioned as a crude office and as storage for goods and materials for the workshop below, but the amount of coin Reynard had offered to rent the place had prompted the proprietor to vacate the premises the very next day, asking only a single question: "How long shall you be needing it?"

There came a knock on the door. One feature that had attracted Reynard to this particular building was an exterior staircase, providing direct access from an alleyway to his rented room. If he chose to, he could come and go discreetly, unbeknownst even to those working up a sweat directly below.

Another knock came, this time slightly louder.

"Come in!" Reynard called out.

The door opened, and several men entered the room. The light was fading fast, but Reynard could still recognize them. Spiro, the man he trusted most in this business, and the two bruisers who generally accompanied him, Able and Elijah. They coaxed three men in front of them, occasionally prodding them with a knee to their backsides. As they neared Reynard, Spiro and his cronies stopped pushing and stepped back.

"Good evening, gentlemen." Reynard swept his shoulder-length black bangs behind his earlobes. "How nice of you to be out so late on my account. I swear, were it not important that we meet, I myself would be in bed by now."

"Reynard—" said the only man with spectacles.

"Now, now, Kasparr." Reynard stepped closer to him. "Please don't."

Kasparr opened his mouth to speak again, then bit his lip and swallowed.

"Joshua... Jonathon. It's good to see you." Reynard placed both hands on the shoulders of one, then the other, skipping over Kasparr as though he were not there. "You've traveled far. You must be weary. Spiro, some chairs for our guests, if you please."

Spiro's shadow moved silently across the room. As he made his way back toward Reynard, the sound of chair legs scraping against the floor accompanied him. Able and Elijah moved to the door, their large silhouettes framing either side.

"Thank you, Spiro." Reynard grasped the two chairs, turning them as he motioned. "Joshua... Jonathon. Come, sit here. Please."

All three of Reynard's guests exchanged nervous glances, but none dared refuse. Joshua and Jonathon shuffled forward, casting a last look at Kasparr before fixing their eyes on Reynard. Both watched him so intently that they had to feel for their seats with their hands.

"There, there," said Reynard, patting them on the shoulders as he moved behind them. "Best seats in the house. Front row! Reserved just for you. Great theater!" Joshua closed his eyes as though sensing pending doom.

"And you, Kasparr! Our guest of honor. Star of the show, really!" Reynard dragged the third chair to where Kasparr stood, stepped behind him and spoke directly into his ear. "Sit here, please. Center stage, that's where you belong this evening."

"Reynard, if I might explain myself." Kasparr reached for Reynard's hand as he lowered himself into the seat.

"Stop right there, Kasparr. That's nowhere in the script. Have you not studied your lines? Tsk, tsk. This is not a dress rehearsal, Kasparr. This is live theater. Jonathon! Do I not pay you well for your services?"

"Very well, Reynard. Most assuredly," said a shaking Jonathon.

"For your loyalty, Joshua?"

"M-more than enough," stuttered Joshua. "In fact, if you like…"

"You see, Kasparr, even the audience knows its lines." Reynard crouched in front of Kasparr, so that their faces were on a level, then brushed his fallen bangs back behind his earlobes. "You appear to have a bad case of stage fright." He patted Kasparr's knee, then stood to cross the room. "No matter. I'm here for you. When it's your turn to speak, I shall prompt you. How's that?" Through the darkened outline of a small window, Reynard watched the sun sink into the sea. He would need to hurry.

"Jonathon, Joshua, can you still see the stage? All will be for naught if you cannot." He paused at the edge of a long table covered with what appeared to be a tablecloth and waited for a response. "I didn't hear you."

"Yes, Reynard," said Jonathon.

"I can as well," whispered Joshua.

"Very good. And thank you for keeping your voices down. We wouldn't want to upset the rest of the audience, would we?" One of the large men standing guard at the door suppressed a chuckle. Reynard was unsure whether it was Able or Elijah, but either way, it made him smile. It was nice to be appreciated.

"This is very important...the three of you here together. I'm a simple businessman, and I rely on you to make our business profitable. Joshua, you manage our interests in the north. Jonathon, you the south, and Kasparr, you handle the Fostead sector. I, of course, manage the coastal area myself. Between us, we cover the entire inland territory. You three were chosen, hand-picked by me after great deliberation. It's a tremendous honor, really. And a tremendous responsibility. I've placed my livelihood...nay, my very life...in your hands." Reynard stared long and hard at each of the seated men in turn, then rapped the knuckles of one hand sharply on the tabletop. "You see the truth in this, do you not? I must submit the same sum to The Guild each moon, regardless of the amount you send to me. One dire short, one kingshead light, and I must pay the difference. Or pay a different price."

Reynard took a deep breath, exhaling as he closed his eyes. He tilted his face toward the ceiling. "Tell me, Kasparr, do you know what a gaffe is?" He waited, but there was only silence. "This is where you speak, Kasparr. It's your line next."

"A gaff?" Kasparr shifted nervously in his seat. "I suppose so, yes. I mean, it's a hand tool, right? Used to hook large fish—"

"No, no, no!" Reynard was suddenly looming over Kasparr. "Not a gaff, Kasparr. *This* is a gaff, Kasparr." He picked up a large steel hook from the table, held it in front of Kasparr's face, then spelled the word out slowly. "G... A... F... F. I'm not asking about a gaff, Kasparr. I'm asking about a gaffe. G...A... F... F... *E*. You have some schooling. Surely you know the difference."

"Yes." Kasparr wrung his hands, looking longingly at the dark outlines of Jonathon and Joshua. "Of course. If I might explain, Reynard."

"So you do know what a gaffe is."

Kasparr nodded, tears flowing freely now. "Ye-yes, Reynard."

"What is it then?"

"A gaffe is a terrible blunder. Reynard, I beseech you!"

"And do you know the price to be paid for a gaffe, Kasparr?" Reynard's voice suddenly seethed with anger.

"Oh, Gods above, please..." As Kasparr removed his spectacles, Reynard swung the gaff. Kasparr screamed as the steel hook ripped into his throat.

Reynard gave a vicious tug to ensure it was firmly embedded. "When you shortchange me, Kasparr, you shortchange the entire guild!" With a firm grasp on the gaff, Reynard pulled Kasparr from the chair and dragged him across the room. Kasparr's legs jerked spasmodically, his boot heels bouncing off the floor. His hands clawed, then gripped the steel shank of the gaff where blood flowed freely from his throat, but there was no dislodging it. Gurgling noises roiled from his mouth and neck as Reynard hoisted him roughly onto the tarp-covered table. "Spiro!"

Instantly, Spiro appeared at Reynard's side, a dagger in his hand. He thrust it violently once, twice, three times into Kasparr's chest, and the gurgling subsided. The kicking became twitching, then stopped altogether.

Reynard wrested the gaff from Kasparr's throat, leaned against the table, and exhaled a deep breath. Spiro wiped his dagger on Kasparr's trousers, then sheathed it. Reynard placed a hand on Spiro's shoulder, still slightly out of breath. He swept his hair back out of his face as he motioned to their audience. "Take a bow, Spiro." As Spiro did so, Reynard approached Jonathon and Joshua.

"My apologies. Not very good theater after all. Kasparr should have better learned his lines."

Both Joshua and Jonathon sat wide-eyed. Joshua's teeth chattered uncontrollably and Jonathon instinctively placed his outstretched hands before him as Reynard approached.

"What's the matter?" asked Reynard. "Was it really that bad?" It suddenly dawned on him what they were looking at. He hadn't even realized he still held it. "Oh." He casually tossed the gaff behind him. It bounced off Kasparr's body, landing on the floor with a clatter. "Well!" He clapped his hands once loudly. "At least you know the difference now between gaff and gaffe, eh? That's something!" He shook a bloody finger in front of their faces. "My advice? Avoid them both. You'll live longer." He patted each man on the head and walked away. Able opened the door for him and Reynard moved rapidly down the stairs, leaving Spiro and his crew to clean the mess up.

It would not be difficult to dispose of Kasparr's body. This time of night, no one would notice a few extra hands carrying a lumpy tarp bound with twine, even if it did drip. *Hah! No one would likely notice were it day!* It was one of the few benefits of sharing this place with a horde of dead and dying fish. A little more blood, another ribbon of entrails, a few more pieces of decaying flesh. Who would be the wiser?

He'd taken care of business. He hoped The Guild was watching.

Reynard's eyes roved the interior of his sitting room. It was a long way from the docks, and a hundredfold more comfortable. The trappings of success were everywhere. A painting by Gereau, vases from the Northern Isles, bookends chiseled from pure carmine. His gaze came to rest on a small glass orb he had commissioned to hold his most prized possession: a soiled, well-worn coin of little value in the marketplace. It was the first dire he had ever captured as a pickpocket. The mastertaker who'd first trained him had gifted it to him, advising him never to part with it.

Reynard quietly drummed his long fingers on the upholstered arms of his chaise. Spiro sat atop a smokewood desk, his butt resting on its blotter, his short wiry legs swinging leisurely in the air.

"What was Joshua's take again?" asked Reynard.

"Twenty-six kingheads."

"And Jonathon? The south?"

Spiro sighed. "Twenty-one."

"And here? On the coast? Our own operations?"

Spiro hung his head. "Thirty-five," he said, as though exhausted.

"What's the matter?"

"You've asked me three times now. The numbers stay the same."

"Mmm." Reynard stood to stretch. "I hope our little theater helps to motivate the Fostead sector."

Spiro grinned. "It was a good performance."

"Yes. I was amazing, of course. You were... well, let's just say, a little aggressive."

"Aggressive?" Spiro frowned.

"Yes, I believe that's the word. Aggressive. I dare say you owe me another table. Surely it was unmarked before you took to stabbing Kasparr." Reynard clasped his hands behind his back as he strolled across the room. He stopped to run his fingers along the grain of a wooden post running from floor to ceiling. "What was he thinking, anyway? Five kingheads, that's a problem."

Spiro shrugged, his thin eyebrows lifting slightly.

"Five kingheads?" asked Reynard incredulously.

Spiro spread the fingers of one hand in front of his face.

"I mean, it's not as though we really need it to make payment to The Guild." Reynard held a hand in the air, palm up.

Spiro nodded.

"Even so, our lifestyle demands a healthy profit, above and beyond what The Guild demands of us." Reynard raised his other hand palm up, then weighed one hand against the other. "Five kingheads!"

Spiro simply watched.

"No," Reynard said, "it cannot be ignored. I mean, what would happen if the others followed suit?"

"Well—"

"I'll tell you, shall I? We would be forced to hold theater every week, and you would continue your aggressive ways and we would quickly run out of performers. No doubt The Guild would demand a lead role as well. No, we can ill afford that. We must nip this in the bud, my friend. Before The Guild catches wind of it. Kasparr's bookkeeper..."

"Lee–oooh." Spiro howled, tilting his head toward the ceiling.

"Leo."

"Lee-oooooh!"

Reynard laughed. "He's not from The Isles, you dolt! How would you like it if I took to calling you 'Sparrow,' eh?" He turned suddenly serious. "We must make a trip to Fostead, I'm afraid, and see to things ourselves."

"That's exactly what I was going to say." Spiro casually inspected his fingernails.

No, it wasn't. Not even close. "Really?"

"Really."

"Pray tell, then. What would I say next?"

"I'm allowed, am I?"

"I insist."

"Very well, then." Spiro cleared his voice, his prominent throat cork bobbing up and down. "I hate traveling inland this time of almon. So dusty! My gawds! So hot! Unbearable, really. And the bugs! So if we must go..." Spiro shook a threatening finger. "Someone on the other end must surely pay!" He raised both hands and flicked them in the air as a show of finality.

A long silence ensued as the two stared at one another.

Finally, Reynard shook his head. "You see? Again, too aggressive."

Reynard waved the carriage off and stretched his limbs. Spiro craned his head back as far as it would go, then flung it forward as he spat into the street.

"Must you?" asked Reynard. "This is Fostead, not the stinking docks." He looked about, relieved dusk had fallen and that most people were indoors. They had left the coast at dawn. The carriage had held together, and they had not encountered any rogue thieves. *Just as well for anyone in that business! Spiro would have proven a nasty surprise.* "You know the best part of that ride?"

"That it's done?" said Spiro bitterly.

"Quite right," said Reynard with a chuckle. "Quite right!"

Spiro rubbed his butt and stretched his back. "I think some of my bones have been jarred loose."

"My head feels like it's been hit with a klubandag." Reynard picked up his satchel and started to walk in the direction suggested by the carriage driver.

"Say again?" asked Spiro. "What in Baelon is a klubandag?"

Reynard stopped in the middle of the street and waited for Spiro to catch up. "Surely you jest. You, of all people. Do you truly not know of a klubandag?"

"Were I to know, would I need to ask?"

Reynard stared at him a short time, then walked on. "A klubandag, my friend, is a club with an iron spike at its end."

"Klubandag." Spiro shook his head in amusement. "Why not just say club, then?"

"Because it's not the same thing, is it?"

"Well, I'm not sure your head would know the difference."

"Oh, wouldn't it?"

"Not if I was wielding it. No. It most assuredly would not."

"Mmm." Reynard used his satchel to point down the street. "Look, I believe that may be the place."

"I mean," said Spiro, "if you were fighting for your life, would you scream, 'Someone throw me my klubandag?' Doubtful. More like 'Someone throw me my gods damned club!'"

"This is why we cannot carry on a conversation. That's just as many syllables, Spiro. You make no sense!" Reynard halted in front of a large, dark building. The sun had set, but it was still light enough to read the hand-carved sign above the door: The King's Inn.

"Please," Reynard said with a sigh, stretching the word, "let me do the talking."

"Of course, my liege."

Reynard lay in the dark, on a straw bed across the room from Spiro, working with his tongue at a piece of bread stuck between his teeth. Despite the late hour, he had convinced the innkeeper to part with both bread and ale—a meager meal which, after such a long carriage ride, was more than satisfying.

"I don't think I could suffer much longer in a contraption like that," he said. "By comparison, even the chamber pot felt like a kiss on the cheeks, eh?"

"I thought we weren't conversing."

"We're not. I'm talking to myself."

"Ah, as I am thinking to myself."

"About what?" *Gods above, do I really want to know?*

"About the klubandag, of course."

Reynard sighed loudly. There was always a risk in adding to the muddle between Spiro's ears.

"I mean," said Spiro, "once you knock someone on the head with it...not just tap them, mind you, but really knock them soundly...how are you going to get the spike out if another man's brains need mashing? Doesn't sound practical at all."

Reynard's better judgment jerked the reins on further discussion. "Good night, Spiro."

"Just thinking to myself, mind you."

Raggett Grymes

Raggett Grymes was unable to stand still. He paced back and forth across a dusty road a morning's ride from Fostead, shaking out his arms and legs.

Before too long, the king's palace would be filled with nobility—dukes and duchesses sitting properly in the great hall, conjecturing among themselves as to what the servants would bring next. He imagined it might be some sort of roasted fowl, basted with a special sauce he'd never tasted. Or a fish he'd never heard of.

He spat at an insect in the road, scratching his scalp through thinning brown hair. Neither he nor any of his companions would ever be invited to the palace, or taste the kinds of food required to impress the likes of those dining there tonight. Nor did they care to. The upper class were snooty and self-important. When he rose to fame and fortune—and he would rise, sooner than later—he would put them all in their place.

Why he was still struggling as a taker was beyond him. He'd been a member of the GOT since childhood. By all rights, he should at least have been afforded the title of mastertaker by now. Were they not paying attention? He had, of course, suffered setbacks—jobs gone awry—but who had not? The GOT was likely unaware of them anyway. The notion that watchers were everywhere, observing every move guild members made, and reporting them to the High Order? Well, it was obviously impossible, no more true than the horrible stories his parents had told him as a child about ghosts to make him stay in bed at night. He'd tested the waters, to be sure, shortchanging his gatherer, Kasparr, a dire here, a dire there, until he was certain no repercussions were forthcoming. But that had started long ago. These days, he withheld at least half of what The Guild expected him to distribute to Kasparr. It was so easy to misrepresent his earnings. In fact, he had of late performed a few side jobs and kept all the profits for himself. The worst he had suffered during past visits to gullible Kasparr was a scowl of dissatisfaction, and he could live with that. How that idiot had ever made it to the position of gatherer was beyond him.

No matter. He was destined for bigger things, and would likely skip right past the roles of mastertaker and gatherer. All it would take was one impressive act. Something so bold and distinctive that watchers wouldn't need to witness it. Something so fantastic that word of it could not help but reach the High Order. It wasn't just the best way to make a favorable impression on The Guild. It was the *only* way to earn the position of overseer. That was a far more fitting role for him anyway—a larger stepping stone than mastertaker or gatherer, as it were, to his rightful place in the High Order. It was just a matter of time. He was smarter than all of them, really. And he had something his fellow takers did not. Ambition. He had big plans. A drawer full, in fact. Plans so outlandish, so fantastic, that the GOT could not help but notice and reward him. Perhaps he would capture their attention today.

He took stock of the men he had selected for this particular job: Shum wasn't much to look at, absent any teeth or hair, but he was always at the ready, and there was none quicker or quieter once inside a house. Edwyn was as handsome as Shum was ugly. He was loyal to a fault, strong as an ox, and just as dumb. And Harolt—the man was little more than a kind face with distinguished wrinkles, but how often had that tipped the scales in Raggett's favor? Quiet and unassuming, Harolt was. Instant respectability.

The four of them had positioned their flatbed wagon to the side of the only road leading to the palace from the manor they watched. When the gentleman who owned the property did finally pass, riding high on his horse with two hirelings trailing behind, Raggett doffed his cap and bowed low to hide his smiling face, for he did appreciate the nobleman's predictability.

"C'mon then." Raggett beckoned to Shum, and together they slithered into the wagon bed, one on either side of two large wooden beams. Edwyn and Harolt covered them quickly with a leather tarp, leaving only two ends of lumber protruding from the wagon's rear. Raggett listened to them tie the tarp, then felt the wagon shudder as they climbed onto the driver's bench. He heard Harolt nicker to the horses, and the wagon's wheels begin to creak.

Soon, they were making their way uphill toward the baron's manor. From his hiding place, Raggett gauged their progress, interpreting the slowing of the wagon even as Harolt advised him in a hushed voice. "Almost there, boss." He lay silent, wondering how many workers the gentleman had left at his estate. If they were extremely lucky, it would be vacant, but more likely, there would be remaining servants. The gentleman was a land baron, with expensive taste and a lifestyle that demanded many helping hands.

Raggett shifted his position so he could peer out a knothole in the sideboard. The wagon had stopped on a fairly steep incline, affording him a decent view of the manor atop the hill.

"Good day, mum." Harolt addressed a stocky woman standing by a hitching post some distance from the house. She wiped her hands on her apron and brushed a few wisps of black hair from her sweaty forehead. Harolt doffed his cap to reveal his graying hair. "Name's Harolt."

The woman acknowledged Harolt with a curt nod, then gave Edwyn a thorough viewing, starting with his chiseled facial features, skin browned by the sun, and thick crown of black curly hair. Her eyes seemed to linger on muscles that could not be hidden by clothes. "What kin I do fer ya?"

"Well, we're here to deliver Baron Treadwell's wood, of course."

The bed beneath Raggett and Shum shook as Harolt set the brake and dismounted the wagon. If they could be sure the woman was alone, they would not bother with this pretense.

"What wood is that?" The woman's eyes narrowed. She folded her arms across her chest.

"Well, the wood in this wagon, madam."

"I don't know nuthin' about no wood. You'd best come back another day."

Harolt kicked a stone with the toe of his boot. "I'm afraid that's not possible, madam. We've come a long way, and the baron is expecting this. I'm not sure what he's building, but he won't be building anything without it. And our boss, well, if we return with this wood still in our wagon, he won't be our boss much longer, eh?" The bed of the wagon lifted slightly as Edwyn dismounted to join Harolt.

"And I suppose you want payment." The woman's hands came to rest on her wide hips. Raggett watched through the knothole as she stood her ground.

"Not at all, madam. This load is already paid for. So if you'll just show us where to put it, we'll be on our way."

What he means, madam, is that he and Edwyn will be on their way, then wait just down the road whilst Shum and I slip inside the baron's house and rob you blind!

"Paid for?" There was a long silence as the woman looked back toward the manor. "I suppose that'd be alright, then," she said finally. "Around back. There's a shed. It's unlocked." Raggett released the breath he had been holding. The wood would be unloaded before Edwyn and Harolt left with the wagon.

"And is there anyone about, perchance, to help us?" Harolt scratched his head innocently as he looked around. Her answer would help to determine the degree of caution Raggett and Shum would need to exercise once inside the house.

"Most o' the help is in the fields." She again wiped her hands on her apron. "But the Gods know why you'd need it with the likes of him around." She gave Edwyn another head-to-toe appraisal before turning back toward the house.

Raggett lay back, listened to her walk away, then felt the movement of the wagon as Harolt and Edwyn climbed back on.

"Hup!" Harolt signaled the horses with a flick of the reins. As the wagon jerked forward, one of the wooden beams between Raggett and Shum began to slide backward. Both men laid hands on it, but the dense smokewood, green and heavy, continued to slide, gaining momentum as the wagon rolled uphill. Raggett swore as a large, jagged splinter pierced the web of flesh between his thumb and forefinger. He let go of the wood.

"Shite!" cried Shum, both arms and one leg now trying to encircle the wooden post. Raggett watched helplessly as the beam slid out of the wagon and onto the dusty ground, taking Shum with it. It landed with a loud thud, accompanied by a muffled groan from Shum .

The wagon stopped. Raggett peered from beneath the tarp as the woman came bustling into view. "Madam!" Harolt cried out. "Madam, please!"

The woman stood over Shum, glaring down at him. "What's this, then?" she asked, before lifting the tarp to scowl at Raggett. "What's the meaning of this!?"

Raggett nursed his bandaged hand as he walked. The splinter's extraction had been more painful than its entrance. Still, he had no desire to trade places with Shum, who limped along beside him, showing the effects of his tussle with the lumber. Nor would he choose to be in the shoes of the woman who had caused them so much trouble. He spotted a few more flecks of her blood on his trousers and rubbed them into the soiled fabric.

He breathed easier as they entered Fostead's south end. Here, he always felt more comfortable, at ease, and in control. The south end was a lot like him, really. Always busy, gritty, working hard and barely scraping by. Determined to make something of itself. At times, confused by its own energy. Always in the shadows of the palace district—main street and town square—but truth be told, it was so much more alive, and so much more essential.

The maze of alleyways and narrow streets was lined by countless shops so tightly pressed together they seemed as one, all sagging in the same direction like some row of trees bent over time by strong prevailing winds. It was easy to lose oneself in the south end, but being lost felt like being home to Raggett.

He stopped in front of a small business squeezed between a bookstore and a candle-maker. Unlike most others, there was no sign hanging from its front. Raggett felt inside his pocket for the few coins he was willing to part with. He opened the tiny shop's door, causing a small bell to announce his arrival. Shum slithered in behind him and shut the door.

Raggett took a moment to absorb a fairly familiar scene. The shop consisted of a modest office with two desks, connecting to an even smaller room containing a crude cot. A bit cramped for most, perhaps, but Kasparr had once told Raggett he felt it suited him. The gatherer had explained that he was allowed to use the smaller room to sleep when necessary. Apparently, the previous tenant had done the same when not tending the front room, which had then served as a bookshop. The place still smelled of musty paper.

Occasionally, Gatherer Kasparr had said, he and his bookkeeper—a mouse of a man usually tucked into a corner behind a tiny desk of his own—turned away lost souls in search of the old bookstore, but they were, in fact, alone most of the time, and they enjoyed the solitude.

Today, however, the little bookkeeper sat behind Kasparr's desk. The gatherer was nowhere to be seen. Perhaps he was sleeping. Raggett stared into the adjoining room, but the cot was obscured by shadows.

The little bookkeeper rose.

Try as he might, Raggett could not remember the man's name.

"Afternoon, Raggett." The little mouse extended a hand across the desk, clearly priding himself on his recall. Raggett ignored the invitation. *Smug bastard! I'll not reward you for your parlor trick!* "I'm Leo, Kasparr's bookkeeper. And who might your friend be?"

"This here's Shum. He's with me."

"That's quite obvious. You've come to make a payment, I suspect." Leo reached for the ledger on his desk, dipped his quill in ink, and began to scribble an entry. "Or should I say... partial payment?" The bookkeeper looked up at Raggett with a smirk.

"What's that s'posed ta mean?"

Leo stopped the ink from flowing. He straightened and looked Raggett in the eye. "I'll explain it to you, shall I? You haven't made your expected payment for several moons running. I don't suppose today is any different."

Raggett's eyes narrowed. It turned out the mouse had a bit of rat in him. "Where's Kasparr?"

"Away, but he wishes to speak with you when he returns. Don't think he hasn't noticed."

Raggett mimicked Leo's tone. "Noticed what?"

Leo leafed quickly through his ledger. "Seventeen dire. Fourteen dire. Eight dire! Shall I continue?" The bookkeeper dipped his quill into its inkwell. "Now, you've come to make this moon's payment?"

Raggett felt a tingling rise through his chest and flush his face. His upper lip curled. His nose began to twitch. "I thought I might. But no, now that you mention it, I haven't."

"Haven't you?" Leo set the pen down and began to nod knowingly. "I see." He closed his ledger and adjusted his spectacles. "Well then, how can I help you? A loan perhaps?" He chuckled, exposing two large buck teeth. He was all rat now.

Raggett snarled. "I'm the best taker Kasparr has ever known!"

Leo snorted. "There are children begging in the streets who take as much as you, and more!"

"Is that right?" Raggett clenched his fists. "Can they clean a baron's manor, as we did just today? Eh? Can they do that? Can they rob the king himself? Eh? Cuz that's what we'll do next! And when we've finished with the king, and The Guild has given me my due, don't think I won't remember you, or what's been said today!"

Leo laughed. "You? Rob the palace? With your little friend here, I suppose? Go on, then. Get out! I've better things to do than listen to the likes of you. You couldn't rob a blind man if he left his doors unlocked. Get out!" The rat opened his ledger in animated fashion, adjusted his spectacles, and retrieved his quill. Raggett's eyes roved the tidy desktop as the bookkeeper blathered on. "I'll let Kasparr know that you stopped by, shall I, and record a giant goose egg for your—"

Raggett picked up the object closest to him and slammed it against the side of Leo's head. The spindle's thin metal spike, still holding pieces of scrap paper, disappeared into the bookkeeper's ear. Leo inhaled sharply, dropped his quill, and began screaming.

Raggett managed to grab hold of one of Leo's flailing arms. The other hit him in the eye. "Help me, gods damn it!" he shouted, spurring a stunned Shum into action. The two men wrestled Leo's slight torso onto the desktop, whereupon Shum sat on the bookkeeper's head.

Raggett found the spindle a good tool for releasing anger. By the time he caught his breath, the rat had taken his last.

Something needled Raggett, making it impossible to concentrate. The past, the present, the future—all fought for his attention. Once darkness fell, he would find his way to The Dragon's Breath, his favorite place to celebrate and stir up trouble. After all, it wasn't every day one cleaned a baron's manor.

Still, something wasn't right. He dabbed at his black eye with a bandaged hand. The baron's bitch and Kasparr's pet rat were still inside his head. *Why is that?*

"Tomorrow at noon, then? In the warehouse?" Young Alden's voice brought him back to the present, to The Raven's Nest, known for its cheap liquor and ability to keep secrets.

"Can't wait," Shum said, sucking gulps of sudsy ale past his toothless gums.

Raggett sat back, stroking strands of his sparse beard. "That's right. Noon tomorrow, in the warehouse." His entire crew would be amazed by his plan to rob the palace. "But until then..." He pointed a threatening finger at Alden. "You don't breathe a word to no one. You're sworn to secrecy, eh?"

He studied Alden's reaction until he was sure his message had been taken to heart. Young Alden with his mane of golden hair and boyish good looks. But what really set him apart from the others was his brain. It wasn't as large as Raggett's, obviously, but it was clearly serviceable. On top of that, the lad could be trusted, which in this business was saying something.

"One more thing, Alden. Swing by the granary at sunrise. I'll meet ya with what we took today. Don't pawn it here in Fostead or we'll all wind up in chains. Understood? Take it to Summerfield, and one of the smaller shops there. Abrigon's, perhaps. He don't ask a lot of questions. All right, then. Go on. Make sure everyone knows 'bout tomorrow's meeting."

Young Alden rose and took his leave.

Raggett sat back, watching Shum raise a cup of ale to his mouth, when suddenly it hit him. He sat bolt upright.

"Ya need ta go back!"

"What?" Shum wiped a frothy cloud from his floppy lips.

"To Kasparr's place. Ya need ta go back and get that book!"

Overseer Reynard Rascall

Reynard walked the main street of Fostead with a much lighter step than the previous evening, well rested and with no bags to carry. A morning with Kasparr's bookkeeper, Leo, was all he would need to determine why this territory's profits were so light. Assuming Leo was not complicit, the bookkeeper could fill in for Gatherer Kasparr while Reynard took his time searching for a permanent replacement. With any luck, he and Spiro would return to the familiar comforts of Waterford the very next day.

"Have you never seen the palace?" he asked, turning down a side street and tipping his hat to a young lady passing by.

"Never," said Spiro, keeping pace beside him.

"It's quite spectacular, really. You know, it's not a taxing walk from here. Perhaps once we've finished with Leo, we should treat ourselves to a peek."

"Instead of tipping a pint at the tavern?"

"We may never be back again."

"Let us pray. Would the king be greeting us with ale?"

"I suspect the king shall be far too busy for us," said Reynard with growing enthusiasm. "I'll supply you a pint for the road, shall I?"

"It's the queen who'll be wantin' to see me." Spiro laughed, cupping his genitals with one hand as he walked.

Reynard stopped, moving aside to let two men pass. "You do know she's dead."

"Who's that?" Spiro halted, hands on hips.

"The queen, you dolt."

"Is she?"

"You know she is."

"How would I know that?"

"How could you not? Any child with half a brain knows of the queen's death."

Spiro shrugged his shoulders.

Reynard blew out a heavy breath. "Perhaps that explains it."

"Explains what?" Spiro's beady eyes narrowed beneath thin brows.

"You're serious." Reynard shook his head in amazement. "You really are a mess up there." He tapped Spiro sharply on the head. "Anyway, your queen's been dead two almons now. Threw herself off a balcony, she did."

Spiro stood silent for a moment. "A shame. Tired of waitin' for me, was she?" He chuckled and walked ahead, turning to make sure Reynard was following.

"Your ignorance knows no bounds," said Reynard. "It really is amazing. If you do not lower your voice or choose your words more carefully, what you mistake as wit may well be the death of us."

They walked in silence for a few more blocks, moving closer to the outskirts of town. The streets grew narrower, the shops smaller. The charming din associated with the hustle and bustle of the palace district had long since faded away, and with it all signs of discretionary wealth. There was not a white glove or top hat to be seen; not one dress with fancy lace. This place belonged to the working class, and it sang a less melodic tune. It had also been a while since Reynard had spotted any soldiers. That gave him peace of mind.

Spiro, slightly ahead of him, suddenly whirled to assume his characteristic stance with hands on hips.

"What is it?" asked Reynard.

"We're here." Spiro's beady eyes drew Reynard's attention to a distinctive sign in the shape of a boot above his head.

"So we are. Just across the street, then." Reynard led the way to a small shop with no distinguishing features or signage.

"What if he's not here?" asked Spiro.

Reynard reached for the latch and pushed the door open. He stepped inside. The shop's curtains were drawn, but he could see well enough to make out two desks with chairs. Behind the larger desk was an open doorway leading to another room.

"Hallo!" he called.

"I told you he weren't here. What now?"

"You didn't tell me anything." Reynard shut the door behind them. "You asked me, 'What if he's not here?'"

"And you've yet to answer." Spiro watched as Reynard rounded the desk and stepped into the much darker back room.

"Leo?" Reynard paused to let his eyes adjust as Spiro joined him. There came no response, but Reynard began to make out a narrow cot against the back wall, and on it, what looked to be a person lying down. "Leo, are you sleeping?"

"Drowned in ale, more like it." Spiro crossed the room to kick the cot. "Wake up, friend! Boss is here!" He grabbed a handful of shirt and jerked it, calling over his shoulder to Reynard. "This one's not sleepin', that's for certain. He's drunk as can be, or...Gods above!"

"What is it?"

"He's dead!" Spiro released his grip, stepping back while gawking at the cot. "He's left the living, this one, and only just made the trip. His head's bashed in, and it's still wet!"

"Do tell." *Who would be so bold?*

"Lookie here!" Spiro lifted a small object from the floor.

Reynard returned to the office, lost in thought. Spiro followed, dropping what he had found onto the desk. Reynard looked at it: a small wooden block the size of a fist, a thin metal spike protruding from its center. He recognized it as a spindle, used to impale business papers. This one was covered in blood.

Spiro closely examined the tool. "It's a baby klubandag, is it not?"

Reynard's attention was suddenly fixed elsewhere. "You're not going to like what I'm about to say."

"Try me."

From a corner of the desk, Reynard picked up a ledger, its cover wet and sticky. "Our trip to the palace...it may have to wait."

THE FEAST OF LORDS AND LADIES

"It is your heart and not this crown that makes me feel a king."
King Axil, age 28, to Queen Isadora on their wedding day.

Sibil Dunn

The quiet of early morning found Sibil Dunn preoccupied with thoughts of those who had helped to shape her life. People who had believed in and supported her. People who'd loved her. A sobering fact hammered away: most were now lost to her.

Her father, renowned architect Adrian Dunn, had been the first to go, crushed by a large stone toppled from a palace scaffold. On learning of the accident, King Axil had sent more than his condolences: a basket of food, a wreath of flowers chosen by the queen, and two promises: her father would be buried alongside dukes and duchesses outside The Keep, one of five royal buildings he himself had designed; Sibil would be granted admission to the prestigious boarding school *Quest* for the remainder of her school almons.

It was there she had met Princess Lewen. From the day they had been assigned to room together, the bond between them had grown. At school, they'd been inseparable, and though Lewen's responsibilities had required her to return to the palace often, she had on many occasions brought Sibil with her. The princess had never made an issue of her title, and Sibil rarely thought of her as royalty. They had just been two girls with similar interests and outlooks. Until Lewen, too, had been swept away by a tragic accident.

When she was young, Sibil had confided her worries to her mother. They would sit for long spells, unraveling the fabric of whatever troubled her, as though it were an ugly quilt that could be restitched into a saner pattern. But since her father's death, her mother had become increasingly distant and withdrawn. She rarely spoke to Sibil now and never left the house. It wasn't as though their relationship was strained in any particular way; it had simply ceased to exist.

Sibil's thoughts turned to her two remaining friends: Tristan and Theos Godfrey, twins introduced to her by Lewen. As squires preparing for knighthood, their training had included attendance at select *Quest* classes. They were athletic, smart, self-assured but unassuming. Funny but not obnoxious, and generally unlike any other boys she had ever known.

One of her favorite memories was of once accompanying the twins home after school, only to be greeted by a disgruntled patriarch. The boys had neglected their morning chores and were condemned by Sir Godfrey to an afternoon of penance. Mrs. Godfrey hadn't the heart to send Sibil away, so she had seated her in the backyard where she could watch the boys till the soil in preparation for spring planting. It might as well have been yesterday—the memory was that vivid.

Both boys shirtless, their lean muscles rippling beneath a sheen of sweat and dirt as they bent to their task. It made her laugh, watching them try to outdo one another with tools meant for something other than cutting flesh.

Every now and then, Tristan stooped to pluck an insect from the dirt and carefully remove it from harm's way.

"What are you doing?" Theos asked. "Just smash them as you go!"

"They're rupples," said Tristan. "They help to work the soil, and they devour the bugs that eat our crops." He bent to pick up another. Half as long as his little finger, it curled into a small ball in his palm.

"Bah!" Theos swung his rowmaker into the ground. "There are hundreds! You're wasting time!"

"They have as much right to be here as us. This is their home as well."

"If you do that for every one we come across, brother, we shall be here 'til the sun sets." Theos stopped to wipe his brow.

"Then let us wish for one worth seeing," Tristan said, gently placing the rupple in Sibil's hand and closing her fingers around it.

Such a little thing. And yet...

It was at that moment she had first decided she loved Tristan, and she had loved him ever since.

An almon ago, she and the twins had graduated *Quest*, shortly before the anniversary of Lewen's death. Together, they had honored the princess' memory by gathering wildflowers and delivering them to The God of Children's House, a tradition Lewen and Sibil had honored almost every moon. But the twins would soon be knighted, and that would mark the beginning of new lives for them. They would have little time for old schoolmates.

But they're here now!

Sibil rose quickly, pulling on her worn leather leggings and a loose cotton blouse. She gave her long dark hair a few quick brushes before tying it back in a ponytail.

The fact that the twins were destined for knighthood was no reason to sit and brood. Their mother sold flowers in Fostead's marketplace, and would no doubt welcome seeing her. Lady Godfrey would at least have news of her boys. Perhaps they would be coming home soon to train with their father, Sir Godfrey, and once again invite her to join them. She slipped the dagger they had gifted her under her waistband just in case. She called out to her mother, stuffed an apple and a piece of bread into her pocket, and set off with firm resolve.

Sibil sat on a large rock on the roadside, entertaining second thoughts. A long walk and fresh air had cleared her head, allowing reality to settle in. Tristan and Theos were most likely with their respective knights. Pressing on to Fostead wasn't going to change that. Still, her alternatives were limited. She could make a day of losing herself in the village crowd, or she could return home, a poor choice given the circumstances there.

Just as she decided to press on, she became aware of movement from the direction she had come—someone shuffling down the road. *Impossible!*

She slid down behind the rock, out of sight, to watch the moving figure. As it grew closer, and its gait became more familiar, she eased herself to sit, bewildered. What was her mother doing walking down this road?

Is she following me? No other explanation was forthcoming. Her mother had not walked to town for the past two almons. Though The Lords and Ladies Feast would be celebrated this day, she could not imagine the woman being drawn to that event. Even when her father was alive, her mother would say on this day each almon: "Why would I stand gawking at the castle? From so far away, mind you, in a crowd, with the hot sun baking me like a biscuit, when your father can take me straight inside any day I please?" And she would raise her eyebrows and smile at Sibil, then peck her husband appreciatively on the cheek.

Sibil raised herself, assuming enough time had elapsed to allow her mother to pass. She considered, for a moment, racing out and asking the woman why she felt the need to spy on her. But prudence and a pinch of doubt restrained her. She settled down again and closed her eyes. She would rest just long enough to ensure her mother was out of sight and then pick up her trail.

Sibil had given her mother a long lead, and that had proven prudent on the road to Fostead. But as she neared the fork leading either into town or to the palace, her strategy turned on her. She watched from a distance as a swollen crowd swallowed the woman.

"The Lords and Ladies Feast," she whispered.

She decided against entering the assemblage. Instead, she climbed a knoll and sat beneath a tree. With an expansive view of the crowd's edge, and from a spot her mother was certain to pass on her return home, she relaxed and allowed her eyes to wander. It did not take them long to focus on the blaze of white stone streaked with blue and gray that interrupted the horizon above and beyond the crowd. The Castle of Aranox entranced her with its towers and turrets connected by long stretches of crenellated battlements. Constructed of pure baelonite, it stuck out against the blue sky like a crisply chiseled cloud. It was more than just a massive presence; it was Lewen's birthplace, and the site of her father's death.

Mari Dunn

Mari Dunn had been awake since dawn. She heard Sibil say she was leaving, but she did not respond, not even to ask where her daughter was going. She walked around inside the cottage, picking objects up at random, depositing them elsewhere, without any real regard as to what she was doing. Though aware of her surroundings, she felt somehow detached, both physically and mentally. She was drifting away, and the sensation was unsettling but eerily familiar. She felt she might throw up, and a prickly heat spread through her. She had felt this twice before, and she dreaded what was coming.

She dropped the silver bowl she was holding and fell to the floor, her body stiffening. Her eyes rolled back, and everything went black.

A spacious, crowded room. Long tables heaped with food and drink. Laughter, music, merriment. Scores of well-dressed men and women. The center of attention: a large bearded man, a crown upon his head! Hands reaching to him. No! Clawing at his neck! A dagger plunged into his back! Another run through his heart!

Mari set off down the road, concerned about the distance to her destination. Her shoes were severely worn. It would be a painful journey if no one stopped to help, but she had little choice. She pulled her shawl over her shoulders and hurried on.

The first time she had blacked out, she had not known what to make of it. With no similar background to draw on, she had thought the vision of her husband with a pained expression, reaching out for help, had merely been a bad dream. When he'd died that same day inspecting a palace building site, crushed by a falling block of stone, she'd thought it a morbid coincidence, nothing more.

The second time, she had been sleeping when it woke her. That same feeling of withdrawal from the real world, followed by nausea, then paralysis, and ultimately unconsciousness. And a vision—this time of two women, one older, the other Sibil's age, both dressed in their finest, both crying out for help. One surrounded by men and a bloody horse. The other flying like a wounded bird, crashing to the ground. It had shaken her initially, disturbing her so much that she had wrung her hands raw while sitting on her bed, rocking back and forth. *Do something*, she had told herself, but she had not known what to do. Or if she had, she had not dared to. She was no longer sure whether uncertainty or fear had gripped her. Perhaps both.

It was not until a day later that she had learned of the queen's and princess' deaths, and her heart had stopped momentarily, frozen mid-beat as the images of the two women reappeared to her. It was not possible, but there was also no denying it. If she had mentioned it to anyone, they would have told her she was dreaming. Or that it was someone other than the queen and princess she had imagined. Or that it was a coincidence. Or that her mind was playing tricks on her; that it had conjured up those images only after she had learned of the women's deaths. Or that she was mad.

But Mari knew better. It had been a premonition. A terrifying glimpse into the future. And now this.

Mari stood at the base of a road on the outskirts of Fostead, along with scores of others drawn to watch an informal parade of nobility make its way to the castle atop the hill. The road led nowhere else. Anyone on it past this point was headed either to or from the palace. Several footmen dressed in gold and red greeted those turning onto the road, checking with white gloves to ensure everyone who passed held a large card embossed with the royal seal. Between the footmen and the palace, the road was lined on either side by soldiers, an obvious and effective deterrent to anyone without an invitation.

Behind the row of soldiers were horses and wagons, with royal staff milling about. And because the castle gates stood open to receive a constant flow of nobles, an additional unit of mounted soldiers sat armed just outside the castle walls. But the sun was high in the sky now, the flow of nobles reduced to a trickle. Most were probably inside the castle already, preparing for their best meal of the almon.

Mari looked anxiously around. A morning of thoughtful travel had failed to produce any plan of action. She had not even thought about The Lords and Ladies Feast being held this day, which only made her task more difficult. Now she was stopped at the bottom of the palace road with little hope of getting any closer to the castle gates. Her feet were blistered and raw; her legs ached from ankle to hip.

She gathered herself. The king was going to die soon if she did not warn him, she was sure of it. Perhaps he would die anyway. Her husband, the queen, the princess—perhaps they all would have perished even had she tried to intervene. She had no way of knowing, but the thought that she might have prevented their deaths gnawed at her constantly, and she refused to sit idly by this time. She was desperate to at least try to warn the king. If she did not, she was certain she would never sleep again, or be of any use to anyone.

Someone pushed her from behind, not roughly, and likely not on purpose, but enough to make her lose her balance and bump the back of the gentleman standing in front of her rather hard.

"Oi!" the large man cried, turning around with a scowl.

"Terribly sorry." Mari pressed past the man before he could further react. A shot of adrenaline rushed through her. She lowered her shoulders and wriggled through several rows of onlookers, ignoring their reactions and hostile remarks. The more progress she made, the more resolute she became, until she nearly stumbled from the crowd's edge into the open road, within earshot of two white-gloved inspectors checking guests' invitations.

"Beg pardon," she said, mustering her courage. "I must see the king!" To her surprise, not even the townsfolk standing next to her reacted. She wrinkled her brow and filled her lungs.

"If you please, I must see the king!"

This time, several passing nobles turned their heads. One of the footmen shot her a quick glance of annoyance.

"Careful, love," an older woman behind Mari said under her breath. "Any louder and you'll have half the army on ya."

Mari's heart raced as she stepped into the roadway, close enough to touch some of those destined for the palace. Where moments before she had blended with a wall of worn and soiled wool, she now stood out amidst colorful silk and linen. A small group of nobles parted to give her a wide berth, while the two footmen checking invitations gave her their full attention.

She strode toward them, mindful that two soldiers had also taken note of her. "The king is in grave danger!" she shouted. "I must see the king!"

She was a spectacle to the crowd now, and a potential threat to the nobles wearing their finest. A young couple hurried through the checkpoint, their invitations never presented, as the footmen prepared to engage the intruder.

"I must see the king!" Mari urged herself forward, prepared now to bypass the checkpoint no matter what it took.

It startled her when a soldier grabbed her arm and yanked her roughly sideways. "Not this king! Not this day!" The soldier hauled Mari off as the footmen went back about their business. A second soldier appeared to assist the first, and suddenly Mari was being dragged across the dirt toward a group of wagons.

"What's this, Damen?" she heard a voice say. The soldiers stopped dragging her, but retained their grasp.

"Just a commoner lookin' for trouble, sir," said the one soldier.

"And now she's done found it, hasn't she?" said the other, tugging a bit on Mari's arm.

"Is that right, madam? Are you looking for trouble?" Mari looked up as the owner of the voice came into view. The first thing she noticed was his shiny black boots and the sword hanging at his side. He was sharply dressed in a tunic of royal colors, clean-shaven, with dark blue eyes highlighting handsome features.

"No sir, I am not."

"She looks quite fierce," the man said to the soldiers. "Good thing there were two of you to subdue her." One of the soldiers nodded, but the other looked sheepishly at the ground. "Gave you quite a struggle, did she?" The man stooped closer to Mari, placing his hands on his knees. "Are you an assassin?"

"No, sir."

"Do you mean the king harm?"

"On the contrary. I mean to save him."

"Do you?" The man straightened himself. "Release her, Damen, and help her to her feet."

"Yes, sir." Together, the soldiers lifted Mari erect.

"Now, leave us."

The soldiers complied without hesitation and headed back to their posts.

The man squared himself in front of Mari. "My name is Erik Carson. I am the king's marshal, and I apologize." He moved his face closer to hers. "But if you take another step toward the palace, I shall have you bound and gagged." He turned toward the wagons. "Please, madam, walk with me."

Mari found her voice. "I must see King Axil, and quickly."

The marshal's boots stirred clouds of dust as he walked. "And why is that?"

Mari hobbled after him. "He is in grave danger."

"Is he?" The marshal paused, glancing back at Mari. "What kind of danger?"

"I-I'm not sure. I think someone means to kill him." *He must think me mad!*

"Do they?" The marshal walked toward a supply wagon, where several soldiers were seated on a bench. A flick of his wrist in their direction caused them to disperse.

He stopped in front of the bench. "Please, sit."

"I cannot." Mari wrung her hands. "I must get to the castle."

"I insist." Carson took Mari gently by the wrist. Mari looked toward the castle, her eyes brimming with tears. "Sit, madam, or I shall have you bound and gagged, regardless."

Mari's chest heaved, and she began to sob as she collapsed on the bench. The marshal looked down at her with a wrinkled brow. Tears trickled down Mari's cheeks. "He's going to be stabbed! Here, in the chest!" Mari placed a hand on her bosom.

"Stabbed, you say? Tell me, madam, how do you come to know of the king's peril?"

"I cannot say."

"Cannot, or will not?"

"Please, sir." Mari grabbed one of the man's hands with both of hers. "I beg you. Warn the king!"

"Of what, madam? You give me no cause, save to have you thrown into the dungeon."

"I fear I have gone mad." Mari sobbbed.

The marshal withdrew from Mari's grasp, removed a kerchief from his tunic, and handed it to her. "Do you have a husband in the crowd, perhaps? Someone to care for you?" Mari shook her head, continuing to cry. "What is your name, then?"

"Mari. Mari Dunn."

The marshal cocked his head ever so slightly, his eyes narrowing. "Mari Dunn, you say?"

"Yes sir, my husband was—"

"Adrian Dunn, the palace architect. I know who you are. I attended your husband's funeral."

"Did you? Please help me." Mari reached again for the marshal's hand. "We must warn the king."

The marshal pursed his lips. "You have me at a loss, madam." He turned his gaze briefly to the palace, then studied Mari once more. "Most unusual," he said softly. A moment passed, his eyes again drifting toward the castle.

"Reggie!" he suddenly shouted. "My horse!" A young groom standing watch over a group of tethered horses sprang to action. "Listen carefully, Mari Dunn," the marshal said, resting a hand on her shoulder. "Stay here whilst I see to this riddle."

The groom approached, leading a white mare ready to ride. The marshal accepted the reins, swung easily into the saddle, and looked down at the young man.

"See to this woman's needs. Food and drink first. Then a physician. No one else is to touch her until I return, or they shall answer to me, do you hear?"

The young man acknowledged him with a vigorous nod.

"Hyah!" Horse and rider disappeared behind a veil of dust.

"Thank you," whispered Mari, with all the energy she had left.

The young groom returned with bread and water. Mari devoured the bread as he watched. "What's your name?" she asked, taking a sip between bites.

"Reggie." The lad clasped his hands behind his back and rocked slowly, heel to toe.

"Ah, that's right." Mari recalled the marshal yelling the name to retrieve his horse. "Is he a good man?"

"The marshal? Yes, ma'am, he is." She gave him a stern look. "The very best, ma'am," the boy said with an earnest nod.

"What is it that you do, Reggie? Care for the horses?"

"Yes, ma'am. I'm the groom's assistant. I help care for the soldier's horses, and the marshal's in particular."

"And do they like you?"

"The horses, ma'am? Or the soldiers?"

"Both."

"I don't think the soldiers like me. Or dislike me," the boy added hastily. "Most pay me no heed."

"And the horses?"

"The horses like me well enough. And I them."

"I'll bet they do." A mixture of relief and accomplishment settled over Mari. She was exhausted, but she had done what she could do. "How old are you?"

"I'm fifteen, ma'am." The boy squared his shoulders. "Old enough to join the army if I like, the marshal says."

"Is that so? Like to die in battle, would you? Feel another man's sword run through you?"

"I'm not afraid to die."

"I wonder," Mari said. "I wonder if..." She paused, staring into the distance. The young groom followed her line of vision, but seeing nothing unusual, returned his gaze to her. Mari let fall the wooden cup she had been holding, and then the bread. The boy retreated a step as she dropped from the bench to the ground.

"Are you well, madam?" he asked timidly.

She did not answer, her limbs stiffening until her entire body was straight as an arrow. The last she saw of the real world was the boy watching her in wonder before he ran, crying out as loud as he could for a physician.

A young woman... a familiar form... in the dark and all alone. No! Not alone. A large shadow suffocating her! She struggles to wrest free! She cannot breathe! Please, stop! A child's toy? A brandished knife! Cobblestones awash in blood!

Sibil Dunn

Sibil watched the assemblage below the palace slowly disperse, focused on those heading in her direction. She studied their clothing and their gait, certain she would recognize— Sibil strained to better see a figure zig-zagging unsteadily between others. She stood, her brow furrowed as much from worry as from squinting. Keeping sight of the meandering form, and with growing recognition, she began to walk toward it.

It was her mother. She was sure of it. Sibil began to run. Her mother was stumbling, righting herself, bumping into others, then stumbling forward again. *Is she injured?* "Mum!" Sibil cried, fairly certain she was out of earshot.

The dispersing crowd impeded Sibil's progress. She dodged one person, then another. "Mum!" she cried again. *What on earth has happened to you? Gods damn it! If only I had followed you more closely!*

Sibil was almost upon her now. She slowed to a brisk walk, skirted another couple, then reached out to support her mother's arm. "Mum, what's happened?"

"Sibil?" Bent over, her mother jerked in recognition of her daughter's voice. She stumbled once again, grasping frantically at Sibil's arm. "Is that you?"

Sibil steered her mother from the throng and toward a shady spot beneath a tree. Both fell to the ground, clutching one another's arms.

"Are you all right?" Mari asked.

"Am *I* all right?! Gods above, mum, what's happened to you?" Sibil scanned her mother more closely, somewhat expecting to see blood or broken bones.

Mari's grip on Sibil's arm tightened. "We must leave this place. And quickly!"

"You've had too much sun." Sibil tried to lay a reassuring hand on her mother's arm. "Let's rest a spell."

"No! We cannot!" Mari struggled to her knees. "We must be off!"

Sibil made no move to rise. Without her assistance, her mother was going nowhere. "What's going on, mum? Is someone chasing you?" Sibil quickly assessed the thinning crowd. "Why are you here? You're not making any sense."

"We cannot stay here, Sibil! It's not safe!"

"Why not?!" *What in Baelon are you talking about?*

Her mother's eyes bore into her and she wept. "I came to save the king, but for all I know, he's dead now!".

Sibil wrapped both arms around her mother and drew her close, resting her chin on top of the woman's head. "It's all right, mum. I'm sure the king is fine." All thought of imminent danger was washed away by sadness. Her mother had been falling slowly into some other world for almons.

"You cannot know!" Her mother sobbed, her entire body shaking against Sibil's. "You cannot."

"It's The Lords and Ladies Feast, mum." Sibil stroked her mother's hair. "He dines even as we speak. I am certain of it."

Mari wrested her head from under Sibil's chin. "He may be dead already. I've seen it, I have! Just like the queen and princess, and your father before them!" She was inconsolable and resisted Sibil's attempts to draw her back into her arms. "And you are next, child!"

"What did you say?" A chill swept over Sibil.

"You're next! We must find a place to hide. Your death comes next!"

Aside from the castle of Aranox, there were but five buildings in Fostead sanctioned and commissioned by the king to be built of baelonite, the royal stone. Her father had designed them all. Their conspicuous white facades with streaks of gray and blue would always remind her of him. How strange that she should have to summon courage to climb the steps to one of their front doors.

It was late in the afternoon. Her mother sat beside her, ranting incoherently about the king's and Sibil's safety. Trying to get her home was out of the question. The woman's shoes were beyond repair, and Sibil dared not try to remove them. Where exposed, her mother's feet were crusted with dirt and dried blood. She could barely hobble, let alone walk, and much of the journey home would be uphill. Dark would overtake them long before they made it back.

Visiting family friends was an option, but they lived on the other side of town, and she could not bring herself to appear at their doorway with her mother in this condition. Perhaps as a last resort. She climbed the stone steps to the building, and took the door knocker in her hand. She rapped twice and waited.

It was not long before the heavy door opened halfway to reveal an old, diminutive woman in a long brown habit partially covered by white cloth hanging from her shoulders. A white wimple surrounded her head, leaving only the front of a wrinkled face exposed. Her eyes, nearly lost beneath flaps of skin, looked with interest at Sibil.

"Yes?"

"Beg your pardon, but my mother has taken ill. We're a long way from home, and I fear she cannot make the journey before nightfall. Her feet are of no use to her. I was hoping you might... I thought perhaps..."

"Oh, dear," the woman said, cackling. "I'm afraid you've lost your way. This is The God of Children's House, you see?" She smiled kindly, pointing to the large inscription chiseled in baelonite above the doorway: *The God of Children's House—Where Only The Small Are Great.*

"You see?" The old woman nodded her head as though it might help Sibil understand.

The God of Children: the only god watching over those under the age of thirteen. Sibil wished she looked a few almons younger. Or that she had not been taught to be so humble. *What would you say if I told you my father built this place?* "Yes, thank you. I was just hoping that perhaps you could make an exception in this case. I really don't know where else to go."

"I'm sorry, dear. I really am."

"Who's that, Sister Mapel?" A male voice was shortly followed by the appearance of a middle-aged man in a loose-fitting brown robe tied at the waist with rope. The hood was laid back, allowing a full view of his roundish face. His brown eyes matched the color of his closely cropped hair and his cheeks were flushed with color.

He placed one hand on the half-open door, above Sister Mapel's, and opened it slightly wider so that he could peer outside. Sister Mapel turned and smiled at him. "Thank you, father," she said, and shuffled off.

"Thank you, sister," the abbot called after her, before turning his attention to Sibil. "I apologize. Sister Mapel means well, but..." He shrugged. "You may have to begin again."

"I'm sorry, father. I was explaining to Sister Mapel that my mother can no longer walk. Her feet are raw and blistered, and we are far from home. I was hoping that perhaps she could stay the night."

"I see. I'm sure Sister Mapel explained to you that we are a children's house."

"Yes, father."

"We are all these children have. We serve the God of Children. You at least have a mother, and more than one god looking out for you, no doubt."

"Yes, father. It's just..." Sibil's shoulders drooped as she wrung her hands.

"We can at least have someone look at her feet." The abbot opened the door wider and stepped outside. He took Sibil by the elbow and led her down the steps.

"Your mother's name?" He separated himself from Sibil and placed his hands beneath one of Mari's arms.

"Mari," said Sibil, taking her mother's other arm.

"Well then, Mari, let's get you inside, shall we?"

The two of them helped her stand, and slowly they began to ascend the steps. Mari winced and inhaled sharply once, but she was otherwise silent until they reached the top landing where all three rested momentarily.

"Thank you," Mari whispered.

"You're most welcome, Mari," the abbot said. "Let's find you a bed and see to your wounds." He shouted into the building. "Someone locate Brother Jessup! And Brother Kane!" Sibil could hear a shuffling of soft soles across the interior floor, then saw the swift blur of a habit through the open doorway.

"You'll stay the night at least," the abbot said firmly, moving forward across the threshold.

"But I thought—"

"You'd be surprised how many people come asking to be taken in. We can never be too careful." The abbot continued talking as two similarly dressed men approached briskly to relieve Sibil and the abbot from their burden.

"Thank you, Brother Jessup, Brother Kane. East wing, please. Find her an empty bed with one beside it for her daughter. Be mindful of her feet, please."

"Yes, father," said one. "Arms over our shoulders, please," he said to Mari. As quickly as she complied, the two men joined their free hands behind her legs, sweeping her off the floor.

"Sibil, child! Beware the dark! Promise me you'll not go out alone!" Mari said.

Sibil's embarrassment colored her cheeks.

Unfazed, the abbot watched the brothers carry her mother away. "As I was saying, we can never be too careful." He studied Sibil's face. "But I know you, do I not?"

"Perhaps. I do recognize you, father, though I do not know your name."

"I'm Father Syrus," said the abbot, smiling pleasantly. "And you...you're the young lady who used to bring us flowers with Princess Lewen."

King Axil

King Axil of Aranox tried to see The Lords and Ladies Feast through the eyes of those he ruled. For the kingdom's nobility, there were few better measures of success than to be invited inside the castle walls this day. Fueled by lavish amounts of food, drink, and entertainment, the feast unabashedly rewarded past support and subtly encouraged continued allegiance.

For the masses, it was a spectacle of opulence, a rare glimpse into a magical world otherwise out of reach. A symbol of the realm's strength and prosperity—a realm they inhabited. It promised better days ahead, reminding them that the wider celebration of Six Moons would follow shortly.

Illusions, one and all.

The feast was but a sharp reminder of the queen's and princess' tragic deaths. What was there to celebrate?

Absolutely nothing.

But it had been two almons since their passing—two almons since the last observance of either Six Moons or the feast—and his advisors had argued that both fests should be revived, if for no other reason than to restore across the kingdom a sense of normalcy and stability.

King Axil nodded to his entourage and commenced a slow walk down the passageway to The Great Hall. The sounds of a restless crowd grew louder. Taking their cue from the approaching procession, two guards tilted their spears toward one another, forming a barrier across The Great Hall's entryway. Immediately, and in unison, twelve musicians raised their herald trumpets to lips. Red banners embellished with the crest of Aranox—a gold half sun rising—hung from their instruments. The trumpets blared, and when the tune announcing the king ended, a hush hung over the hall.

The sentry guards retracted their spears, and the king's entourage moved forward.

Marshal Erik Carson

Marshal Carson entered The Great Hall, quickly surveying the room. There were perhaps two hundred people there, some milling about, most seated at three broad tables which ran nearly the length of the room. Music, laughter, and a steady buzz of conversation filled the air. Servants with trays bustled about. Troubadours, minstrels, and other entertainers flitted from one group of diners to another.

Carson signaled two soldiers standing by the doorway. "With me, to the king." As he walked, he scanned the room. "Have you seen the steward?"

"No sir," said one of the guards.

"In the galley, I believe," said the other.

Focused on King Axil, the marshal neared the head of the middle table. On either side of the seated monarch stood two taste testers, charged with sampling every course set before their lord lest it be poisoned. Behind them, near the entryway to the corridor leading from The Great Hall to the king's living quarters, two of the royal guard stood sentry.

By the time the king spotted him, Carson was near his side. "What is it?" the monarch asked.

"It's likely nothing, my lord. I've just come from—"

A woman screamed. Carson jerked his head up. Something crashed to the floor and the sound of a struggle ensued. "Guards!" the marshal shouted. A wave of bodies hit the taste testers standing to one side of the king, knocking them toward the table. One of them fell across King Axil, preventing him from rising. A chorus of battle cries was met by screams of terror. Several men dressed as nobles crashed against the table. There was the glint of steel as a dagger slashed toward the king. Too many bodies too close together caused the blade to miss its mark. It lodged in the back of the taste tester who had fallen across the king's lap. The stabbed man screamed as the blade was withdrawn and raised again. Before the attacker could strike a second time, the point of a spear pierced his stomach. He dropped his knife and gripped the spear's shaft with both hands. Another man clawed at the king's neck from behind. Carson grabbed the assailant's thumb and wrenched it backward as a sword buried itself in the man's chest.

Carson clambered over the arms of the king's chair and onto the table, where he drew his sword and surveyed the chaotic scene. The soldiers who had accompanied him protected the still-seated king, while the two guards that had stood sentry at the corridor positioned themselves between the monarch and his remaining attacker, straddling the two already dead. The assailant's dagger, all he could slip by the palace checkpoints, would be no match against several spears and swords. He was trapped, his weapon still pointed in the king's direction. Several more soldiers closed in behind him. The guests who had been seated at the table distanced themselves.

"Are you injured, m'lord?" Carson stole a glance toward his king.

"I'm fine. Get this man some help," said King Axil, cradling the stabbed food tester.

The marshal addressed the remaining attacker. "Throw down your weapon!"

Wide-eyed and breathing rapidly, the assailant brandished his knife in the air, lunging forward, crying, "Long live King Tygre!"

"Alive!" shouted Carson, but already one of the royal guards had swung his sword. It met the attacker's throat, nearly severing his head from his body. The dead man fell to the stone floor with a thud amidst gasps and shrieks from the crowd.

"I couldn't stay it," said the large guard wielding the sword.

"That's all right, Garth." Carson jumped off the table, and placed a hand on the young man's shoulder. "I would have done the same. Take three men; escort the king back to his chambers. Stay there the night." Carson lifted the injured taste tester so that two soldiers could assist the king in rising. "I have unfinished business here, my lord, but will join you in short order."

Carson beckoned to another soldier, then passed to him the food tester. "See to this man, and discover his name should he die. You four," he said, pointing to several others, "clear this room of all guests, and station guards at every entrance. No one is to enter but those in service to the king. Alfred, order all ranks back inside the castle, and close the gates."

"And Godwin." The marshal turned to one of the men who had first accompanied him across the hall. "Find the steward. Let him know what has come to pass. Tell him the feast is over. He'll not be happy, but it's done. Do not tarry with him. Go at once to where the horses are being held at the end of the palace road. Find the young groom, Reggie. He's caring for a woman. Bring her here forthwith and wait for me."

Carson entered the king's resting room, still pondering the disappearance of Mari Dunn.

King Axil rested on his back, sprawled across a chaise lounge upholstered in purple velvet, his head supported by the heavy coat he had worn to the feast. His large chest shuddered as it rose and fell beneath a shirt no longer tightly laced. The palace steward, Pryll Fletcher, paced slowly about the room.

If only he would keep his mouth shut.

The marshal's attention lingered on the pair of royal pets lying on the floor beside the king. Though domesticated at an early age, they were still cragens. Had they been present at the feast, they would have ripped the assassins to shreds before a sword could be drawn. The black and gray-striped beasts were tense with anticipation, keenly aware of the plate of half-eaten food within arm's reach of their master. The tips of their long tails twitched in the air.

"The food tester?" Not even a full beard could hide the lack of color in the king's haggard face.

"Dead, I'm afraid," said Carson.

The king sighed. "It's a risky occupation, to be sure. But to be stabbed..." He grimaced.

"Faced with the choice," the steward said casually, "I'd fancy stabbing over poisoning."

"Would you?" Carson met his peer's gaze and held it, aware that when battles were not being waged, day-to-day affairs such as cooking, cleaning, and entertaining dignitaries took center stage within the castle walls. As such, the steward was in the company of the king more often, with greater opportunity to demonstrate his proficiency and loyalty, as well as to influence the king's thinking. Mindful of this, Carson typically took care to hide his dislike of the man. Today, he felt a little less inclined. "I shall have to bear that in mind."

"He had family?" asked the king.

"I do not know, my lord," said Carson.

King Axil addressed his steward. "Find out, Pryll. And if so, see to it they are cared for."

"Yes, sire."

"It may as well be me who's dead. It would be so, Erik, had you not appeared when you did."

Pryll muffled a soft scoff, camouflaging it with a cough.

"We cannot know that, sire," said Carson.

Pryll applauded disingenuously. "I was not present, but I am told the manner in which you leapt upon the table was most impressive. Very gallant. Pray tell, how did they get within striking distance of Our Majesty in the first place?"

"Pryll..." said the king.

"They were dressed as nobles, and came through the front gates with the rest," said Carson.

"The front gates your men were guarding?" asked the steward.

"Pryll!" barked the king.

"My lord, I seek merely to determine how it is possible that—"

"I know precisely what you seek to do, and I tire of it!"

"Beg pardon, sire."

King Axil rubbed both temples. "Had I listened, a man would not be dead, and I would still be eating duck."

"Possibly, Your Majesty," said Carson, "but even had we—"

"Please. I was a fool to argue with you. Let us forget I ever did, shall we?"

"It is forgotten, lord."

"What am I missing?" asked Pryll.

"Erik advised me to have each and every guest searched prior to being granted entry to the castle," said King Axil. "But your king, in his infinite wisdom, forbade it. Unnecessary. Too embarrassing." He raised a finger in the air. "Next time shall be different."

"We shall be most tactful," said Carson.

"With the women, yes. But you can scour the gentlemen's ballsacks for all I care, and tell them it's the king's decree whilst doing so! At the very least, inspect the bottom of their feet!"

"These three have since been checked, m'lord. They had no markings. If they were assassins, they did not answer to The League."

King Axil tossed each of the cragens a scrap of meat from his plate. The beasts caught the morsels in mid-air, swallowing them whole. "These two shall dine with me at next almon's feast. They don't like crowds, but they'll learn. You never did say what brought you to The Great Hall."

"It was not a happenstance, sire."

"What?!" Pryll's immediate reaction caused the marshal to regret his choice of words.

"How do you mean?" asked the king.

Carson considered whether or not to disclose his interaction with Mari Dunn. "I was given cause to check on your well-being, sire. My men gather more information as we speak. In fact, they await me. As soon as I have sorted things—"

The steward threw his hands up. "What kind of answer is that? Do you refuse the king what he asks of you?"

Ignorant meddler! "I would fall on my sword first. Just as quickly as I would run it through a man who placed the king in danger, which is exactly what you do by impeding me. Would you keep me from my men, Pryll?" Carson turned to the king. "Shall I run him through, sire?"

"You try my patience," said the monarch, sighing. "Both of you. See to your men, Erik."

Carson left to the sound of the king's voice: "Married couples argue less than the two of you!"

The tree canopy shading the narrow road let little sunlight pass. Here and there a shaft of gold shone through, highlighting an understory of shrubs and next generation trees. Near the road's edge, the sun penetrated more easily, and patches of wildflowers bloomed in a dazzling array of color.

Marshal Carson took scant notice. He spurred his horse on, recounting a brief and unproductive meeting with Reggie, the stable boy. The lad had told him he'd watched the woman collapse before running to get a physician. When he returned a short time later, the woman had vanished. A few servants working nearby had seen her, but they insisted she had simply walked away.

Carson had no idea how the king or steward would react to hearing of Mari Dunn's hysterics outside the castle. And they would hear, given the prevalence of palace gossip. The two soldiers who had first intercepted the woman had undoubtedly told others of their interaction with the "crazy peasant." They had probably made light of it with comrades when first returning to their posts, but even had they not, they most assuredly had woven a dramatic story after hearing of the king's attempted murder—highlighting their own role, of course, in helping to prevent the king's demise. Some twisted version of that tale was bound to reach the king and steward eventually, and he wished to share his own rendition first.

He hoped to find and speak with Mari Dunn before he did so.

The woman's foretelling of the king's peril was a mystery to be solved. He granted that it was possible for the ravings of a madwoman to simply coincide with supportive happenstance, but the odds of that seemed too fantastic to warrant serious consideration.

Could she have been complicit in the attack? Might she hold the king responsible for her husband's death? If so, why try to warn him? A sudden change of heart? The marshal dismissed the notion as too far-fetched.

A more reasonable explanation was that Madam Dunn had somehow overheard those plotting the king's murder, then done her best to reach the king to forewarn him. It was the most satisfying theory he had developed.

The only other possibility was hardly grounded in logic or science. It was...well, preposterous. That the woman could somehow see into the future? No. He could not, would not, give that theory any credence.

He was, however, equally hard-pressed to explain, even to himself, what exactly had prompted him to act on her convictions. He was not generally inclined to rash pursuits, even when prodded by the fervent beliefs of others.

Of one thing he was certain: had he not acted on Mari Dunn's rants, the king might well be dead. It was imperative that he learn what else, if anything, the woman could share with him. How had she come to know of the attack? Did she know who planned it? Would there be another? Had there really been only three assailants, or had others slipped into the background when the initial strike was thwarted? Were enemies of the king still near?

It had not been difficult to learn where Mari Dunn resided. Her husband, the architect, had been familiar to everyone who labored to maintain the castle's physical structure, and was revered by those who took an interest in its design and engineering. His old residence was a short ride on horseback from the palace, and easily identified as the first house on the road leading out of town toward Dewhurst.

The woods gradually began to thin, trees giving way to an increasingly dense thicket of brush. Further down the road, the outline of a house appeared.

Carson knocked on the cottage door. No answer. He knocked again and waited. Still no answer. He tested the latch, pushed the door open, and announced himself. Greeted by silence, he stepped inside. It took little time to survey the interior. The two rooms were small, and sparsely furnished—not quite what he had expected to find in the abode of a renowned architect, and a good reminder of how fortunate he was to call the palace home. It was lived in, to be sure, but he found nothing out of the ordinary.

And no sign of Mari Dunn.

With a perfunctory nod to the two guards standing outside the king's private dining room, Marshal Carson made his way inside. King Axil, seated at the head of the table, greeted him. "Come, come! The soup's still warm! I wasn't certain you would join us!"

Pryll, seated to the king's left, did not look up.

Carson shared a tired smile with his king. Though hungry and tempted, he was in no mood to spend the evening listening to the steward's snide comments.

"Thank you, sire, but I promised my company to Lady Carson, and I'm late as it is."

"Who can blame you?" asked Pryll. "If my wife were half as handsome as yours, I would do the same." He loudly slurped a spoonful of soup.

The marshal bristled. The king closed his eyes. "I wish the both of you would bring your wives to sup here, as was your habit almons ago. That was delightful."

"I, for one, would welcome that, m'lord." Pryll looked directly at the marshal. "I, too, miss the company of Lady Carson."

Carson glared at him. *Go on! Say what's really on your mind! Cross that line, and not even the king's presence will save you!*

"Must I decree it to make it so?" asked the king. Carson continued to hold the steward's stare. "Let us not keep you any longer than need be, Erik. You've something to report?"

"Yes, m'lord. Baron Treadwell attended today's feast. Whilst he was here, one of his servants was murdered at his manor."

"One of his servants?" The king pushed his soup bowl away.

"A cook, apparently. Stabbed to death, and no witnesses."

"You don't think it's related."

"I doubt it, Your Majesty. But it does seem an odd coincidence."

"Very odd. But possible?"

"Highly unlikely, m'lord."

The steward threw another sharp glance at the marshal. "A pity none of them were taken alive, so that we might know with certainty."

A pity you weren't in the thick of it!

"Yes," said the king. "A pity indeed."

Carson bowed his head. "My apologies, sire, but under the circumstances—"

"Don't be absurd. There's no blame for you to shoulder."

Pryll smiled smugly.

"What more have you to share?" asked King Axil. "Earlier you spoke of something that prompted your return to the castle. Just in time to prevent my use as a pincushion."

Carson had anticipated the question. "There was a woman, sire. Outside the castle walls. She claimed you were in danger."

The king leaned forward. "She what?"

"It really was quite unusual, Your Majesty. In all honesty, my first thought was to have her thrown into the dungeon. I thought her quite mad."

"What did she say, exactly?"

"Only that you were in grave danger."

"And how came she to know this?" asked Pryll.

"She would not say."

"Are you so blind?" Pryll tossed his spoon onto the table and rose out of his chair. "I shall tell you how! She knew of the plot before it was hatched. At best, she overheard it being planned; at worst, she was in league with those who would slay you, then had a change of heart. Either way, she can identify the lot."

"And if neither is the case?" asked Carson.

"There is but one other explanation, and it is worse still for her."

"And that is?" asked the monarch.

"That she is a witch, my lord! In which case, she should be burned at the stake posthaste." Pryll turned to Carson. "You say she is not in the dungeon? I trust you have this woman in chains."

"That's hardly necessary."

The steward sneered. "On what do you base that assessment? Your instincts?"

"You think she meant to help?" asked the king.

Carson adjusted the position of a table setting's knife. "I can tell you only this, my lord. Had she not come forth, I would have been outside the castle walls, encouraging my men, whilst one of those intruders slit your throat."

The king considered this.

"Where is she?" asked Pryll.

Carson ignored him. "A good deal remains unknown, sire. We still seek answers, but she is known to you, and poses no threat."

"Known to me!"

"Yes, m'lord. I did not recognize her at first. But it was Madam Dunn, wife of the architect."

"Adrian Dunn's wife?" It was the king's turn to rise. The striped cragens, Sir Black and Lady Gray, appeared from beneath the table, clinging to his side as he began to pace. "Tell me again. What did she say before the feast?"

"Only that you were in danger, sire. And that she came to warn you."

"Most peculiar. Nothing more?"

Carson chose not to share her specific prediction of a stabbing. "No. That was enough to send me on my way."

"And thank the gods for that!"

"Where is she now?" It was a pointed question from the steward.

"I fail to see how that concerns you," said Carson firmly.

"Gentlemen," said the king. "It's but a question, Erik."

"She lives in Fostead," the marshal said, not wishing to disclose his ignorance of her whereabouts, nor wishing to lie to the king.

"Has she been interrogated?" asked Pryll. "How did she come to learn of the king's endangerment?"

He senses my evasiveness. "Interrogated? First chains, now this. I did not realize the steward had proclaimed her an enemy of the palace. Which method do you suggest, Pryll? Which is your favorite? Shall we flog her? The wife of a good friend of the king?"

"Nonsense." King Axil waved the suggestion away. "I know this woman, Pryll. She is the wife of a good man departed. Surely she means me no harm."

"Then she has nothing to hide, my lord. But we must learn how she came to know you were in danger. What she knew of the attack."

"He makes a point," the king said.

"As I said, your grace, we continue to seek answers."

Pryll snickered loudly in disdain.

Carson glared at him. "You are the steward, Pryll. It would be best if you kept to those tasks with which you are familiar, such as seasoning stews and cleaning chamber pots."

"Erik!" said King Axil. "Enough quibbling! Not another word from either of you! Hear well what I say next, then go about your work." He pointed at the marshal. "You have more important things to do than escort a woman who poses no threat. You shall inform Pryll where to find Madam Dunn, and you..." His eyes bore into the steward. "You shall bring her to me tomorrow. Unharmed, do you hear?"

"Of course, my lord." The steward bowed deeply.

"You've chased away my appetite," said the king. "Leave me. Both of you." A wave of his hand dismissed them.

Just outside the king's study, Carson turned to the steward. "She lives on the outskirts of Fostead, on the road to Dewhurst. It's an easy ride from here. Left at the end of the palace road. First dwelling on the right." He turned to go, but Pryll caught his arm.

"If ever you seek to make me look the fool in the king's presence again, you shall regret it."

Carson spun the smaller man around, pinning him to the stone wall. "You make a fool of yourself, Pryll, without any help from me. Remove your hand from my arm, lest I grow fond of it and keep it for myself." The tip of a knife suddenly tickled the steward's eyelash. The blade rested lightly against his cheek.

Pryll's fingers slowly loosened their grip.

Carson turned and strode away, his boots clacking rhythmically against the stone floor.

The steward spat loudly after him.

Sibil Dunn

Night was falling as Sibil left the cobbler's shop. She turned to watch its front door close, managing to wave before the cobbler's wrinkled face and long leather apron disappeared inside. The small shop was, as the abbot had said, but a short walk from The God of Children's House; she had had no trouble finding it following his directions. The abbot had given her a metal amulet in the shape of a rectangular shield the size of her palm. Its leather thong enabled it to be worn around the neck, but the abbot had told her to present it to the cobbler with one of her mother's worn shoes upon arrival.

She had done so and, as predicted by the abbot, the cobbler—a kindly old man with a mop of white hair—had simply asked, "How do you come by this, my dear?"

And though it seemed a bit odd to her, she had responded as instructed: "Thank you for asking, Master Nash. Father Syrus prays for me."

The cobbler had returned the amulet to her hand, folding her fingers around it. "Then I am at your service, madam. What can I do for you?"

When Sibil had explained her predicament, the cobbler had assured her that if she would return on the morrow at sunrise, he would have ready for her mother a pair of new turnshoes made of soft leather goatskin. There would be no charge.

Sibil retraced her steps down a narrow alley as her thoughts returned to her mother's strange behavior. She had purposely ignored previous impulses to reconstruct the day's events, telling herself she had more important things to pursue. She had first focused her energies on finding shelter, and then busied herself with the abbot's offer of new shoes. Those would help her mother's immediate plight, no doubt, but the woman's physical ailments were clearly nothing compared to what was plaguing her mind. Things had not been right with her since Sibil's father died. And they had gotten progressively worse. It was as though she had drifted away from her old self, and from those she had been close to. Sibil had not had a meaningful conversation with her for almons. There were sparks of life here and there, moments when Sibil dared to hope that her mother might be released from whatever enthralled her, but today's events had seriously dashed any such dream. Aloof and withdrawn was bad enough. Now it seemed her mother was drifting from reality as well. Her irrational rants about the king and Sibil's own safety were a new—

A violent force slammed into Sibil's shoulder, knocking her sideways and into the alley wall. She lost her footing, falling to one knee, dazed. There was the sound of gravel grating under foot.

"Well now, lass, jest where might you be goin'?"

Sibil's heartbeat quickened. She should have known not to take the alley. It was dark, but not so dark that she could not make out the shape of a tall man standing over her. She could smell him as well. Suddenly, he grabbed her by the hair and yanked her head toward his crotch.

Sibil still held the amulet. Instinctively, she drove it as hard as she could up between the man's legs. He gasped and released her hair.

"Bitch!" The man reached once more for her, but Sibil had already drawn her arm back. She struck him again with the amulet, in the same spot, only this time with more purchase and resolve. "Agh!" Too late, the man struggled to shield his privates.

Sibil stood, dropping the amulet as she reached frantically for the dagger beneath her coat. Her fingers trembled as they curled tightly around its hilt. She brandished the blade menacingly, panting as she sought to ward off her attacker.

"Bitch!" The man drew his own, much larger, knife. He lunged as Sibil turned and ran straight into the arms of an even larger man she had not seen approaching from the other end of the alley. She tried to push away, but already he had wrapped a strong arm around her, pinning both of hers and lifting her off her feet. Still holding her, the big man grabbed her oncoming assailant with his other arm and threw him headfirst against the alley wall.

Sibil squirmed, but the big man held her tightly with one arm. With the other, he pried the dagger from her hand.

"I'm going to let you go now. No further harm will come to you."

Sibil found herself standing on her own, unsure of what to think. The big man held her dagger by the blade and offered it to her. "Take it and be off."

What's happening? Sibil hesitated before instinct overrode all else. With another surge of adrenaline coursing through her veins, she snatched her knife and ran.

Rolft Aerns

Fifteen almons of service. Rolft had battled both man and beast, survived both plague and famine. The scars on his right forearm, the burns on his left hand—symbols of his fealty to a benevolent king, a compassionate queen, and a princess who had embodied the best of both. What a glorious reign it had been! How quickly it had all come crashing down.

There was no undoing what was done, no honor in seeking to escape or to forget. The queen and princess had been gone two almons now. He would gladly give his life to make amends, but not until he satisfied his vow. Perhaps then the gods would grant him passage to Baelon above. In the meantime, there was work to do.

Rolft steepled his fingers beneath his chin and stared into a dying fire. Deep in The Wandering Woods, he was fairly certain he had left no trail to follow. Even so, he would keep his guard up no matter how serene or safe his surroundings might appear. It had saved him more than once.

His hair had not been shorn since he'd left the king's army. Long and shaggy, it kept his head warm. He buried the fire's embers and heated stones with dirt, stretched out across the warming ground, and pulled the furry hide of a bortok to his chin.

When he closed his eyes, the procession of memories that haunted him most evenings ran its course:

Queen Isadora thwarting his authority in the presence of Princess Lewen. "You say 'cannot' Rolft, but the princess is of age. If she desires to ride alone, so be it. We shall not speak of this again."

The princess' battered body, limp and lifeless on the courtyard, her boot still caught in a stirrup.

A bloody horse, its tail swishing side to side as it was led away.

The queen sprawled motionless nearby.

A grief-stricken king.

A somber march to a final resting place, Rolft's hands supporting one of two twin caskets.

And always the last image in his visual parade: *his dismissal from the royal guard without notice or fanfare.*

No explanation had been required. He hadn't uttered a word of protest.

He should have argued harder that evening with the queen. That effort failing, he should have accompanied the princess the next morning, despite protestations or personal consequence. *"Above all else, and at any cost."* Recognizing the princess' dilemma, he should have seen to the queen himself. Immediately. But their earlier disagreement had caused him to hesitate, and she had fallen to her death as a result.

Guilt.

His constant companion.

He breathed deeply and waited for sleep to claim them both.

Rolft rode slowly, allowing his horse, Sarah, to set the pace. He was in no hurry. He had but one task left in life. Whether he accomplished it this sun or twelve moons hence was of little consequence.

There were only four towns within a day's ride of the royal retreat in Dewhurst. For the past two almons, he had traveled from one to another, following the same routine: rest his horse and have it groomed; stock up on supplies; spend the rest of his time mixing with the locals, watching and listening for anything that might lead him in the right direction. He would spend the next few days in Fostead, then swing south and head for Chalmsworth.

King Axil's castle was a stone's throw from a road leading directly through the heart of Fostead, where the palace secured most of its goods and supplies, and where the staff who were not housed at the castle lived. It was also where the soldiers went when they had time to kill and money to spend. Rolft had lived in the castle barracks for many almons while guarding the royal family. The town's streets and alleys were as familiar to him as to anyone who lived there.

From the outskirts of town, even Sarah knew the shortest route to the livery. Without coaxing, she found the expansive grounds fronting that large structure. The familiar smells of leather, straw, and horse dung further thickened an atmosphere clouded with the dust churned by a multitude of boots and hooves.

Rolft began to survey the men who wore those boots as soon as they came into view. *Always people first!* By the time he dismounted, he had assessed them all, paying particular attention to those wearing the colors of the king. He still knew a fair number of those who called the palace home, but the army was large, with turnover every moon, and the three soldiers standing idly to one side of the livery were unfamiliar to him. Just as well. At least one of them had observed his arrival, so Rolft watched the group until he was satisfied that their conversation continued unaffected by his presence.

He recognized only one man outside the cavernous building. Bohun Barr was large, stocky, and easy to spot. Almost always dressed in a soiled and torn undershirt, he towered above those around him, his dark hair cropped close to his boulder of a head, his arms bulging with the muscles of one who had handled horses and heavy tools all his life. Those meeting him for the first time likely found him an imposing figure, but he was the gentlest of souls. One had only to watch the way horses took to him to know that.

Bohun had operated the livery since before Rolft had known the place existed. As a royal guard, Rolft had considered the stablemaster both capable and fair. Since retirement, he had come to know the man even better. Bohun had first offered to shelter him moons ago, when Sarah had not been feeling well. Rolft had found the stables as comfortable as any tavern, and far more suited to his comings and goings. Bohun had proven to be informed regarding local occurrences, and his four-legged clients were better-natured than most townsfolk. The stables had become Rolft's bed of choice when traveling through Fostead.

After being told Rolft preferred not to have his presence in town announced, the stablemaster had stopped hailing him loudly upon his arrival. Instead, he stepped out to meet him with a quiet handshake, as he did today. The man's grip was firm.

"How are you, Bohun?"

"I'm well. And you?" Bohun used the back of a heavily calloused hand to wipe sweat and dirt from his broad brow.

"The same." Rolft handed Sarah's reins to the stablemaster. Sarah nuzzled the man's broad shoulder, leaving a thick strand of spittle draped across it. Bohun paid no attention.

Rolft patted the horse's rear quarter. "Sarah says yours is the finest livery of them all."

"Does she now?" Bohun cupped the animal's muzzle in his hands, planting a kiss on her nose. "Well, that's an extra ration of hay for you, that is!"

"No news?"

"None to speak of. Not many new to town, and single riders mostly. No one of interest to you, so far as I can tell. Big day today, though. Lords and Ladies Feast, I'm sure ya know."

Rolft grunted. "I'll settle when I leave."

"Keep yer coin." Bohun laughed as he led Sarah away. "I'll keep the horse instead!"

Rolft started what he knew would be a short walk, listening to Bohun's laughter fade away. He had forgotten the feast would be celebrated this day. He headed for The King's Inn, where he would speak with his friend Jarod, find a secluded table, and settle in for the evening.

Rolft sat slumped forward in the dark, as though dozing at a table near the back of The King's Inn, his eyelids all but closed, his head resting on his arms. He had held the same position since his arrival. The tankard on his table was still full.

Four men sat huddled nearby. They had started drinking early, conversing in hushed voices. Slowly, the establishment had filled with patrons paying little attention to anything or anyone outside the reach of their own drinking arm. The more they drank, the less they seemed to care what others might hear or think. By the time the four closest to him had started on their fifth tankard of ale, they were practically shouting at each other.

One of them said something that caused Rolft's head to clear. He held his breath, his heart pounding, listening more intently. Had he heard right?

"Shut your mouth, Kole!" The skinniest of the four, a young man with hair of gold, suddenly shot out of his chair, seething. "One more word, and I'll gut you here and now!" He glowered at the big man seated across from him. "Go on—I dare you!"

The young man's three companions sobered quickly. The one called Kole tried to calm him with a raised hand. "Rest, Alden, rest. I forgot, is all."

No! Say it again, I beg you!

Alden glanced quickly about the room, then scowled at his companions. He pointed at the one called Kole. "And that is why Raggett don't share stuff with the likes of you."

"All I'm sayin'," said Kole, "is that we've heard it all before. Never mind the particulars." He lowered his voice such that Rolft could barely hear and spoke sarcastically. "Big job, big take. The Guild can't help but see it."

The Guild!

The big man called Kole displayed his empty hands. "And look what's come of it."

"Twice now," said one of his companions.

"Fine," said Alden. "This is why Raggett talks to me."

"But you weren't on today's job neither. Who got to go if you're so smart?"

"Raggett always takes Shum when he needs a greasy snake, don't he? And Edwyn just in case he needs the muscle. Took pity on poor Harolt, I suppose. But you'll be workin' soon. Biggest job ever. Needs us all."

"He told you that?"

"He tells me everything."

"Pigs' slop."

"Think what you like. I'll jest let Raggett know you want no part."

"What? I never said nuthin' of the sort!"

"You've as much as said you don't believe him."

"Jest said I don't believe you!"

"But I'm only tellin' you what Raggett told me, so if you don't believe me, well..." Alden let the inference sink in.

"Well...what kinda job then?"

"Can't tell ya." Alden raised his eyebrows and the tankard of ale. He filled his cup once more. "Sworn to secrecy, I am." He placed both palms on the table, leaning forward as he spoke. The other three leaned in as well.

Rolft strained to hear, his eyelids nearly closed.

"Biggest... job... yet." Alden paused for effect. "Which means a big payday." He leaned back and locked his fingers behind his head.

The others leaned slowly back as well. "Huh," said one.

"A toast," said Kole, raising the tankard rather than his cup. "Big payday!"

The others laughed and raised their cups, ale sloshing onto the table. "Big payday!" they cried together.

"Just be there tomorrow," said Alden, lowering his voice. "Everyone, this time. Noon. Same place as always."

"Ready t'work!" said one of the four, rubbing his palms together.

"I'll tell ya what needs work." Kole took one last swig from the tankard before rising to his feet unsteadily. "My cock!" He laughed, nearly losing his balance as two men walked briskly past. "An' you just stay where you are," he said pointedly to Alden. "There's some things a man should do with no one watchin' over him!"

"Go on, then," Alden said. "No one wants to watch you rub your knob!"

Rolft lay awake, his head lightly touching one side of a stable stall. It was the middle of the night, yet he could not sleep. Sarah's large chestnut eyes looked down at him from the adjacent bay.

He lifted by its leather thong the metal object the young woman had dropped, watching it twirl in the night air until it stopped. It was rectangular, convex and shaped like a shield, its backside polished and smooth save for an inscription. He struggled in the dark to make it out: *Protector of Innocence.*

Whispers of cool air entered through chinks in the livery wall.

There was much to think about. He had watched the one called Kole make a poor choice in an alley. The young woman he accosted had been agile, quick, and armed. *What if she had killed the wretch?* As it was, Rolft had pried from Kole's lips the names of five others before sending him to Baelon below.

Five names, none of which he had ever heard before.

He had used Kole's blood to scrawl their initials on his arm, and recited the names until they were etched in his mind as well.

Five men.

Courtesy of Kole's last words, he knew where they would meet with others on the morrow. His foot felt for the pack he had dumped in the corner of the stall.

THE CROSSING OF PATHS

"Protect the royal family and defend its honor, above all else, at any cost, and under any circumstance---so do I pledge." Rolft Aerns, age 19, reciting the Royal Guard's oath before his king and queen.

Overseer Reynard Rascall

Reynard had yet to settle on a plan of action. Leo's murder was an unpleasant complication. At the very least, it meant a longer stay in Fostead. Bad enough. But it also warned of issues darker and more troubling than the siphoning of profits from Gatherer Kasparr's operations, which was itself unacceptable.

He lay pensive on his cot, the dead bookkeeper's leather-bound ledger resting on his chest. The pages of its first half were well worn, their edges softened and crumpled by repeated handling, their surfaces riddled with black ink that had flowed from a steady hand with decent penmanship. In stark contrast, the pages of the second half were stiff, crisp, tightly pressed together and devoid of ink.

Reynard had skimmed the ledger before leaving Kasparr's office. Since then, he had carefully examined its first half several times. Each entry consisted simply of a date, followed by a first name, then a monetary sum. There were dozens of takers' names in Leo's book, each entered once a moon, though not always in the same order.

Reynard had dwelled so long on the last entry that he could not help but picture it now, even with his eyes closed. Made the day before—the day of Leo's murder—it consisted only of that date, followed by a first name: Raggett. No monetary sum. The entry was cut short, as though the author had been interrupted. A review of previous moons' entries, however, revealed Raggett's largest contribution to have been seventeen dire. His most meager, only six!

Whoever he was, Raggett deserved to die, if only for shortchanging Kasparr and The Guild. Six dire for a moon's work? Unheard of! Yet Raggett's meager offerings had been fairly consistent for the past two almons.

Reynard was certain he had heard the full names of all of Kasparr's takers at one time or another, but he had never bothered to memorize them. He had, in fact, told all three of his gatherers he preferred the use of first names only. He knew that Joshua in the north and Jonathon in the south maintained similar ledgers—no doubt filled with unfamiliar names. *Noggods!* He did not even know Joshua or Jonathon's last name!

Mistakes! They were adding up, and they were getting costly.

He frowned, tossing the book onto the floor.

Spiro remained motionless on his back, staring at the ceiling.

"You know what I think?" Reynard asked.

"That this is the most boring hunt you've ever been on?" said Spiro bitterly.

"What's that?"

Spiro's hands stretched toward the ceiling, quivering. "Eat hearty, Spiro! Drink your fill, Spiro! Tomorrow, we hunt!"

"We are hunting," Reynard said, annoyed as much by his own lack of progress as he was with his companion.

Spiro scoffed. "Hunting requires a certain amount of movement. Stealth, to be sure, but the bookkeeper is moving no less now than you."

"Really?"

"Really. And where there's hunting, there's generally some catching and killing involved. I think you may have over-promised."

"Perhaps I should have said investigating. It's really much more a thinker's game. Not everyone is capable of it, to be sure."

"I see." Spiro rolled off his bed to stretch. "Still no clues in your little book?"

"Nothing useful. Remind me to arrange another meeting with our gatherers when we return to Waterford. Kasparr is excused, of course. And have them bring the names of all their mastertakers. We need to change our operations."

"I'll try to remember, but that, too, seems a thinker's game. Are you certain I'm capable?"

"Not at all. But when all you have at your disposal is a dull tool, well, you don't just toss it aside, now, do you?"

Spiro stooped to pick up the ledger by its binding, rifling through the exposed paper edges with his thumb. From between the pressed, crisp pages near the back, a scrap of paper fell, wafting its way to the floor. It landed between the two men.

Spiro picked it up. Reynard stared at it from over Spiro's shoulder. Both sides were covered in tiny print, which close inspection revealed to be a list of hand-scrawled names. Full names.

Reynard soon spied one beginning with Raggett.

His gaze gradually shifted to Spiro.

Spiro clicked his tongue. "If ever you do dispose of me, be careful you don't cut yourself."

Reynard dropped a coin onto the bartop from such a height that it could not help but be heard by the large man sweeping the floor. Reynard recognized him as the one who had welcomed them to the inn—the same man who had watched them from behind the bar the previous night. There were few others in the room this time of day. Most were probably at work or recovering from drinking the night before. Those present had their heads buried in bowls of porridge.

The innkeeper stopped sweeping and leaned on his broom. "You thirsty?" he called from across the room.

"We are not," Reynard said. "But the coin is yours, just the same." Spiro leaned casually against the bar, his hawk-like eyes returning the innkeeper's stare.

"Be direct, or be on your way," the innkeeper said. "I've work to do."

"My apologies," said Reynard. "No offense intended. We seek information, is all."

"What kind of information?"

Reynard held up the scrap of paper from the ledger, dangling it in front of his face. "You know them or you don't. Simple as that."

The big man continued sweeping as he made his way to the bar. "If they live in town, I know them." He accepted the paper from Reynard's outstretched hand and began to digest its script. "What is it you want with them?"

"They work for the man!" said Spiro.

"What he means," said Reynard softly, "is that we have business with them, is all."

Reynard stepped into the street, stopping and turning to flaunt a wide grin. "There, you see?" He slapped his palm triumphantly with the folded piece of paper. "We're on taker Grymes' trail. And that, my friend, is how it's done."

"Most impressive." Spiro brushed Reynard as he walked past. "And all because of that little slip of paper? However did you come by it?"

"Ah." Reynard hung his head momentarily, then quickly followed his associate. "You want credit, do you? For causing this to fall out of that book?" He laughed, pocketing the paper. "Let me ask you something, Spiro... If I build a wall, do you seek credit for putting one stone in place?" Spiro waved him off. "A stone, I might add, which you picked up out of curiosity, then dropped into place by chance?"

Spiro stopped on the other side of the street, hands on hips. "You're building a wall now, are you?"

"Well, so to speak. It's an analogy. To be fair, we're building a wall together. But make no mistake, Spiro, I am the architect."

Spiro rolled his eyes.

Reynard placed a hand on the shorter man's shoulder. "Really, be honest now. Would you have found this paper had I not taken Leo's ledger in the first place?"

Spiro's arms slowly dropped from his hips. "So, you're the architect. What's that make me?"

"Why, you're the mason, of course!"

"The mason." Spiro's beady eyes narrowed to slits.

"Yes. You're the mason. And do you know why you're the mason, Spiro?"

"No, why?"

Reynard slapped him on the back, leaning down to whisper in his ear. "Because you like to get your hands dirty, that's why."

Raggett Grymes

Raggett watched, mildly amused, as the granary came to life. Men scurried in and out of its large mouth like so many ants with shovels, rakes, and other implements he had no interest in wielding. Listening to their banter on countless mornings had taught him more than he cared to know about the building. In its bins was stored a variety of threshed grain and seed, protected from both sun and rain by a double-layered thatch roof. It had been built on stone footings to deter entry by wild animals and to allow air to circulate beneath its floor. Rodents and the damp were most unwelcome here.

Raggett eyed the two sacks slung across the back of his tethered horse. Full of household items too costly for the common purse, they were a little bulky and misshapen to be holding grain. Their contents were courtesy of Baron Treadwell, of course—candlesticks, cutlery and whatnot. All made from precious stone or metal, like carmine or alacacia. And jewelry with gems he could not identify. But outside the granary at sunrise, amidst countless other horses with grain sacks, who would ever notice?

He could hardly wait for noon. His full crew was a dozen now, and every one of them was going to be impressed. Perhaps he should have joined the king's army. Though he did not like being told what to do, he would certainly have made a good commander. Business was picking up as a direct result of his leadership, was it not?

He spied Shum down the road, little more at first than a bald noddle slowly winding its way past horses, men and carts. The closer the taker got, however, the more of him came into view.

Raggett frowned. Shum's hands were empty. As if that weren't obvious enough, the taker made a show of it by raising them in the air and displaying his palms as he approached.

"'T'weren't there," Shum said matter-of-factly.

"What do you mean?" asked Raggett. "The book? It had to be! We left it there. Right on the desk. Did you look?" *Of course he hadn't! No brains, this one!*

"'Course I looked! Why else did I go? It wasn't there, I tell ya."

Clumsy bungler! "Did you look all around? On the floor? Under the desk? Perhaps it fell whilst we were...you know."

Shum pursed his lips over toothless gums and slowly moved his head from side to side. "Nope. I looked high and low. Got on my hands and knees and crawled that whole place three times over. You're welcome ta do the same."

"Raggett!" The sound of his name from behind gave Grymes a start. He turned to see young Alden standing a short distance from him, laboring and obviously excited.

"Alden! What's got into you? You look a fright."

"I've just come from some of the others." The young man tried to catch his breath. "It's not good."

"What's not good? Explain yourself."

Alden looked guardedly around before approaching Raggett to whisper in his ear.

Raggett swore as Alden backed away. "Kole?" he asked. Alden nodded vigorously. "You're sure of it? You saw with your own eyes?"

"I did not. I heard from Edwyn. But he would know. The two were good friends."

"Where? When?"

"Had to be last night. After he left The King's Inn. I was with him there."

"Noggods!" Raggett's mouth twitched.

Alden waited, his breathing slowly returning to normal.

Raggett exhaled angrily. "Change in plans. Take these." He patted one of the sacks on his horse. "Stash them somewhere safe. Don't pawn them today. Spread word instead. Today's meeting is canceled. I need time to think. Once you're done, come find me at The Raven's Nest. And Alden... bring Edwyn with you."

Rolft Aerns

The abandoned warehouse had once been a hub of activity, hosting a constant flow of goods to and from its belly. It had been built, however, between a road repeatedly washed out by heavy rains, and a stream that threatened to take the warehouse's foundation with it each time it flooded. The road had eventually been rerouted and a new warehouse erected on higher ground. Few people used the old road now. Almons of neglect by all but nature had left it a deeply rutted swath of dirt, rock, and hardy scrub brush.

Having left Sarah tethered to a bush deep in the woods, Rolft sat behind the trunk of a large felled tree, trying to match the men he had seen enter the warehouse to scant descriptions provided by the alleyway thief, Kole Cantry. He rubbed one finger against another as he considered leaving. It was well past the appointed meeting time, and there had been no visible activity for a while. Only five men were in the warehouse—far fewer than he expected. Had Kole given him bad information, either purposely or because his mind was clouded by pain?

Kole had told the truth about the meeting's location—Rolft was confident of that. It would be too coincidental otherwise for men to visit this abandoned and desolate site. The number of men he had anticipated would have been a challenge. Five was much more manageable. It was, in fact, conceivable that every man now in the warehouse had helped Kole send the princess to her death. Unlikely, and yet... if that was the case, such an opportunity might never come again.

It was not as though they could be lying in wait for him. None of them had carried obvious weapons. Nor could they know that he was stalking them. Kole had been shocked to learn that fact himself. As far as anyone knew, the princess' death had been a tragic accident.

No, the element of surprise still belonged to him.

Standing to remove his coat, he checked the accessibility of two daggers at his waist. He hefted his arming sword in one hand, a shorter sword in the other. He had been sitting for so long that he took a few moments to shake his legs and get his blood fully circulating. Drawing a long breath, he started down the path once used by wagons to load and unload cargo. The warehouse's loading doors were closed. The men inside had entered through a narrow door to the right.

Rolft listened to dirt and stone grind beneath his feet, convinced it was not loud enough to carry far. He hesitated just outside the door. Unable to distinguish words, he could hear men talking, and was reassured by their good-natured banter mixed with laughter. They were clearly not preparing for conflict. Their voices mixed together, and came from far enough away that he was unlikely to find himself within sword's reach upon entry.

He pushed the door inward with his foot and stepped inside.

The building's interior was not well-lit, but a shaft of sunlight streaming through the opened door enabled Rolft to see the silhouettes of five men. They stood loosely grouped near the center of the building. Their banter sputtered to a stop.

"Who's that?" called one.

"That you, Kole?" asked another.

Rolft approached the group slowly, his eyes adjusting to the lighting. He began to make out physical attributes. The man furthest to his right was of medium build and height, and older than the rest. The young man next to him was a bit taller, and the skinniest of them all. In the middle was a broad-shouldered barrel of a man with a red beard bushy enough to nest a flock of birds. The shortest of the lot by far, he seemed to swagger even while standing still. The fourth man was of average size, younger, his dark hair tied back in a ponytail. The last was a muscular giant in the prime of life, and Rolft's eyes lingered on him. He had yet to speak, and he returned Rolft's stare impassively. *Dangerous if allowed to get too close.*

"Identify yourself!" the stocky, bearded man demanded.

"Thet ain't Kole," muttered the young man to his right.

"Kole's not coming," Rolft said, stopping far enough away to monitor all five men.

"Why not?" asked the bearded man. "Where is everyone? We was told this meeting was required. Where's Raggett?"

Raggett Grymes? I wish I knew!

The bearded man grew impatient. "Bloody bysh! I asked you a question. Where is everyone? And who in Baelon are you?"

One of the lanky youths eyed Rolft leerily. "And what are them swords for?"

"I'll have your names," Rolft said.

"Your mother's arse! I don't know who you think you are, or what game Raggett's playin', but we don't intend to stand around takin' orders from some stranger, do we?" The bearded man glanced right and left.

Rolft brought his two swords violently together, the sharp clang of steel on steel resounding through the warehouse. Before anyone could react, he closed the gap between himself and the group. The tip of the sword in his outstretched hand rested in the hollow of the bearded man's throat. The hands of the short man rose into the air.

"Tell your friends to hold steady, or you'll swallow this blade."

"Easy, friend." The bearded man leaned back as far as he dared, but the point of Rolft's sword stayed pressed against his skin. "Don't no one move."

"Now, your name."

"Brock. Brock Haden."

"And your friends?" Rolft pressed the sword a bit further into the man's flesh.

Brock tilted his head ever so slightly left, his eyes moving in that direction. "That's Harolt on the end."

"Shut up, Brock!" said the young man between Harolt and Brock.

"You shut up, Lane!" Brock said fiercely. His eyes met Rolft's. "That's Lane with the mouth."

"Lane Taylor?"

"Do I know you?" asked the younger man.

Rolft held his gaze on Brock. He tipped his head slightly to the man's other side.

"Bailey Bonaparte next to me," said Brock between clenched teeth. "And the big man—that's Edwyn. Don't know his last name."

"Blythe." The big man glared defiantly at Rolft. "Edwyn Blythe."

Rolft's heart beat a little faster. He took deep breaths to slow it. "That's it, then," he said, lowering his arming sword as he stepped back. He pointed the shorter sword at

Brock. "You can go. So can he." He gestured toward the older man, Harolt. "The rest have business with me."

"And if we choose to stay?" asked Brock.

"Idiot," muttered Harolt, already on his way toward the door.

"But what if this business has to do with the next job?"

"Idiot!" yelled Harolt, nearly out the door.

"Blood will be spilled," Rolft said evenly. "Choose quickly."

Raggett Grymes

Raggett had spent considerable time in The Raven's Nest, but he had never appreciated its cloak of darkness more. He sat alone at a table against the back wall. Kole dead? *Murdered?* Was that really possible? If so, by whom? Was someone exacting revenge for Leo's murder? Or the baron's servant? How could that be? Who on earth could know about that besides Harolt, Shum, and Edwyn? Not even they were stupid enough to talk about it. Or were they? Well, if they were, it would be the last time they talked about anything—Raggett would see to that.

Because that's what a good boss did.

He chewed a ragged fingernail, spitting bits onto the floor. Kole must have done something unrelated on his own. That would be just like him. Probably deserved whatever he got. *Good riddance to a loose cannon!* Raggett would find a replacement.

Because that's what a good boss did.

The pub's door opened, momentarily displaying the silhouettes of two men, neither tall enough to be Edwyn Blythe. They moved together slowly, as though searching for a particular party. Just as Raggett was losing interest, they approached close enough for him to recognize their faces.

"Alden!" he whispered loudly. "Brock!"

Alden stopped, peering through the dark. A moment later, the young man was standing in front of Raggett's table with his companion.

"Sit! Sit!" Raggett watched as both men complied, his patience quickly fading as Brock made several attempts to maneuver his broad-shoulders and barrel frame into a comfortable position at the table. All the while, the man's wild eyes peered at Raggett from behind a tangle of red, shoulder-length hair and like-colored bush of a beard.

Raggett glared at Alden. "What's Brock doing here? Where's Edwyn?" Alden and Brock looked at one another. "I asked you a question. Did I not tell you to bring Edwyn?"

"Uh..." said Alden.

Brock cleared his gravelly voice. "Edwyn won't be comin'."

"What? Keep your voice down! Was I talking to you? Why won't Edwyn be coming?"

"Are you talking to me now?" Brock asked, holding Raggett's gaze.

"Gods damn you! Yes, I'm talking to you now, Brock, because Alden here appears to have lost his tongue. Why, pray tell, won't Edwyn be joining us? And keep your voice down!"

Brock leaned in over the table to whisper loudly. "'Cuz he can't."

"What d'you mean, can't?"

"I mean he can't."

"I did like you said. I spread word the meeting was canceled." Alden glanced nervously at Brock. "Only I couldn't find everyone, so some didn't get the message." The young man swallowed. "Brock here, Harolt, Bailey, Lane, and... and Edwyn. I couldn't find none of 'em, and so..."

"And so we went to your meetin'," Brock said.

Raggett's heart began to pound. "There was no meeting. I told Alden to cancel it."

"Yes, well, we know that now, don't we?" Brock said. "Only not everyone got the message."

"So what? So you showed up. I don't understand. What about Edwyn?"

"Well, we weren't the only ones who showed up, were we?"

"What d'you mean? Who else was there?"

"Some giant of a man. Never seen him before. Wouldn't give us his name, but he sure as shite didn't just stumble in there. Barged in like he owned the place. Like he knew all along we'd be there. Asked us all our names. 'Ah,' he said to me, 'you and the old man can go.' So Harolt and I, we lit outta there, but not before the giant cut off one of Bailey's arms."

"He what?" The words were barely audible.

"You heard me."

"And then?"

Brock's beard swept the tabletop as he leaned further forward. "I told you. We didn't wait around to see. Harolt went his own way. Said to tell you he's done. I run into Alden here outside The King's Inn, and together we headed back to the old warehouse." Alden's hands, resting on the table, began to tremble.

"And?"

"Well, the meetin' was over by then, wasn't it?" Brock laid a burly arm across Alden's hands, preventing them from rattling the table. "I don't think the lad here's up to talkin' about it."

Raggett swallowed hard. "Tell me."

"Well, Bailey's dead, ain't he? Lyin' there on the ground minus his arm. And your friend, Edwyn, also dead. Only he doesn't look as tall as he used to, on account of he's missin' his head."

"What?" Raggett's face contorted. "And Lane?"

"Well, the only good thing we can say about Lane is that he's not missin' any parts. But he's as dead as the rest."

The three men sat in silence.

"Who was it?" Raggett finally asked. "What was his name?"

"I told you he never said." Brock's wild eyes were glistening.

"Well, think, dammit! What did he look like?"

"Big. Almost as big as Edwyn. Dark, shaggy hair. Full o' piss. No messin' about."

"That's all you recall?"

"Thet's all?" Brock said angrily. "I was a little busy watchin' them swords of his."

"Think, then. Did he say anything else before you left?"

"Did he say anything else? Mm-hmm. Yes, he did." Brock sat back with a nervous laugh. "He said...'Blood... will be spilled!'"

Raggett averted his gaze. *First Kole. Now Edwyn, Lane, and Bailey! What in Baelon is going on?* "The Guild won't stand for this," he said.

Not because he believed it, but because that's what a good boss would say.

Raggett was still trying to make sense of what Alden and Brock had told him as he left The Raven's Nest. Images of Lane and Bailey came and went. Swords slashing through air and flesh. A pool of blood. And poor Edwyn. Not all of him. Just his head. The image of that dark curly hair and toothy grin that made women swoon now made Raggett shiver.

First Kole, now this. It could hardly be a coincidence, could it?

He turned his coat collar to shield his neck from a cold, stiff wind, and nearly leapt out of his shoes when a low voice from the dark called out his name.

"There's no cause for alarm, friend." A tall man stepped out of the shadows. "We just want to talk."

"Who's we?" Raggett tried to make out a face.

"My friend and I." A tall man with shoulder length dark hair moved directly into Raggett's path.

"What fr—" Raggett tensed as the point of a knife touched the small of his back.

"That would be my associate," the man blocking his way said casually. "The name's Reynard, but you can call me 'boss.'"

"Boss?"

"Quite right. You're Raggett Grymes. You work for gatherer Kasparr, do you not? Your name's in Leo's book." The lost ledger was suddenly inches from Raggett's face.

Noggods! "You're Reynard Rascall? The overseer? Leo works for you?"

"Indeed." The overseer stepped close enough for Raggett to see his face. Was that a scar on his forehead? "Until his untimely death, that is."

Gods above! "I don't know who killed him."

"I wasn't asking, was I?"

Raggett felt the tip of the knife push harder against his back. He bit his lip, his heart racing. "N-no, you weren't. But now four more of my men are dead. Kasparr's men, I mean. Your men." *Think, think!*

"What's that?" The overseer moved a hand as if to signal something.

Raggett felt the knife retract. "So I'm told," he said. "Three of 'em butchered by some giant in a warehouse just today."

"Really? And their names?"

"Edwyn Blythe, Lane Taylor, Bailey Bonaparte," said Raggett quickly.

"Killed by a giant, you say. And they all worked for Kasparr?"

"Well, yes, in a manner of speaking. They all worked for me." Raggett wiped his mouth with his sleeve.

"I see. And all killed today, you say?"

"Yes. And that's not counting Kole, killed yesterday."

"Another one of yours?" asked the overseer.

Raggett nodded. "Someone slit his throat in an alley. There's but a handful of us left, I'm afraid."

"Most troubling. And little wonder that we frightened you so!"

"Y-yes! I thought perhaps—"

"It was your turn?" The overseer laughed and waved his hand again. A short, wiry man appeared suddenly beside him. Raggett looked for evidence of the knife that had been thrust into his back, but it had, to his relief, disappeared. "Instead, you find yourself presented with two friends. Say hello to Spiro."

"Friends?" Raggett shivered uncontrollably.

"Indeed. Surely you have put the pieces together by now. We are both plagued by the same affront! Whoever dispatched poor Leo most certainly did your friends as well. What other conclusion is there?"

"Well, yes—"

"You know," the overseer said, sidling up to Raggett and laying a long arm across his shoulders, "we almost took you for the man who murdered Leo!"

"What? I—"

"Yes, yes, it's true. We came this close, I'm ashamed to say, but you can see how things might have looked to us. You being the last entry in his ledger, and all. We thought perhaps, you know, a little attempt by someone in the ranks to take control."

Raggett shook his head.

"But now we know," said Reynard, "it's not that at all. Much worse, in fact. No, what we have here is some outsider looking to displace The Guild. I've dealt with this before. Nasty business. The key is to nip it in the bud. Before the sickness spreads. And already, you say, this giant has killed four of us. No, five including Leo. Is that right?"

"Five, yes," said Raggett. "Five including Leo."

"Well, that's far too many. This will have to stop. What say you, Spiro?" The shorter man simply grinned. "What's the matter, Raggett? You look sick with worry. Chin up, friend! Your problems are now solved."

"What do you mean?"

"Well, your gatherer, Kasparr, is also dead, I'm sorry to inform you. Most unfortunate, of course. But it does mean we'll be needing a replacement. You're next in line! Interested?"

"What? Are you serious?" *Gatherer at last?* "I-I suppose. What about all the killings?"

"Bah! We're going to take care of that as well." The overseer pulled Raggett closer, nodding toward his short companion. "You'd never know it by lookin' at him, but that's our giant killer, that is!"

Overseer Reynard Rascall

Reynard lay in the dark at The King's Inn, fully clothed save for his boots. He could picture what he was listening to—he had seen it often enough during the day—a knife released from Spiro's outstretched arm, falling point-first to the floor before Spiro retrieved it to repeat the cycle. It was the smaller of a pair of custom blades with black hilts sculpted from carmine in the Northern Isles. Reynard had purchased both as a show of appreciation for Spiro's handiwork early on in their relationship.

"You're disappointed," Reynard said.

"Am I?"

"Are you not? Bored, then."

"If you say so." Spiro's knife kissed the floor.

"Patience, my friend. Your time is coming."

"Is it?"

"Oh, yes. Most assuredly so. Someone's got their fingers in our pie. All we need do is determine whose hand they belong to. Then you will be free to ply your trade."

"I thought it was the Grymes fella with his hand in our pie."

"As did I." Reynard winced. "I did almost have you kill him, you know. That would have been a mistake."

"Wouldn't have been your first." Spiro's knife pricked the floor. "I was just thinkin' about poor Kasparr."

Reynard suppressed irritation and regret. "Grymes has been stealing from us, no doubt, and he'll have to pay for that. But he's a small fish, Spiro, and we have a whale to catch first. Someone's trespassing on our property."

"You're sure of it, are you?"

"What other explanation is there? If all we had to go on was the word of taker Grymes, that would be one thing. But his story rings true, and once he introduced us to that Haden fella, well—"

"Haden? That Brock fella?"

"Yes, 'that Brock fella.' What did you make of him?"

"Liked him."

"Of course you did. Short. Crotchety. A handful in a fight, I'll wager. Let's see, who else do I know like that?"

Spiro released the knife again.

"Suffice it to say," said Reynard, "he wasn't spinning yarns. Someone's trying to rid the world of Grymes and his crew."

"They're off to a good start."

"Yes, and that pretty much lets Raggett Grymes off the hook, doesn't it? I mean, why would he kill both his gatherer's bookkeeper and the men working with him? How does that make any sense?"

"Maybe one has nothing to do with the other."

"Oh, please. Let's try to stay in this world, shall we? As I said, someone's got their fingers in our pie, Kasparr's slice, at least. We must find whoever that is and let them know we are not pleased."

"You're the architect. I'm sure you have a plan."

The sound of Spiro's blade piercing wood caused Reynard to close his eyes. "Indeed I do. Which is why Grymes and his friends are so useful to us...alive."

"How's that?"

"By all accounts, whoever's up to this has put five of Kasparr's men in the ground already. Why would he stop there?"

"He wouldn't. Leastwise, I wouldn't."

"No, you would not. So think on it. If we keep one eye on Raggett Grymes, who is undoubtedly in line for some unpleasantry himself, and our other eye open for some giant with an insatiable appetite for killing, how long could it be before we are rewarded?"

The length of silence that ensued troubled Reynard. "Still awake?" he asked.

Spiro dropped the knife. "Still thinking."

"Dangerous territory. What about?"

"About the giant and his appetite. Is he eating pie or people?"

Reynard sighed. "Both. The pie is what he really likes. The people are just in his way."

"What if he's not alone?"

Reynard stroked his chin. "We know but one man killed those three in the warehouse. Even so, you're right. Leo was a separate matter. As was the other one Grymes lost. What was his name?"

"Kole."

"Yes, good memory. Kole. A big man himself, apparently. It's not much of a stretch to imagine a giant killed him. My money says this is all the work of one man."

"Even so."

"I've already said you're right. Best not to take too much for granted. There could be a small army involved, for all we know." Reynard propped himself up on his elbows. "Tell you what. I know you like to work alone. I'm sure you're up for whatever lies before us. But let's not take any chances, shall we? Send word to those brothers, the two bruisers who worship you."

"Able and Elijah." Spiro nodded in approval.

"Yes." Reynard pictured them guarding the door during Kasparr's final moments at the docks. "I don't know why I didn't think of them before. If we're going to take issue with a giant, we'd best introduce him to our own."

Sibil Dunn

The sun was not yet visible above the Lumax mountains. A dense fog caused Sibil to avoid the alleyway in which she had been accosted the previous evening. She found another route to the cobbler's shop, feeling a bit self-conscious as she neared. She did not wish to appear overly anxious or presumptuous knocking on his door at dawn. He was, after all, doing her an immense favor, and she had no business expecting he could turn a pair of shoes so quickly. But neither did she wish to be late, especially since it was the cobbler himself who had set the meeting time.

She was greatly relieved when the door opened wide enough to reveal the cobbler's mop of white hair and smiling face. "Good day, lass! Thankee for being sharp! I hope these will suffice." He further opened the door so that Sibil could see what he was holding.

They were oh so beautiful! Perfectly shaped, the color of sand, and without a blemish on them! Sibil reached out to receive them. So soft and supple! Her eyes grew moist. "It is I who must thank you, kind sir. My mother and I are forever in your debt!"

"Nonsense! Your mother has the feet of a child. These practically made themselves." Cobbler Nash winked at her. "Good day to you!" He shut the door, leaving Sibil cradling the shoes to her chest.

She hesitated at the entrance to the alleyway she had traveled the night before. With sunlight now cascading down its length, she slowly retraced her steps in hope of recovering the amulet. Perhaps it was kicked during the scuffle, or propelled down the alley by the feet of later travelers. She stopped and stared at a large patch of discolored cobblestones near the spot where she had been held captive and then set free. The stones had a dull, dark sheen to them; their cracks and divots still moist and glistening. *Someone lost a lot of blood here! I hope it wasn't the man who helped me!*

Sibil hurried on, resigned to the most likely course of events: someone else had discovered the amulet and made it their own. It was, after all, too large to go unnoticed.

She had not even mentioned the altercation to Father Syrus. Rather, she simply told him that the amulet was suddenly wrested from her hand in the dark. The abbot had merely said, "Whoever stole it must have greater need for it."

Sibil wished she knew him better. He seemed a good man with a kind heart, and she desperately needed a confidant. Who better than a priest who had devoted his life to helping children? Still, she could not bring herself to do it. Though he had recognized her, he did not really know her, and what she had to share would sound like the ravings of a lunatic. Also, a part of her was reluctant to burden him with her troubles. He had more than enough of his own, no doubt.

Sibil stopped abruptly. What had her mother said? Not about the king, but about Sibil herself? That she was next? That death awaited her? For a few moments, she stood still, holding her breath while she attempted to connect her mother's words to the previous night's attack. *"Beware the dark!"* Exhaling loudly, she shook her head and resumed walking.

But she could not rid herself entirely of those thoughts.

Father Syrus wished Sibil and her mother well, insisting they take with them a basket filled with bread and fruit. "The more you eat, the lighter your load," he said with a smile, a sheen on his rosy cheeks.

The women hugged him in turn, a wave of sadness threatening to bring Sibil to tears. The abbot opened the heavy door and escorted the women down the steps to the street. "Fare well," he said, his hands clasped at his waist.

"Is that a smile you wear?" Sibil asked. Despite her new shoes, her mother was still hobbling and had to be in pain.

"It is!" Her mother beamed. "Yesterday, I saw my daughter's death, yet here she is beside me."

Sibil adjusted her grip on the basket. "Tell me more about this dream of yours."

"It was no dream, and I do not wish to dwell on it. The good abbot has been our savior these past two days, and now I put my trust in you." She patted her daughter's free hand. "I feel the danger is past. Don't ask me how. But I do sense it. I haven't felt this free in almons."

Sibil hesitated to reply. A part of her desperately wanted to divulge that she had been assaulted the very day of her mother's premonition, but she could only imagine the response that might elicit. Instead, she said, "You've not spoken for so long. It's good to hear your voice."

Her mother kept talking. By the time they reached the fork in the road that would lead them either home or to the palace, she had recounted several stories of Sibil's childhood. But she turned silent as they caught their first glimpse of the castle on the hill. Her feet stopped shuffling, her gaze fixed on the palace.

Sibil prompted her. "You also dreamt the king would be killed?"

"It was no dream," said her mother, still not stirring.

"What would you call it?"

Their attention was captured by the sound of galloping horses. Sibil prepared to allow four riders passage. But as they neared, the lead rider signaled those behind. Their horses slowed to a stop alongside the women.

They were an odd-looking group. The gentleman in charge was of average size, dressed in a white blouse with ruffled sleeves. His trousers appeared to be tailored. His boots were new and polished. The other three men were larger and rougher in appearance. Not in a threatening way, but as though they labored harder for a living than did their companion.

"Good day!" The lead rider's straight brown hair was pulled neatly back in a ponytail. A square jaw supported a thin face. Brown eyes peered out beneath thick brows, a sharp contrast to his otherwise light complexion. He was not unattractive, but the manner in which he focused his attention on Sibil made her uneasy.

"Good day," she said, out of habit.

"I am Pryll Fletcher, steward of the palace, and I travel on an errand for King Axil. I wonder if you might be of assistance."

"We would be honored to assist the king, though I fail to see how we might do so." Sibil set the fruit basket down.

"Might the king not be the best judge of who can and cannot aid him?" The steward's gaze did not waver.

"Of course, your lordship. I meant no disrespect."

"And what might your names be?"

"My name is Sibil. This is my mother, Mari."

"Last name?" asked the gentleman sharply.

"Dunn."

"Ahaa!" The gentleman sat higher in his saddle. "This is most fortunate! You see? You are of great assistance after all!" He looked at Sibil's mother for the first time. "Mari Dunn—it is your company the king desires."

"My company!"

"Yes, madam. And I am charged with bringing you to him posthaste."

"He lives?" Sibil's mother lifted one hand to her chest.

The steward worked to steady his horse. "Of course he lives! You seem surprised. Why is that, I wonder?"

"My mother is not well," said Sibil.

"The king lives despite the well-laid plans of others."

"What?" Sibil's mind began to cloud.

"The king awaits," said the steward.

Her mother looked down at her clothes. "But my garb—"

"Is of no consequence."

"But I—"

"It is not a request, madam. It is the king's command, and we are here to do his bidding." The steward signaled to his fellow riders, and the three of them dismounted.

"What's happening?" Sibil asked.

"How do I make myself more clear? Your mother is to accompany us to the castle."

"For how long?"

"For as long as it pleases the king!"

"And were she to refuse?"

"Sibil," her mother said, "I have no reason to refuse the king."

"There. You see?" said the steward. "You'll ride with Byron, madam." One of the larger men remounted his horse, while the other two hoisted Sibil's mother to sit directly behind him. "Hold tight, Mari Dunn. We can't have you falling off."

Sibil's mother wrapped her arms around Byron, one cheek resting against his back. The two men who had assisted her were already in their saddles.

"Then I'm coming, too!" Sibil stepped into the middle of the road as the riders turned their horses back toward the palace.

The steward reined in his mount sharply, and Sibil lurched to avoid being hit. "What's that?" he said. "Do I hear you make demands?"

Sibil bowed her head. "No, your lordship. But my mother is not well. I would accompany her to ease your burden, is all."

The steward eyed her keenly, the fingers of one hand tapping his pommel. "You're spirited, I'll give you that. And rather fetching for a commoner. You'll ride with me." He extended his hand toward her. "But know your place. One more word out of turn, and you shall rue this day." He extended his hand. Sibil took it, allowing herself to be pulled up until she was able to swing one leg over the horse's back.

"Hold tight," the steward said. Sibil wrapped her arms around his waist. "Tighter. I need to feel you against me."

Sibil complied, glancing regretfully at the basket of fruit left on the road. Shifting her weight uneasily, she imagined her hands wrapped tightly around the steward's thin neck.

Mari Dunn

Mari sat before her king, trying to compose herself. *He is alive, after all!* Not even in her most fantastic dreams had she imagined an audience with him. Where was she? In his parlor? His study? And where had Sibil been taken? Her heart beat rapidly. She wished she were better dressed for the occasion. Not even her new shoes were in style. She smoothed her dress, folded her hands, and then unfolded them.

"How are you, Madam Dunn?"

"Quite well, Your Majesty, thank you." *Why am I so nervous?*

"I do remember you, you know. It was several almons ago we met. Just the once. Do you recall?"

Do I recall? How does he? "Of course, m'lord! How could I forget?"

"It was by the east wall, repairs not yet completed. Mid-morning. Your husband was giving you a tour, and as it happened I was taking my constitutional."

Such a kind voice! "Yes, m'lord. With the queen and princess. It was my great honor to be introduced to each of you."

King Axil nodded. "I fear we've both suffered a tremendous loss since then. Your husband was a great man, and a good friend."

Mari smiled. A royal carpet unrolled for her could not have been more welcoming.

"M'lord." A voice from behind reminded her that she and the king were not alone. *That man who brought us to the castle.*

"Yes, Pryll," said King Axil.

Was that regret?

The king leaned forward. "I'm told, Mari, that I might have joined my wife and daughter had it not been for your actions yesterday."

Mari bowed her head. "I don't know what to say, m'lord."

The man behind her moved to stand beside her chair. "Is it true? Did you come to the castle to warn the king?" His tone was not quite as demanding as it had been on the road, but there was still an edge to it. Not welcoming at all.

"You've met my steward, Mari. He wonders what prompted you to warn me. That's all."

Mari responded directly to her king. "It was a dream, m'lord." *If that was good enough for Sibil, perhaps—*

"A dream!" It was clearly not good enough for the steward.

"Pryll," said the king.

Mari did not begrudge the steward for his skepticism. Not really. But she did not like him, either. He was decidedly unpleasant. "Perhaps dream is too kind a word," she said.

"What kind of dream?" The steward moved closer to her.

Mari refused to look at him. "You should hope to never know," she said, perhaps too quickly. *Choose your words more carefully!*

"It bade you warn the king, did it? This thing you saw? On what merit? What did it show you?" Mari imagined the steward as a foxhound, eager for the hunt, sniffing for a scent, with no idea what he was hunting.

She continued to ignore him. "I saw you in a vision, m'lord. Sitting amidst a merry celebration and at a table laden with food. I watched..." *Go on, you must say it!* "I watched you die!"

"Preposterous!" yelled the steward.

"Pryll!"

"Apologies, sire, but must we really suffer this? A story of convenience without a shred of proof?" The steward bent to place his face in front of Mari's, blocking her view of the king. "Tell us, madam, how you really came to know the men who attacked our king!"

"Pryll!" The veins on the king's temples bulged. "Leave us!"

"But sire!"

"At once!"

Sibil Dunn

Sibil sat on a bed in a servant's quarters, her head spinning. Had it not been for previous visits to the palace with Princess Lewen, she would not have known where she was. The steward had escorted her briskly to the room some time ago, leaving her to entertain herself.

There seemed no end to the mystery surrounding her mother. Supposed premonitions of death had been unnerving enough, but now... an audience with the king? At his request! It was surreal, and Sibil's wildest conjectures did not begin to explain it.

Her attempt to seize control of her own life seemed waylaid once again. She was imagining herself a bit of flotsam from a shipwreck, at the mercy of the ocean's currents, when the steward returned, shutting the door angrily behind himself.

"Where is my mother?" she asked as he approached.

"With the king." Without warning, the steward sat so close to her their thighs touched.

"I should like to see her." Sibil started to rise.

"In due time." The steward caught her arm and pulled her back to the bed.

"What are you doing?"

"If your mother were more forthcoming, you would not be so inconvenienced."

"How do you mean?" Sibil's eyes darted toward the door.

"The woman's hiding something. Perhaps you'd like to tell me what that is."

"My mother has nothing to hide from the king!"

"I could be convinced of that, I suppose." The steward loosened his hold and placed a palm against Sibil's cheek. "There are many ways for you to prove your loyalty to the throne." His hand brushed her breast as he withdrew it. "Are you prepared to do so?" Before Sibil could respond, he leaned in, his lips seeking hers.

Sibil pushed him away, struggling to stand. "How dare you!"

"Need I remind you where you are?" The steward rose, positioning himself between her and the door. "Or who you're talking to?"

"I mean no disrespect, m'lord, but if you—"

"Take off your blouse."

"What?!"

"Like mother, like daughter. Take off your blouse and let us see what you are hiding there."

"I'll do no such thing," said Sibil breathlessly. "And if you lay another hand on me—"

The steward grasped her sleeve. Sibil twisted violently away, her blouse ripping at the shoulder seam.

The steward grinned. "You see? One way or the other!" He started to laugh, sobering quickly at the sight of the dagger Sibil produced. "Put that away before you hurt yourself."

"Take me to my mother!" Sibil waved the dagger at him.

"Did I not warn you about making demands?" The steward lashed out, recoiling as Sibil's blade pricked his arm. He swore loudly as he inspected the spot of crimson staining his white blouse. "You'll not soon forget what I'm going to do to you."

"Touch me and I'll kill you!" Sibil lurched past the steward and onto the bed, clambering quickly over it, but he intercepted her before she could reach the door. He kicked a stool separating them toward her. Sibil grabbed it and flung it back at him. The stool sailed past the steward's head and crashed against the door.

"Make all the noise you want," the steward said. "No one cares!"

Marshal Erik Carson

Carson strode across the castle grounds. A blend of exhilaration and trepidation sharpened his senses. It was not as strong a feeling as what he felt just prior to battle, but similar nonetheless. He had spent the entire morning with his three most trusted advisors, all of whom felt certain that King Tygre of Tegan was behind the attempted assassination. The clues were obvious and damming, but they were shy of proof and would not be well-received by King Axil.

As he left the chapel and stepped onto the inner ward, Carson spied a young servant walking in the opposite direction. "Ho, Bernier! A moment, please!"

The young man looked his way, smiled in recognition, and jogged to Carson's side.

"What is it, Marshal?"

"Has the king entertained guests this day?"

"Yes, sir. Just finishing, I should think."

"A woman?"

"Yes. And the steward."

"Together?" The marshal shot a quick glance toward the king's quarters.

The boy nodded.

"Thank you, Bernier. Most helpful, as usual." Carson began to walk briskly. "Are you able to accompany me?"

"Where to, Marshal?"

"To the king, Bernier. To the king!"

Two large guards barred entry to the king's study. Prompted by a salutation from the marshal, they stepped to either side. "Wait here, Bernier." Carson's eyes swept the room as he entered. King Axil sat behind his desk, his brow fully furrowed. Madam Dunn sat opposite, dabbing her eyes with her fingers.

The king tried to console her. "You must forget everything he said."

"What have I missed?" asked Carson.

King Axil rose and came around the desk. The two striped cragens, Sir Black and Lady Gray, appeared seemingly out of nowhere.

"Madam Dunn has been most patient and understanding, though I fear we've done her an injustice." The king placed a comforting hand on the woman's shoulder.

"Pryll was here?" That would certainly explain things.

"I sent him off," said the monarch, "but not before he opened his mouth, I'm afraid. This was never my intention."

Carson kneeled by the distraught woman's side. "Madam Dunn, do you remember me?"

She looked at him and nodded. "You threatened to put me in the dungeon."

"To my everlasting shame." The marshal offered her his kerchief.

"Though you were ever so kind whilst doing so."

"Come now. This is no time for tears. You've saved the king's life." Carson looked to the monarch. "Surely this is not how we repay such service."

"It is not," said King Axil resolutely. "I should have known better. This was entirely my fault."

"I highly doubt that, sire." Carson received the kerchief Mari handed back.

"It is I who should apologize, my Lord," said Madam Dunn. "I wish I could better explain. The truth is, I cannot—not even to myself." She wrung her hands.

"Many a dream I've had that cannot be explained," said the king, forcing a chuckle. "And many others that were I to try, the people would surely call for my head. Your husband was a good man, and a friend to me. Now his wife has saved my life. How can I repay you?"

Madam Dunn lightly touched her forehead, as though lost in thought. Carson watched and waited. Was she thinking of an answer?

"Yes?" asked King Axil. "What is it, Mari? Please. Anything you ask. You have only to name it."

"My daughter," she whispered.

Carson waited for her to finish.

"I... We..." said the king. "I don't understand."

"My daughter." Madam Dunn rose to her feet.

Carson stood with her. "What about your daughter?"

"Please bring her to me."

What? "Where is she?"

"How do you not know? You brought her here."

"Here?" asked the king.

Carson looked to the door. "What do you mean? Who brought her here?"

"That man. He brought us both."

"Pryll?" asked the king. "The steward?"

"Please hurry!"

"She is here?" asked Carson. "At the castle?"

"Yes!"

"Where exactly?" asked the king.

"I do not know." Mari's hand dropped to her chest.

Carson burst out of the study, startling the guards as well as young Bernier.

"Which way did the steward go?" Both guards pointed in the same direction. "Come, Bernier! Stay with me, now!" The marshal sped across the inner ward, Bernier's spindly legs flailing after him.

"Have you seen the steward?" he asked those they passed. A series of pointed fingers guided them to a narrow passageway leading to servants' quarters. There the marshal halted, unsure of his next move.

He knocked on the first door they encountered, stealing a quick glance at Bernier before knocking again. The door opened to reveal an older man half-dressed, just as a woman came scurrying toward them from further down the hallway. She pointed back in the direction she had come. "Down there!"

The marshal raced to the end of the hallway, Bernier on his heels, where two other women stood outside a closed door, hands over their mouths and clutching aprons. A crashing sound from behind the door was followed quickly by loud voices, then another crash.

Carson tried the door. Finding it locked, he drew his sword, reared back, and kicked it in. The two occupants of the room froze as the door burst open. Pryll was clenching his right arm with his left. Blood seeped between his fingers, turning his white blouse crimson. A young woman with long, dark hair had adopted a defensive posture several paces from the steward, one sleeve of her blouse with a long tear at the shoulder seam. She held a dagger tightly in one hand, her knuckles as white as its bone handle.

"I was escorting her to the king," said Pryll, "when she attacked me!"

"Liar!" The young woman brandished her dagger angrily, spinning toward the marshal. "He lies!"

"Yes," Carson said. "One of many flaws, I'm afraid."

"He attacked me!"

"I have no doubt. Are you hurt?"

"No!"

"She cut me!" said Pryll, starting for the door. He stopped abruptly, the tip of Carson's sword suddenly pressed against his chest. "What is the meaning of this? Let me pass! I'm bleeding!"

"Stay where you are," said the marshal.

"I'll see you in chains!"

"Bernier!" Carson shouted.

The young man appeared, his mouth agape. "Escort this young lady to the king—her mother waits for her."

"Yes, Marshal."

The young woman slowly lowered her knife and cautiously circled toward Bernier.

"And Bernier..."

"Yes?"

Carson's eyes continued to bore into the steward. "Be sure to tell the king all that you have seen and heard here."

"This is outrageous! I am the king's steward!" Pryll stepped back, then attempted to duck under Carson's sword. "Let me pass or I shall—"

A shallow cut appeared on the steward's upper right arm. By the time he stopped screaming, the point of Carson's sword again rested on his chest.

"Sit down, Pryll, and be silent. Or I shall save us all a lot of trouble and kill you here and now."

Sibil Dunn

Sibil and her mother sat behind their young wagon driver, facing the direction they had come. The wagon bed rose and fell jerkily over bumps and dips in the road as it carried them slowly home. Sibil closed her eyes and rested against her mother. She listened to the axles turning, the flick of reins, and Reggie's occasional encouragement to the horse.

She was tired. Her shoulder ached from when the king's steward had grabbed her blouse and wrenched her arm. Had that really happened? She did not remember pulling her knife, but she recalled swiping at the steward in defense and drawing blood. She remembered the marshal's entrance. Being reunited with her mother. Some woman tending to her shoulder. Being escorted to the wagon at dusk.

She remained unsure what to think about her mother. Two days before, she would have said the woman was slowly going mad. Perhaps dragging Sibil into that purgatory with her. But now? Had she really foreseen the king in danger? What of her warning to Sibil before the alley altercation? It was difficult to dismiss both as coincidence. But it was possible. And the alternative, too fantastic to believe. The possibilities and ramifications swirled inside her head.

"Whoa, boy." Reggie's command brought the wagon slowly to a halt.

Sibil turned to see a large gray mare directly in their path, saddled but riderless, returning their stares. It pawed at the ground and snorted.

"Baelon above!" Reggie wrapped the reins around the wagon bench.

Sibil followed the groom's line of sight to spy a man some fifty paces up the road, sitting with his back supported by the steep roadside bank. He was still, his chin resting on his chest.

"Sleeping?" Sibil wondered aloud.

"With his horse wandering free? Drunk, more like it." Reggie set the wagon brake, jumped to the road, and approached the gray mare slowly.

Sibil followed closely. "What are we doing?"

"I'm not sure." Reggie took the reins of the mare and softly stroked the animal's muzzle.

Sibil waited for the stable boy to lead the horse off the road, but Reggie remained motionless. "Gods above!" he whispered, suddenly dropping the reins and walking away.

Sibil glanced quickly back at the wagon and her mother. Reggie began to run toward the figure seated on the roadside. Sibil raised both arms in a questioning gesture before taking the reins of the mare. The horse turned away from her. She reached to reassure it, but her hand froze in mid-air.

A familiar amulet hung by a leather thong from the animal's saddle.

The wagon had been stopped a short time outside what Sibil knew to be the soldier's barracks. Reggie had disappeared into the dark. Her mother was half asleep. When the stableboy reappeared, he was trailed by a hulking shadow.

"Where was he?" asked the shadow. A deep voice.

"By the roadside. He's been bleeding." Reggie moved to the back of the wagon and patted the horse tethered there. "Will the infirmary take him?"

The shadow answered by reaching into the wagon. With surprising ease, he pulled, then lifted, the large body from its bed, throwing him over his shoulder. "You're not to speak a word of this. Not to anyone."

Reggie gestured toward Sibil and her mother. "The marshal instructed me to take them home. It's too late now. He'll want to know why we're back."

"Tell him your wagon couldn't make it."

"He'll know that isn't true. Caleb will—"

A loud cracking sound, accompanied by the shaking of the wagon, silenced Reggie. "Isn't it?" The giant splintered two more spokes of a wagon wheel with the heel of his boot, adjusted his load, and walked away.

Marshal Erik Carson

Carson entered the king's study, unsure why he had been summoned until he saw the steward. King Axil sat, elbows propped on his desk, hands cradling his bowed head. Pryll stood before him, waiting, his forearm bandaged.

The marshal worked to rein in his emotions. He strode to the desk, stopping within inches of the steward, daring the man to return his stare. Pryll started to speak. "Sire, I must—"

The king silenced him with a simple gesture, his head still bowed.

Pryll returned the marshal's glare. Defiant!

Carson's fingers tapped a response on the hilt of his sword.

"I'm in no mood," growled the king, raising his head slowly. "Not a word from either of you." He rubbed his temples. "Not one." He paused, his expression challenging either man to speak. "Very well, then. I have listened to you both. I have given the matter much thought. This will be my final word. We shall not speak of it again. Pryll, you have become too fond of your manhood. Chasing chambermaids and servants. Many of them half your age. A man in your position—it's undignified. And it reflects on me."

The steward's face grew red. His nostrils flared.

"Do you think your dalliances escape me?" asked the king.

"My lord—"

King Axil exploded from his chair. "Not one word!" Both fists slammed down on his desk. "Save your stories for your wife, should the poor woman be so gullible! This has gone on long enough! If you continue to wave your cock around the palace, I shall have it cut off and put in a jar! You can admire it all day long!" Silence ensued until the king regained his composure. "We contemplate war, and I have more pressing matters to attend to. As do you. Get out!"

Still red in the face, Pryll turned, shot a venomous look at Carson, and left. The marshal watched him go, unsure whether he was also meant to leave.

"This is no role for an old man." King Axil sat back heavily in his chair, motioning for Carson to sit.

"Nor for a young one, I imagine." *Ah, but it is good to see your ire back!*

"The Dunns... Mari and her daughter. They never made it home, you know."

"What!" Carson straightened in his chair.

"They're fine." The king waved a hand nonchalantly in the air.

"What happened?"

"Some sort of trouble with the wagon. The gods at work, no doubt."

"How do you mean?"

King Axil shrugged. "They'll be our guests until I've thought it through—assuming they are willing."

"As you wish, sire."

"I would normally task the steward with seeing to their needs, but under the circumstances—"

"Where are they staying?"

"In The Nest."

"I'll see to it, m'lord."

King Axil sat back and closed his eyes. "We were good friends, you know—King Tygre and I."

"Yes, Your Majesty."

"Young men, the both of us. Strong and full of life. Isadora was a noble's daughter, and Tygre's best friend... or so he said when we were introduced. I should have seen how his heart ached for her, but my own was beating far too hard to notice. So many almons ago..."

"M'lord—"

"I cannot even tell you now how it came to pass...the little things that first caused space between us. A space now grown so wide I cannot see across it." King Axil touched his steepled fingers to his lips. "Ah, but his absence from our wedding. I do remember that. Isadora never did get over that."

Carson waited patiently.

"I suppose I grew to accept the loss of friendship—more comfortable in my old age with silence than the thought of breaking it. I was certain he felt the same." The monarch searched his marshal's eyes. "Nearly an almon ago, the chaplain of The House of All Gods came to see me. Someone had draped a large banner over Isadora's burial site in the middle of the night...a banner with the crest of Tegan upon it. I shrugged it off, told the chaplain it was King Tygre paying homage to Isadora. I truly felt that at the time. Now I fear it may have been a message meant for me. Has he blamed me all these almons for robbing him of her? Does he blame me for her death? Would he avenge her?" King Axil chuckled softly. "It would be hard to fault him, really. One would at least have to admire his persistence."

"This is no longer a youth you speak of, sire, but a grown man. And a king at that."

"Grown men and kings are not immune to foolish acts."

"I've come to expect more from my king, sire."

"Have you?" King Axil eyed his marshal skeptically. "You still think the assassins did his bidding?"

"Long live King Tygre!" Carson reminded his king of the battle cry that preceded the attempt on his life. "And they all carried coin with his bust on it. Newly pressed. It does appear to have been a message."

"And you would have us send one back."

"Their heads in a box would say much."

"Yes, it would. It might also lead to war. You know that."

"We are prepared, m'lord."

"I presume you speak of armies to attack and to defend. What of paying the price, regardless of who wins?"

"One can never prepare for that, I fear."

"Just so. We'll split the loaf, shall we? I'll meet you in the middle. We'll send a message to King Tygre, but I shall craft it myself, and there shall be no acts of aggression toward Tegan until he has replied."

"Very well, m'lord. A few more days will only see us more prepared."

King Axil smiled wanly, then scoffed as though at some private thought. "I'm tired, Erik. You'd best be off. I'm sure you have much to do."

"Indeed, m'lord." Carson rose and started his retreat. "Rest well, sire."

"Oh, and Erik—"

"Sire?"

"The girl. Mari Dunn's daughter, Sibil. She was a good friend to Lewen. Same age."

Carson did not know what to say. "Yes, sire."

King Axil's expression was pained. "If Isadora were alive, she would not tolerate it. Even from her grave, the woman commands me."

Carson's brow wrinkled. "M'lord?"

"The next time you have cause to draw your sword against the steward—aim lower."

The smell of burning coal was weaker than that of wood, but just as distinct. The clarion sound of hammers pounding metal into submission. The hiss of red-hot metal kissing water. Marshal Carson would have known he was approaching the palace armory even if he was blindfolded.

He tried to make his presence known to the men and women working there at least once a quarter moon. They weren't warriors. Most had never tasted battle. But where would the kingdom be without them? Their contributions were as important as those of any soldier.

On its periphery, a dozen laborers unloaded carts filled with raw materials. Coal, iron ore, leather, and wood. Most of it would be transformed by hands into helmets, plates of armor, lances, swords, bows and arrows. All the tools of war were fashioned here, from the smallest dagger to the largest catapult. Carson never tired of the place; it was really most impressive.

"It's a good load, is it?" He stopped to help a woman pull the last few pieces of rough-hewn lumber from an ox-drawn cart.

"Oh, my! It'll do, Marshal. If not for bows, then certainly for arrows."

"Well done, then. Neither gets made without you!"

Carson entered a large area shaded by tarps stretched between wooden poles, where bowyers at long tables worked their planes, shaving thin curls of wood from shafts of yew. Some sang softly to themselves as they leaned into their task.

"It helps pass the time, does it—the singing?" he asked a young man reaching for his measuring stick.

Before the youth could answer, an older man next to him responded. "His does, Marshal. It penetrates the wood and makes the bow that hears it sing as well."

"Is that right?" Carson chuckled.

"I swear it! But could you have a word with Argonno?" The old man raised his voice and cocked his head toward his other side. "His singing rises from Baelon below, and is most painful to the ear. It, too, penetrates the wood. Every archer knows to adjust their aim with an Argonno bow."

The singing at the table he referenced grew much louder in response, causing some beneath the tarps to grimace, while others smiled or laughed. It was indeed atrocious. "You see?" said the older man. "More like a wounded beast crying for its mate. Best leave us whilst your hearing is still good, m'lord. He's ruined all of ours!"

"You've only to ask our wives!" shouted a man from another table.

Even the singer laughed at this.

Bemused, Carson rapped his knuckles playfully on the warbler's table. It was a good sign, this cheerful banter, and he acknowledged in passing each artisan who looked up from his task.

Well before reaching the last bowyer's table, he began to feel the heat from "the dragon", a monstrous, dome-shaped furnace serving as the centerpiece of the forge. Ten openings evenly spaced around its circumference allowed ten blacksmiths to work simultaneously, each supported by three assistants. One to stoke the fire, one to breathe air into the dragon's lungs with leather bellows, a third to spell the other two.

The sound of the furnace grew louder as he neared, until it was a constant rumbling accompanied by the scraping of shovel against coal. Someone might be singing here, but it would not reach his ears. Bright embers danced in the air before dying and falling to earth.

From the corner of his eye, Carson spotted Major Stronghart beneath the bowyer's tarps, approaching with a sword withdrawn from its scabbard. He waited, increasingly confident that the major was stalking him.

"What is it, Major?"

"Prob'ly nothing, sir. The gate report—same as most nights on the whole."

"And yet..."

"You know about the baron's help, murdered yesterday? Turns out there were two more."

"Two more of the baron's? We're learning this just now?"

"No, no, not at the baron's manor. Still, I thought you'd want to know. Both in Fostead, same day as the baron's cook. One was a shopkeeper killed in the south end; the other a commoner. Had his throat slit in an alley."

"Mmm. The shopkeeper...killed by knife as well?"

"No, sir, apparently not." The major's expression begged more of the marshal.

"All right, then. How?"

"I'll tell you what was told me, sir. He had several holes in him. Little ones. Like he was stung by a swarm o' hornets."

"That's it?"

"Not another mark on 'im. So they say, sir."

"Huh."

"Then three more killed today. In that old warehouse down by Seastream."

"What?!" *Six murders in two days? Most unusual for Fostead.*

"Yes, sir. Not sure who they were just yet. Whoever did it left a bloody mess. And this." He hefted the sword he had been carrying. "It's no commoner's blade."

Carson's eyes ran the length of the sword. "No, it's not." This was not even a foot soldier's sword. This one was different. "Baselo!" He called to catch the attention of the lead smithy, a huge Black man, before speaking again to Major Stronghart. "All this was relayed by The Hold?"

"Yes, sir. Sergeant Faraday."

"Right, then. We'll visit him tomorrow, you and I, and stop by the Prince of Quills whilst there."

"The Prince of Quills, sir?"

"Its owner penned the palace invitations for the feast. We'll have a word with him as well. We've yet to learn how the assassins gained entry to the castle."

They were joined by Baselo, whose face and arms were smudged with coal and glistening with sweat. His nearly bald head sparkled. "What've you got there, Marshal?" The big man's eyes had already found the sword in Stronghart's hands.

"I was hoping you'd tell us."

Baselo reached out to cradle it. "Oh, it's a beauty, isn't it? Double-edged... the finest steel. Oh, yes, this one's special. Someone took their time with this. Here, look. The way the hand guard curves like that? And the handle, that's spikewood, that is. Whoever wields this asked for that, no doubt. It's got some weight to it as well. Where did you find it? Lost in battle, was it?"

"Something like that. Can you tell where it was forged?"

"Did you not find it in the hands of one of ours?"

"What do you mean?"

"This one's found its way back home, Marshal. It was forged here."

Carson and Major Stronghart exchanged glances. "You're sure of it?" asked the marshal.

"As sure as these are my hands," said the smithy. "It's got our mark."

"You forged it yourself, then?"

"No, that's not one of mine. I'd remember it for certain. And I don't wrap the wire 'round the grip that way. But if you leave it here, I'll find who did. And whichever metalmaster claims it can likely say who wields it."

Squire Tristan Godfrey

Squire Tristan Godfrey rode a horse's length behind and to the side of his knight, Sir Garr. It was a special feeling, always, to ride through the castle gates. The invisible cloak of royalty that covered everything inside fell over him as well. He imagined it strengthening him, protecting him, sharpening his senses. Even the air seemed purer and richer here, and he breathed deeply to drink it in.

He sat a little straighter in the saddle. His shoulders broadened slightly. He knew the knights were a curiosity to nearly everyone, and suspected at least a few eyes were upon him as his horse trailed that of Sir Garr's across the castle grounds. Pretending not to notice, he scanned his surroundings, looking for signs of his twin brother, or his brother's knight, Sir Kraven, and for one young lady in particular who might tell him their whereabouts.

"What ho! Sir Garr! You're late!" The voice was familiar, and Tristan soon spotted Sir Kraven crossing the bailey on foot. Tristan's identical twin, Theos, matched the knight stride for stride.

"Never late!" said Sir Garr, slowing his horse to a stop. "Is that a new squire by your side, perchance? He doesn't look familiar." Tristan rolled his eyes. His brother hung his head. They both waited for the tired ritual to pass.

"I'll trade you mine for yours, shall I?" asked Sir Garr.

"Come, now," said Sir Kraven reproachfully. "Mine is far more handsome. I could never be seen with one as ugly as the likes of yours!"

Both knights burst into laughter, as though it was the funniest, most original joke they had ever heard.

Tristan swung a leg over his saddle and slid to the ground. He returned his brother's strong embrace with equal fervor, slapping him on the back three times before standing back to admire him.

"See to our mounts, and find yourselves a nice spot in the stables," said Sir Garr, handing his reins to Tristan.

Sir Kraven gave his to Theos before walking away with his friend. "Your afternoon belongs to Cogswell, mind you! Do us proud!"

The sun baked both earth and flesh this time of day, with no shade afforded to the line of restless squires. Tristan watched Sergeant-at-arms Arthur Cogswell kick a clod of dirt across the training ground. *He's going to make us wait.* It was, Tristan knew, one of very few remaining opportunities for the sergeant to prepare them.

"The marshal tells me," Cogswell said, pausing for the young men's chatter to cease. "The marshal tells me...that many of you are to be knighted soon." The squires stopped shuffling to listen. Cogswell ran a calloused hand across his gray and glistening, close-cropped hair, then rubbed the matching stubble on his chin and cheeks.

"But I have never seen such a scraggly lot of squires." The sergeant paused again for effect. "'Not this lot,' I said to the marshal. 'There must be some mistake.'"

A ripple of nervous laughter came and went. Tristan snickered, exchanging glances with his brother. Sowing seeds of doubt was clearly part of Cogswell's job.

"What say you?" shouted the sergeant-at-arms. "Are you ready?"

Tristan added his voice to a ragged chorus of "Aye, Sergeant!"

"Are you sure?" The sergeant strode across the bare earth to put his face within inches of a squire's. "That's not very convincing!"

"Aye, Sergeant!" They were in unison this time. Tristan could not suppress a smile.

"Are you ready to go to war?" Cogswell moved down the line to confront another squire.

"Aye, Sergeant!" Their voices were louder now.

The sergeant slapped his thigh in rhythm with his step as he returned to the center of the training ground.

"Without your mothers and fathers to hold your hands?" He continued to slap his thigh and pace.

"Aye, Sergeant!" The squires were even louder now. Tristan joined Theos by shaking his fist in the air.

Cogswell stood still. Stopped slapping his thigh. He had worked the group into a frenzy, and commanded their full attention. "Show me."

A short distance from Tristan, the line of squires broke unexpectedly as two young men standing next to each other fell to their knees, their legs buckling beneath them. Sir Dreddit dealt each another blow from behind, then stepped over their prostrate forms and into the training ground. He carried a staff nearly as long as he was tall, each end heavily wrapped in cloth.

A third squire stooped to assist the two who had fallen. Sir Dreddit was on him instantly, one end of the padded staff thrust sharply into the young man's ribs. The squire let out a loud gasp and crumpled to the ground beside those he had sought to help.

"Are you ready?" shouted the sergeant-at-arms.

A few squires managed a hearty "Aye, Sergeant." A smattering of less enthusiastic answers followed. Initially transfixed by the sight of his fallen comrades, Tristan watched Sir Dreddit stride confidently to stand beside Cogswell.

The knight was an imposing figure, well known to all. Tristan had witnessed his prowess in jousting. He knew his reputation for hard work and rigorous training. And he was keenly aware that one of the squires Sir Dreddit had chosen to lay flat moments ago was his own. The knight stood stoically beside the sergeant-at-arms, a half-head taller, with broad shoulders and long arms. His expression was all business. The scar running from right cheek to jaw was said to have been earned during a tavern brawl his attacker did not survive.

"You, on the ground!" shouted Cogswell. "Stay down!" He pointed toward them while addressing those still standing. "Look at them! They're dead!" Tristan, along with his brother and all other squires, shifted his attention as directed. "And why? Because they were distracted!"

Cogswell acknowledged the knight beside him. "This man has come to kill King Axil! Three of you are dead already! Who among you will stop him? Who among you will save the king?"

Silence.

Tristan exchanged a quick glance with his brother. Theos grinned before giving him a shove. Tristan stumbled forward, righting himself a dozen paces from Sir Dreddit. *Bastard of a brother!* Behind him, the squires began to murmur amongst themselves.

The sergeant-at-arms spoke directly to Tristan. "Who among you would be known as number four?"

Tristan stood his ground. What else was he to do? His gaze shifted to Sir Dreddit. Cogswell hardly mattered anymore.

"What will your poor brother do when you are killed?" asked the sergeant-at-arms.

"He will be known as number five!" cried Theos from the line of squires.

A loud cheer went up from the rest. Tristan rolled his eyes.

The sergeant-at-arms turned his back on Tristan, but what he muttered to Sir Dreddit still reached the squire's ears. "One of Sir Godfrey's boys. Be careful. Lose that stick and you'll have your hands full."

Sir Dreddit did not react. His eyes were trained on Tristan as he hefted the staff in his hands.

Cogswell took a few steps back. "First man to hit the ground is dead!"

Tristan's nostrils flared. He shook the tension from his arms, letting them dangle by his side.

Sir Dreddit stepped toward him, raising the staff in his hands horizontally before bringing it swiftly down on one upraised thigh. The smokewood staff snapped with a loud crack, leaving the knight with a padded club in each hand. He abruptly tossed one piece end over end toward Tristan, who struggled to catch the splintered wooden shaft, and was left cradling the padded end against his stomach with both hands. Sir Dreddit reared back and threw the remaining club as hard as he could. It caught Tristan squarely in the chest, forcing him to step backward awkwardly, even as he realized Sir Dreddit was bearing down on him. He had not regained his balance, nor found the shaft of the club he held, when the full weight of Sir Dreddit crashed into him, driving him back and onto the ground.

He slammed into the earth, Sir Dreddit's weight crushing his chest so hard he thought his lungs would explode. When he did manage a breath, the stench of the knight overwhelmed him. He closed his eyes, allowing his entire body to go limp.

It was over, and he imagined that a real death might feel no worse.

The squires all were silent, shocked and disappointed by how quickly things had ended.

A loud battle cry startled them. Tristan strained to peer out from beneath Sir Dreddit's chest. Before his comrades could react, Sir Parrish barreled into two of them from behind, driving them into the ground. "You're dead," the Black knight said with satisfaction, lying on top of both.

Sir Dreddit pushed himself off Tristan, grinning.

Sir Parrish rose to his feet, dusting himself off while straddling the squires he had flattened. He stepped on one intentionally as he made his way back to stand beside the sergeant.

"Six dead now!" said Cogswell. "This ground represents your battlefield! How often will you let your defenses down?"

Those squires still standing looked nervously about, unsure if there would be another threat, or where it might come from. The sergeant-at-arms strode toward them, a knight on either side. The line parted quickly. Each knight went out of his way to force an opening wider than necessary to pass. Tristan watched in relief as the three mentors walked further and further away.

"You're on your guard now, are ya?" shouted Cogswell over his shoulder.

With the king's knights summoned to the castle for a fortnight, the barracks were nearly full. For the knights, it was a temporary inconvenience. But for Tristan, relegated to sleeping in the stables on a makeshift bed of hay, it was a rare opportunity to connect with his brother and share stories. He and Theos were lying in an empty stall, airing their knights' eating habits and laughing, when Reggie interrupted them.

Tristan exchanged a knowing glance with his twin. They had been discussing the stablemaster's apprentice moments earlier. Having devoted themselves to a life of servitude, they appreciated the tireless attention Reggie paid the horses, but they were unaccustomed to having it trained on them.

"Is there anything I can do for you?"

"We want for nothing, Reggie," said Theos. "Thank you for inquiring."

Reggie nodded. "I'm sorry about your friend."

"What?" Theos sobered.

"What do you mean? What friend?" Tristan asked.

"That girl. The one who was friends with the princess? From school. I used to see the four of you together all the time."

"Sibil?" asked Theos, rising on his elbows.

"Yes. That's her name."

"What about her?" Tristan asked. "Why do you say you're sorry?"

"You haven't heard? Her mother was here to see the king." Reggie lowered his voice and looked back over his shoulder. "The steward made advances on your friend."

"He what?!" Tristan yelled.

"Is she hurt?" asked Theos.

"I think she's okay," Reggie said. "She gave better than she got."

"How so?" Tristan asked. Both boys rose to their knees.

"She cut him!" Reggie whispered, wide-eyed. "With a knife! Then the marshal kicked the door in, and he drew blood as well!"

"Who told you this?" asked Tristan.

"My friend, Bernier. He saw it with his own eyes. He was by the marshal's side."

"Where is she now?" asked Theos.

"Here. In The Nest. In private quarters with her mother. The marshal instructed me to take them home, but we had to turn around."

"Unbelievable," muttered Theos. "What about the steward?"

"I don't really know, but nothing would surprise me. This isn't the first time, you know."

"What do you mean?" asked Tristan.

"Ask anyone who works for him. He's known to have his way with them. Especially the young ones."

Ruler Two

Ruler Two took the last of his calming breaths and tried to determine exactly where he was. Two noms had escorted him below ground and through a labyrinth of tunnels, where ground water seeped between The Hidor's foundation stones, and giant casks of pungent lyla turned even fresh air stolen by windcatchers into something almost too thick to breathe. *Am I just now beneath the School of Taking? No, this seems too far. Perhaps Taker's Tower?*

"King Axil lives."

It was pitch black inside the chamber into which he had been ushered, but there was no mistaking the magister's raspy voice.

"For the time being," said Ruler Two. "But not for long, m'lord."

"A disappointment. Tell me there is no reason for concern."

"There is not, m'lord. We will succeed in killing King Axil, and King Tygre's death will follow."

"I fear you mistake the cause of my concern. Both kings could live forever. That, too, would be a disappointment. Not a concern. You promised no attribution."

Ah! "I assure you, Magister, there is no way to trace this to The Guild."

"What if your assassins had been captured and tortured?"

"They would have blamed it on King Tygre, m'lord. They were told it was he they worked for, and were paid with his coin. They were advised that once they killed King Axil, they need only hail King Tygre, and a dozen others at the feast would come to their aid. A dozen others that never existed. The 'assassins' were never expected to make it out alive."

"What about the man who penned their invitations?"

How did he know about that? "The Guild's name was never breathed to him, m'lord. He could not possibly share it with others."

"I can think of only one way to be assured of that."

Kill him? "Yes, of course, m'lord. It is as good as done."

"As good as done. Hmmm. Let us assume, then, for the moment, that I have no reason to be concerned."

You don't! Why put it that way?

"Let us parse your plan. Three men to kill one king?"

"It was not my plan, m'lord, but—"

"Really? Whose plan was it?"

"Ruler Five. He—"

"Ruler Five? You are the leader of this project, Ruler Two. 'Self-governance' was your idea. Ruler Five is but a tool at your disposal. Are you unhappy with the performance of this tool? Or the lack thereof?" The magister continued before Ruler Two could answer. "Perhaps you would like Ruler Five removed from your team."

Ruler Two hesitated. *What do you mean by 'removed'? Surely you are not offering to terminate Ruler Five!*

"Well?" In the dark, the tapping of the magister's yellow fingernails was as recognizable as his voice.

"No, m'lord." *You're testing me. You have no intention of killing Ruler Five, and the last thing I need is that lunatic lurking around with a chip on his shoulder.*

"Then his plans are your plans, are they not?"

"Yes, m'lord."

"Three men to kill one king. Three men undone by one woman."

Where was the magister getting his information? "That is but a story, m'lord."

"Is it?"

"Are we to believe she can see into the future?"

"Are you certain she cannot?"

"If she could, m'lord, would the king's army not be here now?"

"The king has shared his plans with you, has he?"

Sarcasm from the magister! This is not going well. "No, Magister, but—"

"You think I am wrong to be concerned?"

"No, m'lord."

"I can tolerate disappointment, Ruler Two, but not concern. All cause for concern must be eliminated. Do you understand?"

"Yes, m'lord."

"Even so, you wish to proceed?"

What? Is this a trap? What choice do I have, really? To abandon the project and admit defeat so soon would surely label him a failure and a permanent disappointment. Whereas success—would it not make him the obvious choice to succeed this skeleton in a shabba?

"Of course, m'lord."

"Be certain! If you choose to continue, progress must be assured. The first king must die before the moon is full."

"Before the moon is f—"

"Fifteen suns! Do you still wish to continue?"

The words spilled out of Ruler Two's mouth before he could fairly judge whether they should be set free. "I do, m'lord. Most certainly I do."

Ruler Two shifted uncomfortably in his saddle, his buttocks nearly numb. He had long ago lost track of time. Someone had once told him you could monitor its passage with the movement of the stars, but he could not remember how. Nor could he recall the last time he had left the GOT on horseback. It had certainly not been like this—in the dark of night, unsure even of his destination, accompanied by a lone companion the likes of Ruler Five, whose uninvited comments about the habits of prattlers seemed intended to unnerve him. He could not help but imagine a horde of the giant black arthropods scuttling across the sands behind him, just waiting for the right moment to strike.

"Did I mention this is when they are most active?" said Five. "I shouldn't worry, though. They rarely venture this far from the canyon. And we reek of lyla." He laughed out loud. "Still, if caught, you should try to close your eyes, or cover them. They won't eat unless they're looking into the eyes of whatever they're consuming. Man or beast, it doesn't matter. That's something, eh? Can you imagine?"

That's a pile of bysh, but one can never be too careful! Ruler Two slid a hand into the cloth pouch hanging from his saddle. He rubbed a small handful of the powdered lyla it contained into the sweat clinging to his neck. *Oh, what I'd give to be in the comfort of my own bed right now, soft covers pulled up to my chin. But what choice do I have? The first attempt on King Axil's life was all Five's doing. And yet the magister holds me accountable for its failure. Whatever happens next, it's my neck on the chopping block! Five can no longer be allowed free rein. I at least need to know what he's up to.* "How much longer would you say?" A reflection of the full moon bounced back and forth across the swaying rear end of Ruler Five's black mount.

"To The Cauldron? No time at all. Can't you smell the smoke? Just over that ridge and we'll see its flames. Ten more miles and we'd find ourselves in Aranox. We'll stop just shy of that. The Cauldron sits on the edge of the Lawless Lands, just beyond King Axil's rule, but close enough to woo his subjects to its door. Bear in mind, it's not what you're familiar with. Best be silent and look as though you're in a mood."

"And leave you to do the talking?" Ruler Two scoffed.

Ruler Five stopped his horse. His white teeth gleamed in the moonlight. "In public, most members of The Assassins' League are civil-mannered, much like you. But when it comes to taking pleasure in killing, some are but a step removed from the gates of Baelon below. Please don't encourage them." Five spurred his horse on.

Arrogant arse! Most annoying! He knows full well the position he has put me in! Now he controls my destiny, and without so much as a stitch at risk himself!

Even so, it was impossible to get too angry. After all, the man had supported him in front of the magister during the Reckoning... *'No challenges, m'lord!'*

Wait.

Ruler Five could have orchestrated everything that followed—including the failed assassination attempt—knowing full well that Ruler Two would take the blame!

No, not even Ruler Five was that devious!

Was he?

He had heard a lot of tales about The Cauldron and thought them all far-fetched. But now he was forced to reconsider. The structure loomed ahead, an odd protrusion from sweeping desert sands. A dozen torches flickered from the balcony of each of its four floors, helping to distinguish it from the night's sky. The stories had certainly not exaggerated its size. Outside of the GOT compound and King Axil's castle, it was the most impressive structure he had ever seen. It might not be as tall as The Hidor, but its footprint surely covered as much ground.

Between The Cauldron and the border of Aranox, six large pyres burned, throwing flames and colored smoke high into the sky. They were no doubt a beacon and a greeting to travelers, perhaps a symbol of the impassioned and unrestrained activity the premises were known for. Ruler Two imagined they were also a fiery message to King Axil; a reminder that here, the monarch held no sway. But mostly, he appreciated their protective power; the prattlers were known to hate fire as much as the odor of lyla. He could feel the pyres' heat from thirty strides away, and marveled at the shirtless men roaming their perimeters, poking them with metal poles and repeatedly heaving logs and branches into their centers. An occasional explosion of trapped gas and steam sent red-hot embers flying, and plumes of purple, blue, and pink smoke rising.

"If ever we run out of smokewood trees, we'll know where they've all gone, eh?" said Ruler Five.

They hitched their horses to a rail that appeared endless. Ruler Two estimated two hundred horses stood tethered to it. On its other side was row upon row of some indiscernible crop sprouting from the soil like an army of cigars. It seemed so out of place, he could not help but chuckle.

"Is that a garden?" he asked. "Really?"

Ruler Five slapped him unexpectedly. "It was your idea to accompany me here, and it was a bad one! Have I been talking to myself this entire day's ride? Have you not heard a word I've said? A short time back I pronounced you sharp, but I rescind that. You seem incapable of grasping even the simplest of concepts. I am known here by all who matter. By the time we step inside, news of my arrival will have spread to every corner. When they see me, they are reminded of the magister... that's how this works. If you stay at my side and keep your mouth shut, you've a good chance of leaving in one piece. But if you venture off, or say something out of turn, you forfeit my protection. Do you understand? Everything about you screams, 'I don't belong here and I'm vulnerable. Do what you will with me.'"

Nonsense! More theatrics designed to keep you in control! Ruler Two rubbed his cheek.

"One last word before we go inside. I doubt you'd be so foolish, but if you try whilst here to ply the trade at which you are so good, whether just to line your pockets or to impress your students back at The Hidor, you're on your own. The Guild takes ten percent of every coin that passes through here. If you are caught stealing even one, it will dishonor our arrangement and destroy the trust between The Cauldron and The Guild." Five cocked his head toward the strange crop behind the hitching rail. "And I will not stop them from adding your hands to their collection. That's no garden, friend. Follow me!" He ducked beneath the hitching rail and walked briskly into the night.

What? Ruler Two stumbled after him, careful not to tread on what he now recognized as fingers reaching from the ground. *Barbaric!* Those who would never visit The Cauldron called this place by another name. What was it? Oh, yes—Den of Depravity! Or was it Debauchery?

He kept watch on Ruler Five's back as they joined others leaving the hitching rail and making their way toward The Cauldron. Laughter. Shouting. A steady stream of shadows. Someone going in the opposite direction bumped his shoulder.

"It's like this always, is it?" Ruler Two closed the short distance between himself and Ruler Five.

Five responded without bothering to look back. Whatever he said was drowned by the banter of those around him.

"Say again?" asked Ruler Two, further challenged by noise coming from The Cauldron. It was a dull, steady drone, growing ever stronger, punctuated periodically by raucous and shrill laughter. They were at its doorstep now, and there was pushing and shoving ahead of them. He shuffled his feet to stay close to Ruler Five as they made their way inside.

It was loud. Chaotic. Someone placed a hand on Five's shoulder, whispered in his ear, and pointed across the room. Was he indicating a particular person? If so, there was no way to discern who that was.

Ruler Five was in motion again, shouldering his way through the crowd.

Bastard! Are you trying to lose me? Ruler Two tried to keep up, one eye on his surroundings. More evidence that the stories he had heard were true! This was clearly "the cork room," where one could supposedly procure most any drink imaginable. The bar that bordered the room was interrupted only by the building's entrance, a staircase leading to other floors, and large fireplaces centered on each of the three walls lined with bottles of various sizes and colors.

But mostly there were people; boisterous, jubilant, intoxicated. Celebrating what? One didn't stumble on The Cauldron by mistake. You went there for a reason, if only to say you once had been inside. Women, outnumbered ten to one, seemed out of place, and his eyes settled on one seated just ahead, whose beauty made her all the more conspicuous. She was dark-skinned, slim, and dressed in fur leggings ending just below her knees, leaving her sleek calves for all to see. A matching fur vest left her arms exposed and glistening in the firelight. A narrow band of gold encircled her left arm four times, one end fashioned in a serpent's head; the other in a tapered tail.

She was impossible to ignore. Her face was smooth and sculpted, her hair so closely cropped it showed her shiny scalp. She had full lips, high cheekbones, and thin black brows atop large brown eyes.

Is she looking at me? Ruler Two tried not to stare. *Concentrate!* They were, after all, here to meet an assassin.

He was surprised when Ruler Five stopped to take a seat at the enchantress' table. Even more surprised when she spoke.

"Ayla." She greeted Ruler Five without taking her dark eyes off Ruler Two. "Who's this?"

"Ruler Two," said Five, motioning to an empty seat. "He reports to the magister, the same as I."

"Is that right?" The woman smiled at Ruler Two. She was beguiling!

"He doesn't say much," said Five.

Ruler Two took a seat next to the woman, unsure just what was going on.

"Sometimes that's best," she said, searching his face. "What is it you do?"

Five was quick to answer for him. "If The Guild were a person, he would be its heart."

Was that a compliment?

"He teaches the many ways of taking at The Hidor. There isn't a grandmaster who can hold a candle to him."

"Ooooo." The woman's smile broadened. "I am impressed."

"Charise," said Ruler Five, introducing her to Two. "I dare say she is as adept at killing as you are at taking."

Gods above! How could I have been so blind?

"You flatter me," said Charise, placing a hand on Ruler Five's. "But then, you always were a gentleman." She withdrew her hand before another of Five's could descend on it. "You have a task for me, do you?"

Ruler Five nodded. "You've heard about King Axil?"

Charise looked at him askance. "Three loonsters tried to slay him in his own house. Don't tell me that was you. I won't believe it."

"It's complicated," said Ruler Five.

"It was you!" Charise grinned. "Whatever were you thinking? And who was it that you sent?"

"Irrelevant," said Five. "But there remains a job to do."

"The king?" whispered Charise. "Are you serious?" She looked from Five to Two.

"No, at least not yet. You've heard about the woman?"

"What wom—" Charise caught herself mid-sentence. "The one who saw it all before it happened?" She smiled broadly, waiting for a reply.

Ruler Five nodded.

Charise fluttered her hands in the air. "The one they say can see into the future?"

"The same."

"You've swallowed that story, have you?"

"Let's say we're being thorough."

"Where is she?" asked the assassin.

"She lives just outside Fostead. On the road to Dewhurst."

"You want her gone? It's going to cost you."

"Why? If you don't believe her story?"

"Come now. Women always command a higher price." Charise glanced at Ruler Two. "We're special, you know. And she, a friend of the king's, no less!"

"Two hundred kingshead," said Ruler Five matter-of-factly.

Charise scoffed, then was silent.

"Two fifty," said Five, "and not a dire more."

"I might frighten her for that amount, but if you want her to stop breathing..."

Five resisted. "The woman and her daughter live alone, and by all accounts, she can scarcely walk."

"Then do it yourself, and pray she doesn't see you coming!" Charise fluttered her hands again.

"How much?" asked Ruler Five.

"Four hundred kingshead."

"Four hun—"

"Done," said Ruler Two. Five glared at him.

"Oh, my. He speaks after all. And such a pleasant voice at that." Charise looked to Ruler Five. "We're settled then."

"We are." Five grimaced, still glaring at Ruler Two.

"Very well, then. I'll take—"

"There's more," said Ruler Two.

"Whatever are you talking about?" Five looked like he might strangle Two.

"Is there?" asked Charise.

"The Prince of Quills," said Ruler Two.

"Who's that?"

"A simple shopkeeper. He penned the invitations to the Lords and Ladies Feast. He must die as well."

"Spelled someone's name wrong, did he?" said Charise.

"I hope you know what you're doing," said Ruler Five.

"The magister expects it." Ruler Two said crisply.

Charise looked from Two to Five, then back again, bemused.

"You'll have to hunt him," said Ruler Two. "He's left his shop in Fostead, said to be headed south. Perhaps to Stonybrook. His last name is Penniluk; he has relatives there. Name your price."

"Name your—" Ruler Five stifled himself and sat back with his arms crossed. He shrugged in response to a quizzical look from Charise.

"Three hundred kingshead more," said the assassin.

"Done," said Ruler Two. "Seven hundred kingshead for the two, but both must die before half-moon."

"So be it. I like this one," said Charise. "Where have you been hiding him?"

Ruler Five exhaled dismissively.

"Shall we celebrate?" asked the assassin. "Me, I'm going to the third floor." Was that her hand coming to rest on his leg? "Who else is coming?"

Wait. Isn't gambling on the second floor? The third floor is where one goes to...

Ruler Two felt her fingers press into his upper thigh.

Charise smiled mischievously at him. "Both of you, perhaps?"

THE FANNING OF FLAMES

"Fed too little, a fire dies; too much and it devours you. Just when you think you have it right, then comes the wind!" Marshal Erik Carson on managing emotions during battle.

Rolft Aerns

"How do you feel?"

Rolft heard the words, but they seemed distant. Not directed at him. He struggled to open his eyes.

"You've lost a fair amount of blood." The same voice. Closer now.

"Blood?" The word felt like a small stone passing through Rolft's throat. He jerked at the sudden recollection of the warehouse slayings, but a great weight prevented him from rising.

"You can speak." The voice was deep. By his side. Someone was holding him down. The heavy weight slowly lifted. "We thought the gods had taken you. Should have known they'd spit you back!"

"Fereliss?" Rolft coughed, relaxed, and fought again to lift his eyelids. This time they opened. Vague images slowly became familiar shapes. He was lying on a cot in the castle barracks. His side ached.

"Who else would take pity on such an ugly carcass?" Two almons had not altered Fereliss' appearance. He was still mostly hair from the neck up. Unruly straw-blonde locks cascading to his shoulder blades, thick brows twisting like vines above his dark green eyes, a mustache and beard so full they hid whatever was going on beneath them.

Rolft snorted, wincing at the pain it caused. "Help me sit up."

"Sit up, sure." Fereliss' large hands guided Rolft's legs across the cot. "But I'd think twice before standing."

"Would you, now?"

"I would. Someone sliced you proper."

"Hmmpf. Who patched me?"

Fereliss chortled. "Yurik. Take a look. You've never seen so many knots! The wound was clean cut, though. Sharp blade, but deep."

"I've suffered far worse."

"As a young man. You forget, I was there. You've salt in your hair now. Be mindful."

Rolft winced again. He laid a hand gently on his wound, hoping it would ease the pain. It did not.

"Who was it?" Fereliss asked.

"No one I'd met before."

"Why would someone want to open you?"

"Never did say. They drew first blood, and there wasn't much talk after that."

"They? How many?"

"Three, I think."

"You think!"

"It was rather dark. And it happened quickly. I don't remember everything."

Fereliss raked his mustache with his lower teeth. "I don't suppose they're talking?"

"They would find it difficult."

"Perhaps a conversation with the gods?"

"Baelon below, perhaps. Not above, I can assure you that."

"All this in Fostead?"

"Mmm. The old warehouse. How long have I been out?"

"No way to know. You were out when you arrived. Came in last night. Are ya hungry?"

"Thirsty."

"I'll have bread and water brought." Fereliss rose. "Yurik will want to admire his handiwork, and Garth knows you're here. He'll want to see you as well."

Rolft managed a smile. "All still here. I'm pleased."

"Pfft. Where else would we be?"

"And Sarah?"

"Your horse?" Fereliss laughed. "Bein' cared for by the same lad who saved your sorry arse. That stable boy, Reggie."

"Reggie? How did he—"

"Runnin' some errand for the marshal. Said you was lyin' like some drunk beside the road, half dead. He wouldn't have stopped, 'cept Sarah barred the way, and he said once he seen her, he knew exactly who you were. Wrestled you into his wagon and knew to seek me out."

"Smart lad."

"Smart horse! Offered me a proper greeting, she did, soon as she saw me. 'Fereliss,' she said, 'is that you? Gods above, how long's it been? I'm so sorry my master has been such a stranger and an arse all this time!'"

Rolft hung his head.

Fereliss shook a finger. "If it weren't for that horse and stable boy, you'd still be lyin' in that ditch, a dead man. And your friends?" He pointed to his feet. "Here... just down the road! And none the wiser!"

"I'm sure you're right."

"I'll tell you something else. If now and then you'd let your friends know what you're up to, you wouldn't have been lyin' there in the first place. And you wouldn't have that hole in your side. Because your friends would never have let that happen."

Rolft nodded in resignation. "I have failed you, friend."

Fereliss' visage softened. "Yes, well, all right, then. You're not the only one who likes to wield a sword, you know."

Sword! Did I leave one in the warehouse?

"Three men! All by yourself." Fereliss shook his shaggy head. "Plenty to go around."

"Agreed. Next time."

"Next time." Fereliss turned to go. "Get some rest. I won't be long. We'll likely all be knee-deep in blood soon enough. There's talk of war, ya know!"

Rolft struggled to rise and dress before his friends could return. He silently begged their forgiveness. They would only ask more questions, and he did not wish to lie to them. Telling the truth was out of the question. They would only throw away all that they had built to join him. Outside the barracks, he walked head down, slipping across the bailey through a veil of mist.

He entered the livery thinking he might be alone, until a young stable boy stepped out of a stall to look him over.

"You okay?" the lad asked. "You want your horse? You've come for Sarah?"

Rolft swallowed. His throat was still sore. "You remember her name?"

"Of course. Do you forget the names of your friends?"

"I do not... Reggie."

Reggie's cheeks flushed. He motioned for Rolft to follow as he walked.

Rolft trudged after him. "I'm told you care for more than horses now."

Reggie turned and beamed. "It was nuthin'."

"Nuthin' saved my life."

Reggie passed a few stalls before stopping to proclaim proudly, "Here she is—rested, and ready to ride!"

Rolft could not remember much from the warehouse. He recalled slaying three of the five men whose initials had been scrawled on his arm, and how one of them had managed to run a dagger across his side. Stumbling out the door. Struggling to mount Sarah. Difficulty riding. Nothing after that.

The lone short sword hanging from his saddle confirmed he had lost a weapon somewhere between the warehouse and wherever he had been found. Perhaps it had yet to be discovered. He could search for it come nightfall. But where was the girl's amulet he had slung over his pommel? Might Reggie have removed it whilst grooming Sarah?

It was a mercifully short ride to town. Each sway of the saddle tested the stitches in his side. When he dismounted at the livery, he did so gingerly, wincing as his feet hit the ground. He drew his coat around him to hide his bloody shirt.

Bohun stepped out of the building's shadows. "Well, well. Thought mebbe you'd run off with my horse!"

Rolft managed a weak smile.

"You all right?" asked Bohun. "Sarah looks better'n you."

Rolft handed him the reins. "No news?"

The stablemaster continued to assess Rolft's condition. "Ah, yes, now that you mention it. There was an attempt on the king's life."

"What?"

"During the Lords and Ladies Feast, if you can believe it. Didn't go so well for them involved, as someone such as yourself might imagine."

Rolft remained silent.

"Been a few killin's in town, too." Bohun's eyes widened as he awaited Rolft's reaction.

Rolft feigned ignorance. "Killings?"

"Mm-hmm. Six, I believe."

"Six?!"

"Baron Treadwell's cook. I think she was the first. Kole Cantry, then a fella named Leo. Edwyn Blythe, Bailey Bonaparte, Lane Taylor. I think that's it. Anyone you know?"

The name Leo was unfamiliar to Rolft. He considered asking Bohun whether he knew Raggett Grymes or Shum Ingram, the two men mentioned by Kole Cantry that he had yet to meet. He shook his head instead.

"Didn't know the cook, or the shopkeeper," Bohun said. "But the rest was always up to no good. Not an honest day's work among 'em."

"Huh." Rolft turned to go.

"The marshal, on the other hand," said Bohun, causing Rolft to look back, "he's a good man, as you know. He won't stop tryin' t' find who done it."

There's truth in all that. But not even the marshal can stop me now, and once finished with my task, what have I to live for? What do I care what the marshal does to me? "As it should be," Rolft muttered, walking away.

He entered The King's Inn intent on locating Jarod, and was relieved to spy him busily tending bar. The burly innkeeper acknowledged him, tossing a rag onto the bartop. "Karla! Take my place. I won't be but a minnit."

The two men soon stood outside a small storage room, out of sight of any patrons.

"Where've you been? The dam's broke loose!" whispered Jarod.

"I heard about the king. What else?"

"Three days ago, someone killed a baron's cook and bashed a shopkeeper's head in. Two days ago, another murder. Yesterday, three more at the old warehouse. That's six turned toes up in just three days!"

"By who's hand?"

"Thet's just it. No one to bear witness. But I've my suspicions."

Rolft waited for the innkeeper to continue.

"There's a pair new to town. They come in the same day you arrived. Late that night, off the coach. Didn't think much of 'em. A little odd, is all. Lords and Ladies Feast, don't forget. And Six Moons on the way. Didn't really notice 'em 'til yesterday, when they come askin' questions."

"What kind of questions?"

"Gave me a list of names. Wanted help findin' 'em."

"And?"

"Only one they really cared about... Raggett Grymes."

Raggett Grymes! Stay calm. "Who's that?"

"Good-fer-nuthin' trash is what he is. Common thief."

"Did these men say what they wanted with 'im?"

"Said Grymes worked for 'em, if you can believe that. But here's what matters: Raggett was cozy with those that got themselves killed in that old warehouse yesterday. Friendly with Kole, too—he's the one murdered two days ago in an alley. And now these two gents are looking for Raggett Grymes? You catch my meanin'? Let's just say, it won't surprise me none if Grymes is the next to meet his end. Ain't none o' my business, mind ya. I hope they kill each other."

"What'd they look like, these two?"

"One of 'em kinda fancies himself. Tall fella, my height, but not near as much weight on 'im. Dark hair, slicked back. Scar on his forehead." Jarod's finger ran across his brow. "He's the one did all the talkin'. The other? Small skinny fella, like a stray cat, ya know? Lighter hair, funny nose, tiny little eyes that look right through ya." Jarod shook his head. "Somethin' not right about that one."

"You tell 'em where to find this Raggett Grymes?"

"Told 'em what I know. He comes and goes. Don't know where he lives now. But he's in town a lot. Most likely find 'im hangin' 'round the south end tiltin' a jug at The Poor Man's Pub or The Raven's Nest."

"What about the two lookin' for 'im? You know where they are?"

"Right now? Couldn't tell ya. Haven't seen 'em all day. But come night, they'll be sleepin' under this roof."

"They're stayin' here?" Rolft suppressed his excitement.

"They are. Come with me. I'll show you their room."

Overseer Reynard Rascall

A dense fog had settled over Fostead during the night. It clung to the ground, blanketing buildings and seeping into alleys as the town's inhabitants began to stir. It was too early for most shops to open, but already there was movement in the streets.

Reynard turned his collar up. It did little to keep out the cold. He shivered, blew into cupped hands, then shoved them back into pockets. The fog disclosed little more than the rough shapes of two men down the street. The fact that one had been loitering near

The Raven's Nest, and that he had been willing to engage Spiro in discussion, were both good signs.

"Come on, come on," Reynard grumbled. As if on cue, the men he watched separated, the smaller of the two heading back toward him. Spiro emerged from the mist. "Well?" asked Reynard.

"Done," said Spiro crisply.

"He knows where to find them?"

"Of course."

"How will he recognize them?"

"Able and Elijah? You're joking, right?"

"And what did that cost me?"

"Less than you thought."

"Ah, well then, you can use what's left to buy us something warm. Let's find a fire, shall we?" Reynard wrapped his arms around his chest. "While you were making friends, I nearly froze to death."

The knock on the door was unexpected. Reynard stood to listen. Spiro, lying in bed, craned his head. Another knock, louder. Reynard made his way to the door, glancing back at Spiro before opening it a crack to reveal a sliver of a man in colored garb.

"Yes?" Reynard maneuvered to get a better look. Definitely the king's uniform. The man was alone. Plenty of gray in his hair, wrinkles in his leathered cheeks.

"Beg pardon, sir. Sergeant Faraday of the king's army. I wonder if I might have a word."

"A word?" *Best not to overreact!* "Most assuredly. Why not?"

"Thank you, sir." The sergeant waited for the door to open wider, but it did not. "Might I come in, then?"

"Of course, Sergeant. Of course. Please do." Reynard pulled the door open. Spiro swung his legs to the floor and sat up. Reynard shot him a look telling him to stay put.

The sergeant advanced to the threshold and stopped. "You'll step back where I can see you, please."

Cautious fellow! "As you wish." Reynard presented himself by backing into the middle of the room, his hands spread wide before him. "Have we somehow given offense? I assure you it was unintended."

The sergeant looked him over, then turned his attention to Spiro. Spiro returned the soldier's stare.

"How can we help you, Sergeant Faraway?" asked Reynard.

"Faraday," said the sergeant. "What brings you to Fostead?"

"The Lords and Ladies Feast, of course."

"That was two days ago."

"Indeed, and we've been enjoying your fair city ever since."

The sergeant scoffed lightly. "You arrived by coach?"

Reynard's eyebrows lifted. "Is that important? How we arrived?"

The sergeant waited for an answer.

"Yes," said Reynard. "We came by coach. Is that a problem?"

"No. No, it's not. You've friends in Fostead, have you?"

Reynard spread his hands wide again. "We're new to town."

"No, then?"

"No."

The sergeant took a step further into the room. Reynard moved aside to allow him passage. The soldier returned his attention to Spiro, and the two men locked eyes.

"You don't know Leo Bartlett, then?"

The bookkeeper's last name was Bartlett? Who would have thought? "Bartlett? No," said Reynard. "The name is not familiar."

"Uh-huh. Kole Cantry, Edwyn Blythe, Lane Taylor, Bailey Bonaparte?"

"Never heard of them." *Another truth!*

"And I don't suppose you know Baron Treadwell, either."

"Do we look like we know barons?" Reynard forced a chuckle. "Might I ask what this is all about?"

"You might. There's been a lot of killin' goin' on of late."

"Killing! You don't say...here in Fostead?"

"Un-huh. You don't know Raggett Grymes, then?"

Noggods! "Raggett Grymes... Raggett Grymes... Ahhh! Yes! Spiro, was that not the name of the gentleman we shared drinks with at the pub last night?"

Spiro shrugged.

"Yes, I'm sure of it now." Reynard smiled at the sergeant. "As I said, new to town, but making friends the best we can whilst here."

The sergeant stared at Reynard. "First time you met?"

"With Raggett? Just so. Our first encounter."

"Never heard of 'im before last night?"

"That's right. Why do you ask?" *I'm genuinely curious!* "He's one of those killed, is he? Or perhaps he's the killer you're after?"

"You know the man what owns this establishment?"

"The innkeeper?" *Where's this going?*

"Mm-hmm. Tells me you was asking after Raggett yesterday mornin'. Askin' where t' find 'im."

"Well, yes." Reynard moved closer to the door with a finger to his head. "We met last night. Had drinks. We quite enjoyed ourselves. Today, in fact, we thought to try and find him for another round."

"But that was yesterday."

"What was?"

"When you asked where to find Mr. Grymes."

"What of it?"

"A minnit ago you said you never heard of 'im before you met last night."

"Ahhh." Reynard sighed, his smile fading. "I fear I must have confused my days and nights." He nodded slightly as he and Spiro exchanged glances.

"Well, that's strange, that is," said the sergeant. "You say you never heard of 'im, but the innkeeper says you told him the man works for you. I think perhaps the two of you should take a walk with me." He took a step closer toward the bed Spiro sat on. "What's that?"

Spiro turned to look at the wooden object lying by his side. He ran his fingers along the metal spike rising from its center before picking it up. "What, this?"

"What is that?" the sergeant asked again, his attention drawn to the dark stains mottling the block.

The door to the room clacked shut as Reynard leaned his back against it. Sergeant Faraday turned at the sound, just in time to watch Reynard's smile reappear.

"Show him, Spiro."

Reynard checked to make sure the bolt on the door was engaged, then turned to survey the room. Spiro sat on the edge of his bed, breathing heavily, the dagger in his right hand still dripping blood. Sergeant Faraday lay at his feet, no longer moving. The paper spindle from Kasparr's office protruded from the soldier's head at an awkward angle, only a small length of its spike visible beneath the wooden block. Blood spatter surrounded the dead man, a thin stream still trickling from a gash in his neck.

Reynard acknowledged the blood smears Spiro wore. "Any of that yours?"

Spiro looked himself over, focusing on his left hand. "Don't think so, but the cur did try t' bite me."

Reynard shuddered and laughed. "What did you expect? If someone clamped a hand over your mouth and took to stabbing you with a metal prick, what would you do?"

"I'd kill 'im."

"No doubt." Reynard looked about the room. "Whew! You've made a bloody mess this time, you have."

"'Cuz I was right about the klubandag."

"What?"

"The baby klubandag." Spiro pointed to Sergeant Faraday. "I was right. Went in and out his ear like a greased pig, but when I stuck it in his head, that was it. Nearly broke it off tryin' ta get it back out."

"I fear you've lost me."

"Your 'bloody mess' wouldn't be so bloody if your klubandag had done its job. But no, it didn't, so I had to improvise." Spiro held up his dagger.

"That's not my klubandag. It's not anyone's klubandag, you idiot! It's a godsarse spindle, used to collect papers, not stab people in the head!"

"Oh, really?"

"Really."

"So when the good sergeant here asked me, 'What is that?' what was it you said? 'Show him, Spiro!'"

"Ah... point taken."

"What now?"

"Well, there's no cleaning this up. This isn't the Waterford docks. We can't just feed him to the fish." Reynard wiped the sweat from his neck. "And with this heat, he'll be ripe in no time. We need to find new lodgings."

"Ready when you are." Spiro wiped his dagger on the bed and started to rise.

"No, no, relax. Rest a moment more. We need to think this through. Things just got complicated."

"How do you mean?"

"One has to ask: what did Raggett Grymes do to bring a soldier here? What have we done to warrant the king's attention, besides befriend Mr. Grymes?"

"We've killed one of his soldiers, for starters."

"No, you miss my point. Why would his soldier come here in the first place?"

Spiro shrugged, then used one hand to hold Sergeant Faraday's head against the floor, the other to try and pull the spindle out. "I'm sure this wasn't what he came for."

"I'm sure not."

"You see?" Spiro tugged twice more at the spindle before giving up. "His skull may as well be made of smokewood."

"We must speak again with our friend, Grymes. In the meantime, we've another matter to attend to. Who knows that we stay here?"

Spiro shook his head. "You didn't tell Grymes, did you? No one I can name, for sure."

"Not quite true. Think, Spiro. Who could have told the sergeant exactly what door to knock on?"

A look of realization spread across Spiro's face.

"That's right. And who knew that we were looking for Mr. Grymes?"

Spiro's beady eyes were slits. "The same."

Marshal Erik Carson

Carson tilted the sign hanging from the printer's door, as though that might somehow change its simple message: *Closed.* He released it, letting it swing from a cord tied around the door handle. He shot a look of frustration at Major Stronghart before pressing his face to the shop's front window. There was little to see inside. Mostly dark, and certainly no movement. He frowned at the major.

"Did you need the printer, Marshal?" A middle-aged woman, half as tall as Major Stronghart and twice as wide, stepped out of the adjacent shop's doorway.

"Indeed, I do, madam. Do you know his whereabouts?"

"I don't, but you'll not find him in there. He left with a wagon loaded with belongings three days past. I asked where he was off to, but he didn't answer. Laughed, he did! Said his workin' days were over. I don't think he'll be back."

Major Stronghart raised his eyebrows.

"Thank you, madam." Carson nodded to Major Stronghart and stepped away from the printer's door.

Major Stronghart took one step forward, raised a knee to his chest, and kicked the door in. It crashed to rest at an awkward angle inside the shop, freed from but one hinge.

"Oh, my!" said the portly woman. Several others passing by The Prince of Quills' shop stopped to stare.

The marshal addressed them all. "Fear not! The king will make it right. Go about your business, please." He followed Major Stronghart into the print shop. One long work bench filled the middle of the room. Behind and to its sides were shelves cluttered with tools and supplies. One wall was filled with bottles of ink; another mostly quills. There were stacks of paper and envelopes, rolls of ribbon, scissors, measuring sticks and templates of sundry shapes and sizes. The workbench was littered with materials; the floor strewn with paper and quills. Several of the bench's drawers were half-opened.

"Doesn't look like a fight," said Major Stronghart.

"No. Nor robbery," thought Carson aloud.

"Robbery! Gods, no! He did that himself!" It was the portly woman again, standing in the print shop's doorway.

"Is that right?"

"Left in a hurry, I tell ya! Without so much as a fare thee well!"

"You're certain he didn't say where he was headed?"

"No, Marshal, but his wagon rolled on that way." The woman pointed south. "And if it was me lookin' for 'im, I'd start in Stonybrook. He's got family there."

"Does he? By what name?"

"Same as his, Marshal. Penniluk."

"Thank you, madam. You've been most helpful."

The woman twisted her body out of the doorway to let the marshal pass. Major Stronghart followed.

Carson strode down the street. Sometimes all it took was one small clue. Like a name... Penniluk. Or a sword left beside dead bodies. He felt certain that Baselo would know the owner of the weapon left inside the old warehouse by the time they returned to the castle. A little more time, a little more digging, and he would solve the riddle to all these murders—the bookkeeper, the baron's cook, the commoner in the alleyway, the three in the warehouse. And the king's attempted murder! Might they all be related?

He was so deep in thought that he almost passed The Hold, but its white stonework streaked with blue and gray caught his eye. He motioned for Major Stronghart to enter the small palace outpost. "Let's see what else Sergeant Faraday can tell us. Perhaps it's worth a ride to the old warehouse."

The sun had not had time to fully warm the marshal's back before the major returned, alone.

"Out and about, I suppose. Cell's empty, but his turncoat's there. He can't be far."

The marshal and major followed Jarod down a narrow corridor leading to rooms for rent.

Jarod looked from the major to the marshal before knocking on one of the doors. Hearing no response, he knocked again, louder. "Open up in there! It's the innkeeper!"

"Is it locked?" asked Carson. "Do you have a key?"

Jarod tried the latch, pushing against the door. It opened but a few inches. "It's not locked. But they've shoved somethin' up against it. Here, help me." Jarod leaned his shoulder against the door. "We're comin' in!" he cried, as the marshal and major lent their weight to the effort.

The door swung slowly inward, the three men nearly falling over one another as their scrabbling feet became entangled. Jarod was the first to stumble into the room, the major and Marshal Carson on his heels.

"Gods above!" said the innkeeper.

Carson kneeled beside the body that had prevented the door from opening freely. The man's face was downturned, but he was still easily identified. Sergeant Faraday's bloody throat displayed a gaping wound, and an odd object the size of a fist protruded from the top of his head.

Jarod surveyed the floor, mesmerized by the amount of blood and the story told by the various marks it had left. "Looks like he put up a helluva fight. Started over here. Then they dragged him over there to block the door."

"The men staying here. You know their names?"

"No. I don't take names, Marshal. Just their coin."

"What is that?" asked the major. "Stickin' out his head... a block of wood?"

"You might call it that." Carson tapped the block with his finger. "You remember what was said about the shopkeeper and his wounds?"

"Bunch of small holes about his face and neck."

"Quite right." Carson sighed, one hand still resting on the body.

"And you think that's what done it?" asked the major.

"Indeed I do. It's a shopkeeper's tool. And I'll wager Leo Bartlett is missing his."

"Bloody bysh," whispered Major Stronghart.

The marshal rose to his feet. "You don't know their names, but you'd recognize them, eh?"

"In a crowd, and from a distance," Jarod said. "One's tall with slicked back hair. A scar on his forehead that's hard to miss. The other's no bigger than a boy, but there's sumthin' not right about him. You can see it in his eyes."

"I'm afraid we've no time to tend to Sergeant Faraday now. They can't have gotten far. With any luck, we'll find them before dark. Are you with us, Jarod? We can't do this without you."

"Try and stop me. Just let me tell poor Timmil he's on his own with the ale."

"Right. Meet us down the street, then. We've got to let the stationmaster know—no coach leaves town until we've seen its passengers."

"I won't be but a few minnits."

"And Jarod..."

"Mmm?"

"Arm yourself."

Innkeeper Jarod Kelter

"Timmil!" Jarod tapped the end of the stout cudgel he had picked up from behind the bar against the palm of his empty hand. He stared at the number of casks still littering the alleyway behind the inn, suddenly wishing he had counted them before he'd left Timmil on his own. "Timmil!"

He started down the stairs into the cellar, mumbling angrily to himself. "I swear to all gods, if you've been at the ale again, I'll take it outta your pay!" The sun warmed Jarod's back, illuminating the stairs until he was halfway down. By the time he reached the bottom, the musty coolness of the cellar had enveloped him. He was relieved to see Timmil sitting on a cask, his back supported by several others, a bottle in his lap.

"Best get at it, lad. You're on your own now. I've got other chores to tend to."

Jarod heard the soft sound of something scrape the dirt behind him, then the crack of a solid object as it slammed into the back of his head. Searing pain! *Has my head split open?* He fell forward, dropping the cudgel and hitting the earthen floor hard, first with his chest, then with his jaw. His eyes fluttered open, then closed. His nostrils flared as he took in a shaky breath. A second blow jarred his head. His body trembled uncontrollably, but the pain was duller now, somehow disconnected from his body. He did not even feel the third blow.

Sibil Dunn

Sibil dressed quickly and quietly so as not to wake her mother. It had been her first night sleeping in the palace without the company of Princess Lewen. She felt at home and a stranger at the same time.

Outside, the bailey seemed nearly overrun with men and women bustling about, but none took any interest in her. Relieved, and blessing Lewen for her ability to navigate the palace grounds, she set a course for the soldier's barracks. The man she and Reggie had rescued from the roadside had been in possession of the abbot's amulet now pressed against her chest, strongly suggesting that he was one of the two men in the alley when she had been accosted. But which was he? Reggie had recognized him as a former guard of the royal family. As such, he might have known Lewen, reinforcing Sibil's hope that he was the one who had befriended her. The steward's actions, however, had made it clear that service to the king was no guarantee of honor.

If she could only speak with the injured man, she would know.

One of the barrack's many doors was open when she arrived, so she stuck her head inside. Two chatty maids were tidying the cavernous sleeping quarters, but all the cots were empty. Her eyes roved over them multiple times.

She thought for a moment, then started back across the bailey and toward the stables in search of Reggie. Absorbing the activity around her, and keeping one eye out for any sign of the steward, she nearly bypassed a young couple standing against the chapel with their backs to her.

"Theos?" He, more often than his twin brother, Tristan, wore his long blonde hair tied back. Both figures turned abruptly, caught off guard.

Theos' worried expression turned to one of relief. "Sibil? We heard you were here. How are you?"

"I'm well." Sibil tried not to stare too long at his petite companion. Not even the young woman's obvious discomfort could hide her beauty. She, too, had long blonde hair, a braid on either side falling to her lower back. Pale skin, flushed cheeks, and beautiful blue eyes.

"Oh!" Theos gestured awkwardly. "This is Emili."

Sibil could not decide whether he was nervous or embarrassed.

Emili made an effort to smile. "How do you do? I'm sorry, but I must be off."

Theos turned apologetically to Sibil. "Both of us, I'm afraid." He took Emili by the elbow and led her gently away, calling over his shoulder. "We sleep in the stables, Sib. Come see us tonight. Tristan will kill me if you don't!"

How strange! Sibil watched the couple continue to converse until they disappeared from sight, and her thoughts remained with them until she reached the stables, where a familiar voice drew her behind the building. She spied Reggie standing by the wagon he had driven the previous night, an older man with white hair on his knees beside him, inspecting the damaged wheel. But what really caught her eye were the vehicles beside the wagon—bright and shiny coaches in the colors of the realm. Even from a distance, they demanded one's attention.

"A rock, ya say?" The old man's gnarled fingers prodded various parts of the wagon wheel's splintered spokes.

"Yes," said Reggie, catching sight of Sibil as she approached. "Tell him, Sibil."

"What?" She reluctantly diverted her gaze from the coaches.

"About the rock." Reggie, canted his head toward the damaged wheel.

"Oh, yes," said Sibil. "Ummm. More like a boulder, I should think. Wouldn't you say?"

"Yes! A boulder is what I meant."

The old man looked askance at Reggie, then back at the broken wheel. "Uh-huh. Well, I don't suppose it matters. What's done is done." He turned his gray eyes to Sibil. "And you're the king's guest, I'm told, so that's the end of it."

Sibil repeatedly circled the bailey's perimeter, growing more and more at ease as she reacquainted herself with the castle's layout. Each time she passed the soldiers' barracks, she stuck her head inside. Finding them empty a third time, she sat to rest, disappointed and perplexed. *How far can the wounded man have gone? Just the previous evening, he was slung like a sack of grain over the shoulder of a giant shadow. Of course!* Sibil rose at the recollection of Reggie's query: "*Will the infirmary take him?*"

A chorus of triumphant cries stilled her. Young men's voices, including—she was sure of it—those of the Godfrey twins. When another outburst followed, she turned in its direction and set off to find its source.

She was rewarded as soon as she rounded the barracks. Bare soil sloped from its rear to a spacious level ground that stretched to the castle's wall. Gathered near the center of that open space were twenty to thirty young men standing in a circle. "Squires," Sibil whispered, quickly picking out Tristan and Theos.

Two uniformed men sat talking under a large tarp stretched between raised timbers. Occasionally, they turned their attention to the squires, pointing and laughing before returning to their conversation.

"Who's next?" A short man with gray hair standing in the center of the squire's circle held two wooden swords, one of which he lowered until its tip touched the ground. It drew a circle in the dirt as he spun slowly around. "Come now, lads. Take pity on an old man. Who'll dance with me?" A smattering of nervous titters escaped the squires' lips.

"You're too ugly, Cogswell!" shouted one of the soldiers from under the shade structure. "Perhaps if you put a dress on!"

"Was I addressing you, Sergeant Lagos? Perhaps you'd like to show the lads yourself! Well?" The old man in the circle waited for an answer, glowering, until Sergeant Lagos raised both hands in surrender.

"I'll do it," said a slim squire standing next to Theos. His voice carried easily across the open grounds.

"Ahhh!" the man called Cogswell said with satisfaction. "Squire Axold, is it? Already more courage than our Sergeant Lagos, though that's not sayin' much. Let's see what else you've got." Cogswell handed the squire one of the wooden swords and stepped back. "Whenever you're ready, lad."

Sibil sank to sit with her back against the barracks. Axold was not the tallest squire, but he was a good six inches taller than Cogswell. And he had long arms. They were always an advantage in a sword fight, this much she knew. The two men adopted fighting stances and raised their swords to touch tips.

"Lower base!" shouted Cogswell, patting one of his own thighs to demonstrate. The squire spread his legs a bit further. "Bend your knees!" Cogswell suddenly lurched forward and struck the young man with his sword. "How are you going to move like that?"

Shaken, the squire adopted an even lower stance. "Better!" said Cogswell. "Now, I'm waiting, son. Strike when you're ready!"

Squire Axold glanced nervously toward the ring of young men watching. He took a deep breath, steadied himself, and studied Cogswell carefully. When he lashed out, Cogswell slipped easily out of harm's way. Axold followed him, striking again. Cogswell evaded the blow with little apparent effort. "Not bad," said the old man.

Inspired, the squire attacked once more, lunging and thrusting his sword toward Cogswell's mid-section. Sibil tried to follow the old man's movements, but he was suddenly at the squire's side, positioned to strike him in the back with the flat of his sword.

Sibil's eyes widened as the ring of squires erupted in a cheer of admiration. She watched Cogswell lay a hand on Squire Axold's shoulder and offer him some words of what she assumed to be advice or encouragement.

"You are of no use to our king dead!" the old man shouted at all the boys. "Attack and defend! You must learn to do both! But one is far more important than the other!"

Sibil shifted her seat and settled in, all thought of giants and shadows momentarily erased.

It was dark by the time she arrived at the livery. The barn's back doors were closed, prompting her to hope the Godfrey boys were outside, waiting behind the stables. They were not. She crossed the grounds for a closer look at the royal coaches she had seen earlier in the day. Even in the dark, they were magnificent to behold! She walked slowly down a line of them, running her hand along their embossed and gilded doors. *What would it be like to travel from place to place in—*

"Boo!" A hand reached out from above a door sash to grab her wrist.

Sibil gasped, wrenched her hand away, and staggered backward. Laughter spilled from the carriage. She took a cautious step back toward it. "Tristan?" The laughter grew louder. "Theos?" She was near the door again.

"Princess Sibil Dunn," a deep voice said with obvious inflection, "pray come inside!" A sputtering of repressed laughter followed.

I'll kill them! Sibil threw open the carriage door. The twins each held out a hand to assist her. She slapped them away, grabbed the doorframe, and pulled herself inside. "Think you're funny, do you?"

"Ah, Sib, sorry." Tristan turned to hide his face.

I'll show you sorry! Sibil kicked him in the shin, causing him to erupt in gales of laughter. She plonked herself down next to Theos. Despite his serious countenance, she elbowed him roughly in the ribs, causing Tristan to laugh even harder.

"You'll never be knighted! Either of you! You're still six almons old, the both of you!"

"A-hah-ha-ha!" cried Tristan, wiping tears from his eyes. "So true! So true!" Sibil kicked him again. "Oww! Gawds! All right, enough! Enough! I surrender!"

Sibil jammed her elbow into Theos once more for good measure. "If the two of you could joust half as well as you jest, you might someday be knighted...but I watched you fight today, and I'm afraid there's little hope."

"Aw, c'mon, Sib. I won both my challenges today," said Tristan.

"Against someone half your size. I was watching."

"We saw you, too," said Theos, surprisingly serious. "You're all right, are you? We heard about the steward."

Ah, that explains it!

"Were you hurt?" asked Tristan, sobering. "The way Reggie tells it, you gave better than you got. But if he hurt you—"

"I'm fine." Sibil really did not care to talk about the steward. "But it's the second time in as many days I've had cause to draw the dagger you gifted me."

"The second time!" said Tristan. Both twins were serious now.

"The night before my mother was summoned to the castle, a man attacked me in an alley."

"What!" said Tristan. "Are you serious? I'm so sorry, Sib, for scaring you. I had no way of knowing."

"What happened?" asked Theos. "You fought him off, did you?"

"I did, aided by a stranger. But now I need your help."

"How so?" asked Tristan.

"Promise me you won't laugh."

"We won't," Theos said.

"I would learn to better defend myself. I want the two of you to train me."

"I don't see how we can, Sib. Not here, anyway," Tristan said. "They wake us early in the morning and work us 'til the sun goes down."

"Just a little?" said Sibil. "It needn't take long."

"Tristan's right, Sib. They give us no time to ourselves. When we aren't being herded with the other squires, we serve our knights."

"What about your training with the other squires? Behind the barracks. Might I join you?"

"You're not serious," said Theos.

Sibil maintained her silence.

"Our practices together have been fun," said Tristan, "but it's nothing like the training here, Sib. You'd be hurt."

"And don't think Sergeant Cogswell hasn't noticed you," said Theos.

"Has he?" Sibil asked, hope rising again.

"How could he not? He can't hold the squires' attention while you're watching. He's not going to invite you closer," said Theos.

He might as well have slapped her. It hurt that much.

"Very well, then." Sibil rose suddenly from her seat. "I must be getting back." She jumped from the coach.

"What? You've only just arrived," said Tristan, following suit. "Can you come again tomorrow night? We've missed you." He stepped forward to hug her.

Sibil was too busy wrestling emotions to receive him or his brother properly. By the time she sorted her feelings, regret was her only companion. She stood staring at the livery, listening to crickets.

Alone again.

"I've missed you, too," she whispered.

Marshal Erik Carson

Marshal Carson sat in his private quarters, hoping dusk and solitude would help him bridge the gap between those things he knew and those he did not. The body count in Fostead had risen to nine. Whoever had slain Sergeant Faraday had doubtless killed the innkeeper and his young associate in the wine cellar as well. And under his and Major

Stronghart's very noses! Who were the two men staying at The King's Inn, looking for Raggett Grymes? Where were they now?

And what of the sword found in the old warehouse? It had been identified by Baselo as belonging to Rolft Aerns, a former royal guard! Known to wander now from town to town like some lost vagabond, could Rolft somehow be involved in the recent killings? Could his sword have fallen into the hands of others? How many of the Fostead murders might be related to each other? And where had the Prince of Quills really gone? Carson sighed. The attempt on King Axil's life deserved his full attention. The printer needed to be found and questioned. And yet...

He stared at the door to his quarters. His wife had gone to the kitchen in search of supper. He had warned her to avoid the steward should she see him. The man would be in a foul mood, and more inclined than ever to hurt the marshal in any way he could. *"Next time, aim lower!"* Had the marshal known what he would encounter when he'd kicked the servant's door in, he might have left the steward alone with Mari Dunn's daughter a few moments longer. The image of her squared off against the man was sharp in his mind—not just the fighting stance she had adopted, but the look in her eyes. Angry, resolute. She might well have killed the steward herself. And there was still the mystery of Mari Dunn and her premonitions. The suddenness and certainty with which she had proclaimed her daughter's peril was unsettling, particularly when paired with her foretelling of the king's attempted assassination. *Ah, yes, back to the king!*

There was a soft rapping on the chamber door. His wife returning from the kitchen? "Who's there?"

"It's Garth, m'lord. Garth Browne."

Carson recognized the voice. Opening the door, he was reminded that the youngest of the royal guards was also the largest. Garth loomed over him, his barrel chest rising and falling.

"What is it, Garth? It's late."

"My apologies, sir. I didn't want to bother you. And it's probably nuthin'. But it's botherin' me a good deal, and you're the only one to tell." The young guard's hands fidgeted at his waist.

"What about Fereliss, or Yurik?"

"Mmm. That's just it. They already know."

Steward Pryll Fletcher

The steward was prepared, should his wife wake, to fabricate a situation requiring his presence in the servant's quarters. But this night, she slept soundly. He dressed hastily, not bothering to lace his shirt. He did not, after all, intend to wear it long.

He closed the door quietly behind him, and was soon making his way across the inner bailey. A warm summer breeze did its best to usher out the lingering heat of day. He gave a quick glance back toward The Shaft, recalling his last communication with the king and marshal.

It had been a mistake to bring the Dunn girl to the castle, but she had been hard to resist. He still pictured her on the roadside. Raven hair falling to her hips, tied back to reveal an oval face with high cheekbones and a thin nose slightly turned up beneath dark eyes. Her skin had been the color of honey, glistening in the sun.

Fletcher spat his memory of her into the night. The aftermath would soon blow over. He worried less about the king in that regard than he did the marshal. *That persistent butt rash!* For a price, he could rid himself of the self-righteous meddler. *So be it!* First thing in the morning, he would pay a visit to someone who could manage such a task.

The steward expelled a deep breath and clicked his tongue. The thought of finally acting on his brother's advice brought tremendous relief, allowing him to turn his full attention to what awaited him this evening. He tightened the cord holding his ponytail as he headed down a dark corridor leading to the servants' quarters. To the room where he had hoped to bed the Dunn girl. It was like any other on this wing of the castle, except that he had kept it vacant for his own use these past few almons. He remembered how it all had started, absent any preconceived design—one young maid accused of theft, willing to sacrifice her modesty for forgiveness. It wasn't absolution, but it was sufficient to keep her in the steward's employ.

It had gotten easier over time. Easier to spot the young women who would comply. Easier to orchestrate those situations that left them at his mercy. Easier to find the right words to manipulate them and to ensure their silence.

He paused in front of the door. He remembered this particular girl. They had first met when she'd broken an expensive kitchen vase. She had been nearly inconsolable and desperate to make things right. She was not his favorite type. Her breasts were too small, her hair too light. But she was timid and easy to manage.

It was she who had sought him out earlier this day to confess her role in staining the upholstery of two library chairs. Again she had begged his forgiveness, and he had promised to grant it this evening. It was, perhaps, her most attractive quality: she already knew the rules.

He pushed the door open, thankful that its latch had been repaired, and stepped inside. He gently closed and locked the door. Devoid of light, the room revealed little to his eyes.

"Emili," he whispered. "Where are you?" He heard movement where he knew the bed to be, accompanied by a sniffle, then a whimper. He stretched his arms in front of him. "Don't cry, child. Reach out to me. Let me feel you."

Something brushed one of his arms, then clawed at it, and he instinctively jerked back. "What in—" A strong hand grabbed him by the shirt as a body pressed hard against his.

"Feel this!" a male voice said.

The blade ripped through Pryll's flesh, glancing off a rib on its way to more vital organs. He gasped, frozen by excruciating pain. "No!" *Survival at any cost!* His arms flailed as his assailant drove him roughly into a wall. He clutched the man's clothing in an awkward embrace—*who are you!?*— but a dagger already hovered near his face, and now it pierced his neck, instantly clogging his throat with steel and blood. He could not breathe. He struggled frantically to escape, his legs kicking at the dark. But it was only moments until panic turned to disbelief, and then to resignation. His limbs would not obey him. His grip on his attacker loosened. His legs gave way beneath him. *Is this really how it ends? How unfortunate! What a shame!*

Ruler Two

Ruler Two walked briskly down the Hidor's corridor. He and Ruler Five had met the assassin at The Cauldron only two days earlier. They had not expected to hear from her so soon.

To be entirely honest, he was eager to see her. She had been on his mind a lot since his visit to The Cauldron. There was something irresistible about her. It was largely physical, to be sure—those long, slender limbs; her revealing garb. But there was also something about the way she spoke to him, the way she looked at him, that hinted at a playful, sexual nature. The way her fingers had dug into his thigh; the suggestive invitation to join her on the third floor of The Cauldron. He had checked with more than one reliable source since his return to The GOT compound. The third floor was indeed where one went to explore and satisfy one's animalistic urges. He could not help but imagine, over and over again, what might have happened had he accepted her advances that night.

Have I gone mad? The woman is an assassin! She probably kills her lovers in the act! Far better for Ruler Five to engage her in the throes of passion. Perhaps he has already!

No sooner had he exited The Hidor than Ruler Two spotted the pair sitting close together on the stone bench that encircled and contained the courtyard's central fountain waters. In another time and place, they might be two young lovers, showered by sunlight and a shimmering mist.

But the closer he drew, the less enchanting they appeared. Charise's arms were folded across her chest. Ruler Five's expression did not belong to a bearer of good tidings.

"What's happened?" Two asked.

"Nothing's happened." Five used a kerchief to wipe the sweat from his brow and neck.

"What's that supposed to mean?" Ruler Two looked to the assassin for a better answer. "Ayla, Charise."

"Ayla," said the assassin coyly.

"It means nothing has happened," said Ruler Five. "We might as well be starting anew."

"Noggods! What about the woman?"

"The one who sees into the future?" asked Charise. "The woman you said lived just outside Fostead? I journeyed there. I found her house. Empty."

"Empty! So you left? Why didn't you wait for her? What are you doing here?"

"Would you like me to go back and wait? I thought you had a deadline."

How exasperating! "Yes, we have a deadline! All the more reason for you to have seen this through! You should go back and wait for her return."

Charise smiled knowingly at Ruler Five. "I could be waiting a long time. She may not return."

Five said, "Apparently, she's staying at the castle as a guest of King Axil."

What? Ruler Two's stomach churned. "The castle? For how long?"

"No one seems to know," said the assassin. "So what I'm doing here is waiting for payment. And further instruction, if you have any."

"Payment!"

"For my time and travel. This outcome is not my doing. My time must still be paid for."

Ruler Five intervened. "She's right. That's how this works."

"The castle is but a stone's throw from the woman's house!" said Ruler Two.

Charise shrugged. "Were the castle just another cottage, I wouldn't be here. But it's not. You hired me to kill a woman living in a house with her daughter. That is a far cry from killing a friend of King Axil whilst she sleeps in one of his beds. Under his wing, so to speak. If you want that done, you'll need to say so, and it will cost you dearly."

"Bloody bysh! What about the Prince of Quills?"

"What about him?"

"Did you at least kill him?"

"No. You told me the woman should die first." Charise raised her eyebrows. "Did you misspeak?" Ruler Five hung his head. "Perhaps the two of you need time to reconsider what you really want. And while you're at it, Five, you'd best explain to your friend here how the League of Assassins works. It's not that complicated." She looked directly at Ruler Two. "We do what it is we're tasked to do—nothing more, nothing less—for a price agreed upon in advance. Since you're new to this, and I still like you, I'll settle for half of what we agreed upon for my time and trouble thus far. If you still want the woman dead by full moon, the new price is one thousand kingshead; if you want the Prince of Quills to die, the price remains the same. You know where to find me."

Ruler Two's attention was captured by movement in The Hidor's uppermost breeze-way, adjacent to Takers Tower, where the supreme leader resided. Was that the magister standing there now, watching them? "No, wait. We know what we need."

The High Order had met once before in the magister's private garden, the Leaveum, but that had been a special occasion, not a general business meeting. This was unusual. General meetings were held every time the moon made a quarter turn, either in The Chalice Room or The Blade. Surely this change in venue had nothing to do with moratorium. He made his way to the fifth floor of The Hidor, then stopped for a moment at the spot where he thought the magister might have stood watching his meeting with Five and the assassin, Charise, the day before. He told himself there was no cause for alarm. The moratorium was still well in hand. Even so, he started his cleansing breaths much sooner than usual.

A last look down the breezeway, followed by a search of the grounds below, revealed no sign of Ruler Five. Even a few words with him before the meeting would help to affirm they were still in this together.

The breezeway led directly to Takers Tower, the magister's personal domain. There were only two ways to get to the Leaveum. One was to go directly through the tower. The other was via a narrow, enclosed corridor that skirted the tower's exterior. The passageway's gate, typically locked, was held open this morning by a young male nom cloaked in a white silk shabba.

Ruler Two entered the corridor, keeping to one side to avoid puddled water. Sunlight streamed through narrow openings in its upper wall, illuminating his way. By the time he was half-way around the tower, the Leaveum became visible, its outer door held open by another nom, allowing him a clear view of foliage and figures. He took the last of his cleansing breaths.

It was pleasant inside the glass-paneled Leaveum. The air was somehow different here—fresher, lighter, cleaner, if that was possible. Lush plants crowded the room, vying for space and sunlight. Most were not native to the Lawless Lands, or to Aranox, for that matter. Ruler Two recognized only one: inkollar, a climbing vine common to the Southern Isles, easily identified by and named after its prolific black tendrils in the shape of a hangman's noose.

The entire place was a dazzling array of colors, shapes, and textures. Fascinating and beautiful, really. It was enough to make one think Ruler One knew what he was doing. Surely the magister did not maintain the Leaveum himself. Portly Ruler One stood next to Rulers Three and Four at a cluttered potting table; One with his hands folded, Three with her fingers flitting back and forth like a large insect's wings, practicing her math. Ruler Four appeared somewhat inconvenienced, and all three looked at Ruler Two as though they knew something he did not. *What is it? Has the magister spoken to you privately? And where is Ruler Five?*

As though in answer, the rear door to the Leaveum opened, presenting Ruler Five followed by the magister. What had they been doing on the other side of Takers Tower?

"General business," said the magister. "Ruler One?"

Ruler One nodded, his jowls jiggling as he spoke. "Progress on all fronts, m'lord. The new route to Tegan's border is fully mapped. Repairs to the cisterns are complete. The GOT's surplus storage silos have been filled. I remind everyone that next quarter we will undergo a purge. Please tidy those facilities in your care beforehand. This will save time and prevent the destruction of items you wish to keep. Takers Tower is exempt, of course, magister, unless you wish it included."

The magister swatted that notion away, as though it were a moth targeting his shabba. "Ruler Two?"

"We look forward to graduation ceremonies in two moons, m'lord. I anticipate the release of two dozen mastertakers. All are spoken for. Candidates for next almon will begin arriving shortly thereafter. Once your lordship has determined whether operations are to expand, contract, or remain the same, we shall estimate the number of candidates needed."

"You and I shall deliberate that together," said the magister through wheezing breaths.

Together? You and I? An honor! Ruler Two shot a quick glance to his cohorts.

"What else?" asked the magister.

"Grandmaster Sylak grows too old to teach," said Ruler Two. "His mind is sharp, but his hands no longer work—not well enough to demonstrate the art of taking, that is. He will need to be replaced."

"His understudy is ready?"

"Yes, m'lord. Grandmaster Everts."

The magister's fingernail tapped the side of a large clay pot. "Very well. Does Grandmaster Sylak wish to continue serving in some other capacity?"

"I have not broached the subject with him, m'lord."

"Mmm. Continued silence then, for now."

"As you wish, m'lord." *What might he be thinking?*

"Anything else?"

Ruler Two signaled there was not.

"Three?"

The old gray owl looked at home in the Leaveum. Ruler Two imagined her perched in one of the shrubs whose branches rose to the glass ceiling. "Collections, normal. No adjustments warranted, m'lord, though the inland sector is once again under review. Collections there have not varied since last we increased its target."

Ruler Two rolled his eyes. The overseer responsible for the territory in question was not very bright. At least once every almon, his collection target was raised. Why? Because he consistently produced a predictable payment that went above and beyond his target. If he would only vary it—a little above the target one moon, slightly less the next—the raises would not come so quickly. Even The Hidor's dullest student could make sense of that.

"Six moons ago," said the magister thoughtfully.

"Just so, m'lord," said the owl.

"Overseer Rascall? The same who fleeced the Duke of Isles and his entourage?" Was that a hint of laughter that escaped the old man's hood?

"The very same, m'lord," said Ruler Three.

"And he continues to submit a surplus of ten percent?"

"To the dire, m'lord," said the owl. "As he has the past four almons, regardless of the target."

Again, the finger-tapping. "What else?"

Ruler Three glanced at Two. "Expenses for the moratorium near ten thousand king-shead."

"A pittance for the promise of untold wealth," said the magister. "Anything else?"

Hah! Feather your nest with that!

Three bowed her head. "No, Magister."

"Ruler Four?"

"Nothing to report, m'lord."

"Five?"

Ruler Five shook his head.

"Very well. The moratorium moves forward. Withdrawals from the treasury for that purpose shall be noted, but are unrestricted. Ruler Two has shared his plans with me. King Axil shall die before the moon is full. Ruler Two has guaranteed it."

Ruler Two felt all others' eyes upon him. He looked to Five, seeking some sign—any sign—of support. Nothing! He could not even read the man's expression, heavily shadowed by his shabba's hood. Was that on purpose? It was all dark in there.

Ruler Two and Five walked side by side in silence until they emerged from the tower's external passageway. There, Ruler Two grasped the sleeve of Five's shabba and steered him toward the edge of The Hidor's breezeway.

"Is there something I should know?" he asked.

"I don't know," said Five. "Is there?"

"Something you want to tell me?"

"Nothing comes to mind."

"You're meeting with the magister in private now, are you?"

"Oh, and you are not?" asked Five.

"What are you talking about?"

Ruler Five glanced toward Takers Tower, then lowered his voice to mimic the magister. "'Ruler Two has shared his plans with me! The king shall die—he guarantees it!'"

Ruler Two met Five's accusatory stare, then slowly nodded. "My apologies. That was not my doing. He asked to be updated. I complied. There was naught said that would surprise you."

Five flashed his predatory smile. "You needn't be concerned either. We discussed nothing to do with you or your moratorium. The magister wanted to know more about a particular overseer. He wants him watched. That's all. I swear it."

THE SHOWING OF HANDS

"If only you could see into the hearts and minds of others, then might you wish to be blind." From the Scriptures of All Gods, attributed to the God of Virtue's nemesis, Asperine.

Marshal Erik Carson

Carson stood patiently, hands clasped behind his back, wondering just how many books the king had read. From floor to ceiling, the library's every wall was lined with them. So many different works. He had himself read many, mostly to do with philosophy or the strategies of war. But it occurred to him that even were he to read one each moon, he would die well before he made it through them all. And none would name the king's would-be assassins, solve the Fostead murders, unravel the mystery that was Mari Dunn, nor find the Prince of Quills or Rolft.

Someone knocked on the library's door. Carson glanced at Major Stronghart, seated in a nearby reading chair. The major did little more than raise his eyebrows.

"Enter!" Carson called.

"You sent for me, Marshal?" Fereliss' large frame squeezed into view. The royal guard shut the door and looked about the cavernous room with apparent reverie and awe.

The marshal waited for the guard's attention. As soon as he received it, he asked, "Do you read, Fereliss?"

Fereliss' eyes flitted back to the shelves, then to Major Stronghart. "No, m'lord. Never learnt."

"Pity." Carson gestured toward the books. "There is so much to learn from them. And we are disadvantaged by what we do not know. Do you not agree?"

"You know more than I, m'lord."

"Do I? How long have you served His Majesty?"

"Thirteen almons now, Marshal."

"Thirteen almons. Eleven in the Royal Guard. You took an oath?"

"Protect the royal family, m'lord—above all else, at any cost."

"Above all else?"

"That is the oath, m'lord."

"Then we find ourselves on even ground thus far."

Fereliss waited silently.

"That is the same oath—the very same, word for word—that Major Stronghart and I swore to our king." Carson paused. "Yet you would complicate our efforts."

"Marshal?" Fereliss swallowed.

"You've heard, no doubt, we seek a killer?"

Fereliss' eyelids lowered slightly.

"A killer in no mood to stop, it seems. The count rises every day. Your friend, Rolft. How many did he say he'd slain?"

Fereliss rolled his eyes, glancing once again at Major Stronghart. "Three by his hand, m'lord."

"For what reason? What is he up to?"

"I do not know, sir. He did not say—only that they drew first blood."

"It would appear you do know more than I. Six people killed in Fostead. Murdered. At least three of them killed by one of ours; a man retired from the king's army. Yet this gave you no cause to seek an audience with me? In fact, you harbored him! And now...three more dead since last you saw your friend! That's nine!"

"Three more?"

Carson felt the ire rise in him. "Sergeant Faraday among them!"

Fereliss shook his head. "I had not heard, m'lord. I'm certain Rolft—"

"Where does your loyalty lie, Fereliss? With your friend... or with your king?"

Fereliss took too long to answer.

"Above all else!" Carson shouted. Major Stronghart remained motionless. The marshal adjusted the placement of several books on a shelf. "Where is your old friend now?"

"I don't know, Marshal. I swear it. He's injured. Can't have gone too far."

"Mmm." Carson plucked a book at random from the shelves. "Then you shall help us find another."

"M'lord?"

"The Prince of Quills. The man who penned the invitations for The Lords and Ladies Feast. He's gone missing, too. I would speak with him. Take Garth and Yurik. Find the Prince of Quills and bring him to me."

"All three of us?"

"His last name is Penniluk. He's said to be traveling south. Perhaps to visit relatives in Stonybrook. Start there."

Fereliss grimaced. "It is a just punishment, m'lord."

"Punishment?" Carson glared at Fereliss. "Do you know the penalty for treason? I should have you drawn and quartered. This is far from punishment. In fact, just the opposite. Has your friendship blinded you completely? I save you from yourself!"

"M'lord?"

"Tell me that the bond of friendship does not pull at you. That you are not about to act on foolish thoughts."

Fereliss hung his head.

"That is a temptation I now remove from you. And from others you might influence. Gather Garth and Yurik. You leave this very evening."

"As you wish, Marshal." Fereliss backed out of the library. His bootsteps sounded down the hall.

Major Stronghart looked up at the marshal from his seat.

Carson sighed. "Have them followed, at least until they make first camp. If Fereliss knows Rolft's whereabouts, he may try to warn him."

Carson passed maids sobbing in the hallway, then elbowed his way into the same room where he had discovered Mari Dunn's daughter fighting off the steward. A small group of soldiers and castle staff were gathered to gawk in disbelief at a lifeless body.

It was a spectacle so surreal that it commanded silence. The ghastly scene conveyed to even the dullest mind that this had been no accident. Murder on the castle grounds was shock enough...but the killing of the king's steward? Sheer madness!

"Clear the room!" Carson cried. Several onlookers turned. "Sergeant Lagos! Clear the room!"

"You heard the man!" A large, bearded soldier gave those standing next to him a shove toward the door. "Look lively now!"

Carson waited just inside the doorway as the small crowd jostled past. He nodded in appreciation as Sergeant Lagos neared. "Send them on their way, Sergeant. I don't want them here. All except the maids who found him. I'll want a word with them."

"Yes sir, good as done." Sergeant Lagos disappeared into the hallway behind the last of the onlookers. The marshal listened to the barking of orders as he shut the door. He made his way toward the bed, noting it had not been slept in.

Pryll Fletcher lay on the floor, fully clothed, his blood-stained shirt unlaced. Carson kneeled beside him. The steward had been stabbed several times in the upper torso, but the jagged opening in his throat appeared to have sealed his fate. Carson glanced around the room. There were blood smears on the floor adjacent to the body, and on the wall closest to it. Nothing on the bed.

The marshal rose to his feet, staring at the steward. "You really were a smellhole, Pryll. What did you expect?" He took a deep breath and exhaled loudly, nudging the steward's body with his boot. "At least it wasn't poison, eh?"

"I spoke with him just yesterday," King Axil said, dumbfounded.

"As did I, m'lord."

"In a servant's quarters, you say? Who would be so bold?"

"It was unoccupied, m'lord. By Pryll's design, apparently—kept vacant for his evening entertainment."

"What?! How is it these things escape me?"

"The same room to which he took Madam Dunn's daughter."

King Axil closed his eyes. "I cannot make sense of it! The steward murdered! On palace grounds, no less! And no one heard a thing?"

"A servant's quarters are next door. He heard a row, but said he'd grown accustomed to it."

"Accustomed to it?"

"Yes, Your Majesty. 'The sounds of strenuous activity,' he called it. He knew the steward's ways and conditioned himself to ignore it."

"We chart our own course." King Axil sighed, his brow deeply furrowed. He met the marshal's gaze and held it. "Tell me you had no hand in it."

"I did not, m'lord."

"What I said the other day... aim lower? It was in jest. You know that."

"I did not take you seriously, m'lord."

"You did despise the man."

"Yes. But were I in the habit of killing those I despise, I would be a busy man indeed."

"Do you despise me?"

"M'lord?"

"I would not blame you. I saw the way he looked at your wife. All women, I suppose. I should have dismissed him almons ago. I don't know what prevented me. His father, I suppose. I respected him. He was like you in many ways, though I think now perhaps he should have spent less time serving me, and more time with his sons. Pryll has a brother, you know. Percival. A loathsome character, and a bad influence on Pryll when they were young." The king shook the memory away. "You'll find the man responsible, of course."

"If it was a man, m'lord."

"Gods above, you don't think..."

"It is entirely possible, m'lord. Given half a chance, my own wife—"

"Enough." King Axil held up a hand. "You make your point. What about Pryll's wife? Does she know?"

"She is aware, m'lord."

"How is she taking it? What did she say?"

"Not a word. She hardly seemed surprised. More relieved than grieved, if I am not mistaken."

"To live like that. Poor thing. I'll visit her myself. What of the attempt to have me killed? Any progress?"

"No, m'lord. I do wish we'd taken one of them alive. No one's going to claim three men who missed their mark, I'm afraid."

"You still think it was King Tygre."

"Until a better thought arrives." Carson waited for the king. He considered mentioning Rolft's actions, but decided now was not the time.

"Let me know when it does. In the meantime, what do you make of Madam Dunn?"

"I don't know what to make of her, m'lord. But there is something there to wonder at."

"Twice now." The king held up two fingers. "She foresaw the feast, of course, but then that business with the steward and her daughter. You witnessed that yourself."

"Twice now, yes. I witnessed both."

"I'm thinking of inviting her to live here."

Carson raised his eyebrows.

"Were she living in the castle," said the king, "might she not warn us in advance of pending doom? An enemy's attack? Another plague or fire? Perhaps foretell the next to die in Fostead?"

Carson ran his fingers through his hair. "I had not thought of that, m'lord." *Might the notion have some merit?*

"I pondered it all night," said the king. "If she can benefit the realm, why not? What have we to lose?"

Carson felt uneasy. The sooner Fereliss and the other guards left in pursuit of The Prince of Quills, the better. He entered the livery, immediately catching sight of Caleb's assistant, Reggie, a short distance down the center aisle, tending a black stallion with a curry brush.

He hailed the young groom. "A moment if you please, Reggie."

"What is it, Marshal?"

"Has Fereliss been to see you?"

"He has, Marshal. Garth and Yurik, as well."

"And?"

"I'm told they leave tonight, sir." The young groom motioned to the stallion. "Thunder here belongs to Garth. Master Bull and Victor are next. All three are to be ready before the sun goes down. That's right, is it?"

"Just so. They're not to leave the stables before then, not under any circumstance, do you understand?" *Just to be sure!*

"Yes, Marshal. Whatever you say."

Carson patted the stallion's backside as he praised Reggie. "We're in good hands with you, as always. I've been meaning to thank you, by the way, for the aid you rendered Rolft. Garth told me what you did."

"It was his horse I recognized, Marshal. It was nothing, really."

"Modest to a fault. Good lad. You are henceforth my eyes and ears around these stables, and wherever else you go. Whatever you see... whatever the horses tell you... anything unusual, anything at all, report to me at once. Can you do that?"

"Of course." Reggie hesitated, his eyes growing wide. "There is one thing. I'm not sure if this is what you mean."

"What is it, then?"

"Blood, Marshal," the boy said somewhat excitedly. "In the stables just this morning. Does that count?"

Sir Kraven was sitting on a block of wood, honing a collection of blades, but Carson's focus was on the squire who worked nearby, inspecting shields and lances. Sir Kraven noticed the marshal's approach and stopped his sharpening mid-stroke.

"I hope you've come to entertain us," the knight said. "We rot, sitting here idly."

"Bored?" asked Carson. "The king was nearly killed. Three assassins are dead as a result. Last night, our steward was murdered while we sleep." He shot a glance at Theos. "Nine killed now in Fostead, including Sergeant Faraday, and we may well be at war by fall. It seems to me you would be hard pressed to miss some action even were you hiding. I trust you make yourself ready."

"For whatever you require, Marshal. You need only command it."

"For now, a word in private with your squire will suffice."

Sir Kraven looked at Theos. "Is he in some sort of trouble?"

"A word is all I need. I've just finished with his brother. We won't be long. When we're done, you and I shall speak."

Sir Kraven turned away, waving an arm to signal his blessing or his lack of interest. Carson could not tell which. He turned his attention to the squire.

"Walk with me."

Theos carefully rested the shield he was inspecting against others in a large wooden box. Carson watched his every move, waiting to make eye contact. Theos approached with eyes downcast, so the marshal started walking. He led the squire behind a tent and out of view of any others.

"You know why I must speak with you?"

The young man shook his head from side to side, but his eyes betrayed him.

"Show me your hands."

Theos held them out, unable to control their shaking. Dark markings beneath his fingernails and in the crevices of his cuticles were evident.

"Soles of your boots."

Theos swung his left foot backward, catching the top of it and raising it to his buttocks.

"Now the other."

Carson could not believe his eyes. Even the sides of the young man's boots displayed numerous spatters of dried blood. *You must know the penalty for this! How could you have been so careless?* "Listen to me carefully, Theos. As if your life depends on it. If Sir Kraven questions you, tell him that I asked only whether you are prepared to die for your king."

Despite his apparent confusion, Theos nodded slightly.

"Are you?" asked Carson.

"Prepared to die?" whispered Theos.

"For your king."

"I am, m'lord." Theos swallowed.

"Let us hope it does not come to that. I'm off to see Sir Kraven. Give us some time to ourselves. Go give your hands a better wash...there's dirt beneath your fingernails. Clean your boots. And Theos... dispose of anything else of yours that is not clean, do you hear? You represent the king."

The sun had set. A driving rain danced off the marshal's head, muddying soft earth. He tried not to think of how tired he was, or of rest or sleep, and fought to focus on the task at hand. There was the sound of boots and horses' hooves.

"Evening, Marshal." Reggie appeared from the stables with a horse in tow. Four others stood already hitched to a long rail running parallel to the side of the barn.

"Evening, Reggie. Where's Caleb?"

"Inside. Do you need him? He was going to come out, but I told him to stay warm. The rain was unexpected." Reggie tethered the fifth mount to the rail.

"No. Let him stay dry."

"They don't like the thunder. But they're mostly settled now." The young groom cocked an ear toward the sound of footsteps. They grew louder and more steady as members of the royal guard, followed by Sir Godfrey's sons, trickled into view. Each carried one or two light sacks.

Carson greeted them, his gaze lingering on the Godfrey twins. Theos had helped the steward meet his end, no question. But Tristan? He could not be certain. Distancing both from the castle until the steward's death blew over was the right thing to do. Was it not? *Am I condoning murder? Dishonoring our king?*

There was little talk as the men found their mounts along the rail and fastened their sacks to saddles. A few coarse words rang out, followed by muted laughter. Reggie hurried down the rail, moving from horse to horse, gently stroking the muzzle or cheek of each as he bid them a safe journey.

Carson watched the animals' breathing, small clouds billowing from their nostrils. He noted that Fereliss, despite the awkward circumstance, took time to speak with the young groom.

"Marshal!" called a voice from behind.

Carson spun, wiping the rain from his eyes as Major Stronghart lumbered into view. "What is it?" he shouted.

"There's two more dead in Fostead! And Rolft's been spotted, Marshal!"

Carson swore before addressing the mounted search party, the rain beating down on him. "Gentlemen! Find the Prince of Quills! Put him in chains! Bring him here to me!"

Sibil Dunn

Sibil knocked on the door of The House of Children, certain Father Syrus would appreciate the return of his amulet, as well as the bouquet of flowers she had picked that morning.

As she prepared to knock again, the latch clicked, and the door swung open to reveal the same nun who had greeted her the last time. The old woman's eyes and smile nearly disappeared amidst the wrinkles on her face.

"Sister Mapel?"

"Why yes, child. Do I know you?" The slits of the nun's watery eyes twinkled, but not in recognition.

"My name is Sibil. I seek an audience with Father Syrus."

"Not today, I'm afraid. Father Syrus is away."

"When will he return?"

"Only the gods know, child." Sister Mapel nodded assuredly. "Only the gods know."

Sibil presented the flowers with an outstretched hand. "Would you see that he receives these?"

Sister Mapel gathered them somewhat awkwardly. "Of course, child."

"Thank you, sister." The two women stared at one other. "They could use some water."

"Of course. Will that be all, dear?"

Sibil hesitated, feeling for the metal amulet beneath her blouse. "Yes. Thank you, sister. You've been quite helpful. Please tell Father Syrus that I'll call again."

She scurried down the steps, her feet with a mind of their own. '*Only the gods know!*' It was probably true. No doubt all seven gods watched over Father Syrus. How could it be otherwise? All seven had once watched over her. When she had turned thirteen, and the God of Children released her, the local priest had proclaimed it so. But more importantly, she had felt it to be true. These days, she was not so sure. Neither the God of Good Fortune nor the God of Happiness had made their presence known in any lasting way for quite some time. Had they abandoned her?

Sibil bypassed the road leading to her parents' house—there was nothing there worth going back for. She turned left at the fork below the palace, choosing to head west rather than return to the castle.

By mid-morning, she had arrived outside The House of All Gods, a massive building commissioned by the king and constructed entirely of baelonite. It was the last of several buildings her father had designed as palace architect.

She stood for a moment outside its gates, marveling at his handiwork: rounded cornerstones and spiral, fluted pillars; a broad, crown-shaped band encircling the building just below its roofline; sculpted drapes drawn and tied to frame the entryway, their folds forever frozen in elegant repose. And above its front doors, a chiseled greeting to every visitor:

The House of All Gods: For All People For All Reasons For All Time.

Several men labored in the well-kept gardens out front. Sibil recognized one by the hat he had worn the day Princess Lewen was laid to rest—a wide-brimmed shield of straw with colored ribbons dangling from its back. She kept her eyes on it until she entered the building. Finding herself alone there, she quickly exited through a rear passage, taking a path leading through more gardens and open grounds. The path eventually turned to earthen stairs cut into a steep hill leading to a broad plateau.

Large statues of the seven gods, all carved from baelonite, encircled the plateau's perimeter, protecting the royal graveyard. It was the God of Happiness who seemed most intent on watching her weave through a maze of mounded earth and headstones to a familiar spot before dropping to her knees.

"Ayla, Lewen." She curled her legs beneath her, and absent-mindedly plucked at blades of grass. "So much has happened this moon. I wish I knew what you could see." Sibil turned her face skyward. "Your father was nearly killed, and my mother is said to have saved him. Can you imagine? I really don't know what to make of her these days. We're staying at the palace now...for how long, I do not know. But oh, how I wish that you were here, in the flesh, with me.

"There's talk of war. The twins are at the castle with their knights, helping to prepare. They've both grown older, even taller, I think, though I doubt you'd see much change in them. My heart still aches for Tristan, though I've not told him yet. You're the only one who knows. I cannot bear the thought that he might not return my feelings. Does he love me? One look at him, Lewen, and you would know, I'm sure of it. What should I do? He's to be knighted soon, and then when will I see him? Tell me, please. I cannot bear to live like this much longer!"

Sibil picked up the pace, her heartbeat quickening in anticipation of her rendezvous with the Godfrey boys. She imagined them waiting for her, and she resolved to maintain a cheery disposition in their company. It wasn't their fault they had no time to train her. And if Tristan's arms encircled her this night, she would return the embrace until he asked to be let go! She had sought the twins earlier in the day, but had not even seen them among the squires training behind the barracks.

She wondered as she neared the stables how best to alert them to her presence, and was relieved to discover Reggie preparing two lanterns outside the doors. She hailed the young groom just as one of the lanterns fluttered to life.

"Sibil!" he said. "Tristan told me you might come."

"Am I too late? Too early?"

"No, this would be the time, all right." Reggie moved to light the second lantern. "But they're not here, I'm afraid."

"What?" Sibil's brow furrowed. "Where are they, then?"

"Sleeping with the royal guard! They leave before first light!"

"Leave! Where to?"

"Didn't they tell you? They hunt a man for the marshal!"

Sibil's stomach turned. "Are we at war, then?"

"Not yet, but Caleb says it's brewing."

Sibil stared into the night, praying that the gods of good fortune, health and strength would watch over both the boys. "When will they return?"

Reggie shrugged. "A half moon, perhaps? Five men to capture one—I shouldn't think you need to worry."

"Thank you, Reggie." Sibil trudged away, disconsolate. She had imagined Tristan would be as eager to see her as she was him, but now? She was, no doubt, the furthest thing from his mind.

Rolft Aerns

Rolft woke with a start, instinctively grabbing at the metal that pricked his throat. He flailed at it while scrabbling away, until his back was pressed against the stable bay and he could retreat no further. He stared down the handle of a pitchfork into the wide eyes of Bohun Barr.

"The truth!" said the stablemaster. "What have you done?"

Rolft sat motionless. How long had he been sleeping? What day was this? "What do you mean?"

"Jarod was a good friend!" The muscles in Bohun's arms rippled as he gripped the pitchfork tighter.

"To me as well. What's happened?"

"He's dead, that's what! Murdered in his cellar! And you want me to believe you didn't know?"

"Jarod's dead?" Rolft could not believe it. Had he not just spoken with Jarod? Was that yesterday?

"Damn right! Timmil Childs, too! And one of the king's men! Some sergeant!"

"When was this?"

"Yesterday! At The King's Inn. You were there! The sergeant was killed in one of Jarod's rooms!"

Rolft tried to piece things together. The room Jarod had showed him? Where two suspicious men were staying? He tried recalling his last words with Jarod.

"You've got one last chance before I start callin' for soldiers," Bohun said. "Where'd all that blood come from?"

Rolft glanced down at his side. "You sure you want to know?"

Bohun tightened his grip on the pitchfork.

"Kole Cantry," said Rolft, "and those in the warehouse. Dead by my hand. One of 'em cut me pretty good. But that was days ago. Look, it's been stitched." He lifted his shirt.

"Uh-huh." Bohun's eyes narrowed. "I knew you was hurt when you come in that day."

"And I've a good idea who killed Jarod."

"I'm listenin'."

"There were two men stayin' at the inn. Two Jarod didn't trust. One with a scar on his forehead. The other smaller, like a stray cat, Jarod said. Raggett Grymes works for 'em. Sound familiar?"

"No, but I know Raggett Grymes. Snake in the grass, he is."

"Jarod showed me the room where they were stayin'. I need to go back and see for myself."

"We've got to tell the marshal." Bohun relaxed his grip on the pitchfork, lowering it slightly.

"No." Roflt shook his head, placing a hand on his injured side. "He'll only try to stop me."

"Stop you?"

Rolft gently pushed the pitchfork aside. "I'm going to kill them, too."

Stablemaster Bohun Barr

Bohun weaved his way through the narrow streets of the south end, fairly certain he had left his good sense back at the livery with Rolft. This was a place to avoid whenever possible. Little good came from the south end. Still, he moved surely, resolutely, driven by a strong desire to help avenge his good friend, Jarod. He trusted Rolft, and the name Raggett Grymes was not new to him. If there was a war between those two, his allegiance was not in question. Surely there was no law against simply locating the scoundrel and pointing Rolft in his direction. Bohun tried to set all doubt aside. If misgivings plagued him on the morrow, he would pay the marshal a visit.

Earlier, he rather than Rolft had gone to The King's Inn, because he was known there and could engage the staff without raising suspicion. The barmaid, Karla, had taken him to the room where the king's sergeant had been killed. Karla had confirmed that two men matching Rolft's descriptions had stayed there. The motive for the killing was unclear, but everyone suspected that the same two men were responsible for Jarod's and Timmil Child's deaths as well. The marshal and his soldiers were searching for them.

It was early afternoon when he entered The Raven's Nest. There were few customers this time of day. The barkeep looked up out of boredom at the sound of the opening door. Bohun recognized him as a man who frequented the livery with his horses and his questions.

"Bohun? Do my eyes deceive me?"

"Peter! It's good to see you." Bohun approached the bar and the two men shook hands energetically.

"Kin I get ya sumthin' ta drink?" asked Peter. "My coin, of course!"

"A little ale, then, if you please. But just a touch—it's early."

Peter poured two drinks. "What brings you ta the south end? I never thought ta see you here."

Bohun drew a finger across a wet spot on the bar. "I'm lookin' for someone."

"Who's that?" Peter sipped his ale.

Bohun glanced around the small establishment. "Raggett Grymes. You know 'im?"

"Course I know 'im. Not the kind the likes of you pass time with. You in some sort of trouble?"

"I'm not."

"Is he?"

Bohun considered this. "Would you miss his business?"

"Would I..." Peter's wrinkled brow smoothed. "Most of those what comes in here wouldn't be missed by their own mother. I never liked the man."

Bohun tilted his glass to his lips. "You wouldn't know his whereabouts, would ya?"

Peter eyed him silently.

"What is it?" asked Bohun.

"You certain you're not in any mess?"

"What makes you ask?"

"Ain't none of my business," said the barkeep, "but me an' the horses owe ya. You don't talk like a man in trouble. I've got an ear for that. But unless I miss my mark, there's trouble lookin' for you."

"How's that?"

"Two men come in last night. I'm s'posed t' let 'em know if anyone comes askin' after Grymes. In particular, a big man like you."

"What'd they look like, these fellas?"

"The one did all the talkin' was a tall fella. Long black hair. Smooth talker. The other was lots shorter, never said a word."

"The tall man...scar on his forehead?"

Peter shrugged. "It's dark in here come night, and we didn't get cozy."

"How are ya s'posed t' let 'em know? Where are they stayin'?"

"They're smarter than that. I'm s'posed t' let Grymes know. He's just across the street at The Good Knight's Rest."

"What! I was just there. Innkeeper said he never heard of him."

"Gabriel? Course he did! Cut from the same cloth, that one. Trust me, Grymes is there. Him and Shum Ingram been in and outta here like lovebirds these past couple o' days. You see that table in the back? Take a seat...come nightfall, they'll be sittin' on your lap."

Bohun drained his drink, then wiped his mouth with the back of his hand. "Would ya point 'em out to someone who wanted to pay his respects?"

"I might, if he was a friend of yours."

"How would he find you?"

"How would he not? It's only me works here. Every day 'til I lock up. How will I know him?"

Bohun thought for a moment. "He'll give my name."

"Good enough."

"That's it, then." Bohun offered his hand.

Peter grasped it firmly. "You watch yourself. Gabriel or someone else is bound to tell Grymes you've been askin' after 'im. Like as not he already knows. And you know 'bout all the killin's, eh?"

"I do. I'm obliged. Bring the horses 'round when you get a chance. I'll see to them myself."

Bohun entered the livery excited and out of breath. He caught his young assistant by the shirtsleeve and spun him round. "Listen carefully, Bertram. I'm gonna close the stable doors. No one's t' set foot in here but you and me, and that fella Rolft, sleepin' in the back. You need t' take the horses in and out, that's fine, but you open and close the doors each time, you hear? I know it's a bother, but that's the way it's gonna be, so long as he's stayin' here. No customers inside. All right?"

"Whatever you say. Shall I close them now?"

"Please, Bertram, on your way out. That's a good lad. I'll join you soon enough."

Overseer Reynard Rascall

"What is this place again?" Reynard moved about the room to keep his blood circulating. He rubbed his palms together while searching for the origin of a draft tickling his neck.

"The Bull's Horns," said Spiro, motionless on his bed of straw.

"An apt name for what I slept on. There were vermin scuttling across the floor last night." Reynard arched his shoulders and back. "What would I give for a feather mattress! Bull's Horns, indeed! Named after the wrong end of the beast, I'm afraid." The King's Inn was far more to his liking, but they could not go back there. Not after Spiro's performance with the sergeant who had questioned them about Raggett Grymes. Or his riddance of the innkeeper in the wine cellar.

Reynard brushed his bangs back. "A sleepless night has me thinking. The fact that taker Grymes has somehow drawn the attention of the law does not bode well for us. If the king's men catch up to him, I should think it's only a matter of time before he points a finger our way."

"It's time for him to meet the mason, is it?" asked Spiro hopefully.

"Not just yet. We still need him to lure our giant out of hiding. But that reminds me…why did our mysterious giant kill just three at the warehouse? If he means to put Kasparr out of business, why not kill them all? Why spare that Brock character and the old man?"

"Mebbe they're friends with the giant. Mebbe they're part of it."

"Maybe. Or perhaps they had nothing to do with it at all. Maybe it's something personal between the giant and those he's killing."

Spiro cocked his head. "You know what I'd do?"

"Of course I do. Really, Spiro, it's not as though your strategy ever changes."

"Doesn't it, though?"

"No, it doesn't. But I dare say this time you're right."

"Am I?" The corners of Spiro's mouth turned slightly upward.

"Yes. Yes, you are. Kill them all, just t' be sure. I swear, Spiro—" Reynard silenced himself at the sound of a knock on the door. He motioned for Spiro to rise as he moved across the room. "There is but one who knows we stay here."

Spiro was quickly to his feet.

Reynard opened the door and ushered Raggett Grymes in. "Quickly, friend. You've news?"

"He's been seen!" Raggett struggled to catch his breath.

"Our giant?"

"Yes!"

"Where?"

"At The Good Knight's Rest...where I'm tucked in!"

"I knew it! What did I tell you, Spiro? How long ago was this?"

"Not long. The time it took to get here!"

"What does he look like? How will we know him? C'mon, man, time's wastin'!"

Raggett held up a hand. "There's no rush, we know 'im!"

"How's that?" Reynard placed a hand on Spiro's shoulder, stopping his companion's progress toward the door.

"I said we know 'im! Gabriel recognized 'im when he come askin' after me."

"Who's Gabriel?"

"The innkeeper where I'm stayin'. And he'll be wantin' the money you promised him, too."

"Ah, yes. He'll have it. Twice over if he can put a name to the man."

"It's Bohun Barr, the stablemaster."

"Stablemaster! What did your lot do? Steal from him? Sod his wife?"

"I've no idea. Don't really know the man. Makes no sense, him lookin' for me."

"He tires of working with horses, does he? Dreams of greater riches? I don't suppose it matters what his reasons are."

"What now?" asked Raggett excitedly.

"Don't stray from The Good Knight's Rest. We'll find you when we need you."

Spiro

Spiro sat across the street from the livery, dividing his attention between the activities outside that business, and the soldier stationed a few shops further down the street. Boots and hooves stirred up a constant cloud of dust in front of the stables. Horses there outnumbered men, but Spiro paid the animals little attention. Men came and went, staying just long enough to deliver or retrieve their horses. Few had been there the entirety of Spiro's watch. Fewer still had gone in and out of the barn with any regularity. And only one of those had been a big man.

With a furtive glance toward the soldier, Spiro made his way across the street, keeping one eye on a rider who had just mounted his horse outside the stables. Spiro measured his gait so that he nearly ran into the horseman on the other side of the street.

"Beg your pardon, friend, but can you tell me where I might find Bohun Barr?"

"The stablemaster?" The horseman looked down at Spiro, twisting in his saddle to answer. "Big man leadin' the black stud. There!" He gestured toward a large man across the livery grounds.

Spiro waved casually in appreciation, already focused on the man identified as Bohun Barr. It was the same man he had assumed to be the stablemaster, so he stared just long enough to be confident of future recognition. Then he went back across the street to bide his time.

Spiro's eyes widened as the large stable doors swung open. His pulse quickened when the stablemaster stepped outside. The livery grounds were nearly deserted. The sea of people once packing the street had been reduced to a slow-moving stream. The sun had disappeared behind the western mountains, and with it the soldier who had been standing post just down the street. It would be some time before dusk gave way to dark, but already it was quiet.

Spiro sat with his elbows on his knees, his head cradled in his hands, eyes peering out from behind splayed fingers. He watched the stablemaster and his young companion cross the livery grounds, then stop at the street's edge. They spoke briefly, then went their separate ways—the young man into town, the stablemaster in the opposite direction.

Spiro stood, stretched, then stepped into the street. His right hand moved instinctively to confirm the presence of his knives.

Stablemaster Bohun Barr

It was dusk when Bohun went to wish Rolft well.

"You're sure you don't want company?" he asked.

Rolft shook his head. "I am already in your debt. Go home to your family."

"Family!" Bohun laughed, looking up and down the stable. "This is my family!"

Rolft smiled. "So the horses tell me."

"Well then." Bohun scratched his head and looked around the barn. "You know where the key is. If perchance you cross paths with those that killed Jarod... kindly give them my regards."

"That I will."

Bohun trudged down the stable corridor, stopped half-way to the doors, and looked back. "You're quite sure?" he asked.

"Off with ya!"

"Hmmpf." Bohun resumed his march. "Mind yourself, then, for Sarah's sake. I'll see you on the morrow."

Bohun had walked the same route home every night for fifteen almons. He had done it in the pitch dark and in the driving rain—in poor health and, on occasion, while drunk. So he paid little attention to his surroundings, letting his feet find their own way out of town. His mind was preoccupied with what he had learned at The Raven's Nest. He would have liked to help Rolft face his enemies, but he knew it was not in him to take part in any killing. He wondered just what it was that allowed Rolft that luxury.

He covered the distance so quickly that he nearly passed his house, a small one-bedroom bungalow he had built with his own hands. It was set back off the road, tucked into the woods atop a slight incline so that he would not lose sleep during the rainy season. He was half-way up the long pathway to his door when a voice from behind startled him.

"Mr. Barr?!" Though obscured by trees and fast-fading light, the figure striding up the roadside caught Bohun's attention. *Was I followed?* It occurred to him that he would have seen or heard something earlier had he not been lost in thought. The man came into full view, stopping at the bottom of Bohun's pathway. Bohun could not discern his facial features, but he was certain he did not know him.

"Mr. Barr?" the man called again.

Bohun hesitated. "Who's that? Do I know you?"

"No, no. I'm new to Fostead, but I'm in need of your assistance."

"How's that?" *Sumthin's not right here!*

The stranger started up the pathway. "My horse, it's—"

"That's far enough." Bohun tried to inject an air of authority into his voice. Torn between courtesy and caution, he looked around to ensure the man was alone.

The stranger stopped some twenty paces away, raising his hands in deference to Bohun. "I'm told you're the man t' see."

Bohun assessed the man's physical capabilities. He was short, perhaps two heads shorter than Bohun, and skinny. The stablemaster judged he could throw the man a few body lengths if need be, and he was fortunate to hold the higher ground. "Why's that?"

"Thet's what all the townfolk say...horse's got a problem, you go see Bohun Barr."

"Hmmpf. What kind of problem?"

"Sickness, I'll wager." The man took two more steps up the path, stopping when Bohun retreated one step himself. "She's not herself. Won't eat."

Bohun shifted his weight uneasily. "Bring her 'round the livery. First thing tomorrow. I'll have a look."

It was getting dark now, trees and ground starting to blend together.

"Evenin' then. I'm much obliged." There was the shimmer of a brief smile.

Bohun exhaled in relief as the man turned to leave. He resolved to keep him in his sights until he disappeared. But the man stopped moving. Bohun squinted to better see. The shadowy figure turned back toward him, exposed teeth reflecting the moonlight.

"The name's Spiro, and we've a touch more business."

"What?"

Bohun stared in disbelief as the man suddenly bounded up the pathway toward him. He froze, aware that if he tried to run, the man would be on him well before he reached his house. Terror welled in him. The man had already closed half the distance between them. Bohun glanced quickly at the ground. There was nothing there he could use to defend himself. Looking back at the onrushing figure, he braced himself for contact. If he could catch hold of the bastard, he would fling him as hard as he could into nearby tree trunks.

Bohun yelled in defiance, reaching out to greet his attacker. He grabbed fistfuls of the night air as the little man dropped to his knees, sliding a short distance into Bohun's legs and driving his knife straight up into the stablemaster's crotch. Bohun screamed, found the man's head with his hands, and sought to tear it off.

The shorter man rose rather than resist. He plunged his knife into Bohun's stomach. Bohun gasped, releasing his grip on the man's head as the knife entered him again. He clutched his stomach in an attempt to stem the bleeding. His attacker stepped back, watched, and waited.

One of Bohun's knees buckled as he attempted to turn toward his house. He stumbled, crashing to the ground awkwardly. His loud groan ended in a gurgle, a strange mixture of pain and resignation. "Son of... a whore."

"I'm the mason, if it's all the same to you. Or you can call me Spiro." The little man stepped next to Bohun, then lowered himself nonchalantly onto his haunches. "You don't look so good. Painful, is it?" He patted one of Bohun's legs. "Take heart, at some point the suffering is spent. Not yet, I'd say. Can you feel this?" He drove his knife into Bohun's thigh.

"Ahhh!" Bohun writhed on the ground. His ragged breathing stirred the leaves beneath his nostrils.

"Good for you." Spiro chuckled. "And this?" He jabbed the blade back into the same leg.

Bohun jerked, his anguished cry turning to sobs.

"I could end your misery." The little man held his knife up to the moonlight for a casual inspection. "You'd welcome that, I s'pose." He rose to his feet, wiped the blade on his pants leg, and tucked it into his waistband. "Bide your time. What's left of it."

Rolft Aerns

Rolft reflected on all that he had learned from Bohun Barr. Both Raggett Grymes and Shum Ingram were staying at The Good Knight's Rest! He pictured the place—the streets and alleys he knew would take him there. And just across the way, The Raven's Nest, where the pair would likely spend their evening.

He had but a vague description of Raggett Grymes—one that just as well belonged to any number of men: average height and build, thin brown hair, sparse beard, no distinguishing features. Shum Ingram, on the other hand, would be relatively easy to spot. Bohun had likened him to a snail, bald and without teeth. It was more than enough to go on, given the stablemaster's assertion that the keeper of The Raven's Nest would be working all night, and that he would be willing to identify both men.

The most surprising news from Bohun had been that Rolft, too, was being hunted. By associates of Raggett Grymes, no less! He tried to make sense of that, concluding it was the price he paid for having set two free from the warehouse. Or perhaps his stalkers were the men staying at The King's Inn...Grymes' bosses. The man with the scar and his friend. Those responsible for Jarod's death. He removed a large knife from his waistband, turning the blade to inspect both sides.

Night was both a blessing and a curse. Fewer people on the streets made traveling easier, but there was no multitude in which to hide. And while the dark shielded him from others, it hid them from him as well. If the soldier had waited any longer to step out of the pitch black into the shadowy street, Rolft would not have seen him in time to adjust his own path.

It was not the first of the king's army he had spotted. The other soldier had also been alone, and neither moved with the carefree swagger of a man relieved of duty. It caused Rolft to hug the entrance to an alleyway before deciding to alter his route to The Raven's Nest. He ducked down the alley, knowing a more circuitous, less traveled course would take him but slightly longer.

He made good time, passing freely from one narrow passageway to another, paying close attention to the few men he encountered. They, too, had chosen the dark, secluded alleys for a reason. They reminded him of Kole Cantry and the girl with the amulet, but tonight, those he met shrank from him in search of solitude.

A cool breeze whipped down the alley, carrying warm night air and the faint sound of revelers. Thunder rumbled softly in the distance. Rolft glanced up at the sky. The moon was full, obscured now and then by fast-moving veils of cloud. A few scattered drops of rain hit his face.

Sudden peals of laughter drew his attention to dark figures moving past the alley's juncture with a larger passageway. He made his way there, and stopped to catch his breath. The memory of Princess Lewen being dragged across rocky ground by her horse assailed him. He placed a palm against his injured side, vowing to ignore it until the evening's task was done. The Raven's Nest was but a few doors to his left.

Outside The Raven's Nest, it had been dark and loud, but inside it was louder. Darker. Crowded. Rolf jostled his way past unfamiliar faces to force an opening at the bar. The men on either side of him moved their drinks to make room. The barkeep was a short, burly man whose voice rose above those of his needy customers. Hands full, he shouted, cursed, and laughed as he dispensed both drink and entertainment. It did not take him long to notice Rolft was without glass or bottle.

"What will you have?"

Rolft leaned into the bar. "You're Peter?"

The entertainer turned serious. "Who's askin'?".

"Bohun Barr."

The barkeep stepped back, studying Rolft as he rubbed his hands together. "Wait there!" He grabbed a jug from the floor and walked the length of the bar before disappearing into the dark. A few moments later, he reappeared near Rolft's side, still carrying the jug. He was a full head shorter than Rolft, stocky, and bow-legged. He cupped his free hand around his mouth. "Follow me!"

Rolft fell in behind, scanning the room ahead and to his sides as the barkeep pushed his way through the room. When he stopped, so did Rolft.

Peter motioned with his chin, as though he had something to say. Rolft lowered his head to listen.

"Not here," the barkeep said. "You understand?"

Rolft did not respond. He was focused on a pair of men at the back of the room, their heads thrown back in laughter. One of them was bald, his lips glued to his mug so that Rolft could not tell if his teeth were missing. The other had thin brown hair and a sparse, ratty beard.

It was only when they erupted in appreciation of the jug the barkeep presented them that Rolft realized Peter had continued to their table. The bald man stood to slap the barkeep on the back. Peter threw a meaningful glance Rolft's way as he retreated. He brushed past Rolft without acknowledging him, gruffly repeating two words just loud enough to hear: "Not here!"

What would be the king's reply to that?

Rolft stared a moment longer at the two men before moving to stand impassively in front of them.

When they realized he was not simply passing by, they set their drinks on the table and acknowledged him. "Help you, friend?" The straggly haired man wiped his sleeve across his mouth, erasing both drink and grin.

Rolft's fingers closed around the hilt of the dagger beneath his coat. "Raggett Grymes? Shum Ingram?"

"'At's me!" the bald man said.

His companion's eyes grew wide with sudden realization. He stood, nearly falling backward as his chair scraped against the floor. He righted himself, his back pressed against the pub's wall, a small dagger he had withdrawn from his waistband clutched at his side.

Shum Ingram placed both hands on the table and began to rise. Rolft's dagger came down fast and hard, driving easily through the back of the man's right hand before embedding a full inch in wood. Ingram screamed. Rolft let go of the knife as the bald man dropped back onto his chair and tried unsuccessfully to remove it with his free hand.

The room grew markedly quieter. Several patrons near Raggett and Shum's table backed away.

"I bear a message from King Axil!" Rolft shouted at the stunned and silent. He pointed at the impaled bloody hand. "That was for his daughter, Princess Lewen! This," he cried, brandishing a much larger blade, "this is for his wife, Queen Isadora, who watched her daughter die!"

Shum screamed in terror, his cry cut short by the blade ripping through his windpipe. He collapsed forward, his forehead hitting the table with a thud.

Rolft held his bloodied knife high and turned his attention to Raggett Grymes. "And this—"

"She was alive!" said Raggett, thrusting his dagger nervously in front of him to ward Rolft off. Rolft swatted Raggett's hand. The knife flew from the man's grasp, clattering on the floor. "I'll pay you!" Raggett reached out, both hands shaking.

"This is for the king, and the suffering of a kingdom!" Rolft drove the blade swiftly past Raggett's outstretched arms and into the man's chest. Raggett gasped, his eyes wide with fear, his hands clasped around Rolft's forearm. Rolft jerked the blade free. Raggett wheezed and slumped to the floor, his back supported by the wall. His head lolled forward until his chin rested on his chest.

And there was silence.

Rolft turned to stare at the men standing closest to him. Most averted their gaze and shifted their position uneasily. It was not until Rolft noticed a seated old man staring blankly at him that he said quietly, "Long live King Axil."

"Long live King Axil," the old man said.

Overseer Reynard Rascall

What's Spiro doing, taking so long? What if he's no match for the stablemaster? Nonsense! Spiro has never failed to catch or kill his quarry. Ah, but the stablemaster has proven to be more elusive and dangerous than most! Does the giant know we stay here? Might he be on his way right now? What if—

Reynard bridled his imagination as Spiro slipped into the room, unannounced and in one piece. "Well?"

Spiro closed the door. "Well what?

"The stablemaster, you idiot! Our giant! He's dead?"

"I think not."

"You think not! Did you track him down?"

"I did."

"But he's not dead?"

"I mean, he may or he may not be. I really wouldn't know."

"Confound it, Spiro, you went to kill a man! Either he is dead, or he is not. Which is it?"

Spiro smiled wryly. "Impossible to say. Better you should ask if he will die."

"I see. You are the master of the spoken word now, are you? Will... he... die?"

"He will. Without a doubt."

"Ahh, I am so greatly relieved. Why must you—"

"Unless, of course..."

"Yes?"

"Unless he's dead already."

Reynard rolled his eyes. "We should celebrate! A hearty meal. What say you? And please, I beg of you. Do not say mutton stew. I know how you enjoy it, but really, it is not worthy of a celebration. And we do still have a problem. Your friends will be none too happy with you."

Spiro wrinkled his brow.

"Able and Elijah." Reynard began to chuckle. "They should arrive by carriage this evening. Can you picture that? They're much bigger than you or me. Imagine how they're feeling now, stuck in those cramped quarters for so long. Their big bones bouncing up and down all day...." Spiro began to smile as Reynard continued. "I'm only just recovering from that ride myself, you see? After days of walking about and lying flat, no less. Imagine their surprise when they step off that fiendish contraption only to be told that you've finished all the dirty work. That it's time to turn around and get back on!" Reynard began to laugh. Spiro chuckled. "That they've traveled all this way for naught!" Reynard burst into hearty laughter. Spiro beamed.

Reynard waved a hand, trying to compose himself. "So, I've been thinking, you see. That simply won't do. I mean, it would be you delivering that message, of course. They love you so, those two...don't think I haven't noticed. But even so, Spiro, I fear that if you did not choose your words just right, well, they'd be apt to tear you in two and stuff you in their mouths." Reynard began to laugh again, barely able to finish his thought. "A snack, if you will, to sustain them on their ride." Spiro was no longer chuckling. His smile began to fade. "No, no, bear with me." Reynard gulped for air. "This is where your strategy, 'kill them all', comes in."

Spiro's hands went to his hips.

"Really," said Reynard. "Raggett Grymes' fate is sealed now, I'm afraid. The man is clearly not all there. He's already drawn the king's attention. Do you know what he told me before he left? He plans to rob the palace! Can you believe that? Not that it couldn't be done, mind you, by a mastertaker or someone such as ourselves. But by him? No, he's a serious liability. He'll bring the entire army down on us. We must do ourselves and The Guild a favor and dispose of him. Quickly, I might add. We'll let Able and Elijah have him, shall we?" He smiled broadly again, trying hard not to laugh. "So they don't eat you, you see?" Reynard put a hand to his mouth demonstratively. "We'll drop in on Mr. Grymes before we feast this evening and invite him to meet your large friends tomorrow. Then we'll be off. Back to good ol' Waterford!"

"You're finished, are you?" Spiro asked.

"I am." Reynard drew a deep breath to steady himself. "What do you think?"

"I'm ready."

"You're ready." Reynard dabbed his eyes with his sleeve. "For what are you ready, my friend, eh?"

"Mutton stew, you daft arse!"

A steady rain fell. Reynard stood outside The Good Knight's Rest, watching with growing unease a small crowd across the street. Three soldiers in front of The Raven's Nest kept the restless throng at bay. Spiro had disappeared into that sea of gray in search of information. Reynard shivered and blew warm air into his cupped hands.

Spiro emerged from the gathering and crossed the street. Rain matted the small man's hair and flowed freely down his face.

"Well?" asked Reynard. "Did you see Mr. Grymes?"

"No, but he's in there all right."

"How do you know? What's happening? Don't tell me the soldiers are here for him."

Spiro's expression made it clear they were. "Gods damn it!" Reynard seethed. "I told you this might happen! I should have let you kill him that first night. Now he's going to pull us into the fire as he burns."

"No, he's not."

"Oh, he's not? I'll wager he will." Reynard brushed his hair back angrily. "Trust me, the man lacks any mettle. He'll finger us in a heartbeat."

"He won't. He's dead."

It took a moment for Reynard to respond. "Dead?"

"Killed, they say. Him and another of his men."

"Raggett Grymes, dead," thought Reynard aloud.

"Along with another. Someone took a knife to them."

Reynard sighed. Spiro waited. The rain grew heavy. It was a long while before Reynard wiped his cheeks and sighed again.

"What now?" asked Spiro.

Thunder rumbled.

"I'm of two minds," said Reynard. "This too could be cause to celebrate. No doubt Raggett's given others cause to do him harm. Perhaps we were not the first in line. If so, someone has done us a favor. Able and Elijah are robbed of their opportunity, of course, but that's a small price to be rid of the man—with no possible way for anyone to tie his death to us."

"I s'pose."

"Possible, but far too convenient, I'm afraid. More likely, we've been on the right path all along. Whoever killed poor Leo in his office—and since then, what, four others of Raggett's crew? He's simply making progress. Is this not why we've kept Raggett close? To lure the giant and his friends to us?"

"Ah! I did learn sumthin' else from that gaggle over there."

"Pray tell."

"Whoever killed Grymes and the other was a big man."

Reynard spread his hands. "You did kill him, did you not?"

"Who's that?" Spiro wiped his face.

"The stablemaster, you dolt!" Reynard jerked a thumb back over his shoulder. "The man asking after Raggett Grymes in this very inn today!"

"He's dead. I'm sure of it. The stablemaster had no hand in this. I'll stake my life on it."

"Then we must assume he had a partner. Another giant, no less! A sobering thought, as it means extending our time here in this chamber pot."

"Chamber pot, is it?" Spiro walked away. "Perhaps," he called over his shoulder, "you might join me on a visit to the castle! A delightful trip, I hear. Quite spectacular, and so close!"

Reynard shot a look across the street, where the crowd had begun to disperse. "There's no mutton stew where we're headed!" he called after Spiro. "I guarantee you that!"

Reynard kept a hand on Spiro's shoulder to discourage him from leaving the protection of the alleyway. Main street appeared empty, but they could ill afford to take chances. A light rain continued to fall, and it was growing ever colder. *Even The Bull's Horns offered more comfort than this!*

He watched the body of the carriage lift visibly as two large forms dismounted. Each carried a small satchel, just big enough to hold the tools of his trade. The two travelers looked up into the rain, down the darkened street, then at each other as the carriage rolled away. One shrugged, the other followed suit.

Reynard could not be certain that it was Able and Elijah, but a confident nod from Spiro assured him it was them. He watched the two behemoths stretch, then walk to the far side of the street. They sat down next to their satchels.

Reynard hesitated. Who else might be watching from some other shadowed spot? Twice he held his breath for as long as he could before removing his hand from Spiro's shoulder.

Mari Dunn

There were no visible stars. A soft mist fell from the dark sky. Orange and yellow flames danced behind sconce torches on the inner bailey wall.

Mari neared the castle gate, stopping at the base of the steps leading to the battlements. A sentry at the gate took note of her and approached, stopping abruptly upon recognition. "Oh, it's you, madam. Beg pardon."

Mari lifted her dress just enough to allow its hem to clear her shoes, then started up the glistening steps.

"Them's the battlements, madam," said the sentry. "There's naught to see up there."

Mari continued her climb. She had no idea where she was going, no sense of what compelled her to place one foot in front of the other. Something other than her own will guided her, but she felt no desire to fight it.

She reached the top of the stairs. The wind blew freely above the castle walls, whipping free strands of hair about her face.

A soldier on the battlements approached her. "Can I help you, madam? Is everything all right?"

Mari did not respond.

"Do you need help getting down?"

"No, thank you." Mari laid a comforting hand on the soldier's shoulder as she passed. She moved slowly down the battlement, dragging her fingers along the parapet's crest.

THE PARTING OF WAYS

"If a bortok wants the path you're on, you must stand aside and let him have it. He has no brain, so you must think for both. But if he paws the earth and bares his teeth, if the hairs on his back rise, then you must fight to keep your path and use your brain to best him. So it is with loud and angry people---you must treat them like the bortok, for they are much the same." Ribald Aerns to his son Rolft, age 15.

Marshal Erik Carson

Carson's search for King Axil ended in the chapel. The monarch stood with his back to him, seemingly transfixed by stained-glass windows high above his head.

The marshal cleared his voice.

"I came to count my blessings," said the rooted king. "It took no time at all. Tell me you have come to add to them."

Where to begin? "Perhaps I should come back another time, Your Majesty."

"Nonsense. I'm already in a foul mood. You've naught to lose."

"Perhaps I do have one bright piece to share. The Prince of Quills—he's taken flight."

Whatever had captivated the king set him free. He turned to face the marshal. "We're trying to find the bright side of a pile of krep, are we? How is that possibly good news?"

"The manner in which he left is most unusual, and hardly a coincidence, I should think. It points to his involvement. The bright side is we're on his trail. Once captured, he may well lead us to those who sought to slay you."

King Axil sighed. "What of the Fostead murders?"

Carson saw no way to turn this into good news. "The count has risen to eleven, Your Majesty."

"Eleven!"

"That is not the worst of it, I'm afraid. At least five were by one familiar to us. Rolft Aerns."

"The royal guard! You're sure of it?"

"Three by his own admission, m'lord. Two more last night, I'm fairly certain."

"Impossible!" The king shot a glance toward the door where two guards stood, then lowered his voice. "The man helped carry Isadora to her grave!"

"Yes, m'lord. Apparently, he spoke her name last night. Yours as well when he was finished."

"You have him here?"

"No, but we shall."

The king snorted.

Was that disbelief? Anger? Disgust?

"What of the steward's murder?" asked King Axil.

"As I suspected, m'lord." *Let us not go there!*

"As you suspected. And you would share what you suspect with your king?"

"I would, m'lord.... if he commanded it."

"And if he did not?"

"Some doors are best left closed, m'lord."

King Axil hung his head. "No real progress with the Prince of Quills or those who sought to kill me. The queen's favorite royal guard stands accused of murder. The steward's death remains..." He paused, looking up to make eye contact with his marshal. "A mystery, shall we say? Have you nothing positive to share with me?"

"In truth, m'lord... I do not."

Another heavy, royal sigh. "You've heard of Madam Dunn's wanderings?"

"If you speak of last night, sire, I have."

"What do you make of it?"

"Given all else, I've not given it much thought, m'lord. But I will admit it has caused a stir amongst the men. An evening stroll along the battlement? Not a common pastime."

King Axil stared at nothing in particular. "No."

"But common is hardly what we have come to expect from Madam Dunn."

King Axil's gaze remained fixed. "What were you told about last night?"

"Only that she climbed the battlements on her own. One of my men greeted her, and she refused assistance."

"And then?"

"She leaned against the parapet, just above the castle gates, and spoke to herself. That is all I know."

King Axil snorted disdainfully.

"Is that not right, sire?"

King Axil exhaled heavily, a nervous laugh escaping his lips. "It is an apt description, I suppose, from those who knew not what they were watching."

"M'lord?"

"She was not 'leaning against the parapet.' She was laying her hands on a stone."

"I don't—"

"The stone that killed her husband."

"What?"

"Yes. A stone she had never before laid eyes on. A stone she had no way of knowing was on the battlement. No way of knowing it had ever been used at all. We are surrounded by thousands of stones. Thousands! And yet she made her way to this one in particular. In the dark of night. How do you explain that?"

"I am lost, m'lord." A shiver ran up Carson's spine.

"You know the story of her husband's death."

"It is common knowledge, sire. But I had not heard the stone had a story of its own."

"Precisely my point. No one knows. There is no story. I had that stone set aside the day Adrian was killed. No fanfare. It was just another rock. Weeks later, I showed the masons where I wanted it to rest. No one said a word. They had no idea what they were handling. Just another rock. I don't know what I was thinking. That his contributions here should not be forgotten? A fitting tribute to a friend, I suppose. I have not passed through those gates—not once beneath that stone—without at least a thought of him. Something I have kept entirely to myself for fear others might think it morbid. Not a word to anyone. Not even Mari Dunn." He raised three fingers in front of the marshal's face.

Squire Tristan Godfrey

The damp morning air had turned warm, then hot. The silhouettes of scraggly spikewood trees dotted an otherwise barren landscape with the only shade in sight. Far into the distance, the Fekle Forest promised a more hospitable environment. And just beyond those woods lay the town of Stonybrook, where Tristan hoped he and his companions would find their quarry, The Prince of Quills.

When first given his assignment by Sir Garr, Tristan had been pleasantly surprised. Two squires traveling with the royal guard in service to the marshal? It was unheard of.

Together with Theos, no less! But the guards' surly dispositions and his brother's quiet demeanor had since dampened his enthusiasm. The timing was also suspicious—directly on the heels of Theos' moonlight escapade outside the palace stables. The same night the steward had been slain. Tristan had thought of little else since observing blood on his brother's hands and clothing the following morning.

"I still don't understand it," said Yurik. The guardsman's repeated complaint had gone unanswered all morning, but it lent credence to Tristan's theory that the marshal had not been doling out rewards when deciding who should hunt The Prince of Quills. "Would someone please explain to me what we are doing here? How is this the work of the royal guard?"

"We seek an enemy of the king. Does that not protect him?" Fereliss seemed annoyed.

"Perhaps at arm's length. But where is our king now? Do I see him here? No. Who watches over him? The royal guard is always close at hand. Is it not so?"

"Does the marshal need a reason or your blessing to order us thus?" asked Fereliss. "Can you not just put your shoulder to the work? The squires are doing a better job of that than you!"

"Broad as my shoulders are," said Yurik gruffly, "they do the bidding of my head, and it requires reasoning."

"Does it?" Fereliss laughed.

"It does."

"Nonsense! You knocked yourself unconscious chasing chickens whilst blindfolded! Was that the bidding of your reasoned brain?"

Before Yurik could respond, Garth interjected quietly. "I fear it is my doing."

"How so?" asked Yurik.

"I told the marshal of Rolft's presence at the castle. But only after he was gone. It ate at me inside. I could not bear it."

"What of it?" asked Yurik. "What has that to do with—"

"I, too, discussed Rolft with the marshal," said Fereliss with a sigh.

"What! Everyone but me is best friends with the marshal now, are they?!" Yurik squared his shoulders proudly. "You are forgiven, Garth." He turned in his saddle to face Fereliss. "You are not. I still fail to see why we are here. So the marshal knows of Rolft. Why should he care? And what has that to do with us? What does he know?"

"What little we know," said Fereliss. "What Rolft himself declared. He killed three in Fostead. Who or why we do not know, but it is still the king's realm. The marshal will see him in chains. Don't think he won't."

"Is this our penance for being so tight-lipped?" asked Garth.

"Tight-lipped! By your own admission, both of yours have been flapping like a bird's wings!" said Yurik.

"It isn't that," said Fereliss.

"What then?" asked Yurik. "He thinks we had a hand in it?"

"No."

"What then?

"Think on it! He worries we might help the fool and seeks to distance us."

"Ahhh." Yurik nodded as he thought things through. "We would, you know, given half a chance. He's a smart one, the marshal is."

"Indeed," said Fereliss, furrows creasing his forehead. "Always thinking, that one."

The guardsmen fell silent. Tristan slowed his horse, allowing them to continue out of earshot.

"Reggie claimed Sibil gave better than she got."

"What's that?" Theos slowed his mount as well.

"When the steward attacked her. She gave better than she got."

"Do you doubt it? She's trained with us enough."

"She cut him, no less! With the blade we gave her, I'll wager!"

"I should like to have seen that, all right."

"Do you fancy her?" asked Tristan.

"Sibil? Don't be daft! She's more a sister to me." Theos shot his brother a wry smile. "But don't think I haven't noticed how you look at her. It's getting old, and so are you. If you don't confess your love to her when next we meet, I swear I shall do it for you!"

Tristan was unmoved. "Did you do it? For Sibil?"

"Do what, brother?"

"I saw the blood on you!" Tristan whispered. "Did you do it?"

Theos took a moment before responding. "Do you recall when we were little? That giant hornets' nest behind the barn? What did I always tell you? Use your lance, Tristan. Use your lance!"

A smile turned Tristan's lips.

"But no, not you." Theos turned in his saddle with a reproachful stare. "You had to pierce its heart with your little wooden sword. But it didn't die, did it, brother? Do you remember the price we paid?"

Tristan closed his eyes, but his smile did not fade.

"This is what you do now with your questions. You wield them like a little wooden sword, poking at a hornets' nest."

"It's a dangerous game, is it?"

"It is."

"Ah. And what would you call slitting the throat of the king's own steward?"

Theos waited a long time to answer. "I'm to be married soon, brother."

"Do you take me for a fool?"

Theos reined his horse in. "Emili Beckridge."

"The servant girl," said Tristan, following suit.

"We are promised to each other."

Tristan studied his brother. "No, you are not. Nor does the moon follow only us. Do you remember trying to convince me that was so? You seek shelter behind falsehood now, as you did when we were children."

"When we were children, yes," said Theos.

"Just so. It is beneath you even more now, and an insult to Miss Beckridge."

"It is the truth, brother. Every word."

"Is it?" Tristan could not hold his anger. "Then you have chosen a poor time to reveal it! What should be cause to celebrate is lost. I speak of the steward's murder! Why drag Miss Beckridge into that? If you are indeed betrothed to her, why—" He stopped abruptly as the pieces came together.

"What if Sibil had not been so fortunate in dealing with the steward?" asked Theos. "What would you have done?"

A long silence followed.

"If the marshal finds out..." Tristan whispered.

"I suspect he already knows, brother."

Overseer Reynard Rascall

"It's quite pleasant out, really. Don't you think?" Reynard drew a large breath as they reached the top of the hill. He turned to survey the view and spread his arms, a bottle of wine in one hand, a chunk of cheese in the other. "Behold!" To his right, and at higher elevation still, sat the castle, an impressive display of white stone rising into the sky. The city of Fostead was spread below.

Spiro refused to look. The course they had taken up the hill was clearly visible—a swath of darker green where their bodies had brushed the morning dew from long grass. "I'm soaked from the waist down," he said.

"And I from the knees." Reynard laughed. "What of it? Fresh air. An unobstructed view. A little wine and cheese. It all helps me to think." He handed the bottle to Spiro and collapsed on the trunk of a large fallen tree.

"It's helping me to think as well," said Spiro. "To think how fargin' cold and wet I am."

"I am of two minds." Reynard picked up a rock and flung it down the hillside. "One is telling me it's time to leave."

"That again?"

"Intuition, my friend." Reynard tapped his head. "A faithful companion of the thoughtful. Little wonder you've not met."

Spiro opened his mouth in feigned laughter, snatched the cheese from Reynard, and plopped himself down on the tree trunk.

"I know I trumpeted the castle to you," said Reynard, "but Fostead really is a smellhole. You were right. I see that now. I shan't miss it once we're gone."

"A krephole if ever I saw one." Spiro cut a piece of cheese with his knife. "I was ready to leave before we arrived. I'm ready still."

Reynard continued to contemplate out loud. "Truth be told, the inland has not made us wealthy. Early on, it helped us prosper, but of late, the profit hardly warrants our effort. If someone else wants it, we could let them have it and be little worse for it. Meanwhile, someone could be robbing us blind in Waterford."

"If you say so."

"And there is that." Reynard pointed through the mist to a short column of specks winding its way from the castle into the city. "More soldiers. The risk increases every day."

Spiro spat in the castle's direction. "Risky for whoever killed Grymes as well, don't you think? What are the chances the soldiers find the stablemaster's partner first?"

"If they do, he'll hang. Wouldn't that be droll?" Reynard was lost in thought for a moment. "But we shan't count on that."

"Why not?"

"Let's see. If I seek to find someone, who do I send: a dozen soldiers stuffed into their uniforms to stumble and bumble about with rules and a code of conduct? Or do I send 'the mason'—free to blend in with the crowd, to move like a cragen, and to use whatever means and methods he so chooses?"

"I thought you said we was leavin'." Spiro tore at the bread with his teeth.

"I said I was of two minds. The one compelling us to stay has since silenced the other. Shall I tell you why?"

Spiro chewed enthusiastically, motioning for Reynard to continue.

Reynard held up a finger. "First, there is the matter of pride. Have we ever tucked our tails and run? Left loose ends untied?"

Spiro shook his head vehemently.

"No. It's not in our nature, and there's no changing that." Reynard held up a second finger. "Then there is the mystery of it all. Who is this new giant we are hunting, and why does he torment us? If we leave now, these questions will haunt us the rest of our days."

Still chewing, Spiro shrugged.

Reynard displayed three fingers. "Payback for Leo Bartlett, Raggett Grymes, and his friends. They were, after all, in our employ."

"We did speak of killing Grymes and his lot ourselves," Spiro said, his mouth full of bread.

"A fair point, but how we choose to treat our own employees is our business, is it not?"

Spiro wiped a trail of crumbs from his upturned lips. "Like Kasparr."

"Precisely. Like Kasparr." The two men shared a chuckle.

Reynard unfolded a fourth finger. "The money and discomfort this trip has cost us... *tsk, tsk, tsk*. Unforgivable. Worse yet..." Reynard spread wide all the fingers on one hand. "What if the bookkeeper disclosed our identity or whereabouts before he died? What then? Do we care to be watching our backs the entire march to our graves? No. And as if all that were not enough! I've run out of fingers and haven't even stated the most obvious."

Spiro waved the block of cheese at him, urging him on.

"The Guild, Spiro! I don't believe it's always watching any more than I believe in Baelon below. But we can't abandon an entire territory and leave it to someone else. The Guild would notice that soon enough, believe me, even if we did make normal payments."

"Why don't we ask The Guild for help, then? If it's so worried about its precious territory, won't it help us to secure it?"

Reynard held his hand out for the bottle. "The Guild is like your smellhole, Spiro. You wish you didn't need it, but you do. And you need it to work well. In fact, we pay them more each moon than they demand. Ten percent, to be exact. And why do we do that?"

"So they'll leave us to our business."

"Precisely. Crying for The Guild's help is out of the question. I'd be embarrassed, frankly, and it might well get us killed. No, we need to see this through ourselves." Reynard rose briskly from his seat. "And let us not forget Able and Elijah. I still don't fancy putting them straight back on that carriage. No. We must first give them what they came for. Starting with the keeper of The Good Knight's Inn. He's one of the few left to identify us."

"They'll enjoy that," Spiro said.

"They can pay a visit to The Raven's Nest as well," thought Reynard aloud. "Another little tidbit to keep them occupied. Surely after last night, a better description of our new giant is in the offing from the owner there."

Mari Dunn

Mari stood patiently waiting for King Axil to speak, increasingly aware that her presence, though requested, made him anxious. The monarch fidgeted with a quill, then shuffled several slips of paper from one spot on his desk to another.

"Please, Mari," he said at last, motioning for her to sit. "You're well, I hope."

"Quite well, Your Majesty."

"I would speak with you about a matter most important."

"The stone that killed my husband." Mari had sensed it the moment she entered the room.

King Axil's eyebrows rose.

"You are concerned by my visit to the battlements."

"No, I... That's not why I summoned you, though I do find it curious."

"What...that I would converse with a stone?"

"It is but a stone, Mari. It cannot talk or listen."

"Yet when you pass below it, you are reminded of my husband. Your friend, Adrian."

King Axil leaned forward. "How could you know that?"

"Is it not so?"

King Axil nodded. "Every time."

"You speak to the stone? Or it speaks to you in some manner? One or the other, surely. How else could you be moved by it?" The king stared silently at her. "It is, as you say, but a stone, Your Majesty, yet it moves you when you near it. Does it not? Did someone hear the stone speak words to me? Am I to be judged for speaking to the stone that killed my husband? If one day our king mutters to himself as he passes beneath it, 'Rest well, Adrian,' shall we deem him unfit to be our king?"

"But how—?"

"Did I find it? I cannot explain that... any more than how I came to know Your Majesty was in danger. What does that matter? What harm has come from it? I pose no threat, sire. Quite the contrary, I assure you."

"You will forgive an old man's prying, but this gift of yours—it's been with you always?"

"No, m'lord. Unless it has lain dormant. The first I knew of it was when Adrian was killed."

"And since?"

Spare him any mention of his wife and daughter! "Yourself, of course, at the feast, m'lord. And most recently, my daughter, Sibil... three times these past few days." Mari's eyes grew moist.

"Three times!"

"Yes, m'lord."

"And each time... in peril?"

"Yes, Your Majesty. As with the others. Pending doom is all that I have seen."

"But why me?"

"I have wondered that myself, and at best can only guess."

King Axil's gesture encouraged her.

"My husband spoke so highly of you, and so often! Even absent that, you are my king, so when we were introduced, I was most honored. I can only say, m'lord, that each vision has been of someone I hold dear, or someone I feel connected to in one way or another."

King Axil nodded, though his brow remained deeply creased. "This is why I asked to speak with you, Mari. I thought perhaps... if you were to live here at the castle... you might help to see the kingdom's future. Shine a light on brewing darkness, so to speak."

Gods! Did he think she could call upon it at will? Or that it was with her always? Mari averted her eyes, hoping he would continue—give her time to think.

"Your daughter would be most welcome to join you, of course. You would want for nothing, Mari, both of you free to come and go at will. No burden would be placed on you."

"I do not wish to seem ungrateful, m'lord. I have never been so honored, but neither would I pretend to be something I am not. I fear you may exaggerate my abilities. There is something inside me, no doubt; something you know I cannot explain. It is nothing I can sway. I cannot make it start or stop. I cannot bend it to my will. Quite the opposite. It comes and goes, arriving unannounced. It takes control of me. Not for very long, and never to my detriment. It shows me things. People. People in danger. And always people I know. I don't think it's going to show me what might befall the kingdom or the castle, m'lord. The visions are not that grand or sweeping."

"I am under no illusions. You have been most forthright. Should you never have another vision, your presence here will be most welcome."

"It is a most generous offer, m'lord."

"Nonsense, Mari. You'll find the palace commonplace soon enough. Consider this small thanks for having saved the life of your king."

"I don't know what to say, Your Majesty."

"Say nothing, then. I would rather you not answer in the moment. Let us speak no more of it today. Just promise me you'll think on it. Perhaps discuss it with your daughter."

"Thank you, Your Majesty." Mari stood and curtsied. "The next time you see fit to walk the battlements, you might lay your own hands upon that stone. Who knows what it might..." She brought a hand to her bosom as a prickly heat spread across her chest. "Who knows what it might say to you." The room began to spin. *Gods, no! Not here, not now!* She reached out to steady herself just as her legs gave way. She heard the king call out her name, then Marshal Carson's even louder.

Then everything went black.

Sibil! By herself... No! In a crowd! Amidst soldiers and... pushing, shoving... wielding a blade! Fighting for her life!

Sibil Dunn

Sibil made her way toward The God of Children's House for the second time in as many days, praying Father Syrus would be there to greet her. Were he not, she would journey to the Fostead Keep. It had been a while since her last visit to her father's grave, and she needed something to occupy her time while waiting for the twins' return from whatever mission they were on.

"Sibil?"

Sibil turned to survey those traveling behind her.

"Sibil!" A young man on horseback waved to catch her attention.

"Reggie?" Sibil waited, allowing others to pass as the young stable boy guided his mount toward her.

"I thought that was you!" Reggie cheerily dismounted.

"What are you doing here?" Sibil asked.

"I carry a message for Rolft...the man we found on the roadside." Reggie began to lead his horse alongside travelers making their way into town on foot.

Sibil kept pace beside him. "He's here? In town?"

"So I'm told."

"He's well, then?"

"I should think. Well enough to travel, anyway. You know who's not so well?"

"Who's that? Not the king, I pray."

"No, it's the steward. The man who attacked you. He's dead!"

"He's what?" Sibil's feet stopped moving.

Reggie reached back to pull her along. "It's true. I didn't think to tell you last night. Someone slit his throat! Serves him right, if you ask me. It was bound to happen sooner or later, the way he treated everyone."

The two plodded past The God of Children's House.

"Where's Rolft?" asked Sibil. "Where are we going?"

"The other end of town."

"Where is he? Staying at The King's Inn?"

"No idea. Keep your eyes open. We could get lucky and spot him. Otherwise, I'm doing all I know to do."

"Which is?"

"Look for his horse, Sarah, at the livery. Talk to Bohun if he's there."

"Bohun?"

"He runs the stables. I worked there as a boy. He helped me get my station at the palace. If Rolft's about, he prob'ly knows where."

Rolft Aerns

Rolft propped himself on one elbow, then raised himself to a sitting position. He shifted again to better support his back against the rear of the stable bay. It was an effort, and he grimaced as he moved. Sarah snorted and pawed the earth.

"It's all right, girl. Just a bad scratch." Rolft tried to lift his shirt to inspect his wound, but the blood-soaked fabric was matted and dried to his stitches. He began to peel the shirt from his skin, stopping when fresh blood seeped from beneath it.

He took a deep breath, preparing to resume, when sounds from the livery entrance froze him. Unfamiliar voices, followed by footsteps. He tensed and readied himself to rise, but when two youths appeared in front of him, he relaxed, slipping back into the straw.

The young man beamed at him. "It's Reggie, sir. From the palace stables."

"So it is." Rolft's eyes flitted between the stable boy and the young woman at his side.

"This is Sibil. She helped bring you to the castle."

"Then I am indebted to you both. How did you find me, and how did you gain entrance here?"

"Fereliss thought you might be in town. I thought only to check the livery for Sarah. I know Bertram well enough, so he let us in...though he said he really shouldn't."

"Where's Bohun?"

Reggie shrugged.

"Well done," said Rolft. "What business have you with Fereliss? And what has it to do with me?"

"Fereliss sends a message: 'The marshal knows.'"

"Eh?"

"That's all he said...'The marshal knows.'"

"The marshal knows," said Rolft.

Reggie shrugged again, turning to gaze at the barn doors. "That's all he said, and I'm afraid I must be off. They'll be missing me at the palace."

"My thanks again to both of you." Rolft hung his head in thought, listening to Reggie's retreat. When he looked up, he was surprised to see the girl still standing there, as still as stone. "What is it?"

The girl slowly withdrew an object from her waistcoat and held it out in front of her. She let it drop. It dangled in the air, suspended by a leather thong around her finger.

Rolft recalled the last time he had seen it. *Reggie must have given it to her.* The girl stood silent. "Thought I'd lost that," he said finally.

"As did I."

"What?"

The young woman lifted the leather thong and hung the amulet around her neck. "I thought I'd lost it, too."

Rolft's brow furrowed. *The girl in the alley!*

She waited while he thought.

"That was you?" he asked.

"There were two men there that night," she said.

It was her! Rolft nodded slowly. "The other no longer bothers anyone."

Sibil's eyes strayed to Rolft's bloodied shirt. "You were hurt that night?"

"What? No, I...What is it you want?"

"You were once a royal guardsman?"

"Who told you so?"

"Reggie. Is it true?"

"What does it matter?"

"Did you know my friend? Princess Lewen?"

It seemed to Rolft that time stood still. "You knew the princess?"

"She was my best friend. Did you serve her?"

"What's your name again?" Rolft squinted to better see the young woman's features.

"My name is Sibil Dunn. Did you serve her?"

"I did," said Rolft. "I serve her still."

Rolft moved swiftly, a watchful eye on his surroundings. He could ill afford a repeat of the previous night, when he had almost stumbled into a soldier crossing the street. All the while, Reggie's short message from Fereliss rang in his ears: "The marshal knows."

Knows what? That he had been to the castle? No, that was not worthy of a message from Fereliss. Besides, too many had seen Rolft at the castle for that word not to have gotten back to the marshal. That he was responsible for the deaths of those in the warehouse? Most likely. His friends, though loyal to their bones, could easily have told others of his exploits. He should have kept his own mouth shut, or sworn Fereliss to secrecy.

No matter. After his performance at The Raven's Nest, it was no surprise that the marshal was hunting him. He would likely hang for what he had done. For what the king had once counted on him to do. He should probably have moved Sarah before leaving the livery. He could not stay there any longer. If Reggie and the girl could find him so easily, well... the marshal might be there now.

The girl. Sibil. He remembered her. He had not gotten a good look at her in the dark alley, but in the stables—as soon as she had mentioned the princess—he had placed her. No longer the young schoolgirl Lewen had kept company with so often. Older. Sadder. But he remembered her. Sibil Dunn, daughter of the architect. He could picture her now, laughing at the side of a mirthful Princess Lewen. How strange that she should cross his path three times in just the past few days. It had to be a message from Lewen, telling him it was time.

Rolft breathed easier as he ducked into the alley. He was at peace with it all. He had little left to live for. If the gods would only let him finish what he had started, he would go willingly. The man with the scar and his companion—if they were the bosses of Raggett Grymes and his gang, they could not go unpunished. And even were they not, Rolft felt certain Jarod's blood was on their hands. He could not let it pass.

He had only the description Jarod had provided. Not much: one with dark hair and a scar on his forehead; the other a short man, "like a cat with a funny nose." The fact that Bohun had returned from The Raven's Nest with news that these same men were hunting Rolft now spurred him on. With any luck, the barkeep, Peter, could provide a better description of the pair. Regardless, the south end was a good place to let his presence be known. If he could not find them, it would not be the end of the world.

They would, given time, find him.

Barkeep Peter Terrick

"You fellas all right?" Peter called from behind the bar.

The two old men raised their glasses to salute him. They were not the first that morning to have asked to sit at the table where two men had been killed the night before. One of them jabbed the tabletop with his finger and said something to his companion. The other laughed. "You should hang a sign!" he yelled to Peter. "*This is where they died!* Good for business, mind ya!"

Peter rolled his eyes. Despite his best efforts, the bloodstains on the tabletop remained. As soon as he could spare the time, he would pay Bohun a visit and complain about his violent friend. "'Not here,' I said," he muttered to himself. "More than once, I did!"

A shaft of daylight flooded the bartop as the pub's door opened to two men. They entered one behind the other, each stooping to avoid hitting his head on the doorframe. Peter tried not to appear unduly impressed by their size as he watched them lumber to the bar. "Can I help you gents?" He laid both palms on the bartop.

"Gents, he says!" One of the big men shoved his partner playfully.

"That's us!" said the other, smiling to reveal a missing tooth. "I'm Able!"

"Elijah!" said the other just as proudly.

"What'll ya have?" asked Peter, bemused.

"Beggar's Ale, 'course," said Able.

"Boss is payin'," said Elijah gleefully. He tossed a silver coin onto the bar. "Best give us the bottle!"

Peter chuckled. There was little to distinguish one colossus from the other. "Cause to celebrate, is it?" He slid the coin into his hand, then fished a bottle from the shelf behind him. Pulling the leather knot from its top, he placed it on the bar. By the time he'd found two mugs, the one called Able had picked the bottle up and put it to his lips. Peter watched the man's throat cork bob up and down several times before the bottle was relinquished to his companion.

"Brothers, are ya?"

"We are!" Able laughed, slapping Elijah on the back. "The Brothers Bortok!"

Unable to contain himself, Elijah sprayed the bar with a fine mist of ale and spittle.

Peter shook his head good-naturedly as he wiped the counter with a rag.

"We'll be needin' another bottle," said Elijah. "This one's half empty."

"We have some questions, too." Able took the bottle from his brother's grasp and returned it to his lips.

"Questions," said Peter.

"About last night," said Elijah.

"Last night," said Peter, wearily. "What kind of questions?"

"About the killin's," said Able.

"What about 'em?" Peter's gaze drifted to the two old men still sitting at the blood-stained table.

"You was here?" asked Able.

"You seen it happen?" asked his brother.

"I'm always here," said Peter.

"Him what done the killin'," said Able cryptically.

"Tell us about the killer," said Elijah.

Peter looked from one man to the other. "What about him?"

"Yes. That's what we need to know," said Able.

"What can ya tell us?" Elijah took another swig from the bottle.

"Not much. Big man. Bad temper."

"That's it?" asked Able.

Elijah drained the bottle. He set it forcefully on the bar.

"That's it," Peter said.

"What'd he look like?" asked Elijah.

"Like I said—a big man. Not as big as you two, mind ya, but big enough."

"A big man," said Able. "That's the best ya can do?"

"It's dark in here at night."

"Uh-huh."

"What about his name?" asked Elijah.

"You know his name?" asked Able.

"No. I didn't ask his name."

"Seen 'im before?" asked Able.

"Know where he lives?" said Elijah.

"Where we might find 'im?" said Able.

Peter studied the inquisitive pair. "Why?"

"Well, thet's our business, innit," said Able.

"*Our* business," said Elijah.

"No," said Peter, decidedly.

Able scowled and clenched a fist. "No?"

"No, I don't know where he lives."

The door to the pub creaked open. Sunlight spilled into the room, then disappeared as a tall man closed the door behind himself.

*Wait, is that...*Peter stared, slack-jawed, as the man moved to the end of the bar in silence. *Noggods! It's Bohun's friend, in the flesh!*

"Ain't ya gonna help him?" asked Able. "Man's probably thirsty."

"Bar's closed," Peter said to the newcomer. "This here's a private conversation. Best go the way ya came."

"I'll wait."

Able scratched his head. Elijah followed suit.

"You need," said Peter, "t' go." He cocked his head slightly toward the brothers.

"Who are you, fella?" asked Able.

"What business is that of yours?" asked Bohun's friend.

Able turned to Peter. Peter hung his head, refusing to look at him. *Oh, Gods above!*

"Well, that depends now, don't it?" said Able.

"On what?"

"On whether you was here... last night."

"What if I was?"

"Well, that might make your business my business."

"*Our* business," said Elijah.

"Sorry, brother. Our business."

"I'm lookin' for someone," Bohun's friend said, no longer exhibiting as much interest in Peter as he had when he'd first entered.

"Well, ain't thet strange. So's we!"

"Is that a fact?"

"It is. What's this fellar's name—the one you're lookin' fer?"

"Two fellas. Don't know their names."

"No kiddin'. We don't know the name of the man we're huntin' either. Just what he looks like." Able raised his eyebrows. "A big man... the likes of you."

"All right, all right!" said Peter nervously. "Bar's closin', lads. I mean it!" He tossed his rag onto the bar and turned to leave. "You wanta keep this up, you do it outside."

Able reached across the bar and grabbed him by the shirt, pulling him roughly back. *Noggods!* From below the bar, Peter produced a wooden cudgel, but as he raised it, Elijah seized his wrist. "Oh no, you don't! You've woken the sleeping bortoks, now, you have!"

The two brothers pulled him easily onto the bartop, sending their empty bottle crashing to the floor. One of them wrapped an arm around Peter's neck and squeezed. The other twisted the barkeep's arm until the cudgel fell from his hand.

Stretched out on the bartop, his head locked in the crook of a giant's arm, Peter had a view of the two old men sitting at the blood-stained table. They stood up.

"Sit down!" yelled the brothers in unison.

The two old men sat slowly.

"You've good seats for good theater!" said one brother.

"That's right. Good theater!" laughed the other.

"Let him go," Peter heard Bohun's friend tell the brothers.

"What? This one?" Able tightened his hold on Peter's neck and twisted it in the direction of Bohun's friend. "Is that 'im? Is that the big man you saw last night?"

"Let him go," Bohun's friend said again.

"You don't look so big to me." Able sneered. "But tell you what—we're gonna let 'im go. 'Cuz you asked nice, and 'cuz we're told you've got a bad temper. We don't want to see thet, now, do we, brother?" He yanked Peter by the head, dragging him horizontally until only his feet were supported by the bar.

Fargin' bastards!

When the brothers let go, Peter cried out, his body crashing to the glass-strewn floor. His chest burned. Searing pain shot through one arm. He lay still on the crushed glass, groaning.

Rolft Aerns

"Oh, krep!" Two old men sitting at the table where Shum Ingram had met his end stood and shuffled quickly to the corner of the pub furthest from the bar. Neither they nor the barkeep lying on the floor appeared to interest the two 'brothers bortok' any longer.

One of the giants grinned at Rolft. "Name's Able, and I know who you're lookin' for."

Able. Not a name he'd heard before. "Do ya now?"

"Mmm. Funny thing…they're lookin' for you, too."

"Are they?"

"I'll tell you what. I'll take you to 'em." Able nudged his sibling, pushing him an arm's length away. "Me and my brother, here, Elijah. We'll take you to 'em."

Elijah... also unfamiliar.

"We will?" asked Elijah.

"That we will. As soon as he stops breathin', brother. As soon as he stops breathin'."

"Ohhh!" Elijah cracked the knuckles of both hands.

Rolft kept his eyes on Able as he moved toward the middle of the room, where chairs and tables might help him avoid grappling with both men simultaneously. He wanted to keep at least one alive, and had settled on killing or disabling the one who talked the most. Big mouth, big brother, he surmised.

But it was the other, the one called Elijah, who stooped to pick up Peter's cudgel and make a beeline for Rolft. He overturned chairs and tables in his way, flinging some with his free hand as though they were toys.

His brother was right behind, warning him as they advanced. "Be careful with this one 'lijah! He's got a knife, you see?"

They moved faster than expected, building momentum as they neared. Rolft picked up a chair and flung it toward them. Elijah batted it easily away. "He wants t' play!" the big man cried.

When a table was the only thing remaining between the onrushing brothers and himself, Rolft kicked it violently into Elijah's thighs. Elijah stopped quickly enough for his free hand to blunt the impact, but his brother plowed into him from behind, propelling his torso forward and onto the tabletop. Rolft was on him in an instant, one hand pinning to the table the wrist that held the cudgel, the other bringing his knife down into the big man's back. Elijah screamed. Able swore. Elijah jerked up and spun spasmodically into his brother's arms, the hilt of Rolft's knife still protruding from his back.

The cudgel lay on the table. Rolft grabbed it and swung it at Able's head, but the brothers were still spinning in an awkward embrace. The cudgel cracked against the side of Elijah's skull instead. The younger brother went fully limp, his dead weight dragging him out of his brother's embrace and onto the floor. Able roared his brother's name and picked up a nearby stool as Rolft prepared to deal another blow from across the table. The cudgel and stool met in mid-air, sending painful vibrations up Rolft's arm. The stool shattered into several pieces. The cudgel flew from his hand.

Able spotted the knife protruding from his brother's back and stooped to retrieve it, but before his fingers could wrap around it, Rolft kicked the table again. It slammed into

Able, knocking him off balance. Rolft was over the table quickly and on top of him. With a roar, Able found his footing and rose, dislodging Rolft and hurling him into an adjacent post. Half-dazed, Rolft stood and staggered to stand with his back against the timber, only to catch Able's fist in his side. His stomach flew into his chest as the stitches Yurik had sewn burst open. He dropped to his hands and knees as Able cleared the furniture between them.

Rolft felt it beneath his hand, looking at it only as his fingers wrapped instinctively around it: a piece of chair leg, its broken end sharp and jagged. As Able's lower half came into view, he lurched forward, driving the splintered shaft into the giant's thigh.

Able screamed in agony. He tried to withdraw the spike, but it was slick with blood and firmly embedded.

Rolft rose to his feet, bringing his fist up under Able's jaw. It rocked the big man backward. Able regained his balance, turned, and limped toward the door.

Rolft stumbled after him.

Marshal Erik Carson

The throng in the street parted slowly ahead of his horse, like water before a ship's bow. With Major Stronghart by his side and a pair of soldiers close behind, Carson headed for the south end, where the odds of learning the whereabouts of Brock Haden, or others associated with Raggett Grymes, were highest. The rest of the troops in Fostead, including four more dispatched from the palace at sunrise, were combing the city under the guidance of Sergeant Lagos. They were all searching for any sign of Rolft, or two others described only as a tall man with a scar on his forehead, and his short companion with a beak for a nose.

As the crowd gave way, it quieted. He was certain everyone had heard about the murders. Fingers pointed and voices whispered. This was no routine reminder of royal might. Women pulled children tightly to their bodies, sheltering them in the folds of their dresses. The presence of the soldiers no doubt brought both comfort and unease. They must be wondering: could the killers be nearby?

Marshal Carson and his troops turned simultaneously at the sound of another rider. The marshal watched with interest as the soldier drew alongside.

"It's Sergeant Lagos, sir!" the young soldier said excitedly. "He's requesting that you join him."

"Where? What's happened?"

"Just south of town, off the road to Chalmsworth." The soldier leaned forward in his saddle, lowering his voice. "It's number twelve, sir."

Carson cursed under his breath.

"He said to tell you it's Bohun Barr."

The marshal released a louder curse. "The stablemaster?" He spurred his horse before the soldier could answer.

Carson slid to the ground before flying dirt and rock could settle. Handing his reins to a soldier standing in the road, he bounded up the pathway. It was Bohun's place, all right. Sergeant Lagos stood near a body halfway up the path. Two soldiers walked the perimeter of a small house in the background.

"It's him, innit?" muttered the sergeant, stroking his coarse beard.

"How long?" asked Carson.

"Sometime last night, I s'pose. Stabbed several times. One in the gut did most of the damage. Another in his privates must've hurt sumthin' fierce. Those in his leg... I dunno. Strange."

"Strange how?" Carson kneeled to get a closer look, as Major Stronghart came up the path to join them.

Sergeant Lagos shrugged. "When was the last time you saw someone stabbed more than once in the same leg? Or in the crotch, for that matter?"

"Find anything else?"

"No, Marshal. Nuthin' in his pockets. We've looked around a bit. I reckon it happened right here. House is still locked."

Carson glanced at the cottage. "Makes no sense."

"No, it doesn't. But he was good friends with Jarod Kelter," said the sergeant.

The marshal thought out loud. "Sergeant Faraday stumbles on the killers at The King's Inn and pays the price. Jarod and his helper are just goin' about their business, but they see too much. That makes sense as well. So what's Bohun doin' here? Someone had to chase him out here for a reason."

"Or be lyin' in wait," said Sergeant Lagos.

"Either way, we may have to start all over."

"Maybe he was with Jarod at the inn and saw too much," said the major. "He got away, or at least this far, before the killer caught up with him."

Carson let out a long, slow breath. "It's possible, I suppose." He scratched his head. "It's just him and young Bertram at the stables. Lad's there every day. I'll take Cyril and have a word. He should know Bohun's comings and goings from the livery." The marshal motioned toward Bohun's house. "Force it open, Major. Have a look inside. Then find us in the south end, will you? What was that barkeep's name again? Peter?"

"That's right."

"The two who were killed there last night...perhaps he can tell us how long they were there before they died. It might help us to know whether they had a hand in this." *Wait a bit!* "Where are their bodies?"

"Those killed at The Raven's Nest?" asked Sergeant Lagos. "They'll be with the undertaker, Wainwright. Southwest corner of town. Why?"

"Find him. Tell him not to touch the bodies any further. I want an exact accounting of everywhere there's blood on them. Where, and how much. Especially their hands, under their fingernails. Everywhere! You understand?"

The sergeant hesitated.

"What is it, Sergeant?"

"Beggin' your pardon, sir. But what if there's no blood on their hands? You don't think that—"

"Rolft?" *Indeed!* He turned and started down the path. "Honestly, I don't know what to think anymore."

Carson dismounted in front of the livery amid a number of patrons waiting their turn to speak with Bohun's assistant, Bertram Collier. Several of them took note of the marshal and his uniformed companion, still astride his horse. They stopped what they were doing to watch.

The marshal had picked Bertram out of the group before entering the stable grounds. He had watched the boy grow from a skinny child into a strapping young man under Bohun's tutelage. He knew him to be a hard worker with a genuine fondness for horses and a fierce loyalty to the man who had taken him in. Though he could not imagine Bertram's involvement in Bohun's death, neither could he help staring at the young man's hands as he approached. He got a good look at them as Bertram accepted a horse's reins from a customer turning to leave.

"Tomorrow, then," Bertram said to his client, rubbing the horse's cheek.

"How are you, Bertram?" asked Carson.

"I'm well, Marshal." Bertram grinned. "But I'm barely keepin' up. Bohun isn't in yet. Do you need sumthin'?" He led the horse toward the barn.

Carson followed. "Bohun won't be comin', lad."

Bertram turned around. "Why not? Is sumthin' wrong?"

"I don't know how to tell you, son." Carson paused, trying to find better words. "Bohun's dead."

"*What?*" Bertram's grip on the reins slackened.

"Come with me." Carson put an arm around Bertram's shoulders and guided him toward the barn. "Cyril, I may need your help!"

Cyril was swiftly off his horse.

Carson pushed one of the barn doors open and ushered Bertram inside. "That's it, son. You're done for the day." He turned to address the curious onlookers outside, most of them with horses still in tow. "There's no more business to be done today. Not here!"

"My horse is in there!" yelled a stout man.

"It can't be helped! Try back tomorrow!" The marshal began closing the barn doors.

"But I've already paid! Where's Bohun?"

"You heard the man!" yelled Cyril, striding quickly to place himself between the barn and the confused onlookers. "It can't be helped!" He extended an arm and pointed at the stout man. "Would you challenge the marshal? Neither he nor the king himself will suffer that, I guarantee you!"

Carson latched the barn doors. "I'm sorry, Bertram. Really, I am. Bohun was a good man. He thought the world of you."

"He's really dead?" asked Bertram weakly.

"He lies just up the road. Outside his house."

Bertram cradled the top of his head with both hands. "I don't understand. When? How?"

"Last night. Murdered, I'm afraid."

"Murdered! By who?"

"We don't know as yet. But you can help, perhaps."

"How?"

"When did Bohun leave here yesterday?"

"We left together. Closed up at dusk, same as always."

"You were with him?"

"Only to the road, like always. I live in town. He goes the other way."

"You think he went straight home?"

"Where else would he go?"

"You've heard about the murders at The King's Inn?"

"Everyone has. You think they're tied?"

"It's possible. That was two days ago. Do you remember where Bohun went that day? Any chance he visited Jarod? Maybe went to the inn for some other purpose?"

Bertram thought. "No, Marshal. We spent all day puttin' up new boards together. I remember because it was so hot inside. That was the day Rolft came as well."

"Rolft!" *Gods above, of course!*

"Him and his horse. This is where they stay. Every time he comes to town. Once or twice each moon—back o' the stable there." Bertram motioned down the corridor.

Carson's hand reached for his dagger. "He's here now, is he?"

"No. Left a bit ago."

"Left town?"

"No. His horse remains. Left on foot for I don't know where."

The marshal ran a hand through his hair. "Listen carefully, Bertram. You go home now, you hear? Lock up, and don't come back until I send word for you. Right now, lad!"

"Are you certain?"

The marshal was half-way out the door. "Cyril!"

Overseer Reynard Rascall

Reynard had found the only shade available in front of The Good Knight's Rest. He and Spiro struck a common pose for men passing time in the south end, leaning against the building with their heads bowed. They watched Able and Elijah lumber across the street, then disappear into The Raven's Nest.

Spiro suppressed a chuckle.

"What is it?" asked Reynard.

Spiro shrugged. "You should see your face."

"They're your children. But if they bungle this...."

"You said 'Don't kill 'im' while it's light out' a hundred times if you said it once. I think they got that part, at least."

"They know what to do, you think?"

Spiro continued his parroting. "Talk to the barkeep. Find out what he knows about the giant from last night. His name, what he looks like, where he lives... anything!"

"Bravo." Reynard sneered, his eyes still locked on The Raven's Nest. "It's not your memory I'm worried about."

Reynard watched and waited with bated breath as the small gathering outside The Raven's Nest grew larger. The noise attracting those passing by had grown loud enough to reach across the street. He strained to hear as best he could.

"It's a scuffle, all right," whispered Spiro, his beady eyes flitting back and forth between Reynard and The Raven's Nest.

"Stand fast." Reynard pressed a palm against Spiro's chest, his own attention shifting between The Raven's Nest and those areas from which he expected soldiers might suddenly appear.

A brave soul in the crowd flung open the pub's door, turning muffled sounds crisper and louder. A sudden guttural cry of anguish rose above all else, silencing everyone outside. It jolted Spiro, and Reynard placed an arm across the smaller man's shoulders. "Not yet!"

He watched wide-eyed as the spectators in front of the doorway scattered, retreating to form a semi-circle into which the pub spat two large men, one clinging to the neckline of the other's shirt with both hands. "Spiro!" one of them cried in distress.

"Able!" Spiro broke free of Reynard.

"Spiro! Spiro! I beg of you!" Reynard looked up and down the street. "Gods damn it!" he cried, trotting after his companion. By the time he reached the outer edge of the crowd, Spiro had disappeared. In the distance, the faint sound of horses' hooves on cobblestones began to drum.

"Oh, gods!" Reynard shouldered his way past others to a point where he could better see and hear the two big men wrestling on the ground, grunting and wheezing, each straining to find purchase on the other. When the combatants rose to their knees, the smaller of the two moved more quickly, locking his arms around Able's neck from behind and pulling backward with all his might. Able arched, seeking relief, his face turning red, veins bulging. His hands clawed at his assailant, who, maintaining a vise-like grip, rose to his feet, towering over his captive. With a final violent jerk, he lifted Able from the ground, twisting the giant's neck until it cracked.

Those watching gasped. The victor loosened his hold, and Able slumped to the ground. His killer—*no doubt who we've been hunting!* —dropped to his knees, head bowed, exhausted.

Spiro emerged from the throng of onlookers to confront the kneeling giant, the blade of a knife glistening in his hand.

Not here! Gods above, not here!

Another murmur rippled through the crowd as Spiro advanced with singular purpose, halting when the tips of his boots reached Able's lifeless body.

The spectators grew deathly silent.

The sound of horses' hooves grew louder.

"I wish I had the time to do this right," Reynard heard Spiro say.

The exhausted giant slowly lifted his head. His dark, wavy hair clung to his untamed beard.

Spiro's hand flicked out, his blade slashing across the big man's face. The giant winced, his arms rising instinctively but much too slowly to ward off the attack. Blood streamed down his cheek as he rose unsteadily.

Spiro's hand darted back and forth, jabbing the point of his blade into one of the big man's thighs. The giant cried out, dropped back to his knees, his hands fumbling awkwardly in search of a weapon. When they came up empty, they moved instead to cover his wounds.

"This next one's gonna hurt," said Spiro.

A blood-curdling scream startled everyone. A dark figure appeared out of nowhere, slamming into Spiro, knocking him off his feet and onto his back. By the time he hit the ground, the figure was on top of him. Spiro rolled and scrambled to his feet, dagger still in hand. Reynard judged his attacker to be even quicker, already on his feet, crouched low in a fighting stance.

Reynard was stunned. *Her* feet! It was a young girl, dressed in black, her hair tied back in a ponytail! She hissed at Spiro as she moved, her body slinking between him and his prey. She flicked her dagger toward him, warding him off like a cat displaying its claws.

The sound of horses' hooves turned to boots on cobblestone, accompanied by coarse shouting and the unmistakable clanking of steel blades. The crowd parted. Reynard was jostled roughly, then shoved so hard he fell. By the time he was back on his feet, a swarm of soldiers had surrounded Spiro, who looked in no mood to surrender. Three of the king's men stood poised to run their swords through him. A fourth tapped Spiro's black-handled dagger with the tip of his sword.

"I wouldn't," the soldier said.

Marshal Erik Carson

Carson set off for the infirmary, ruminating as he walked. The castle's defenses were in place. There was time to further contemplate Fostead's rash of murders. Fourteen! Rolft Aern's responsibility for at least half of them was difficult to accept. Garth's third-hand telling of the warehouse slayings had been anything but conclusive, leaving the door open to different accounts. He had hoped for them, actually. But the subsequent killing of Raggett Grymes and his crony by a man not only matching Rolft's description, but spouting allegiance to the royal family, had fueled the marshal's fears. Witnessing Rolft strangle a man outside The Raven's Nest had erased all remaining doubt and likely sealed the former guardsman's fate. Given his past status, Rolft would answer to the palace for his murderous actions. And not even his ties to the queen could save him now. Not even were she alive.

Also apprehended, and sitting behind bars in the Fostead Hold, was the little man described by Jarod as a "cat with a beak for a nose." He had been staying at The King's Inn when Sergeant Faraday was butchered—in the same room, no less! —so it was no stretch to imagine he had killed Jarod and Timmil Childs as well. Carson assumed the man had also killed Bohun Barr; the telltale wounds inflicted on Rolft's leg were proof enough of that. The wee man would have killed Rolft, too, were it not for Sibil Dunn.

Only two of the recent executions were not reasonably attributed to either Rolft or "the cat," and those were the bookkeeper and Baron Treadwell's cook. Two mysterious murders in a town the size of Fostead? Carson could live with that, and they might yet be explained when the prisoners began to sing. And sing they would.

Sergeant Fields would help to guard and interrogate the prisoner at The Hold. If he could not loosen the cat's tongue during the next few days, the prisoner would be dragged to the dungeon and introduced to more effective forms of persuasion.

Sergeant Lagos would resume the hunt for the prisoner's associate, the man with dark hair and a scar on his forehead. Temporary assistance would be provided to the overwhelmed undertaker, Drixle Wainwright, and to Bertram at the livery. But enough progress had been made that the marshal once again considered Fostead less deserving of his attention than the attempt on King Axil's life. The town would slowly settle back to normal. With any luck, the celebration of Six Moons three suns hence would help to bury the past.

Marshal Carson noticed Madam Dunn's daughter, Sibil, as he crossed the bailey. She sat outside the infirmary's doors, her knees pulled to her chin, her back resting against the wall. He had spoken with her outside The Raven's Nest just long enough to gain an appreciation for her interest in Rolft, and to understand why she had followed him there. He hoped she would not be unduly distraught when she learned the guardsman's fate. She was as intriguing as her mother, and he welcomed the opportunity to speak with her again. He acknowledged her with a wave well before he reached her.

"Good day to you, Miss Dunn!"

"And to you."

"You're well, I trust?"

"I am."

"And your mother? How is she faring?"

"Much better, thank you, though it is still not clear to me why we have been asked to remain."

"That is for the king to share, but I trust you have been made to feel welcome. You are both free to come and go at will, I assure you. In the meantime, you are to be provided whatever you need."

Sibil was on her feet immediately. "I need to see Rolft. But I am told he is allowed no visitors."

"My doing, I'm afraid."

"Then you can grant me access."

"Perhaps."

"I would be most grateful."

"There is one thing of which I myself remain unclear. You say you defended Rolft outside The Raven's Nest because of your encounter in an alley?"

"I told you...he saved my life that night."

"You sought to aid a friend in need. Repay a debt."

"You make it sound as though I planned it, when in truth, there was little thought involved."

"And the steward? I wonder. Had I not interrupted, might you have killed him?"

Sibil hesitated. "Perhaps. As any trapped animal might seek to save itself. How is that unclear?"

The marshal shrugged. "What is unclear to me is how you came to possess your skills. I have seen them twice now on display, and it was not merely the instincts of a cornered animal I observed."

"I suppose Sir Godfrey is to blame for that," said Sibil, defensively.

"Sir Godfrey!" *How could that be?*

"His sons are friends of mine. I've trained with them a fair amount."

"Sir Godfrey!"

"And his sons."

Carson closed his eyes, raised his chin, and massaged the back of his neck. "I suppose I should not be surprised. Yet I am at a loss for words. Let us say the training shows, shall we, and leave it at that for now?"

"As you wish. And Rolft?"

Carson knocked on the infirmary door. "Tomorrow, perhaps. Has he woken, do you know?"

"How could I? The nurses will not let me enter."

A small aperture in the door at eye level slid open, then shut.

"Again, my doing, I'm afraid. Try back tomorrow, why don't you?" The door opened and he slipped into the infirmary before Sibil could respond.

Sir Black's and Lady Gray's heads lifted off the floor, their ears laid back, their muscles tensed. But as soon as the cragens recognized the marshal, their tails began to wag. Their bodies relaxed. They laid their heads back down.

Carson shut the study door behind him, glancing around the room. "No response from King Tygre?"

King Axil sat relaxed in a chair next to the cragens, away from his desk. He shifted in his seat. "Not as yet. Any day now, I suspect. Regardless, the answers you seek lie elsewhere, I'm sure of it. What about the Prince of Quills?"

"Also any day now. And I pray you're right."

"I'll wager he's the better source of information. What of Rolft? Any change?"

"He remains unconscious, m'lord."

"What does the physician say?"

"He's lost a lot of blood. He has several wounds, but one of them is older than the rest. It's badly infected. They do not know if they can root it out."

"But he'll live."

"They cannot say. It might be best for him if he did not."

"Hard to fathom what he's done. The queen would not believe it."

"I dare say."

"Were she still here, so would he be. You know that as well as I."

"I do."

"Three almons running she refused you his retirement." The monarch chuckled. "I don't know what you were thinking."

"That he was of age, m'lord. And that he should be treated the same as any other."

"As any other what? Man who saved her from a madman with a pitchfork, and kept Lewen from drowning?"

Carson sighed and closed his eyes.

"That is the same face you wore when she refused to give her blessing." King Axil smiled broadly as he kneaded the folds of skin on the scruff of Lady Gray's neck, then patted Sir Black's head. "Rolft was their favorite too, you know. They would have died in that fire were it not for him."

"Also true, m'lord."

"What were you thinking?"

Carson merely shrugged. The king followed suit, still smiling. "My apologies. The memory amuses me, but I do not mean to take pleasure at your expense. I've interrupted you. Please..."

"I told you earlier how Madam Dunn's daughter came to Rolft's defense."

"Yes, yes. Like a cragen unleashed, you said."

"And why?"

"Because she was with the stable boy when they found him on the roadside. She helped to bring him to the castle. You told me this."

"So I thought, but there is more. It seems that she was with Rolft when he killed his first in Fostead."

"What!"

"She was accosted in an alley, and Rolft came to her aid."

"I don't understand. What was she doing there?"

"A coincidence, Your Majesty. She could not even say who saved her... until she and Reggie picked Rolft up on the roadside. It was then she saw that Rolft was in possession of an amulet she'd dropped in the alley."

"This is too much. What am I to believe?"

Carson shrugged. "There is no reason to doubt the girl. We know a man—a thief, in fact—was killed in the alley she describes. We know Rolft killed three more in a warehouse the next day, the very day Reggie and the girl found him wounded on the roadside. Several, if not all, the men dispatched by Rolft were members of The Guild of Takers. And I myself watched Sibil draw a dagger in Rolft's defense outside The Raven's Nest. She would have killed for him, I'm sure of it."

"Because he helped her in the alley."

"It would seem enough, but there is even more."

King Axil snorted in amazement.

"She sees in him a kindred spirit, Your Majesty."

"Kindred spirit! How so? Is she in love with him?"

"Hardly, sire. I believe it to be a bond of loyalty and common purpose."

"You've lost me, to be sure."

"You told me Sibil was a good friend of the princess, and I have since recalled her presence here on numerous occasions."

"Best friends. That's true, so what?"

"Rolft told Sibil he is still in service to the princess."

"What?!"

"Yes, m'lord. As we speak, Miss Dunn sits outside the infirmary, awaiting his recovery."

"Serves the princess how?"

Tread lightly here! "When he killed the first two inside The Raven's Nest, several there heard him say he did it for his king, his queen, and the princess."

King Axil's nostrils flared. "Were they known to us?"

"No, Your Majesty. Again, common takers. But does it not make sense?"

"It makes no sense! Isadora and Lewen are dead two almons now!"

"Yes, m'lord, and Rolft was charged with keeping them alive. I dare say witnessing their deaths destroyed him. Nor did he welcome forced retirement. I'm told he wanders now from town to town, like a vagabond, no longer right in the head."

"But even so..."

"I think perhaps he has convinced himself that he avenges the queen and princess' deaths."

The king could only shake his head.

"It would explain a lot," said Carson.

"That he might be so tortured by their deaths. Far be it from me to question that," the monarch said finally.

"It's not too great a stretch, knowing Rolft."

"Remind me, how many has he killed?"

"Eight I am certain of, Your Majesty, but who knows how many more?"

"Gods above, you think there may be more?"

"It's most unlikely there are not. The bookkeeper? The baron's cook? The stablemaster, Bohun Barr, who Rolft was staying with at the time. Who knows what else will come to light as we investigate?"

"All killed in the name of the crown?" King Axil shook his shaggy locks. "It cannot be ignored. What are we to do with him?"

Carson maintained his silence. *You know as well as I!*

"It is the cruelest twist of fate that he should hang for this," muttered the king.

"We should pray, perhaps, he does not wake."

The king stared at Carson for a long while. "If it were you lying there, what would you wish?"

"If it were me, lying at death's door, under similar circumstance? Would I wish to be woken, only to be hanged by those I would have died for, by the crown to which I swore allegiance? Would I wish to be branded a traitor and a murderous lunatic...for acts I was certain were in the realm's best interest? No, my lord. If I were nearly gone and could be left to simply drift away, forever remembered as a loyal servant who died for king and country, my honor still intact, what choice would that be, really?"

Again, King Axil held the marshal's gaze a long time. "Are we not in a position to help him make that choice?"

So here we are at last! Wait for the king to finish it.

"We are agreed, then," said King Axil. "It's for the best, and I cannot stomach the thought of hanging him. Isadora would never forgive me for that."

"As you wish, Your Highness. He may yet go of his own will. If not, I will see to it. There are, however, pieces to the Fostead puzzle that only he may know. If he wakes, I would speak with him before he dies."

"So be it. Should he wake, you are at liberty to decide when he dies, so long as it is quick and painless, and while he is in the physician's care. Let all of Baelon remember him as the loyal guard he was."

THE POINT OF NO RETURN

"Don't waste time trying to retrace your steps or slow your progress. Neither is possible once you've left the cliff's edge. Focus instead on surviving what awaits." Sergeant-at-arms Arthur Cogswell

Squire Tristan Godfrey

Tristan rode behind the Prince of Quills, trying not to judge him. The man was nothing like what he had imagined. He was small, pale-skinned, and timid. Not the sort one pictured plotting to kill a king. He was a sorry sight, really, still dressed in his nightgown, now soiled from krep he had expelled while shackled on his horse. Plucked from bed the night before, intimidated by the royal guard— *Well, who wouldn't be?* —he'd offered no resistance. Just a steady stream of statements proclaiming his innocence. Yurik had gagged the man a short time back, accusing him of being "worse than Fereliss." All six riders had been silent ever since.

Don't pity him! He's brought this on himself!

But had the "prince" committed any greater offense than that of murdering the steward? What fate awaited Theos? Tristan could not bear to think of it. What was happening? Life had been so simple and so clear. One path for both him and his brother. They would follow in their father's footsteps: be knighted, marry, serve the king and raise their families within a day's ride of each other. They had promised!

He stole a glance at his twin brother—so grave!

And what of Sibil? Theos would make good on his threat to disclose Tristan's feelings for her. He could not suffer that! They would be back inside the castle walls by dark. He would show his brother; he would confess his love to Sibil straight away. What did he have to lose?

"And what about the two of you, eh?" It was the voice of Fereliss, loud but playful. "What did you do to deserve this dubious honor?"

Theos spoke before Tristan had a chance. "We serve our knights, our king, the kingdom."

Fereliss burst into laughter. "Are you certain you haven't already been knighted? You talk like one, to be sure! Though I'll wager you did something more suiting one of us to land you in this spot! No matter...keep it to yourselves. We really don't care to know."

The sound of an arrow hitting its mark broke the silence.

"Archer!" Garth cried out, clutching his shoulder where a feathered shaft protruded.

"The prisoner!" shouted Yurik.

Tristan reached in vain for the Prince of Quill's mount. Another arrow sizzled by him. Then another, so dangerously close he felt it stir the air beside his cheek. He struggled to control his panicked mount as the prisoner's horse broke away.

"Get low!" yelled Fereliss, nearly knocking Tristan off his horse. Tristan lowered his head behind the animal's neck, instinctively glancing back to check on Theos, just as an arrow slammed into his brother's chest. Theos let go of his reins and tumbled backward, as though he'd been hit by a blacksmith's hammer. He hit the ground like a sack of grain before jittery horses' legs and swirling dirt hid him from Tristan's view.

"The prisoner!" someone shouted.

There was more yelling as Tristan slid from his horse and scrambled in the direction he had seen his brother fall. "Theos! Theos!"

He found him lying awkwardly on his back; the tip of an arrow that had pierced his chest propped him slightly off the ground. The squire's eyes stared blankly back at Tristan. Blood trickled from his nose and mouth. Tristan dropped to his knees beside him.

Theos coughed, blood spraying from his mouth. His breathing was ragged as he gripped Tristan's shirt.

What should I do? Break the shaft off where it enters! Tristans's hands shook as he grasped the arrow. *Do it!* But another cough from Theos startled him, and he recoiled.

"Leave it...brother." Theos gagged, his grip on Tristan's shirt loosening.

"Help me!" Tristan shouted to the guardsmen. "Help me!" The surrounding chaos had settled into quiet, but he could not move. Could not think. *This isn't real. It isn't happening!* His twin brother's eyes were closed. *Wake up!* Tristan held his breath as he waited for Theos to show some sign of life.

"He's gone, lad." A heavy hand descended on his shoulder.

Impossible! Impossible!

But his brother did not stir.

Sibil Dunn

Sibil was halfway across the bailey when she saw Marshal Carson leave the infirmary. Her hopes of seeing Rolft rose, but the marshal kept his brisk pace in passing, saying only, "It's not a good time for him, I'm afraid."

She thought for a moment to trail the man—several questions prompted her—but there had been an edge to his voice that warned against it. She watched his back until it was obscured by men and horses, then turned away, her planned vigil outside the infirmary now pointless.

She wandered aimlessly. She had declined her mother's invitation to visit with the wives of King Axil's senior staff. The twins were still away. The livery was so quiet she knew before she reached its doors that all the squires were elsewhere. Still, she peeked inside hoping to find Reggie. There was no one, just horses, but the sound of muted voices drew her around the building.

Several soldiers and the old stablemaster, Caleb, were gathered near the group of colorful coaches. Before she could decide whether to approach, Reggie appeared from behind one of the carriages. He hailed her and broke into a trot.

"Sibil! I was hoping you would come!" A broad grin brightened his face.

Sibil withstood the impact of an unexpected hug and wrapped her arms around the shorter boy. She glanced toward the coaches. "Did you get in trouble for the wagon's wheel?"

"Never mind that!" said Reggie. "Are you okay?"

"Of course. Why would I not be?"

Reggie released his hold and stepped back. "There's a story going 'round 'bout you and your friend, Rolft."

"What story?"

"They say you fought two giants together! Killed them both after I left you! Is it true?" Reggie's eyes were wide with wonder.

"No, it's not."

Reggie remained excited. "They say you saved Rolft's life!"

Sibil ignored the remark. "Do you know how badly he was hurt? They won't let me see him."

"No, but it can't be good. Bernier tells me they've tied him to his bed."

"What!"

"You know, so he won't further injure himself. You didn't tell me you were going to war with him!"

Sibil frowned and bit her lip. "Can you ask Bernier?"

"About Rolft's condition? Indeed! He'll know, or he can find out. He's in and out of all the quarters, delivering linens, running errands, or some such. And he knows people."

"Thank you, Reggie." Sibil stole a quick glance toward the soldiers before walking away.

"Hey!" Reggie called out. "They say your mother can see the future!"

"Don't believe all you're told!"

"I like your mother! Did you know I met her before I met you?"

Sibil raised a hand in the air and kept walking.

She had not been sitting long. Just long enough for sunlight to creep up her shins and warm her knees. If the squires did not arrive to train behind the barracks by the time the sun had found her face, she would head to the infirmary.

In the meantime, she was content to watch the old man move beneath the tarps adjacent to the training grounds. His presence gave her hope that the squires would soon appear, but also stirred in her mixed feelings. Respect. One wouldn't think it possible just watching him putter about, but she had seen him school the squires in combat with an assortment of weapons, toying with them as though they were lost children.

Cogswell, that was his name. The sergeant-at-arms stopped puttering, moved to the edge of the weapons shelter and stood, staring...at her? Theos' words came back to her: *"Don't think he hasn't noticed you. He's not going to invite you closer."* She was certain the old man was too distant to make out her expression, but she stared back with resentment, nonetheless. She felt for the knife tucked beneath her blouse, vowing never again to be without it.

"Sibil! There you are!" Reggie's cries and sudden appearance startled her. She abandoned Cogswell's stare. The young groom was quickly by her side, struggling to speak.

"What is it, Reggie? Is it Rolft?" It hadn't been that long since she had—

"No! It's your friends!" His expression was so pained.

"What's happened? Are they back?" Sibil rose anxiously to her feet. The young groom looked away from her. Was he crying? "What is it!" she yelled, grabbing him by the sleeves and forcing him to look at her.

Marshal Erik Carson

Carson was accustomed to Major Stronghart's approach. There was something in the soldier's stride that divulged whether he was bearing good news or bad. The manner in which he used his hands. The number of times he cocked his head from side to side.

These would not be welcome tidings.

Carson steeled himself, taking a seat on the same block of wood that Sir Kraven had rested on while honing his blades. "Don't tell me more are dead in Fostead," he said in somber greeting.

"You're going to wish that was the case." Major Stronghart jerked his head in the direction of the castle gates. "Yurik's just returned with the Prince of Quills. The printer's dead, Garth is wounded. Took an arrow in the shoulder. He'll be fine; the infirmary has him now." Stronghart took a deep breath. "But one of Sir Godfrey's boys...." Carson closed his eyes as the major continued. "Dead, I'm afraid. Yurik claims it's Theos. They were ambushed. Don't know by who. Tristan hunts his brother's killer... Fereliss chases him. They're still out there."

The castle gates began to open. A loud voice outside said, "On your best behavior! You represent King Tygre!"

Four riders entered slowly, assessing their surroundings.

"Welcome to Aranox!" Marshal Carson greeted them from the bottom of the battlement stairs. "You're a long way from home!"

The lead rider stopped. Carson quickly appraised him as those behind followed suit. Slightly older, more gray than black in his short hair and trim beard. A weathered face, heavily creased by sun and, no doubt, worry. Light gray eyes, alert and penetrating. "We're welcome, are we?" the man asked guardedly.

"Of course!" Carson said. "Why would you not be?" He paused, allowing for an answer that did not come. "I'm Erik Carson, marshal to King Axil."

"Geralt Ademar, marshal to King Tygre of Tegan," said his counterpart.

"I know you by reputation only." Carson smiled, extending his hand as Ademar dismounted. "All good, I might add."

Ademar accepted the proffered greeting. "I could say the same. You prepare for war, do you?"

"We are always prepared to some degree. Never fully, I might add."

"It would be foolish to think otherwise. Who are you expecting?"

"To be honest, we're not entirely sure. Perhaps you could help us solve a riddle."

"Not sure! What sort of riddle?"

"A quarter moon past, three men tried to slay our king during the Lords and Ladies Feast." Carson eyed Ademar steadily.

"So we were told. I trust their efforts were thwarted."

"They were." Carson paused. "They shouted, 'Long live King Tygre!' during their attack."

"Wha-at?!" Marshal Ademar bristled. "So that's what this is all about, is it?" He locked eyes with Carson. "King Tygre has no quarrel with King Axil. In fact, he considers him a good friend. What possible motive could he have for killing him? Trust me, if King Tygre had had a hand in it, I would be aware. Your king would now be dead, and we, too, would be making ready for war, not standing here, defenseless. How witless do you think us?"

"It was not an accusation. I don't suppose whoever is behind it would want to be standing where you are."

"No. They most certainly would not." Marshal Ademar cast a quick glance toward the archers on the battlement.

"But now you know the riddle, what do you make of it?"

"I don't know what to make of it, but we are not King Axil's enemy. Of that I can assure you!"

"You pose no threat, I'm sure of that."

"Not among supposed allies. Were that not the case, you might be made to feel less comfortable yourself."

The two men continued to assess each other.

"Perhaps," said Carson. "Let us hope it never comes to that."

"Agreed. They're dead, I presume, the three? They gave no other clues to their allegiance? This is how wars start!"

Carson dug a hand into his waistcoat pocket. "So it is." He offered what was hidden in his fist to Ademar. "They all carried several."

Ademar turned the coin over in his hand.

"We don't see a lot of those," said Carson. "Ours bear the profile of another man."

Ademar nodded slowly, frowning. "This proves nothing, of course. Anyone can come by these."

"Three men, all with several coins newly pressed? It's possible, I grant you, but under the circumstances..." Carson produced a small leather pouch for Ademar's benefit.

"What's that?"

"More of the same. Carried by the man who granted the would-be assassins access to our king."

Marshal Ademar smiled. "I carry one or two myself. As well as this..." He withdrew a large envelope bearing the royal seal of Tegan from beneath his waistcoat. "Which would you prefer to present to your king?"

Carson returned the smile. "Follow me. You can choose yourself. King Axil will be most pleased to receive a friendly face."

"A friendly face, indeed! I'll thank you to remember that the next time I come knocking at your gates!"

Wrestling with his boots, Carson stumbled out the door of his quarters and into the middle of the night. Major Stronghart stopped to wait for him. "Go on!" said the marshal, tugging a boot into place. "Go on!" He was still groggy, unsure if he had truly awakened from his first sound sleep in several nights. The disruption was his own fault—he had asked to be notified as soon as Fereliss and Squire Tristan Godfrey returned.

"They're unharmed?" He tucked his shirt into his trousers as he trailed the major toward the castle gates.

"I've not spoken with them, Marshal. I came as soon as I was notified."

A shroud of mist enveloped the bailey, whipped one way then the next by swirling winds. Carson wished he had donned a coat. He laced his shirt, then folded his arms across his chest. Even from a distance it was clear something was different. Any activity at the gates was unusual this time of night. He noted the two horses, but their riders had dismounted and were difficult to distinguish in the midst of a growing number of greeters. Coarse words rang out. Then a good sign: laughter. A large figure broke free of the small gathering and strode toward the marshal and the major with one arm raised in salutation.

"Marshal! Major!" shouted Fereliss.

"You're all right?" asked Carson. "What about Squire Godfrey?" The three men stopped to greet each other.

"I'm fine, but Tristan...the lad's unharmed, but he's worn out."

Carson looked to Major Stronghart. "Have Squire Godfrey taken to the infirmary for a day or two's rest. Notify Sir Godfrey and Sir Garr of his return."

He addressed Fereliss as the major hurried off. "You found his brother's killer, did you? What happened?"

Fereliss stroked his beard. "We only caught a glimpse of him before he vanished. It was planned, m'lord, make no mistake. We had just left the Fekle Forest, but it gave him ample cover. He picked the perfect spot to ambush us; his bow was true from a great distance, and his mount was swift. By the time we found his trail, he was long gone. We were never going to catch him, but Tristan would not stop the hunt."

Carson looked closer at Fereliss. "What happened to your face?"

The guardsman rubbed the cheek below his swollen eye as he glanced back toward the gates. "The lad's a handful, Marshal, but I'm all right. He's not himself, as one might well imagine."

Spiro

The back of the burly soldier's hand landed squarely on Spiro's mouth. The blow sent him hobbling backward in his shackles to sprawl against the jail cell wall, a bloody smile spreading across his face.

The soldier doubled over to catch his breath.

"Perhaps he's had enough, Sergeant," said a second soldier standing just outside the cell door.

"Enough?" The sergeant scoffed. "I don't think either of you dullards understand what's going on here." He wiped his nose and arched his back. "If you understood," he said to the other soldier, "you'd be in here helping me with all you've got." He turned to Spiro. "And if you weren't so stupid, you'd be talking as though you'd just learned how...You do know how, do you?"

Spiro spat a bloody mist toward the soldier. *I would not want to be in your shoes...not when Reynard comes for me!*

"Have you ever visited the castle dungeon?" asked the sergeant. "Don't talk to me, see if I care. But that is your next home, my friend. And it will be your last. You know why the dungeon keeper wears a hood? It's not because he's ugly. No. It's because no man ought to be seen doing the kinds of things he's going to do to you. You have no idea. You'll think fondly of our time together when you're in his hands. You're going to scream at first. And then you'll cry. Then you'll beg to be back with me. You have no idea." The sergeant straightened and took a deep breath. "Just your name. Just your name, and I promise you, we're done this day."

Spiro's bloody smile grew wider. He spat at the soldier again.

"Have it your way." The sergeant lumbered forward, his meaty hand pinning Spiro against the wall.

Overseer Reynard Rascall

It was the same hill he had climbed two suns earlier with Spiro. But today, the trek seemed longer, and decidedly less enjoyable. Upon reaching the top, Reynard collapsed onto a familiar fallen tree to catch his breath.

He could not let his mind wander in the city, where his continued freedom demanded constant vigilance. He had been tempted to think things through in bed, but that would have been especially ill-advised with a bloody corpse for a roommate. He studied the city below, fairly certain he could identify The Good Knight's Rest, where he expected the body of the innkeeper, Gabriel, would soon be found. He would need to find other accommodations for the evening if he was to stay another night.

What to do about Spiro; that was the question. Reynard's gaze shifted to Fostead's main street, and the prison to which he had watched his partner dragged. The gods only knew what they were doing to him there. Reynard gnawed at a loose piece of cuticle and spat it into the air. He could leave Spiro to fend for himself. The fool's current predicament was, after all, his own doing. Always so impetuous!

Yet allowing others to determine his companion's fate might have dire consequences. Despite his unquestionable allegiance, Spiro would eventually tell his captors whatever they wished to know, including Reynard's name, and where he lived and worked. Unacceptable, under any circumstance.

Spiro's absence had also called Reynard's attention to another fact that both amused and annoyed him. It was not something he could ever share with Spiro, or anyone else, for that matter. But it was increasingly difficult to ignore. It had, in fact, been on his mind even as he stabbed poor Gabriel Solomon to death. He missed the little bastard.

"A pinch or two each night until the sweating stops?" said the woman, nervously. She dropped the small pouch into her purse.

"Just so," the apothecary said with confidence. "With plenty of water, mind you. Your husband will be good as new."

"Thank you, sir. I pray you're right." The woman handed the old man two coins.

"Three days at most. Good as new!" the shopkeeper called after the woman as she rushed away. Adjusting the spectacles on the bridge of his nose, he turned his attention to Reynard. "Yes? What can I do for you?"

Reynard quickly surveyed the room. The shelves behind the apothecary were littered with bottles of various sizes; the floor nearly covered by bins and barrels. "I need something to put a horse down." He wiped a sleeve across his mouth. "Two horses, actually."

"Put them down?" The old man squinted. "Do you mean to put them out of their misery, or simply put them to sleep?"

"Out of their misery. And quickly."

The street urchin had claimed to be ten almons old, but Reynard doubted he was more than seven or eight. Thick curls of straw-blond hair and big blue eyes adorned the boy's cherubic face. But someone had dressed the tiny prince in tattered clothes, rolled him in the dirt for several almons, then set him squarely down on a path leading only to ruin. Reynard felt certain that for the silver coin the child had received, and the one he'd been promised upon completion of his task, he would do most anything.

Cloaked in darkness, he patted the boy's blond curls. "You know what you're to do with that, then?" He used his boot to nudge a small black kettle resting by the boy's feet.

"Yes, sir!" said the child in a high-spirited voice.

"It smells good, doesn't it?"

"Awful good, sir!"

"But you're not going to eat any of it, are you?"

"No, sir."

"Not even one bite, mind you, or you'll not receive your coin. Understood?"

The child nodded vigorously.

"Tell you what. You do exactly as we agreed...nothing more, nothing less...and I'll give you not one, but two silver nobles. How's that?"

"Two, sir? Yes, sir! Thank you, sir!"

Reynard picked the kettle up, making sure its lid was secure, before handing it to the urchin. "All right, then. Off you go! And not one bite! I've eyes on you!" He watched the boy leave the alley and traipse down main street lugging the small kettle in one hand. *Just a few doors down...that's it!* The child stopped in front of The Hold and set the kettle down.

The boy knocked softly on the door; so softly Reynard strained to listen. Silence ensued. Three more soft knocks. There was some mumbling from inside The Hold that Reynard could not make out.

"It's me, sir!" the child's voice rang out.

"Say again?" A man from within the jailhouse cleared his voice.

"It's me, sir!"

Reynard heard the distinct sound of a small aperture in the door being opened. "Are you lost, son?" a gruff voice asked. "Go away! This is no place for a child."

"Please, sir. Me mum'll beat me proper if I don't give you this."

Good lad!

"Eh? What's that?"

"Stew, sir. Hot stew! Me mum made it special for you." The child took a deep breath. "She says it's for the soldiers, and the prisoner's not to have *any!*"

Bravo! Well done!

"She did, did she?" A short silence. "You're all alone, are ya?"

Reynard imagined the soldier pressing his face hard against the aperture in an effort to widen his view.

"Yes, sir. Please, sir. I'll just leave it by the door, shall I?"

Reynard staggered into an alleyway and collapsed, out of breath. Spiro pulled up beside him, doubled over, hands on knees.

"We must leave this place," said Reynard through gasps.

"Not now. Not yet," said Spiro resolutely.

"Don't be absurd. We leave at once!"

"I'm not going anywhere just yet."

"Is that so? Have you lost your mind? Have you not been paying attention? The man I just killed to free you... he wore the King's uniform. We are no longer common thieves at risk of spending the rest of our days behind bars. No, Spiro. If we are caught, we will be hung or have our heads chopped off. Whilst crowds cheer, no less. Do you understand that?"

"Even so—"

"There is no *even so*!"

Spiro dug his heels in. "What happened to all them reasons for stayin'?"

"You've buried them so deep in your krep they are no longer recognizable!"

"What about the money?"

"Money! You're worried about money, are you? I'll tell you this: money isn't going to help you where you're going!"

"Oh, ho! We don't tuck our tails between our legs!" chided Spiro.

"You're not listening, my friend. Have you no imagination? Do you know what it means to be tortured? Not to death, mind you, but to the very edge of it, where you can still feel everything they do to you? And when that's finally over, they'll not be done with us. We won't see anything once blindfolded, but I for one can already feel the fibers of a rope tightening around my neck. Or will it be the cold, worn surface of a wooden block they rest our heads upon? Either way, the moments anticipating what comes next will not be pleasant, and they will be our last."

"I thought we didn't want to be looking over our shoulders."

"Ah, yes. Well, at least we will have shoulders to look over."

"But Able and Elijah—"

"Are dead! Gods dammit, Spiro! I beg you! There is no longer reason to stay. The king's soldiers will kill our giant for us. They know what you look like and will be hunting us as well. If we're caught, we will be killed. The king will post a reward; those who would otherwise befriend us will be the first to turn us in. We can't buy anyone's silence—we've precious little money left. Barely enough to pay our way back home. Even with the coin, where would we stay? No one will take us in. We'll catch our death of cold out here."

Reynard glanced down the alley while he waited for Spiro's response. When there was none, he took it as a good sign. "Listen to reason, friend. A good life waits for us in Waterford. Let us go back tonight, and I promise you, the first meal there will be a bowl of mutton stew!"

"I may know a place."

"What's that?"

"Where we can stay. I may know a place." Spiro turned his head. A shaft of moonlight lit one side of his face.

Reynard's eyes widened at the sight of extensive swelling and multiple contusions. He hung his head in resignation. "You may know a place."

He could scarcely discern the outline of the building into which Spiro had disappeared. Not even the light of a full moon could make its way through the layers of forest leaves above him. He chewed the ragged edge of a fingernail and waited. When Spiro's slight frame reappeared, he spat in relief. "Where are we? What is this place?"

"It's the stablemaster's home." Hands on hips, Spiro brought his bruised and swollen face closer to Reynard and grinned. "Or used to be."

"He had no family? No wife or children?"

Spiro stared blankly at Reynard, his smile fading.

"You have no idea, do you! Quickly man, count beds! One stitch of a woman's clothing, one child's toy, and I swear I'll take my leave!"

Reynard adjusted the pile of clothes serving as his pillow. "We shan't freeze or starve this night, I'll grant you that," he said begrudgingly.

"Someone was using his noggin," said Spiro.

"Fishing for a thank you, are you? Words one might have thought to hear upon your release from prison. Someone was certainly using his noggin there. Not to mention his lock-picking skills. And sticking his neck out for you to boot!"

"Did I not thank you?"

"Hah! I suppose you did in your own way. What was it you said? Ah, yes: 'What took you so long?'"

"There. You see?"

Impossible! "Be that as it may, we must be off at first light. There's no telling who might come knocking on the morrow."

"The stablemaster's dead! Who might we expect?"

"Again you flaunt your lack of imagination, Spiro. Perhaps someone hired to cook or clean for the man. The tax collector. A relative seeking to settle the estate? A curious neighbor. The marshal or his men seeking clues to a murder. Please, there may not be room enough to accommodate them all."

Spiro did not respond. Reynard adopted a less condescending tone. "We are at a serious crossroads, my friend."

Silence.

"I would ask you a question, Spiro." Reynard waited a moment to let that find its way through the dark. "A serious question which deserves a serious response. Not your customary wit. Do you think yourself capable of such a thing?"

"I shall try, but the wit comes naturally."

"Granted."

"And is most difficult to bridle."

"Hardly a promising start. Tell me, please, what binds you to this place? What is so important that we risk our lives for it?"

"You said yourself... my strategy never changes."

"Ah, yes. Kill them all. We're back to that, are we?"

"I was never of another mind."

"It's as simple as that, is it?"

"It is."

"Kill them all, and you are finished with Fostead?"

"Finished."

"Very well, then. Might we be more specific?"

"The giant."

"Yes, of course. A thorn in our side from the start. And now he's killed your friends... Who else?"

"Anyone who gets in the way."

"That's it? 'Kill them all' has been distilled to one man?"

"One giant, and all who get in the way."

"And once he draws his last breath, you will return with me to Waterford?"

"Why would I not?"

"This is most important, Spiro. Whether I stay or go tomorrow depends upon your answer. You must swear it. The very moment the giant's heart stops beating you will leave this place?"

"I swear it."

"No matter how he dies."

"How do you mean?"

"How he perishes—the manner of his demise—can be of no consequence. You must leave regardless. You mustn't say that it can only be by your hand or with a gods damn baby klubandag, do you get my meaning? The king holds the giant now, and will likely cut his head off for all the murders he's committed. You're not going to be invited to wield the axe. Do you understand? If we are exceptionally lucky, you may watch him die. One has to wonder why you didn't kill him whilst you had the chance."

"That bitch!"

"What? Nonsense! I'm speaking of the opportunity that presented itself before she introduced herself to you. You pricked the giant two or three times in the legs, at your leisure, when one good thrust in the chest would have finished him."

"You were watching, were you?"

"Everyone was watching, you dolt! You nearly got us both killed with your theatrics."

"My what?"

"Your stupidity!" yelled Reynard. "What were you thinking? The giant is still alive. And you're now recognizable! Having you by my side is akin to..." Reynard paused at the sudden recollection of the bruises on Spiro's face. "I may as well go walking about with a signed confession, is all. Listen, we'll need to disguise you if we're to venture into town. It's impossible to make you any taller. Far too much work to make you pleasing to the eye. Come now, friend. Where's your sense of humor? You know, it was mutton stew that killed that soldier. It was all I could find to put the poison in."

A loud sigh ended Spiro's silence.

Reynard chuckled. "Thank the gods he didn't offer you any!"

Ruler Two

Ruler Two was not partial to the borderlands that separated desert from forest. It was as though they tried too hard to be too many things and failed to be anything worthwhile as a result. The Lawless Lands were desolate and mostly barren, but their undulating dunes were beautiful, and there was something earnest in their lack of pretense. The realm's forests were primal and majestic; scented and alive.

But here, in the transition between pure sand and fertile soil, sparse clumps of struggling grasses grew like weeds beneath twisted spikewood trees. Stunted shrubs took what little shelter scattered boulders could provide.

There was nothing attractive about it.

It seemed only fitting that the prattlers would have feasted here. The disturbing signs of their past presence were difficult to ignore.

Ruler Five laughed. "You worry too much, friend." He kicked a sun-bleached human skull across the ground. It bounced several times before clattering to a stop amidst a pile of skeletal parts.

"And you too little." Ruler Two was convinced that Five was choosing meeting sites he thought likely to make his companion uneasy. *Don't give him the satisfaction!*

"Relax," said Five, flashing teeth whiter than the dried bone he picked up. "They're underground this time of day." He shielded his eyes from the sun and wiped his brow.

"How reassuring." Ruler Two scanned the horizon. A lone rider appeared to shimmer in the distant heat.

"Charise." Ruler Five tossed the bone end over end into the gruesome stockpile. "Good thing we weren't here when this happened. We're just lean and tough enough to suit the prattlers' tastes. They'd fancy us, you know."

"Disgusting. How would you know? You speak their language, do you?"

Ruler Five chuckled. "All you need do is check that pile to know I speak the truth. Surely you can tell by those remains how many women and children were eaten here. Very few, I'll wager."

Ruler Two declined Five's invitation. He watched instead as the horse bearing Charise entered the abandoned campsite. It did not matter how many times he saw her; she was always fascinating. She wore a long thin duster coat made of white linen. It was slit up the sides to her hips, revealing the fact that she wore very little underneath. Her long dark legs were exposed as her sinewy body slid smoothly to the ground. The gold serpent he remembered encircling her arm at The Cauldron now slithered around her ankle.

"You've already eaten, I see," she said, her large brown eyes trained on the jumble of bones. "I was so hoping to join you."

She was only half-kidding, Ruler Two was certain. "Can we get down to business?" he asked.

"Two's a bit squeamish, I'm afraid," said Five.

"Ah, well, business it is, then. The Prince of Quills is no more." Charise cocked her sculpted face as though looking for approval.

"How can we be certain? Have you any proof?" asked Ruler Two. Did she expect them to simply take her word for it?

"Proof!" Charise stiffened. "Was that in our contract?" She glared at Ruler Five.

"It was not." Five raised his hands to calm her. "Ruler Two does not—"

"I told you to educate him!"

"Educate me?" said Ruler Two angrily. "You were hired to kill a man! Now you request payment. Am I not permitted to ask for evidence the job is done?"

"Listen, Two," said Five. "Proof of death must be requested in advance. It—"

Charise put a finger to Five's lips. "You've had your chance." She approached Ruler Two until her mouth was inches from his. "Five is right. Proof of death must be requested in advance. And can you imagine why? Because securing proof affects the manner in which a job is performed, and we don't like disagreements after the fact, do we? How should I know what would satisfy you?" She paused to let him think. "Would you require a full body? Just a head, its face undisturbed? A ring finger, perhaps, with jewelry still intact?" She pressed her chest against his.

Gods above! What is she doing?

"No?" said Charise. "Something more personal, perhaps—"

Two felt her chest rise and fall against his, her hand suddenly groping between his legs!

"An appendage with which you are more familiar, perhaps?" She grinned as her fingers squeezed his genitals through his trousers.

Gods help me!

"You can see why it would be important to determine what constitutes proof of death in advance. Obtaining it can be difficult; it requires close contact with the victim. And it affects the price of the contract. A ring finger is far cheaper than a full body, as you might imagine."

Ruler Two swallowed hard as Charise backed away, a mischievous glint in her brown eyes.

"Consider yourself educated," said Ruler Five, looking on in amusement. "Charise is a much better teacher than I, don't you think? For what it's worth, I've never asked for proof of death. It's a worthless frill, a crafty ploy by The Guild to prey on the emotions of its clients. In my experience, the word of an assassin is proof enough. Their reputation is at stake, and any failure would soon become self-evident. Let us concentrate on more important matters. Two more must die before the moon is full."

"The woman and the king," said Charise knowingly. "You have two quarters. More than enough time if used wisely."

"What would you suggest?" Ruler Two did his best to appear unruffled.

"Wait for the king to leave his castle. Slipping inside is possible, but should be considered a last resort. It would be quite challenging... and costly."

"And if he doesn't leave?" asked Two. "How long before we pursue him in the palace?"

"One quarter, I should think. Until just after Six Moons."

"Is there some way to entice him out?" wondered Five aloud.

"I doubt that will be necessary," said the assassin.

"Why's that?" asked Ruler Two.

"Six Moons is nearly upon us. The royals always make a showing that day. They like to parade themselves through the streets. A perfect time to send him to the gods. Plenty of cover, lots of distractions. Easy." Charise cocked her head. "If he leaves the castle before, so much the better. There's no cover near it, but if he distances himself...goes into town, or visits his loved ones at The House of All Gods, which he is wont to do quite often...we will have him."

"You'll need to be watching, then," said Ruler Two.

"Yes. Eyes on the castle gates as soon as possible, starting tonight, and remaining there until the king is dead. It might seem a bit much, but just watching doesn't cost you terribly, and it'll ensure we're ready if an opportunity presents itself. One never knows, the king might entertain a sudden urge to go riding, or to visit some noble's manor. And should he venture out at night, for even just a stroll outside the castle gates, the dark will gift him to us."

Ruler Five nodded. "And the woman?"

Charise scoffed. "First off, I don't believe the stories, so if it was me... Well, I wouldn't worry much about her. If she shows her face, kill her for good measure, but otherwise..."

"It's not you," Ruler Two said, "so..."

"In that case, you'll want two assassins, one focused on the king, the other watching for the woman. Neither distracted from their task should the other get busy. You don't want the king slipping through your fingers just because your lone assassin is occupied with putting the woman down. This way, should the king and his seer leave the castle together, but then go separate ways, you still can hunt both down."

Now we're getting somewhere!

"Let's be clear," Charise said. "We don't want any further misunderstandings, do we? What if the king should offer himself to us before the woman does? If you continue to insist that she be killed first, well, you'll have missed that opportunity. Can you afford that, given your deadline?"

Noggods! It's an excellent question. How might the magister answer? "What do you think?" Two asked Ruler Five.

Five bared his snow-white teeth and shrugged. "It's your plan, Two. Whatever you decide."

Oh, so now it's my plan, is it? "Very well then. The woman first, as long as that can be arranged before the celebration of Six Moons. Beginning that day, both she and the king are marked, and the order of their deaths shall be of no consequence."

"Clear enough," said Charise. "What about proof of death?"

Ruler Two bristled. "I've been educated, haven't I? If I want proof, I'll ask for it."

THE SEAMSTRESS OF THE DARK

"Sorrow is like quicksand, Sibil. The more you struggle, the more it drags you down. Let go, and you will be released much sooner." Adrian Dunn to his brooding daughter, one moon before his death.

Sibil Dunn

Theos dead? Killed by an assassin? Tristan in mourning with his family? None of it was real. It simply was not possible. Sibil hoped at some point she would waken from her nightmare, much relieved. Laugh about it, even, with both twins by her side. Until then, it was best to keep inside herself, eyes closed, and not allow distractions. Stay blind, silent, numb, and let the bad dream run its course.

But she could not shut out the sound of dirt and gravel grinding under boots, threatening to invade her safe cocoon.

From her seat against the wall, she allowed herself the narrowest of eyelid slits to watch a trio of big men lumber to the infirmary's door, then try to open it. One of them, his shoulder bandaged, looked as though he might belong inside. She shifted her position, resolved to rise and follow on their heels should they succeed in entering. The one person she would talk to now still lay inside, wounded.

The trio tried the latch a second time and, finding the door locked, banged upon it with their fists. "Open up in there!" one of them said. His companions grunted in approval.

A small aperture in the door slid open, allowing a woman's curt voice to escape the infirmary. "State your business."

"We've come to see Rolft Aerns," the man closest to the aperture said forcefully.

Rolft! Sibil's eyelids lifted to allow a better look at the speaker. His unruly hair and full beard disappeared into a long fur coat, making him appear like some creature of the woods.

"You'll kindly let us in so that we don't have to break the door down." The creature nodded at his comrades, who nodded back at him.

Ruffians!

"You'll have to see the marshal. No visitors." The aperture closed with a crisp clack.

"Hmmpf." The largest of the three expelled a loud breath.

"Same as last night," said one of his friends disapprovingly.

"That's it then," said the creature. "Do we know where the marshal is?"

"He won't allow it," Sibil said. Dispensing bad news felt strangely satisfying.

"What's that?" asked the creature.

Wait! His voice is familiar, is it not? "The marshal. He won't allow it," she said confidently, commanding the ruffians' full attention.

"Why not?" said the largest of the three.

"He wouldn't say, but I know that Rolft is badly wounded."

"How would you know that?"

Were they really doubting her? She was in no mood for that. "I was there! He fought three men! It was hardly fair."

"Three men!" The creature clenched his fists. "What did I tell him? Plenty to go around!"

Again, that familiar voice! "He killed two of them!" said Sibil. "The one I saw was bigger than any of you!"

"And who might you be?" asked the creature.

It came to her then; it was the shadow from the night she and Reggie had brought Rolft to the castle!

"I'm Sibil."

"Thistle?"

"Sibil! Are you friends of Rolft?"

"Since before you were born, by the looks of you," said one.

"We're friends of his, all right," said the shadow. "And what might your business with him be?"

"The same as yours, I suppose."

"All right, lass. If you say so." The shadow eyed the dagger Sibil held as he motioned to his comrades. "Come on, lads. Thistle's going to keep watch over Rolft while we hunt down the marshal."

Sibil watched them leave, the largest shoving his friends good-naturedly. One of them said something about paring potatoes and the others laughed. Her brow furrowed. They were not worth further thought. She examined the dagger gifted to her by the Godfrey boys. Theos had fashioned its bone handle, embedding in its base a small red jewel supplied by Tristan.

She closed her eyes and drifted back into her cocoon.

Overseer Reynard Rascall

"G'day, friend."

The sound of Reynard's voice clearly startled the apothecary. The bottle in his hand froze mid-way on its journey to a shelf.

"Where'd you come from?" The old man squinted behind his spectacles.

Frightened you, did I? Thought you'd locked that door? "Ah, well, you were kind enough to assist me yesterday."

The shopkeeper brought the bottle back to the counter. It clattered as he set it down. "Did I?" His mouth hung open.

"Most assuredly. Do you not remember?" Reynard moved close enough for the shop-keeper to make out his features.

"No, I don't." The lump in the old man's throat appeared to clog his airway.

"No?" Reynard removed his hat and raked his long black hair back across his head.

The apothecary stared at the scar that action disclosed. He shook his head.

"Pity. I find myself in need of your assistance once again. What was the name of that poison you gave me yesterday?"

"Mullwyd," whispered the old man.

"Ah yes! Mullwyd! I thought you didn't remember me."

"What? Oh. Yes, I do now. Of course. Yes, it was mullwyd. Mullwyd, yes. For your horses, right? It did the job, did it? You need more? I'm sure I have it. Yes...in the back. I'll just take a look, shall I? You stay here...I shan't be long."

Reynard leaned against the counter and watched the apothecary stumble into the dark recesses of the shop. It could not be helped. He closed his eyes and listened to the old man's shuffling footsteps, the back door opening, boot soles scraping the floor, a muffled cry, soft grunting, something falling to the floor.

The sounds of Spiro introducing himself.

Rolft Aerns

Rolft drifted in and out of consciousness, struggling to distinguish between what he dreamed and what was real. The line between those two worlds seemed to ebb and flow until, at last, he was certain he was awake.

And no longer in physical danger. The last thing he remembered was the sensation of supportive hands beneath his body. Lifting him, transporting him. Friendly voices. People tending to his wounds. His wounds! He tried to move his limbs. They were restrained. Leather straps bound him spread-eagle to a bed. Pain in his legs made him wonder if they would work even were they free. Bandages around his head covered one eye. Still, he had been to the palace infirmary often enough to recognize his surroundings. He was in a corner of that large room, isolated from the few others being treated. There was no one near enough to talk to—by design, no doubt.

He recalled only bits and pieces of his fight with two big men at The Raven's Nest. He was fairly certain he had killed them both, and in doing so, compromised his ability to locate the others he had gone there to find. Not what he had planned.

The rest was even less clear. A small man—perhaps the one Jarod had described as a cat—stabbing him in the leg. Someone else knocking the small man over—the Dunn girl? His thoughts were interrupted by the approach of a man he had not seen in two almons.

"This is how you treat retired soldiers, is it?" Rolft asked.

"It is not," said Marshal Carson. "But neither is it the manner in which we treat a murderer of... let's see, I've lost count. Three in the old warehouse, by your own admission, I am told. Two in The Raven's Nest night before last; in front of witnesses, no less. Two more there just yesterday—I saw with my own eyes. And one in the alley, if I have not taken too great a liberty fleshing out Miss Dunn's story. That's eight at least, my friend. By all rights, you should be in the dungeon, stretched out on the rack. The fact that you are not is due to your past service."

"Could it be much worse than this?" Rolft flexed his strapped hands as best he might.

"Yes, it could. Decidedly so. Explain yourself so that you may never know."

"Explain myself." Rolft scoffed.

"Do you deny the killings?"

"I do not. They deserved to die."

"For what offense?"

"You'll not believe me." *But what have I to lose?* "The first six...for the deaths of Queen Isadora and Princess Lewen."

"What's happened to you? The princess died in Dewhurst. Dragged by her horse. The queen fell to her death! You were there!"

"The princess rode that morning. By herself. Six men intent on robbing the retreat waylaid her. Beat her and bound her to her horse. The ties came loose. Her boot was caught in the stirrup. She was dragged to death. The rest you know."

Carson slowly shook his head. "It is not possible."

"I knew you would not believe it."

"Garth, Yurik, Fereliss...all were there with you!"

"They had no way of knowing."

"I have heard them recount that day so many times I can recite it." The marshal's ire rose. "You were at each others' sides. You each saw the same events unfold. There were no thieves. You did not track the princess."

"I went alone the next morning."

"Alone. How convenient! What prompted you? A sudden urge?"

"The blood on the princess's horse. A bloody handprint that could not belong to her. High on the horse's rump."

"Absurd! A bloody print that you alone could see? Where were your friends? They have not once mentioned a bloody print."

"Busy with the queen."

"So you followed the princess' trail. The thieves were still there, I imagine. Waiting to tell you of their plans, and how they beat the princess?"

"The tracks were clear. Six bootprints in addition to Lewen's. Six men."

"You kept that to yourself, did you? Then lied to me when giving your account? I'll finish the story for you, shall I? By some miracle, you found the six. I suppose you tracked them by their bootprints all the way to Fostead two almons later. Then killed them, is that right? That's only six. By last count, we were up to eight!"

"I was looking for the men the six thieves worked for. The two I killed yesterday got in the way."

"Got in the way!" said the marshal doubtfully. "What about Leo Bartlett?"

"I don't know who that is."

"Baron Treadwell's cook?"

"Why would I kill a baron's cook?" *What are you getting at?*

"Sergeant Faraday, Jarod Kelter, Timmil Childs?"

"Killed by those I hunt. A small man, perhaps the one who stabbed me outside The Raven's Nest, and his partner."

The marshal shook his head. "And Bohun Barr?"

"What?" *That can't be right!* "Bohun's dead?"

"They killed him as well, did they?" The marshal signaled the infirmary staff. "Or was that you?"

Rolft fought at his restraints, rattling the bed.

Marshal Erik Carson

Carson kicked a clod of dirt as though it were his enemy. He should not have lost his temper. How could the gods allow a man like that to fall so far from grace? He hoped the physician would administer the toxin soon, that it would work quickly and that the royal guard would feel no pain. He prayed the gods would still grant Rolft access to Baelon above. He hoped the warrior would find peace there.

He was nearly at The Shaft when he noticed Major Stronghart on a collision course with him. The soldier's head rolled from side to side. His hands rubbed his thighs as he walked. More bad news on the way.

"The prisoner in Fostead...he's escaped. Whoever freed him poisoned the man on watch...Sergeant Fields. And—"

Carson swore loudly.

"And you can guess where they got the poison. Old Harley Simpkin, the apothecary. He's dead as well."

Carson shot a quick glance back toward the infirmary. Clearly, this was not Rolft's handiwork. *What in Baelon is going on?*

"Tell me, what has he to say for himself?"

Carson ran his fingers through his hair. "His story stretches one's imagination, sire, and there is no one to bear witness to his accounts."

"Entertain me."

"It is hardly entertainment. It involves the queen and princess. He faults several men for your daughter's death, m'lord. He further claims to have hunted down her killers."

The king became quite still. "How could that be? It was an accident. He was there! As were others!"

"At the royal retreat, 'tis true. But Rolft insists the princess was beaten the morning she went riding."

"Beaten?" The king's jaw dropped.

"By thieves planning to rob The House at Dewhurst. He claims Lewen stumbled upon them by accident."

"What proof does he offer?"

"None, sire."

The king studied Carson's face. "Yet you wish to believe him. His story—it's possible?"

"As I said, sire, it stretches the imagination. But for the same reason what he says can not be proven, neither can it be disproved. And there is the character of the man himself to consider. His devotion to the crown is not in question. Nor do I doubt his own belief in the tale he has spun."

"All in his favor. But the notion that these, these thieves, were somehow involved in Lewen's death. There were others of the royal guard present the day she was killed, were there not?"

"There were. Too preoccupied with the queen's death, if one is to believe Rolft, to notice what he alone observed. It was the princess' horse, sire. Rolft claims to have seen—"

"Claims to have seen what!?" The king raised his eyebrows as the marshal bolted from his chair.

"A thousand pardons!" Carson cried, running from the room.

"Caleb!" Carson entered the stables in such a rush he almost knocked the old man over. Caleb clung to the handle of his pitchfork, its tines providing him a third leg to aid his balance as the marshal grasped him by both shoulders. "Caleb. Two almons ago. The queen and princess...their last visit to Dewhurst. Did you accompany them?"

"Course not." The old man snorted. "You know I don't travel no more! Especially not no overnighter! That's a job for a young man if ever there was one."

"Reggie then, was it?"

"You seen any other young grooms about?"

"Reggie!" the marshal cried.

"Out back," Caleb said. "What's this all about?"

"Reggie!" Carson whirled to exit the barn just as Reggie entered.

"What is it, Marshal?"

"You remember what I said, 'bout bein' my eyes and ears?"

"Yes, sir." The boy's eyes darted to Caleb for clues.

"You remember two almons ago? Your trip to Dewhurst with the queen and princess?"

Reggie stood with his mouth open, nodding slowly.

"You remember the morning of their deaths?"

"Of course. I'll never forget."

"This is very important, Reggie."

"Yes, Marshal."

"The princess' horse."

"Shadow."

"Yes, Shadow."

"She named him that on account of he followed her wherever she went," said the stable boy.

"And he brought her back that morning. The princess. Shadow brought her back. Is that right?"

"He did. I was waiting in the barn for their return. I both heard and saw them coming."

"Did you tend to Shadow?"

"Yes, Marshal. As soon as Rolft cut the princess free."

"Tell me."

Reggie shrugged. "I took him to the barn."

"Did Rolft accompany you?"

"No. He stayed with the princess. And the queen."

Carson's entire frame relaxed. "You never saw Rolft in the barn?"

"No, sir."

"And Shadow?"

"He was frightened, I remember. Took some time to calm him down."

"But he was not hurt? There was no blood on him?" Reggie was silent long enough to cause the marshal to repeat himself. "There was no blood on him, is that right?"

"Shadow was uninjured, but there was blood. So much I went to fetch a bigger pail of water."

"Show me where."

Reggie looked confused. "Where I got the wa— Oh! You mean the blood?"

"Yes, lad. Can you show me?"

Reggie approached a horse tethered outside its stall. "She was dragged a long ways, the princess, you know?" Carson and Caleb watched as Reggie ran his hand along the horse's left flank in a reassuring manner. "Her boot was twisted and caught inside the stirrup. Left side of Shadow. Most of the blood was here, below his rear chestnuts." Reggie looked back at the marshal as he swept his hand across the lower part of the horse's back left leg. "But there was some here as well, along his belly, and some by the saddle, too."

"But none on the other side, is that right?" asked Carson. Reggie straightened, one hand on the horse's back. He again stared at the marshal without speaking. "Reggie?"

"I'm not sure."

"What do you mean, not sure?"

"I mean, I'm sure. It's just that..."

"What is it, lad?"

"There was blood. On the right side. Here." The young groom laid his hand upon the horse's right buttock. "But then..." He looked at the marshal in anguish. "Then it disappeared."

"Disappeared?" Carson looked for help from Caleb, but the old man shook his head.

"I saw it," said Reggie. "I know I did. But then I went for water, and when I returned..." *Don't tell me it was gone!*

"It was gone," whispered Reggie. "It's come to me in dreams so many times, I tell myself it wasn't ever real. But it was. I know because of what it looked like. You can't forget something like that."

"Like what? Tell me."

"Like a bloody hand. On Shadow's rump." The stable boy splayed his fingers and laid his hand on the animal's rear. "Like this."

"It's true then?" asked the king grievously.

Carson nodded slowly.

King Axil closed his eyes and tilted his head back. "All this time..." His shaggy locks trembled as his head lolled from side to side. "Two almons of regret. Tortured by belief that it could have been prevented." He stared at the marshal through welling eyes. "It has been difficult to bear, but this... I cannot live with this." The marshal looked on helplessly. "The thought of some man's hands on my daughter...her blood spilled whilst I was...what, preparing for a farging feast? And Isadora...you know as well as I what they say."

"M'lord. I do not think it—"

"That she blamed herself for Lewen's death! Do you think for a moment that had she known the truth, she would have thrown herself off that balcony? No! She would not have rested until the murderous lot were hanging by their necks!"

"Most are dead, m'lord."

"But two still breathe."

"It would appear so, m'lord."

King Axil's frame shuddered. "I don't care if it takes the entire army. You will bring them here. I would look upon them with my own eyes before they die."

Rolft Aerns

Rolft watched warily as Marshal Carson approached, dagger in hand.

"How are you feeling?" asked the marshal.

"Like a pig, ready for slaughter. You've come to finish the job, have you?"

"I deserve that, I suppose." The marshal managed a smile as he cut the leather ties that bound Rolft's hands to the bed.

"What's happened?" Rolft moved his arms slowly to a position where he could rub his wrists.

Marshal Carson cut the bonds that held his legs. "Why did you remove the blood from Lewen's horse? Why keep that from the other guards? And me?"

Rolft's brow wrinkled as he bent his toes. "You believe me now?"

The marshal sat on the side of the bed. "I am still perplexed. "Why?" he asked again.

Rolft exhaled loudly. "It is a fair question. I have asked it many times myself."

"And your answer?"

Rolft flexed his calves, relieved to find them both responsive. When he tried to bend his knees, however, one thigh cried out in pain. He grimaced, his hands reaching instinctively to cover his wounds. "Rage, I suppose. I was so mad at the queen for not listening. For allowing the princess to ride alone. Angry with Lewen as well. But I knew. I knew I was to blame. I should not have let her go, regardless of the circumstances."

"The queen and princess did not die by your hand, Rolft, nor by your lack of action."

"That's how it felt. Their deaths were on my head. Had I shared that with the others—Garth, Yurik, or Fereliss—they would have thrown their lives away to help me."

"Why not tell me?"

Rolft closed his eyes. "It felt personal. I kept it to myself. By the time I realized that was not for the best, it was too late. The longer I kept it, the less wise it seemed to share. There is no good answer. A mistake. No more, no less. Why the change of heart?"

"Reggie, the stable boy. He remembers it. The bloody handprint—just as you described. High on Shadow's right rear. Too high for Lewen to have reached whilst she was being dragged. Had to have been put there before that."

"Not by her. It was much too large to be Lewen's. It belonged to one of those I killed."

"There were six, you said."

"I knew by the tracks they left at Dewhurst, but the number was confirmed by the first I killed—Kole Cantry."

"The man in the alley."

"Just so."

"You found him how?"

"I overheard some toss-pots bragging at The King's Inn. They were drunk. One of them mentioned the princess. I followed him to the alley. He told me what happened that day in Dewhurst. Gave me the names of the others, and their plan to gather at the old warehouse. The rest I think you can piece together." He waited as the marshal processed this. "Bohun's really dead?"

"I'm sorry to say. Killed the same day you slew those two at The Raven's Nest. Or the night before. Probably by the same little man who stabbed you in the leg. Bohun had similar wounds."

"Where is the wee man now?"

"He was taken to The Hold in Fostead, but he's since escaped. If he had anything to do with the deaths of the queen and princess, though, he won't get far."

"It was Raggett Grymes' lot that killed the princess. Members of The Takers Guild. Jarod told me Grymes worked for two men. Your prisoner, the wee man, fits the look of one. The other's tall with dark hair to his shoulders. A scar on his forehead. They killed Jarod and the others at the inn as well, I'm sure of it."

"Dark hair and a scar. It's not the first time I've heard that," said the marshal. "Jarod said the smaller one was like a cat with a beak for a nose."

"The barkeep from The Raven's Nest...how does he fare?"

"Peter? Not well, but he'll live."

"He can better describe them. The little man and his partner with the scar."

"Get your rest. The king will want to speak with you when time allows. Meanwhile, another waits to see you."

"Fereliss? Yurik?"

The marshal laid a reassuring hand on Rolft's shoulder. "You have more friends than you know."

The Dunn girl, Sibil, held a small bouquet of flowers in her hands.

"You look better," she said in greeting.

Rolft's good-natured scoff turned quickly into a coughing fit. "Better than what?"

"Better than the last time I laid eyes on you."

"Outside The Raven's Nest?"

The girl smiled. "No. I came by earlier. As soon as the marshal allowed. You were sleeping, but you didn't have as much color in your face." She touched one of his wrists. "Is it true they bound you to the bed?"

"A simple misunderstanding."

"And these?" Sibil gestured to the old scars on Rolft's left forearm. "Another misunderstanding?"

"You could say that. Someone thought long ago to kill the queen. I was of another mind."

"What? Oh! Was it during Six Moons? I know this story!"

"You followed me in town. Why?"

"Because of what you said. In the barn with Reggie. That you still serve Lewen. I have so few ties left to her myself. And because of what happened in the alley. Then finding you on the roadside. Do you not find it odd?" Sibil shifted one foot uneasily. "I suppose I imagined some sort of bond between us."

"Did you? You've only saved my life twice, you know. It takes three to make a bond."

Sibil blushed. "The first time hardly counts. Were it not for Reggie, you might just be a pile of bones by the roadside now."

"Hmpf. We'll call it even, shall we?"

"If you say so."

"There's not many who would have done what you did outside The Raven's Nest. I can count on one hand those I know. I myself have few remaining ties to Lewen. I remember the two of you together. Always laughing. It is a good memory."

Sibil sniffled and bit her lip. She placed a hand lightly on Rolft's forehead. "You still have a fever. I should let you rest." Her hand moved to his shoulder.

Rolft smothered it with his own. "If there was not a bond, lass, rest assured there is one now."

Sibil laid the flowers by his bedside. "They're not from me. Lewen was always the one for flowers. She would have wanted you to have them."

Rolft's eyes opened slowly, his muscles tensing at the sight of three large figures looming over him.

"Marshal said you didn't look so good." Yurik's voice was a welcome sound.

"We reminded 'im," said Fereliss, "you never did look good."

Rolft relaxed and forced a smile.

Garth maintained his serious countenance. "It was I who told the marshal you were here. And about the warehouse slayings."

Rolft exhaled through his nose dismissively. "No matter. I would have done the same."

"You were busy whilst we were away," said Yurik. "Or so we're told."

"By who?"

"Some by the marshal. Some by the young lass who sits outside each morning, waiting for you to heal."

Rolft glanced at Fereliss. "I could have used your help, to be sure. As you say, plenty to go around."

"Giants, no less!" said Fereliss. "Or so we're told. Ah, well, we would have been there and seen for ourselves, wouldn't we, if you hadn't run off again without so much as a word. We would have followed you, except our friend, the marshal, he put his arm around my shoulders and said to me, 'Fereliss, I hear your friend the mischief-maker is about to make more mischief. Don't ask me how I know, but I do.'" Fereliss shot a reproachful look at Garth before continuing. "'I also know,' the marshal said, 'how bad an influence the mischief-maker is on you well-meaning lads.'" Fereliss tapped his chest. "Well-meaning lads...thet'd be the three of us. 'Thus,' the marshal said, 'I send you on a task of great importance, where you cannot be tempted by the mischief-maker.'" Fereliss pointed at Rolft's wounds. "Alas, we were called to serve our king, or we never would've let that happen, would we, lads?"

"And how did you fare?" asked Rolft.

"How do you mean?"

"On your task of great importance."

"Ah. Well, we rode without Major Stronghart, you see, so..."

"The God of Fortune was not with you," said Rolft.

"Most decidedly not," said Yurik, drawing Rolft's attention to his bandaged shoulder. "One of Sir Godfrey's boys, Squire Theos, was killed."

"What happened?"

"Never mind that," said Fereliss. "Was there something you wished to tell us?" He raised his eyebrows expectantly. "About the queen and princess, perhaps?"

"The marshal told you?"

His visitors nodded in unison.

"It was difficult to swallow," said Fereliss.

"It is the truth," Rolft said.

"What happened to the princess and the queen we do not doubt," said Fereliss. "I speak of you withholding that from us."

"Ahh." Rolft sighed resignedly.

"Difficult to swallow," repeated Fereliss.

"It counts for little now, I know, but at the time I thought that if I told you—"

"We would follow you to Baelon below and burn with you?"

Rolft nodded.

"We would, of course!" said Garth quickly.

"Of course we would!" said Yurik.

Fereliss grinned. "Without a doubt, we would! And our friend, the marshal, he would have put us all in chains. Or worse. We understand." Fereliss paused. "Perhaps if you had told him...why did you not? He may have starch in his breeches, but he is wise and fair, nonetheless."

"Agreed. I was not thinking clearly."

"Clearly not."

"The marshal says you killed them...those that beat the princess," said Garth.

"Those who tied her to her horse that morning, yes. But the two they work for wander free. One of them gave me these wounds. As soon as I am able, I'll hunt them down as well." Rolft noted the discomfort on his friends' faces as they exchanged glances. "What is it? What's wrong?"

"We know about the two as well," said Fereliss.

"The one who escaped from The Hold and his partner with the scar," said Yurik.

"Sergeant Fields was killed whilst guarding the little one," Garth said.

Rolft gathered fistfuls of bedding.

"We've just come from the marshal," said Fereliss.

"We're to finish what you started," said Garth.

"How's that?" asked Rolft.

"The two that still walk free. We're to track them down and bring them back."

"Who is?"

"We are. The three of us," said a subdued Fereliss.

"Whilst I lie here in this bed? Not likely!" Rolft gritted his teeth, struggling to raise himself onto his elbows.

"I thought you might say that," said Fereliss. "Lest you forget, my friend, we serve the king. We did not choose this path. The marshal—"

"We all choose our paths!" yelled Rolft. "Help me up so that I may follow mine!"

Sibil Dunn

Sibil's pace slowed upon entering the infirmary, her view of Rolft blocked by the backs of three large figures standing at his bedside. Even from behind, they were easily recognizable. *Ruffians!* Her interest in seeing Rolft waned, but she edged closer nonetheless, then stopped, uncertain. She could leave and come back another time. Or she could join them. Or... they were talking...

She stumbled blindly from the infirmary, her world turned upside down by what she had overheard. Lewen's death—not an accident at all! She found her way behind the soldiers' barracks to collapse in a confused stupor. Queasiness and shock overwhelmed her. *Tied to her horse? Beaten by several men!* It was too horrific to imagine. Sibil vomited, then sobbed until she was spent.

Her ragged breathing slowed. Deep, calming breaths. She felt the dirt beneath her hands. A warm breeze brushed her temples. The emptiness in her began to fill with anger. Where were the seven gods when her friends most needed them? Innocence, naivety, trust that good would triumph over evil—these were things Lewen and Theos had taken to their graves. *Useless baggage! Evil walks boldly among us! The steward; those who had tried to kill the king; whoever murdered Theos. Lewen's attackers...*Sibil gasped. *Was the man Rolft killed in the alley one of them? Of course! How close was I that night to sharing Lewen's fate?*

"Prepare yourselves!" she heard the sergeant-at-arms cry out. "Touch tips!"

Sibil watched through glassy eyes as the old man strolled across the training circle below her. Dust rose from beneath his feet, roiling like the acid in her stomach. *'He's not going to invite you closer.'* Sibil's fingers brushed the smooth hilt of the dagger in her waistband. One leg began to twitch. Her foot tapped the ground repeatedly. It was all she could do to keep from launching herself at him like a stone from a catapult.

Wait!

Out of the corner of her eye, she saw Marshal Carson and a tall soldier round the barracks and stride down the slope behind them. She sprang to her feet and followed, catching them just as they reached the sparring grounds. She made no attempt to hide her reddened eyes or tear-stained face.

"Miss Dunn," said the marshal, "is everything all right?"

Two squires in the center of the circle had just completed their contest, and the marshal's arrival drew the attention of all.

"I wish to be trained!" said Sibil unabashedly.

There were titters from the squires within earshot. The tall soldier accompanying the marshal stared them down as Sergeant Cogswell made his way across the grounds. "Marshal Carson! Major Stronghart! To what do we owe the honor?"

The marshal continued to assess Sibil's state. "We cannot tarry, Sergeant. The major updates me on the castle's defenses, and thinks better in the open air. I trust you prepare a strong and noble future for the kingdom?"

"I wish to be trained," said Sibil emphatically. Even her breathing was determined.

"What was that?" asked Cogswell. A nearby squire whispered something to his neighbor.

"I said, I wish to be trained."

"Now listen here, lass," said the sergeant-at-arms.

Marshal Carson held up his hand, continuing to return Sibil's stare. "The king has been quite clear with respect to Madam Dunn and her daughter. His words: whatever they wish, whenever they wish it."

"I wish to be trained."

"Miss Dunn," said Major Stronghart in a kindly but cautionary tone.

"So be it," said the marshal. "Sergeant!"

"Marshal?"

"You're conducting challenges?"

"Yes, m'lord, but—"

"The young lady is next."

Cogswell's steely gray eyes looked at him askance. "Marshal?"

"Has your hearing gone the way of your good nature, Sergeant?"

"No, sir!"

"Very well, then." Marshal Carson nudged Sibil into the training circle. She reached into her waistband and removed her dagger, handing it to Major Stronghart.

The sergeant-at-arms strode to the center of the circle, motioning for Sibil to follow. The two combatants there had not moved since their fight. Cogswell grabbed the fallen squire by his shirt and lifted him roughly to his feet. "You're not quite dead, after all! Back to the living you go!" The sergeant held his hand out, and the defeated squire surrendered his weapon before rejoining his comrades.

Sergeant Cogswell turned to the victor, who stood grinning at Sibil as he twirled his sword in one hand. "Well done, Squire Earl. But you still leave yourself open to counter-attacks. Squire Talbot would have made you pay several times. Discipline!" Squire Earl nodded curtly.

Cogswell's fingers beckoned Sibil.

She approached, shedding her tunic, her heart racing.

The circle of young men grew more agitated. "Come on, Earl!" said one.

"My sister's next!" cried another.

"Shut it!" yelled the sergeant-at-arms, spinning slowly to challenge all the boys with a menacing stare. "The next to flap his lips will square off with me! And I promise you, I'll not be kind!" The young men grew quiet. Cogswell handed Sibil the wooden sword, exchanging it for her tunic and muttering under his breath. "He's all bite, lass... no defense. Look for your opening."

Sibil glanced at her opponent. He grinned wickedly and winked at her as the sergeant-at-arms stepped back. She hefted her sword. It was heavier than she had imagined it would be.

"Prepare yourselves! Touch tips!"

Squire Earl stepped forward and pointed his wooden blade at Sibil's head. She hesitated, locking both hands tightly around her sword's grip before raising her blade to meet his. As soon as the tips touched, she heard the sergeant-at-arms cry, "Fight!"

And Earl was on her, his sword slashing through the air. It was all she could do to block it, but the sheer force of his blow drove her backward. The squire advanced, using his momentum to swing even harder. Still stumbling, she was late to defend the blow. His sword crashed into hers, snapping her wrists back and forcing her fingers to release their grip. Her sword flew from her hands as she fell backward. By the time she hit the ground, the point of Earl's sword was pressed against her chest. She was pinned to the ground, staring into his devilish grin.

"Stop!" cried the sergeant-at-arms.

The ring of squires erupted in approval.

Cogswell shot Marshal Carson a knowing look before striding back into the circle. "That's enough!" he shouted at the frenzied squires. "Enough, I say!" Squire Earl took a respectful step back as the sergeant approached. Sibil raised herself on her elbows. "All right, lass?" the sergeant asked, extending his hand. She nodded. "Up you get, then." Cogswell pulled her to her feet. She dusted herself off. The sergeant picked up her sword.

Major Stronghart turned to the marshal. "She's got some fire in her, I'll say that much. There aren't many la—"

"Daggers!" the marshal called out to the sergeant-at-arms.

Major Stronghart stood still, his mouth half open. Cogswell looked in disbelief at the marshal. "Beg pardon, m'lord?"

"If it pleases Miss Dunn," the marshal said.

"Daggers." It was as though the sergeant had never said the word before.

"Daggers?" Sibil glanced at the marshal, then turned to the sergeant. "Yes, please. Daggers."

Cogswell stared at her momentarily. He shook his head. "Squire Peters! Daggers to the circle!" One of the younger squires broke from the rest to fetch weapons from a nearby stockpile. He hurried back to present them to the sergeant and left with the wooden swords.

The sergeant tossed one of the smokewood daggers to Squire Earl, then turned to Sibil. "You sure you haven't had enough, lass? You don't have to do this."

"I want to. Please." She extended an open hand.

Cogswell grunted something unintelligible as he gave up the remaining weapon. Sibil hefted it, wrapping her fingers around its hilt. She brushed a wisp of hair across her forehead.

"All right, lass," the sergeant said resignedly. He raised both hands in the air as he stepped away from the combatants. "Naught to the head! And when I say 'stop,' you damn well stop! Prepare yourselves!"

Sibil slid one foot back, crouched low. Squire Earl followed suit, a smirk spreading across his face. He winked at her and tossed his wooden dagger from one hand to the other.

The ring of squires came to life again. "Slay the giant killer!" shouted one.

"Shut it!" yelled Sergeant Cogswell before others could join in.

Squire Earl grinned in approval, tossing the dagger deftly to his other hand.

"Fight!"

Sibil circled warily to her right, her eyes riveted on Squire Earl's knife. As it began yet another flight to the opposite hand, Sibil darted forward, hissing as she feinted. Both the sound and sudden movement startled the squire. His fingers closed too soon, missing the dagger in mid-air. Its hilt glanced off his knuckles, and the blade fell to the ground. He stared at Sibil before diving for the knife. She was on top of him instantly, her legs straddling his back, her weight flattening him against the ground. He clawed at the dirt as she grabbed his shirt with one hand and pressed her dagger against his neck with the other.

"Stop!" cried Sergeant Cogswell.

Sibil jumped to her feet. Squire Earl stood slowly, sheepishly brushing dirt from his clothes. "What was that?" he muttered. "Screaming like a girl. Unfair!"

The sergeant-at-arms was in his face. "Unfair, was it! Unfair?" Cogswell pressed his chest against the boy, pushing him back. "This is not some game of pitch and toss! You're fighting for your life! There's no such thing as unfair! Back to the line!"

Cogswell turned to Sibil. "Well done, lass." He reached out, inviting her to surrender her weapon.

Sibil's arms remained at her side, ignoring the sergeant's outstretched hand, her eyes searching the ring of squires.

"Again."

"What?" Sergeant Cogswell's brow wrinkled.

"Again."

The sergeant's eyes pleaded with the marshal.

"Again," said the marshal.

Cogswell withdrew his hand and yelled, "Squire Talbot!"

An undercurrent of murmurs rippled through the grounds as one of the taller squires broke from the ranks. He was at least as tall as the Godfrey twins. He moved confidently into the circle, appearing neither frightened nor reluctant.

A bigger target. Easier to hit. More flesh to cut. Stay calm! The closer the squire came, the taller he got, until he stopped growing just the other side of the sergeant. Sibil imagined the top of her head might pass below his armpits.

Be quicker. Be small!

"Naught to the head! Prepare yourselves!" Sergeant Cogswell handed Squire Talbot his dagger, then stepped back to join the marshal and major. "Now I'm curious," she heard him mutter under his breath. "Fight!"

Sibil crouched as low as she dared. She circled to her left. Squire Talbot moved with her, even more imposing with a dagger for an ally. She thanked the gods their weapons were not real. Talbot darted forward. Sibil backed as quickly away. Again. And again, as the squire feinted to gauge her reactions. His movements were not slow, but neither were they the lightning quick attacks she was used to from the Godfreys. Was he measuring her?

Baiting her? She waited for Talbot to put his weight on his forward foot, then delivered her first feint. He moved away easily. Smoothly.

"Hup!" Talbot sprang forward, his dagger slashing through the space Sibil had occupied before sidestepping. The two were quickly circling once again. Sibil felt a rush of adrenaline course through her. "Hup!" The squire lunged again, this time anticipating Sibil's sidestep. She narrowly avoided his blade, leaning back and lashing out simultaneously. Her dagger slid across his outstretched forearm.

"Hit!" cried the sergeant-at-arms. A chorus of 'oohs' and 'ahs' arose from the circle of restless squires. They began to shout and gesticulate. The sergeant let them be.

Sibil moved further back, out of Talbot's long range of attack, to stand for a moment's rest. Her opponent watched and waited. Sibil moved more quickly now. She circled right, then left, then right again. The squire moved more cautiously, reluctant to engage, his breathing slightly labored.

Sibil picked the pace up even more, nearly dancing as she circled her adversary. Squire Talbot spun slowly in a smaller circle, watching her, warding off her feints.

"Hup!" Suddenly, he advanced. Sibil darted away. The squire did not slow. He chased her, this way, that way, his momentum building, his large frame bearing down on her. When she abruptly halted, hands on knees, he lunged at her. Sibil dropped her pretense, dodging him. She slapped the wrist of the arm he thrust at her, grabbed a handful of shirtsleeve, and pulled him close. Their bodies pressed together, the point of her dagger between them.

"Stop!" cried Sergeant Cogswell.

Squire Talbot pushed off Sibil, tapping her smokewood blade with his. *Was that a tribute or resentment?* Cogswell intervened, relieving both combatants of their daggers. "Patience, Squire Talbot. When a dagger's all you've got, you must be certain of your enemy before you commit. You don't want to be too close if the rabbit turns out to be a tiger!

"Well done, lass. You're as quick as they come. If you learn when to harness that speed, and when to let it fly, you'll pose a serious threat."

The marshal joined them. "Miss Dunn is to be trained in close combat. Two sessions each day to start. By yourself preferably, Sergeant, but if that is not possible, then a knight proven in battle. Sir Godfrey, perhaps. Sir Dreddit or Sir Parrish. Do you understand?"

"Yes, sir!" Cogswell scratched his head. "It'll be my pleasure."

"If it meets with Miss Dunn's approval, that is." The marshal turned in deference to Sibil.

"It does," said Sibil. "Very much."

"Then I bid you good day," said the marshal, striding off. "Walk with me, Major."

Marshal Erik Carson

Major Stronghart caught up quickly. When they were out of earshot, he asked, "How did you know?"

"What? Daggers? Had you witnessed her defense of Rolft the other day, you would not ask."

"At The Raven's Nest?"

"Just so. Most impressive. How long has she been under Sir Godfrey's tutelage?"

"Sir Godfrey! Whatever do you mean?"

Carson stared back at the ring of squires. "When I asked her where she learned to fight, she answered with his name."

Stronghart shrugged. "And what has he to say?"

"I haven't had the heart to ask, given his son's death."

They both were silent as Sibil came running toward them.

"My dagger, if you please," she said breathlessly.

Major Stronghart reached inside his tunic for the weapon. "It's a fine blade," he said, handing it back to Sibil.

"Whatever I wish, whenever I wish it, is that right?"

"The king's own words, Miss Dunn," said Carson.

"And yet, when I wished to see Rolft?"

"Conflicting edicts from the king, I'm afraid. It happens."

"I wish to join the hunt for those who caused the death of Princess Lewen."

Carson stared at her a long time, first answering his own question as to how she might have learned the hunt was on, and then searching for the right words. "What I say next is not to be taken lightly. I wish that all my men had half your spirit and gods-given talent. Alas, my hands are tied. Your wish cannot be granted. More conflicting edicts, I'm afraid. Enjoy your training, Miss Dunn. I shall be monitoring your progress with great interest."

He looked back at the training grounds, as did Sibil and Major Stronghart.

The squires had begun to chant. "Wisperal! Wisperal!"

Sibil Dunn

Sibil ran from the infirmary, her hopes of seeing Rolft there dashed once more. "Dragged off by those three idiots!" the distraught attendant had angrily informed her. She rushed into the livery, relieved to find the squires had yet to return.

Reggie and Caleb were at the other end of the barn. "Have you seen Rolft?" she asked.

It was already afternoon, and Caleb appeared to welcome an excuse to lean on his pitchfork. "Just missed 'im," the old stablemaster said.

"Can you help me? I need a horse!"

The old man scratched his head.

"You should take Shadow!" Reggie said. "She should take Shadow. No one else will ride him. He needs the exercise!"

"Shadow?" Sibil paused. "Lewen's horse?"

"The boy's right. Would you ride 'im?"

"Why wouldn't I?"

"Some would rather not be reminded of... well, you know."

"I'd rather not forget."

"Others think he's cursed," said the stablemaster.

"He's not cursed!" said Reggie.

"I don't believe in curses," said Sibil.

"Neither does the horse. He's in the back pen. Reggie kin help ya."

"On, boy. Time's come." Sibil whispered in Shadow's ear. She gave the powerful beast free rein on the palace road to Fostead, sensing, as she had with Rolft, a kinship. It was exhilarating to be astride a living thing that Lewen had been so close to for so long. To be moving swiftly, ever closer, she imagined, to avenging her best friend. She blamed the wind for the tears that streaked her face and blurred her vision.

Sibil slowed Shadow's gait, stroking his neck reassuringly as she guided him past the fork leading to her home and to Dewhurst. Soon, Fostead's buildings loomed. Passageways took shape. People became more prevalent. She took one long look down main street before turning Shadow toward the south end of town.

Rolft Aerns

As soon as Rolft was fully outside the infirmary, Fereliss slammed the door with satisfaction.

"Should we let the marshal know you're joining us?" asked Garth.

"I am no longer under his command."

"The physician was none too pleased with your departure," Yurik said.

"I'd not go back to him if I was you." Fereliss clasped his hands behind his back as he walked. "He has all sorts of wicked tools, you know, and you're on his bad side now. You'd fare better with the young lass, Thistle. I'll wager she'd care for you!"

"Who?" Rolft winced as he limped along.

"That skinny lass. The one clinging like a kitten to your side. Thistle."

"The marshal says she's something of a scrapper," said Garth.

"Perhaps with other kittens." Fereliss laughed. "She can't weigh but two bales, can she, lads!" Rolft stopped walking, causing Fereliss and Yurik to do the same. Garth halted behind them.

Rolft waited for the guardsmen's chortling to stop.

"What is it?" Fereliss asked. "You all right?"

Rolft held a finger inches from Fereliss' face. "There are two truths you'd best take to heart. One is that the lass has twice now saved my life. She shares a bond with me, the same as each of you. The second truth I tell you is for your own good. You would do well not to raise her ire. She may not look strong or fearsome, but she is quick, and would relieve you of your privates before you knew what happened."

Garth's hand moved slowly to his groin.

Rolft led the way, his horse moving with the flow of pedestrians in the street. Fereliss, Garth and Yurik followed. Any faster, and they would have little hope of picking anyone out of the crowd. Rolft alone could identify the escaped prisoner dubbed 'the cat.' None of them had ever laid eyes on the small man's partner, the man with shoulder-length dark hair and a scar on his forehead. Rolft had done his best to describe them both, based in part on descriptions provided by Jarod and Bohun. It wasn't much to go on. The guardsmen watched for anything out of the ordinary, waiting for Rolft to alert them.

It was Yurik who first noticed Sibil as he turned to scan the crowd behind. He called to his companions.

"That's Thistle, is it?" asked a squinting Fereliss.

It did not take long to realize she was chasing them. By the time she caught up, all four were sitting on horses at rest, facing her in the middle of the street. Passersby were forced to navigate around the small blockade. The guardsmen shifted their attention between Sibil and her mount.

Garth said what Rolft was thinking. "That's Shadow."

"He suffers, too," said Sibil, "and we are both owed a debt." Shadow pawed the ground on cue. "We're coming with you."

Rolft weighed her words while the guardsmen waited, watching. He nodded. "She can identify the cat. Introduce yourselves." He locked eyes with Fereliss. "Properly."

"Fereliss, m'lady." The grizzled guardsman leaned forward, doing his best to bow on horseback. "At your service."

"Yurik, miss... miss..."

"Dunn," said Sibil.

"It's my pleasure, Miss Dunn."

"I'm Garth. And the honor is all mine," said the youngest guardsman earnestly.

Sibil acknowledged them in turn, her gaze returning to Fereliss as she pronounced her name: "Si-bil."

Rolft reined Sarah back in the direction of The Raven's Nest.

Overseer Reynard Rascall

He was at least a decade out of practice, but the skills necessary to relieve preoccupied wayfarers of their purse were still at Reynard's disposal. He found them remarkably familiar and easy to ply amid a throng peppered with the inebriated. With Spiro waiting in the alley, it took little time to collect the funds he estimated were necessary to extend their stay in Fostead.

He tugged his hat down to his eyebrows and identified his last mark, a well-dressed gentleman with no apparent companion. He approached from behind, sidled up to the man, stole a quick glance down the street, and froze. The mark continued on, and Reynard jostled his way to the roadside, his gaze never leaving the four riders headed his way: three men and a girl. Three very large men, one of whom looked remarkably like...

Reynard bowed his head a bit further, positioning himself behind a gaggle of boisterous men. As the riders plodded past, he peeked from beneath the brim of his hat and swore under his breath.

Reynard paced the floor of the stablemaster's home while Spiro rummaged for food.

"This is not a positive development, my friend. What is the giant doing free? He's killed more men than we can say. The soldiers watched him strangle Able before they hauled him away. Why isn't he in chains? I'll tell you why! Did you look closely at the mounts of those he rode with today? The cloth beneath their saddles?"

Spiro shrugged before continuing to poke around the cottage.

Reynard tapped his head. "If I had been quicker with my thoughts, and not so worried about you, I would have followed them. I'll wager everything I own that those horses found their way back to the palace!"

"Makes no sense. Their riders wore no uniforms."

"What of it? There are all sorts within the castle walls who do not wear the king's colors. When was the last time you saw a woman in uniform, eh? What do you think his knights wear beneath their armor? It's not a soldier's uniform, I can tell you that. No, no, why didn't I see this before? He's been killing for the king all along! Killing with impunity!"

"What's that? Is it better than the klubandag?" Spiro removed an exceptionally large hat from a wall peg and donned it.

"Impunity, you idiot! He's been killing with the king's blessing. Nay, at his behest!" Reynard put both hands to his head. "Of course! Of course! How could I have missed it? The lass as well, it would appear! And now they ride with three others just as big as he is! This krephole's full of giants!"

"And the stablemaster?" Spiro asked from beneath the hat. "What about him?"

"What about him? He may well have tried to take over Grymes' business. It stands to reason, doesn't it? Our mistake was in believing he and the giant who killed your friends were acting together. No, no, no! This one seeks to put us out of business, yes, but for a different reason altogether! He's hunting us because Grymes and his men were half-wits, breaking the king's law right beneath his nose. This one does the king's bidding! What were we thinking, setting up shop in farging Fostead? Gods only know what information Grymes spewed before the giant killed him. Or Able and Elijah, for that matter. Did they tell him our names? What we look like? Where we live? The king's entire army may be looking for us now!

"All the more reason for us to visit The Raven's Nest. What was the king's giant doing there the day you played with him? Not drinking, I'll wager you that. He can't have known he was going to run into Able and Elijah. What could they have said or done in that short time to set him off? Lest you forget, he killed Grymes and that Ingram fellow there as well. Don't tell me he just happened by on both days. No, no, the barkeep there knows more than he lets on, I'm sure of it. And to think he can identify me! He has to go, but not before he answers all our questions. We'll wait until he closes. Follow him home if need be. Get some sleep. I'll wake you when it's time."

Spiro saluted him from beneath the brim of the stablemaster's hat.

"And lose the hat. We're not trying to draw attention, gods dammit! It makes you look like a walking toadstool. And please, when we go back to The Raven's Nest, do pay attention. We can't afford a repeat of the last time we were there."

The stablemaster's hat nodded.

Reynard sighed. "You do remember last time?"

Barkeep Peter Terrick

"'Night, Peter!"

"G'night, Simon. G'night, Owyne!" Peter looked up from wiping the bar. His last two customers of the evening stopped briefly at the front door, leaning against each other, laughing. One tipped his hat to the young soldier standing like a sentry there.

Peter took a moment to reflect. The soldier's presence had not hurt business after all. In fact, most customers had seemed at ease with, if not comforted by, Cyril's presence—particularly those aware of Fostead's rash of recent murders.

The king's soldiers had stopped by the day before to notify him of Gabriel Solomon's execution—*just across the street!* —and to warn him to be vigilant. Which he had been.

His attention shifted quickly to where his cudgel lay. His new, improved cudgel. His friend had fashioned it from a piece of spikewood, leaving several sharp ridges encircling its business end. Never out of reach, it was a serious weapon, suitable for wielding with one good arm, unlike the broom he wrestled now with one arm folded and strapped to his chest with linen.

It had been three days since two brotherly brutes had sent him crashing to the floor, breaking his arm and knocking him unconscious. Two elderly patrons had watched the ensuing melee from start to finish. The man who had killed Grymes and Ingram the night before, Bohun's friend, had battled both giants single-handedly, stabbing one to death inside The Raven's Nest, then chasing the other outside to strangle him. Peter had since learned the man was a retired member of the king's royal guard named Rolft; not someone to trifle with. An associate of the two brothers, the one known as "the cat", had appeared and stabbed Rolft repeatedly before being attacked himself by a young girl. The king's soldiers had captured the cat and taken him to prison. His partner, the man with a scar on his forehead, who had visited Peter earlier, was still roaming Fostead. And keeping busy. He had broken the cat out of prison and presumably killed Gabriel. Sadly, someone had also slain Bohun.

"Did you want some help with that?"

Peter looked up. No, the young soldier had not hurt business. But the 'brothers bortok' would have snapped the skinny lad in two, like some spindly piece of dry kindling. Peter was sure of it, so if he had to give up his cudgel or the lad, well...

Something in the alley bumped the pub's back door, causing the burly barkeep to stand motionless for a moment, listening intently. But there followed only silence. Peter leaned his broom against the bar, grabbed his cudgel, and headed for the bolted door.

Cyril raised a cautionary hand. "No! Let me see to that!"

Marshal Erik Carson

Carson halted near the top of the stone stairway. A short distance away, King Axil leaned against the battlement's parapet, either lost in thought or mesmerized. Perhaps both. The Lumax Mountain's far-off snow-capped peaks and shadowed valleys hid the Kingdom of Tegan, wherein lay New Haven and the castle of King Tygre.

"Do you prefer your solitude, m'lord?"

King Axil patted the wall by his side.

Carson accepted the invitation. Sir Black and Lady Gray observed his approach before returning their muzzles to rest on the parapet's crenels.

"They've departed, have they? King Tygre's men?"

"Yes, sire. Well-rested and well-fed."

"Tegan means us no harm. I trust you know that now."

"Marshal Ademar was most convincing."

The king chuckled. "A familiar fool with a crown on his head was not to be believed, but a fellow marshal, albeit a stranger, that's a different story."

Carson placed his hands on the parapet and joined in searching the horizon. "My apologies, sire. Perhaps if the stakes were not so high. Perhaps if I were better at keeping those around me safe."

"Don't be absurd."

"I nearly sent Rolft Aerns to the gods today. He came this close to—"

"The man lives, does he not, and has you to thank for it. Why must you always diminish your accomplishments, Erik? It's most annoying. Speak of something worth hearing, why don't you? If King Tygre is not hunting my head, who is?"

"We know the assassins were aided by The Prince of Quills," thought the marshal aloud. "I think we can dispense with the notion that he penned their invitations unwittingly. The very fact he ran, the pouch of coins he carried, the fact someone sought to silence him...all suggest that he conspired to have you killed." King Axil motioned impatiently for him to get on with it. "Why silence him, other than to prevent his lips from telling truths intended to stay buried? Does it not make sense that whoever killed the Prince of Quills seeks your death as well?"

"I'd say that's a rather obvious conclusion. Does it help to identify who that is?"

"Does it not? Who would be so bold as to execute a prisoner escorted by five men in broad daylight? Armed men, I might add, identifiable if not by uniform, then by the colors of the cloth beneath their saddles. Who would be so bold, Your Majesty?"

The monarch rolled his eyes before returning the challenge. "Who would be so bold as to attack me in my palace whilst surrounded by armed guards? Idiots, that's who! I don't see how this helps."

"Idiots, perhaps, m'lord, but bold nonetheless. And whoever slew the Prince of Quills knew what they were doing. A deadly strike from far enough away that most archers would not attempt it. What's more, they left no trail to follow. Not even for the likes of Fereliss."

"So they're bold, and not totally inept."

"Yes, sire. And backed by heavy coin. How many do we know with the resources for that?"

"Any number of nobles, I suppose. They're not all in love with me, you know. Successful businessmen. The Guild of Takers. The League of Assassins. The list is quite long, really. Meanwhile, where are the takers responsible for my wife's and daughter's death?"

"We'll have them soon enough, m'lord."

King Axil grimaced, cocking his head toward Fostead. "Look at all the little ants. Already stirred into a frenzy for the morrow. We should be calling it the Inebriation of Six Moons, not the celebration."

"Indeed, sire."

"Will it delay your search for them? Their capture?"

"It won't help. We could stop the celebration if you wished, but it would be an effort and there would be consequences. I think it best we wait."

"Consequences?"

"Some would not be moved by words alone, particularly those already taken to drink. There would be injuries. The streets would burn at night. Your Majesty would be reviled for some time."

"The usual revolt, then."

"Just so." The marshal smiled.

"Might they get away? If we tarry?"

"For all we know, they've already left Fostead. Regardless, we are not waiting. Sergeant Lagos leads a small search party now. The royal guard another. Once Six Moons has passed, we will go door to door. And I promise you, m'lord, no matter where they are or where they go, they will not get away."

King Axil grunted his satisfaction. "Need we worry about tomorrow's processional? It's safe, do you think?"

"I thought we had agreed you would not—"

"I don't plan on marching."

"I think that's wise, m'lord. Nevertheless, the procession will be heavily guarded."

"While it is underway, I shall visit Isadora and Lewen."

"What!" *At the House of All Gods? Have you gone mad?* "Your Majesty..."

"It no longer feels like war, does it?"

"What does it feel like, then?"

"More personal, I suppose."

"All the more reason not to venture outside the castle, m'lord."

"You're welcome to join us if it makes you feel more comfortable."

"Us?"

"Madam Dunn has already accepted my invitation. Her feet remain too sore to join the procession. If she foresees so much as a pinch of trouble, I promise we'll not go."

"Could it not wait another moon, sire?"

"She's also accepted my invitation to live at the castle. And she has met with all the senior staff, including your officers. I feel quite secure. Don't you?"

The two men were silent for a moment.

King Axil pushed away from the parapet, taking note of the direction in which the marshal was staring. He laid a hand on his friend's shoulder, then started down the stairs, the cragens at his heels. "Center stone over the gates. Top row. A big crack down it's middle...hard to miss!"

THE CELEBRATION OF SIX MOONS

"Death waits for us all, but it is far less patient with some."
Drixle Wainwright, undertaker

Sibil Dunn

Sibil found herself entranced. Such a strange room! Nothing but tree trunks rising to the ceiling, and so closely spaced together. She might as well be in the forest.

"By design," said her father, suddenly standing next to her.

"How do you mean?" Sibil asked. "I thought you only worked with baelonite." *And aren't you dead?*

"Ahh," Her father shook his shaggy, unkempt locks. "When in service to the king, 'tis true. But this house I built for your mother. Can you not tell what kind of trees these are?"

Sibil looked up at the ceiling, a thick mat of interwoven branches mostly covered by heart-shaped leaves as big as her head. A sudden shower of ornate purple flowers descended on her.

"Euphoria," she whispered.

"Quite right! Where do you think your mother gets her powers? She eats those petals, day and night!"

That cannot be true! Consuming the leaves of euphoria might cause hallucinations, even death, but she had never seen her mother eat one.

"There's much I've done without your knowledge," said her mother from the ceiling, just her face visible amidst a patchwork of leaves and branches. Purple flowers started pouring from her mouth.

"If only you could see what she can see from there." It was an old woman with tangled gray hair, rocking a baby's cradle at the base of a large tree trunk.

"No! Stay where you are!" said Sibil's father. Several branches snaked around his ankles before yanking him away. "It's too soon for you!" he called from the ceiling.

Sibil followed his counsel, stretching out on the floor's soft soil to avoid low-hanging tree limbs. A woodpecker rapped on an adjacent tree. *How did it get into the house?*

"I've come to say goodbye." Theos' voice! Sibil did not want to hear those words from him, nor see arrows jutting from his body. She pressed her face into a cushion of moss and duff.

"The squires are calling you The Wisperal," the voice continued, closer now.

"So what?" said Sibil, her words muffled by the earth. "Where are you going?"

The woodpecker landed beside her, folding its wings before speaking. "To avenge my death."

What? Wait! How does one avenge one's own death?

"There's something I must tell you." The bird hopped back and forth in front of her. "A secret Tristan harbored."

"Tell me, Theos, please!" *Am I really talking to a bird?*

"He loves you, Sib. Loves you and no other." The woodpecker spread his wings.

Oh! If only that were true!

"Fare well! Please safeguard this for me." From beneath its wings, the bird produced an envelope on which were scrawled the words:

FOR EMILI, SHOULD I NOT RETURN

The woodpecker disappeared into the woods, leaving the envelope behind.

Sibil awoke encased in darkness, relieved to find she had not left the confines of the palace Nest, certain nonetheless that she would not go back to sleep. The royal guardsmen would resume their search for Lewen's killers, with her or without her, as soon as the sun rose. She could not afford to close her eyes again.

Sibil swung into the saddle, increasingly concerned with Rolft's physical condition. She watched unobtrusively as he tried twice to mount his horse, only to lean his full weight against Sarah's side. He rested his head on the gray mare's neck and called to Fereliss.

Fereliss sauntered through the morning mist to lay a hand on Sarah's muzzle. "What is it?"

Rolft returned Sibil's unwavering stare as he answered. "Help me up. And be quick about it."

"What? Do you mean to tell me—"

"Do as I say!"

"Aye, your lordship." Fereliss reached down to wrap his arms around Rolft's legs, then lifted him awkwardly onto Sarah. By the time Rolft was fully righted in the saddle, Garth and Yurik were also staring at him from their mounts.

Rolft ignored them all, coaxing Sarah toward the castle gates. Sibil scrutinized him as he passed, then turned from one guardsman to another. "Is he fit to ride? He doesn't look well. What did the physician say?"

"Physician?" Fereliss scoffed, falling in behind Rolft. "He spent last night in the barracks, lass. He's had his fill of the infirmary."

Sibil could not take her eyes off Rolft. Despite the cool morning air, beads of sweat glistened on his brow. Not even a full beard could hide his pained expression as Sarah rocked him from side to side. Sibil struggled to broach the subject of his health.

"The story I was told about Six Moons," she said. "The day you saved the queen." Rolft gave no indication he was listening. "I've been thinking. It's not the only story Lewen told me. Was it you who saved her from drowning in the river?" Rolft did not answer, but Fereliss shot her a curt nod. "I knew it!"

"Trouble always finds this one," said Fereliss. "Or the other way around. You know about the cragens, do ya?"

"Cragens?" asked Sibil.

"I remember it well," said Fereliss.

"Enough!" said Rolft. "We have a task ahead."

Sibil frowned. "You're sick," she said, abandoning tact. "And stubborn! You should be in bed. What do you think Lewen would say to you now?"

The three guardsmen exchanged nervous glances.

Rolft commanded Sarah to stop. He waited for his companions to settle next to him, then turned in obvious discomfort to direct his full attention to Sibil. "Two almons ago, I listened to the princess. And the queen. I knew better, but I listened to them both. Now they lie dead." He prodded Sarah gently with his boots. "I'm through listening."

"That's it?" Sibil called after him. "That's your excuse? What has that to do with caring for your wounds?" Rolft rode on, leaving the others frozen in momentary silence.

Fereliss tried to lighten the mood. He spoke to Yurik. "I told you the name suited her."

"What name?" asked Sibil hotly.

"Thistle," said Yurik. Sibil shot a venomous look at him. "Not my idea," he said.

"Oh, let me think," Fereliss contemplated aloud. "The day that we first met the lass. Outside the infirmary. Do you remember? Who was it who said she should be paring potatoes in the kitchen? Was that me? I'm trying to recall."

"No, that was Yurik," said Garth matter-of-factly.

"Ah, yes, so it was," said Fereliss with great satisfaction. He urged his horse to a trot, slowing alongside Rolft.

Sibil prompted Shadow to follow. "Suits me how?" she asked as she joined them.

Fereliss looked at her, opened his mouth to speak, then turned his attention to the road before him. "As though you've never plucked one," he muttered.

"What was that?" asked Sibil.

A sideways glance from Rolft caused Fereliss to hesitate.

"Perhaps Fereliss speaks of your appearance," said Garth from behind. "Thistles really are quite lovely."

"That's true," said Fereliss. "Beautiful, in fact."

Sibil's expression softened.

"And prickly," he added.

"Prickly!"

"Yes, lass. Prickly." Fereliss suffered another glare from Rolft. "With a dagger in her hand," he said defensively. "Would you deny it? Hmmpf. I thought not. You've said as much yourself, Rolft. And Thistle has a nicer ring to it than Wisperal, does it not?" The grizzled guardsman returned Sibil's look of surprise. "Oh, yes, we cannot help but hear what others say, can we! Do you know how long it takes for word to get from one end of the barracks to the other?" He flicked his fingers in the air. "Just so. And half as long as that when chatty knights make their beds beside us! What's wrong with Thistle, anyway? It suits you!"

Sibil expelled a lungful of frustration. "So be it! If we are to go by names that suit us, then what am I to call you? I shall have to think on that!"

Fereliss smiled broadly beneath his bushy beard. "You do that, lass!" He reached out and prodded her shoulder playfully. "What did I tell you, lads? Prickly!"

Rolft Aerns

He knew they were something of an oddity, sitting on horses outside a bakery, just watching south end revelers pass in both directions. Even so, few took note. A pair of jugglers had assumed control of the street, commanding the attention of nearly all who passed. Many lingered to watch the skillful act infused with humor.

Rolft still considered the south end of town the most likely place to run across their quarry, and had assured his four companions that remaining in one place increased their odds of doing so. It was a convenient truth, as he did not have the stamina to roam the city.

He pressed a palm against his side. At one point, that had helped to ease the pain, but now it had little effect. Some sort of infection had taken root and was feeding on his flesh. It had been days since he'd last peeled back the bandages. The amount of festering and dark discoloration then had sickened him.

The palace physician had tried to stem the decay with burning embers—a useless exercise in suffering. There was no point in looking any more. It was not going to heal. It was only getting worse. At times now he imagined he could smell it—the faint but putrid stench of rotting meat.

"Oi!" It was Fereliss, calling Rolft's attention to an oncoming soldier on horseback, shouting and waving as he plowed a furrow through the crowd. Neither Sibil nor the guardsmen moved. They watched and waited for the rider to draw near.

"It's the barkeep from The Raven's Nest!" the soldier cried excitedly. "Him and his wife...both killed!" The soldier looked anxiously at Fereliss. Fereliss looked to Rolft.

"You three go," Rolft said. "The lass and I will stay and keep watch." Fereliss looked unsure. "Go on! You'll be quicker without us. And don't forget! The king would have them alive!"

Overseer Reynard Rascall

Reynard lay listening to Spiro's soft, rhythmic breathing. It was difficult to imagine such a small and peaceful sleeper was responsible for the previous night's mayhem. But signs of Spiro's handiwork were strewn throughout the cottage. Starting with the unusual cudgel lying on the floor. It had nearly taken Reynard's head off. That narrow miss had sent Spiro into a fit of rage Reynard could only watch. The club had eventually been used to bash in the head of not only the barkeep who refused to say much, but that of his wife, who could not, or would not, keep her mouth shut.

The barkeep had confirmed Reynard's suspicions. The giant was indeed one of the king's men. His name was Rolft Aerns, and he had been a friend to the stablemaster. The barkeep had steadfastly claimed that was all he knew. Why Rolft was stalking Reynard and Spiro remained a mystery.

Reynard's exasperation propelled him out of bed. He prodded Spiro with the toe of his boot. "Let's go. It's Six Moons...the best day of the almon for hunting giants."

Spiro stretched and sat up groggily. "The best day?"

"And our last. If we manage to slay him today, good for us! If not, I give you my word, we'll return before the almon is out, and I'll pay to have it done. Either way, I'm leaving this wretched place before the day is through. With or without you, do you hear? We've pressed our luck too far as it is." Reynard let that sink into Spiro's sleepy head. "You understand?"

Spiro nodded slowly.

"You'll come with me, then?" asked Reynard.

Spiro continued to nod.

"Ah! Wash up, then. The day's upon us." Reynard flung a hat at Spiro. "Here. Try this." He grimaced as he looked at the bodies in the adjacent room. "It's no use to our friends anymore."

They sat outside The Dragon's Breath, peering at passersby from beneath their hats. Reynard was compelled to keep just as close an eye on his companion. He wished the morning sun, or boredom, would put Spiro to sleep.

"This is what you call hunting, is it?" Spiro spat into his hands, then rubbed them together. One leg twitched non-stop.

"Have you ever watched a huntsman, Spiro? A true huntsman? They don't go running about, crashing through the wood and brush, announcing themselves. No. They work slowly. Quietly. Do you know the meaning of the word stealth?"

"All right. But then, should we not be sitting by the palace road? Where he is bound to pass?"

"Out in the open? Where the king's men can get as good a look at us as we at them? Brilliant!"

"I only thought that—"

"Stop there, friend. I am the architect, remember? You are the mason. Why?"

"Because I like to get my hands dirty." Spiro folded his arms across his chest.

"Quite right! Think on it this way: we're no longer building walls. Our roles have changed, but our relationship remains. In this case, I am the huntsman, and you, you are my weapon. The deadliest weapon I have ever wielded."

Spiro grumbled softly.

"As sharp and true a blade as one could wish for," said Reynard. "Perfectly balanced. Always at the ready, and never failing to do its job."

"That part's true enough."

"But I am the huntsman, Spiro. And you must trust me to do my job. As I trust you to do yours. Understood?"

Reynard sank back against the wall. In truth, he hoped they would not cross paths with the king's giant this day. Spiro needed to feel sufficient effort had been expended, but a bucketful of boredom suited Reynard well. He was very much looking forward to the coach ride home. He would enjoy every bump along the way.

Safely back in Waterford, he would swallow his wounded pride and inform The Guild that its operations in Fostead had been compromised by a bungling taker by the name of Raggett Grymes. And he would gladly pay to have the giant named Rolft Aerns killed another day. It would not be cheap, but one didn't haggle with assassins.

His plan was simple: keep Spiro's mind off the king's giant. Whenever his companion showed the slightest sign of restlessness, Reynard regaled him with a tale so outlandish he could not help but devote his full attention to it. By the time the sun was high in the sky, there was little break between stories.

Spiro began to fidget once again.

"Have I ever told you about my days at sea as a young man?" asked Reynard. "The mutiny I led to save us all from certain death?"

Spiro exhaled loudly and rose to stretch.

Reynard was quick to join him. "I'll tell you over a bowl of mutton stew, shall I? We haven't had a bite all day."

Spiro elbowed him, directing his attention toward the opposite side of the street.

Reynard scanned those gathered there, his eyes drawn to a pair in conversation. "Grymes' lot, no doubt about it," he said, stroking his chin. "Well done, friend! Only two, are there?"

"The Brock character," muttered Spiro, continuing to stare. "I don't recall the other's name."

"I do," said Reynard. "Loose Ends, wasn't it? We should have a word, at least."

"They've seen us!"

"Indeed." Reynard, watched the pair across the street separate and move in opposite directions. "You take the bearded one. Be quick! Nothing messy, do you hear?" Reynard stepped into the street. Still wary of soldiers, he kept his head bowed, one eye tracking the Brock character's young companion. *What was his name?* Reynard could not recall. Thank gods the lad was tall; his conspicuous blond hair bobbed through the crowd like a leaf riding on the water. Young legs carried the frightened rabbit quickly down the street. It was a short time before he slowed, then stopped to catch his breath.

"Hallo there, friend!" Reynard's voice, so loud and close, clearly startled the young man. "Fancy bumping into you!"

Before the youth could react, Reynard draped a long arm over his shoulders and began guiding him down the street. "I remember you from that night at the pub. You're one of Grymes' lot."

"Alden," said the young man.

"Ah, yes! Alden! My condolences, friend. I heard what happened to Mr. Grymes. Bad luck. But you know what they say: 'sad endings beget glad beginnings!' Surely our bumping into each other is a sign. You've lost your friend—I'm looking for another! The name's Reynard. Let's talk about the man who killed poor Grymes, shall we? Do you know him?"

Reynard steered Alden from the throng toward a passage between two buildings. The young man resisted, no doubt hoping someone— anyone—would notice his discomfort. "I don't. I wasn't there. Didn't see him."

Reynard pressed his blade against Alden's ribs. "Now is not the time for your memory to fail."

"He serves the king! That's all I know!"

Reynard grabbed Alden's ear and twisted it, dragging him down the passageway. "Are you certain? Does he know our names? Where to find us?"

"I've no idea!"

"No?" Reynard swung his captive around the back of the building and shoved him against it. "But you've a good memory for faces, do you not?" The two men stared at each other.

"I do!"

"As I feared."

Mari Dunn

The warmth of the sun on her back, the gentle swaying of the animal beneath her. She might as well be newly born, swaddled, and rocking in a cradle. Content to keep her eyes closed, Mari listened to the sounds associated with Six Moons. Celebratory shouting and laughter. The cries of a child. The clanking of soldiers' swords against their saddles.

"You're all right, are you?" It was the king's voice, rising above the banter of those along the roadside. "Mari? Are you well?"

Gods! He's talking to me! "Apologies, m'lord! I'm fine." Mari opened her eyes.

"It's not too much for you?" asked the king, riding beside her.

"Not at all, Your Majesty." She patted the neck of her dappled mount. "He's a gentle boy, this one. I'm fine."

Mari took stock of her escorts as King Axil returned his attention to the crowd. She counted a dozen soldiers, including Marshal Carson and Major Stronghart—cut from the same cloth, those two. How had this come to pass? She, an ordinary child born to hardship, now riding in the company of the King of Aranox, surrounded by soldiers, passing countless commoners no different from herself but for a chain of happenstance. What had been the first link in that chain? The day she'd caught the eye of a young architect bound for glory? Had she not married him, where would she be now?

The assemblage of spectators thinned as the royal party departed Fostead. A few long-legged youths ran alongside until spent, disappearing well before The House of All Gods came into view.

It had been almons since she laid eyes on it. Little wonder it should cause her heart to flutter. She had forgotten how stunning and magnificent it was, a tribute to the depths of her husband's talent. How she missed him! The touch of his hand. The warmth of his embrace. Still staring at his creation, she brought a hand to her bosom.

"Most impressive, is it not?" said King Axil. "Be mindful of her feet!" he told the soldiers helping Mari to dismount.

Her shoes gently touched the ground before the soldiers released her, perhaps a bit prematurely. She was lightheaded. *I need a moment!*

"Allow me, madam." It was Major Stronghart, his hand beneath her elbow.

"Thank you." Mari exhorted herself to keep pace as they passed through open gates into gardens ablaze with colorful foliage and flowers. The brilliance of the sun's reflection off a massive backdrop of snow-white baelonite caused her to shield her eyes.

"Would you care to rest a moment?" asked the major.

"Yes, please." A rich fragrance of blended oils assailed her nostrils: fruity praxim, pungent axil, perfume-like silver star-tip. To her surprise, she could identify each flower's contribution!

And the bees! Their continuous drone grew increasingly louder, background to a medley of distant sounds she identified with ease: a croaking toad; the squeak of rusty hinges; stiff bristles swept across a floor... all so clear, as though they were beside her!

How peculiar! What was heightening her senses? Was it the memory of Adrian... the splendor of The House of All Gods? The import of the occasion? *No!* These could do no more than lift her spirits, and this was decidedly physical. She half expected to become nauseous or black out, but instead, an unfamiliar strength flowed through her.

"Tread carefully, madam. There's little light inside," said Major Stronghart as they crossed The House of All Gods' threshold.

What's he talking about? The place is awash with light and color! Mari lifted her elbow from the major's hand and began to walk more briskly, crossing the stone floor as though young again, the pain in her feet gone. *Incredible!* These were not her legs. They could not be! So strong, and not under her control. Where were they taking her?

Outside! Hurry! Outside! Where is the king? Too far ahead! Exiting the building! Now out of sight! A sense of dread jolted Mari. She pushed off the balls of her feet and started running.

"Madam Dunn!" the major called, but she had no intention of stopping. The rear door through which the king had disappeared also beckoned her.

The rustling of desiccated leaves... the snapping of twigs...

Sounds that do not belong here!

She reached the door and stumbled outside, breathing rapidly.

Hurry!

"King Axil!" she cried.

The king's entire entourage stopped and turned as she rushed toward them.

"My king!" *One task now—only one!*

"Mari?" King Axil watched her from the base of the steps leading to the royal graveyard. The soldier nearest him moved even closer, but the monarch waved him off. Breathless not from exertion but from anxious anticipation, Mari continued down the path at a pace that was unsafe.

Gods forgive me!

She brushed past one guard, his mouth agape, then another with his arms outstretched.

The whistling of something in the air!

She crashed into the wide-eyed king, sending him sprawling to the ground.

A searing pain shot from her shoulder down her arm.

"Archer!" cried one of the soldiers.

"There!" yelled another.

"The king! Surround the king!" Marshal Carson's voice.

"Inside! Quickly!"

"Go! Go! After them!"

Was that Major Stronghart?

Someone grabbed her arms and dragged her until another pair of hands found her ankles. She was lifted off the ground and carried.

Pain spread from her shoulder to her chest. She watched sky and leafy branches pass overhead until The House of All Gods' ceiling blocked their view.

"Can you hear me, Mari?" The voice of Marshal Carson. She felt herself lowered to the stone floor, saw him kneeling over her. She sought to answer, but struggled to move her lips. A blurry Major Stronghart appeared beside the marshal.

"What say you, Mari? She's cold as ice!"

"Cover her. Use my waistcoat."

A piece of clothing was draped over her chest; something soft propped her head up from the floor.

"Stunned, no doubt. She came this close."

"It hit her, did it? Meant for the king, no doubt!"

"It's only grazed her shoulder. Mari, can you hear me? Are you all right?"

"Poisoned tip!" said an unfamiliar voice.

"What! Bring it here!"

Mari closed her eyes, suddenly nauseous and wracked by prickly pain. The ceiling began to spin.

"Sibil!" she said, gagging as she spoke. "See to my daughter!"

Rolft Aerns

Rolft clenched his eyelids, then opened them wide, trying to regain his focus. When had he lost his concentration? How long had Fereliss been gone? He could not be sure. He only knew he had been staring vacantly at a blurry stream of passersby without really seeing anything for some time. He was relieved to find Sibil still next to him, sitting calmly astride Shadow, and the jugglers still performing.

The crowd had swelled; the sky had darkened. A tangle of shoulder-length red hair and bushy beard spilled into the open space commanded by the entertainers, quickly drawing Rolft's attention. He sat upright. The short, stocky interloper was one of Raggett Grymes' crew that he had let go from the warehouse! He coaxed Sarah slowly forward, displacing those with an unobstructed view of the jugglers.

"What is it?" Sibil asked.

Rolft paid no attention. The red-head looked anxiously over his shoulder, reacted to something, then bolted, disappearing back into the throng. What had unnerved him? A ripple in the crowd preceded the emergence of another figure, this one clearly on the hunt. Shorter even than the red-head, but just as recognizable. It was the little man who had slashed his face and stabbed his leg outside The Raven's Nest!

The cat!

"Hyah!" Rolft urged Sarah into a sudden gallop, sending the jugglers scrambling in opposite directions as he drew his sword.

"Rolft!" Sibil cried.

The cat's eyes grew wide with recognition. He crouched as Sarah neared, readied himself, then dove out of the horse's path, rolling on the ground before springing to his feet. The assemblage issued a collective gasp, backing away as the gray mare slid to a stop at its edge.

Rolft reined Sarah so hard she reared on her back legs. The cat covered the distance to her quickly, leaping to grab the back of the guardsman's collar. Rolft toppled backward, releasing his hold on Sarah's reins and his sword as the cat tried to wrap an arm around his neck. Both men hit the ground. Rolft groaned as he rose on all fours, reclaiming his sword.

The cat was already on his feet, brandishing a knife and circling. Rolft spun slowly on his knees, warding the shorter man off with his much larger blade, then struggled to his feet. The cat stopped and calmed his breathing, his gaze drawn to dark stains on one side of Rolft's shirt.

Sibil dismounted at the crowd's edge. "Leave him!" Rolft said. Sibil hesitated. "Alive!"

The cat darted forward, feinting to gauge Rolft's reaction. Rolft snorted in disdain, blood spraying from his nostrils. He wiped his face with the back of his hand. "All right," he muttered, dropping his sword to the ground and kicking it away. "Come here, you worthless piece of krep!"

The cat's brow furrowed. He stole a glance at Sibil.

"Come on!" shouted Rolft. He drew a dagger from his waistband, tossing it to the cat's feet. "Mangy cur!" He opened his hands and spread wide his arms.

The little man edged closer. Rolft stood motionless, arms still extended to his sides. The cat feinted once, twice, jabbing his blade into the air but maintaining a healthy distance from his adversary's reach. Rolft waited. His one leg would no longer obey him.

The cat struck, lashing out. Rolft batted the smaller man's arm away and reached for him. *Too slow!* The cat sprang forward again, feinting with one hand, attacking with the other. Rolft blocked the blow with his forearm, the blade cutting him as it retreated.

It seemed Sibil could endure no more. "For Lewen!" she cried, her dagger drawn.

Too careless, too fast!

The cat whirled as Sibil rushed toward him.

"Leave him, lass!" shouted Rolft, but already Sibil was within striking distance. The cat's daggers moved so quickly! Sibil tried to parry his attack, but his blade slid across her shoulder before a boot caught her squarely in the stomach. She inhaled sharply, doubled over, and fell backward.

Rolft lunged at the little man, swiping at his head. The cat darted out of reach. Rolft staggered forward, his breathing labored. The cat moved back and forth repeatedly, each menacing gesture followed by retreat. Several times Rolft felt the little man's clothing brush his fingertips. Twice more the cat's dagger slashed his arm.

The cat watched from the corner of his eye as Sibil rose to her knees, rejecting the assistance of two men. He appeared to measure Rolft's condition, then feigned a sudden move. Rolft flinched. The cat grinned. With a dagger in each hand, he advanced resolutely.

Rolft reached out, surprised to grasp a piece of clothing, then an arm! He locked his grip and pulled. *Too easy!* Still grinning, the cat plunged a dagger into Rolft's stomach, withdrew it, then buried the blade in Rolft's side. Rolft roared, wrapped both arms around the little man and squeezed. The cat's smile vanished. Rolft lifted him off his feet and toppled forward. He slammed into the ground, his arms still locked around his captive. Dazed and wheezing, the smaller man struggled to free himself.

Sibil rushed to Rolft, dagger at the ready. She stomped on the cat's hand, mashing it with her boot heel until his dagger was released. She kicked it away, then dropped to her knees beside Rolft's head.

"May I kill him?" she asked breathlessly.

"Alive!" said Rolft, the cat squirming beneath him. "His legs!"

Sibil drove her knife into one of the captive's calves. A muffled scream rang out. Rolft adjusted his position to better smother the smaller man. Sibil scrambled to stab his other leg. Another suffocated cry.

Overseer Reynard Rascall

Reynard slipped out of the alley and headed back in the direction Spiro had gone. He tried to slow his breathing even as he quickened his pace. A bad feeling lurked inside him. It had been a mistake to separate from his associate. *Just do your job, I said! Nothing messy!* Simple enough, but there was no telling how much had found its way into Spiro's consciousness. Or how long it would stay there.

Three large, drunken louts reminded Reynard of the need to watch his step. They jostled him, laughing and offering him a bottle as he passed. Finding Spiro was going to be a trick. The further up the street he traveled, the more closely-knit and agitated the Six Moons' crowd became. Until there appeared to be no further passage. Reynard swore under his breath. It was a larger throng, but all too reminiscent of the rabble outside The Raven's Nest just prior to Spiro's capture.

His misgivings multiplied as he elbowed his way through a clog of limbs and torsos. He should have sent Spiro after the young man, and pursued the Brock character himself, not the other way around. Spiro wasn't inclined to kill quietly, and the red-head was no doubt putting up a fight. A wave of bodies suddenly pushed him back in reaction to a lone horseman out of control. The rider's mount loomed ahead, rearing on its back legs. Its front hooves pawed the air, threatening to descend on people gaping up at them. The rider leaned back, pulling on the reins. Another figure suddenly appeared in the air, latching onto the rider's shirt and wrenching him off the horse.

Spiro!

Reynard clawed his way frantically toward the action.

"Spiro! Leave it! Spiro!" He could only imagine what was eliciting the repeated gasps and groans of those who could see what was happening up ahead. He buckled the back of one man's knees in order to pass, then elbowed another sharply in the side. He wriggled his way between two spindly women to be greeted by his first clear view of the dusty arena in which two combatants fought. *Spiro and... not the Brock character, but the giant!* A loud collective groan escaped those watching as Spiro stabbed the giant in the side. But the giant had hold of Spiro and drew him close, wrapping his arms around him.

Horrified, Reynard watched from the crowd's edge as Spiro disappeared beneath the frame of the falling giant. A young girl with a long, dark ponytail scrambled around the two men like a large crab, stabbing Spiro in the legs. Reynard took one step to intervene but, at the sight of two soldiers running to the young woman's aid, he shrank back. Someone shoved him roughly from behind, jarring him and sending him into the arena.

"That's his partner!" yelled a gruff voice.

Reynard spun. *That meddling, red-headed Brock character!*

He turned and quickly weighed his options for escape.

To his left were two soldiers and the girl; three more of the king's men barred his way forward and to his right.

"Stand fast!" one of them ordered, as the soldiers by the girl rose to draw their swords.

Reynard turned back toward his accuser.

Brock beckoned him with a dagger.

Sibil Dunn

Two soldiers tugged on the cat's legs. The harder they pulled, the more Rolft's body jerked, but they could not extricate his captive. Two more soldiers came to their aid. They kneeled beside Rolft and attempted to roll him over.

"Oh! Be careful!" said Sibil, blanketing Rolft with her body. She spoke into his ear. "You can let go now; the soldiers have him!"

Rolft's uneven breathing stirred the dirt beneath his nostrils. His arms relaxed. The soldiers rolled him over and dragged the cat unceremoniously away. Sibil stared helplessly at the black hilt of a dagger protruding from Rolft's side. His shirt was soaked with blood. Her hands quivered as she brushed the hair from his face. Rolft's eyes fluttered open, then closed.

"Oh, no!" cried Sibil. "Please, no!"

Rolft's breathing grew more ragged.

Sibil recoiled at the touch of a soldier's hands beneath her armpits.

"Oi! Leave her!" a booming voice yelled.

Sibil felt the soldier brushed aside. Fereliss appeared beside her. Garth and Yurik joined him.

"Help him, please," she cried.

Fereliss observed Rolft's wounds, and the knife buried in his side. He grimaced. "Trouble's found you again, eh, friend?"

Rolft's eyes opened halfway. "Plenty ta go around," he whispered hoarsely.

"Captured both, did ya?" asked Yurik.

"Well done, Rolft," said Garth.

"Well done, indeed," said Fereliss, laying a hand on Rolft's shoulder.

Rolft smiled wanly, wheezing. Blood foamed between his lips. His gaze shifted to Sibil. "I can see the queen... and princess clearly now..." he murmured softly, closing his eyes. "They're happy... together... finally at peace." The fingers on his chest stirred weakly. Sibil clasped his hand, her heart pounding.

Sibil stood sobbing, paralyzed by emotion. Rolft's body was loaded on a cart by his fellow guardsmen. The smaller prisoner, already trussed, had been slung over a donkey. The other was on his knees, head bowed, hands clasped behind his back. Three soldiers stood before him, swords pressed against his chest, while a fourth bound his wrists with leather straps.

Marshal Carson strode toward them, acknowledging the soldiers with a curt nod. "It's him, is it?" he asked, waving off their swords. "Shy, are we?" He grabbed a handful of the prisoner's hair, lifting it to reveal a scarred forehead. The man glared at him defiantly.

The marshal's fist hit the side of the prisoner's face soundly, sending him sprawling. The marshal rubbed his knuckles. "That's 'hallo!' from Sergeant Faraday and Sergeant Fields!"

Ruler Two

Countless grains of sand peppered the lower half of Ruler Two's robe as a light breeze swept unimpeded across the desert. Every now and then, the winds would rise and swirl, lifting spiral sheets of grit to pelt his head. He could pull his hood to shield his face, but what was the point? He should instead relish the stinging sensation. This might well be the last time he felt it.

The deadline to kill King Axil had come and gone, yet still the monarch sat upon his throne, unscathed. How was that possible? He had not slept since hearing Ruler Five's account of what happened during Fostead's celebration of Six Moons. It was not something easily digested. It continued to churn inside him like an unpleasant meal warning that the worst was yet to come.

The magister had summoned him, so he traipsed toward the meeting spot as though he had no will of his own, pushed forward by blind duty and guilt—annoying character flaws he had inherited at birth, most likely from his father. They were as much a part of him as his knobby knees and curling toes. What really bothered him was knowing that, at this very moment, he could be—no, should be—on a ship to the Southern Isles to live out his days in comfort and tranquility. He had sufficient resources to pamper himself and to pay others for their silence and protection. He could easily have slipped away last night unseen. Why hadn't he? What had prevented him? *Ah yes, blind duty. And guilt!*

Ruler Two trudged up one last dune leading to the flat terrain that bordered Reception Canyon. The wind blew fiercely here, but the sand was packed hard, bound by small amounts of darker silt and clay. The firmer footing it provided, coupled by its level grade, made walking seem effortless after climbing shifting dunes. He looked to where the ground disappeared two hundred strides ahead, to where it gave way to sky and nothing else. Half the distance there, a small party of figures—he quickly counted nine—stood waiting well back from the canyon's edge. The magister with a nom on either side of him; two more noms stationed by his empty portered chair; Rulers One, Three, Four and Five.

All nine stood facing him, as though participating in some formal ritual. They were somber, serious, clearly anticipating something extraordinary—some act of importance—to transpire. He was not surprised. He had expected something of the sort, though he had hoped his fellow rulers would not be witness to whatever was in store for him.

Their backs were at least twenty paces from the canyon's gaping mouth, where its steep sides dropped until they kissed the riverbank below. He could not see or hear the tributary, but its path was sharply outlined by the serpentine chasm it had cut into the earth, and which stretched for as far as the eye could see in both directions.

What stood out on the near horizon—what seemed out of place and made him wonder, at least momentarily—was a tenth figure standing on the opposite side of the abyss. This was where the canyon was most narrow. Still, the divide between its banks could have swallowed the entire GOT compound whole, and so the figure appeared quite small. It was, nonetheless, unmistakably a person. *Peculiar indeed.*

Ruler Two returned his attention to those watching his approach. He was close enough now to notice that none of his fellow rulers wore their hood. This, too, was most unusual; it was forbidden to wear one's shabba in the presence of the magister without one's hood pulled fully over one's head. And in the presence of a searing sun, no less! This had to be the magister's doing. No doubt the old scarecrow wanted to ensure they could not shield their eyes from whatever was about to happen. The thought sent a parade of tiny prickles up his neck.

And what was he to do before he met his fate? Raise his hood in deference to the magister, or leave it down like all the others?

He decided it was best to leave it where it was. He most certainly could not displease the magister any more than he already had.

Perhaps the magister would simply dress him down; strip him of his title, banish him from The Guild, and make an example of him. *Wishful thinking!* Leniency was a concept unfamiliar to the magister.

Though standing well away from the canyon's precipitous edge, the nine watching him were not entirely out of harm's way, were they? Winds were known to race across the Lawless Lands at breakneck speed. Winds powerful enough to rip most wooden structures into splinters, or catapult entire herds of sheep from one kingdom to another. And already it was gathering a good head of steam.

Might he not call upon the wind to be his friend this day? Was that too preposterous a thought? *Come now, friend. Just one brief demonstration of your strength... Just one good blow should be enough to sweep them all away! Quickly now, before I reach their sides!*

Instead, the winds that stirred the magister's robe stopped almost altogether. All at once, it seemed, and for no apparent reason other than to underscore the fact that Ruler Two really had no friends at all.

His gaze fell on Ruler Five as he neared the waiting party. He did not know what he was looking for. A nod of understanding, perhaps. A sympathetic shrug would have been nice. But Five stood no different from the noms: silent, impassive, seemingly disinterested and disengaged from the proceedings. Ruler Four looked much the same.

The only signs of emotion came from Rulers One and Three. But it was not sympathy he saw. Ruler One appeared most uncomfortable, his expression pained, his eyes wide with apprehension, his jowls quivering slightly. Tiny beads of sweat littered his brow. The folds of his shabba shuddered even in the still air.

And the owl, perched there on the ground, her big eyes sharp and clear, taking it all in, poised to take flight the instant something went awry. He imagined she alone would survive if a sudden gust of wind did happen along. Unless, of course, Ruler Five was quick enough to hop upon her back and weigh her down. That would be just like him.

"Self-governance for all of Baelon," said the Magister. "This is what you proffered on the day of reckoning."

"Yes, Magister."

"Yet we are no closer to that end than on the day you called for a moratorium. Am I mistaken?"

"No, Magister."

"Why is that? One king dead by now—that was your assurance, was it not? What happened, Ruler Two?"

There was no good answer, so he did not offer one.

"Would you have me believe King Axil still rules Aranox because one woman saw you coming—not once, but twice?" The magister exhaled sharply through his nose. "One woman! Twice!"

Ruler Two looked instinctively to Five. The best response would come from him, but Five refused to even look his way. The man stood motionless, as still as a rock, hoping perhaps to go unnoticed. His hands were clasped behind his back. Even his gleaming white teeth remained concealed. Ruler Five did not know the meaning of the word guilt. Nor had he been saddled with a sense of duty. No, his parents had endowed him with a strong dose of aggression, fortified with an equal measure of self-preservation. *Lucky ballsack!*

But then the magister's focus was squarely back on him, and him alone.

"What did I tell you, Ruler Two?" said the elder. "I can abide disappointment, but not concern. What did I tell you about concern?"

Ruler Two swallowed hard and gently closed his eyes. "All cause for concern must be eliminated."

"Precisely," said the magister, raising one arm high into the sky.

Shhh-whap! It sounded like a wet towel slapped against stone. Then silence. Then a gasping, wheezing sound as Ruler Five clutched at the shaft of an arrow buried in his neck.

Even as he swayed there, teetering, he was spoken to by the magister. "Your assassin missed the king from fifty strides. That arrow in your windpipe traveled one hundred. In the wind, no less! And the watchers of The Guild are mine, not yours! It was silly to think otherwise."

The magister turned to Rulers One and Three. "General business is concluded!"

Schuffling across the hard-packed sand, he brought his face so close to Ruler Two's that the stench of his breath was as disturbing as his words. "My eyes are clouded by age, but still I see more clearly than you. Yours are completely blinded by assumptions. You must work on that." The magister's outstretched arms were immediately supported by two noms, who guided him to his chair.

It was all Ruler Two could do to get his jaw and lips to move. "Yes, Magister." He glanced back to the place where Five lay crumpled and unmoving, then to the opposite side of the canyon. The mysterious figure there had vanished.

"And fix your hood!" the magister said. "Your cheeks begin to burn!"

THE END OF THE BEGINNING

"Why do we wish so hard for happy endings? Where is there to go from there?" Princess Lewen, age 9, reading bedtime stories with her mother, Queen Isadora.

King Tygre of Tegan

King Tygre had made it clear he was not to be disturbed. Secluded in his study—eyes closed, chin resting on his chest, his breathing deep and measured—he allowed his restless mind to wander back in time.

Three small children running through a field of waist-high thredgrass that hid them when they crouched. "Tygre! Axil!" a little girl with hair of gold cried out. The boys held their breaths. Even suppressed laughter would give away their whereabouts. "Show yourselves! Show yourselves and be discovered! Tygre!" The little girl stomped the ground with a tiny boot. "Axil!"

How quickly the almons had flown!

Three young adults lying on their backs beneath the stars, each creating constellations that were anything but obvious. "Can you not see it?" asked an exasperated Isadora. She thrust an arm toward the sky, pointing to a million blinking lights. "There! Right there!" The young men's giggles spurred her on. "A dancing lamb! On its hind legs!" There was nothing in the sky resembling anything close to that. The boys writhed on the ground, howling with glee.

He remembered it so very well, because when Isadora's arm had returned to earth, her hand had found his, and their fingers had interlocked.

Those were days of glorious innocence and a future filled with promise, before either he or Axil was fitted for a crown. Before either knew the true burdens of a king.

What a naïve young man he had been. Caught up in his own world of make-believe. He had not even noticed the blossoming of love between his best friends. It had not dawned on him until he'd seen them for the first time in each other's arms beneath the moon. But when Isadora had returned Axil's kiss fervently and with abandon, it had nearly killed him, and his heart had never beat the same.

He had not seen them since. They had married shortly after, in his absence. King Axil of Aranox and his queen, Isadora. They had conceived a child he had never met—a girl, Princess Lewen, taken from them cruelly when she was just eighteen. And Isadora, who had always given her heart fully, had chosen not to live without her daughter.

King Tygre rubbed his temples.

He was wiser now—at least he liked to think so—still paralyzed at times by thoughts of what might have come to pass had he learned sooner how to nourish friendship. If only he had done the right things, said the right words at the right times. How foolish he had been.

Someone had tried to slay King Axil. "Long live King Tygre!" had been their battle cry. This was not disputed. He had sent word to his old friend, vehemently denying any involvement or ill will toward him, but after twenty almon's silence, how had that been received?

It was a half moon since Marshal Ademar had delivered his message, condemning any act of violence toward the house of Aranox. King Axil had not read his message in the marshal's presence, but had promised to respond.

Since then, during Fostead's celebration of Six Moons, another attempt had been made on King Axil's life.

The large envelope on King Tygre's desk had arrived mid-morning, delivered by special courier. The wax seal of Aranox was unmistakable.

He nudged the envelope, pushing one corner then another before picking it up and turning it over.

He slid a letter opener under the flap to sever the seal. He peeled the edges of the parchment back and laid them flat, revealing a smaller envelope and a white handkerchief. Beneath them was penned a short message.

He lifted the silk kerchief, his fingers trembling slightly as he read:

A keepsake.

From when we three were together.

She would want you to have it.

In Friendship,

Axil

On the smaller envelope were the words: *An Invitation.*

King Tygre brought the kerchief to his face, breathed deeply to inhale its scent, then used his hand to wipe his eyes.

Overseer Reynard Rascall

The ominous beating of drums could be heard even from the dungeon.

Reynard sought to mask the sound with his voice. "When we get out of here, perhaps we should return to a simpler life." Spiro sat beside him, clad in nothing but his undergarments, bruised and beaten nearly beyond recognition. Reynard edged closer to him and reached out to touch his arm. "I mean, these past few days...picking pockets and locks...watching you wield your knives...I haven't felt this alive in years. We'll come back and rob this castle...just you wait and see. We could do that, you know, you and I."

"I've lost the knives you gifted me," said Spiro softly.

Bastards! "No matter. I'll replace them, shall I?"

The beating of drums grew louder. *Did someone just open a door to the outside world?*

"Listen to me, Spiro. Death is nothing to fear. Nothing at all. It is, in fact, the very essence of nothingness. All your senses gone—disappeared. You feel nothing. See nothing. Hear... well, you get my meaning. Death is such an ugly word. We should not use it. We should instead say 'nothing.' He met his 'nothing' on the battlefield. I hope to be quite old when 'nothing' comes for me. You see? Death itself is nothing to fear."

Spiro shook his head. "Makes no sense."

Both men listened as the sound of rhythmic bootsteps joined the drumming.

"It makes nothing but sense," said Reynard, trying to stay calm. "How can you fear nothingness? The manner in which it comes for us...that is all that matters." The bootsteps grew louder, clacking sharply down the dungeon passageway. "I should like to die whilst my knob is gliding up and down some buxom lass' slippery canal, or dreaming of gold sovereigns raining down on me. For you, perhaps, it's fighting dragons with your dagger, or drowning in a bowl of mutton stew. These are the sorts of things you must imagine whilst we are on stage today."

"On stage? Oh, that's rich, that is!" A burly guard laughed, appearing outside their cell. Four soldiers emerged behind him, swords drawn and shouldered. "There's no dragons where you're going, friends. More like a giant blade, dropped from the heavens on your scrawny necks! That's a dream come true for you today!"

"Don't listen to him," said Reynard.

"Oh, that's right. Listen to this one." The guard scoffed. "And look where that's got ya!" He prepared to put the key in the padlock. "Show me your hands!"

Taker Brock Haden

Public executions were rare. Those not presided over by the king, less common still. But two in one day, conducted simultaneously in the town square? Unheard of.

There was no place left to stand or sit. Men and women stood pressed against each other like toothpicks in a jar. Children sat on shoulders. Young people climbed stone walls and wooden fences. All were gathered to witness one act of deadly theater that would no doubt be forever remembered and retold a thousand times to future generations.

Brock Haden stood among them, his hands smoothing the tangles of his fiery red hair and bushy beard. "What did they do?" he asked no one in particular. He was genuinely intrigued. He had heard fantastic rumors that could not possibly be true.

"Have you not heard? Killed the queen and princess," said the tall man next to him, "and that was just for starters."

"As if that wasn't enough!" said the woman clinging to his side.

"The list o' them they killed's as long as my arm," said the man.

The woman began rattling off names. "Baron Treadwell's cook, Sarah Waxing, Kole Cantry, some bookkeeper named Leo Bartlett, Bohun Barr, the stablemaster...Jarod Kelter and Timmil Childs from the inn, one of the king's sergeants... those in the warehouse...was that them that done that?" She wrinkled her brow in thought.

"They had the little one locked up before, they did, then lost 'im!" said the man.

"Oh, yes! Thankee, Earl!" the woman said. "Another soldier watchin' 'im, the apothecary...what's 'is name? Gabriel Solomon from The Good Knight's Rest, Peter Terrick from The Raven's Nest." She looked to her husband for assistance.

"Young Alden Neale," he said.

May the gods watch over you, Alden!

"And let's not forget the king's royal guardsman...the one who finally caught 'em!"

"Certainly not!" said the woman. She gave Brock a meaningful look. "They say he's the same one who saved the queen during Six Moons almons ago! Imagine that!"

"Who knows who would've been next if they hadn't caught 'em," the man said.

Brock shuddered to think.

"Oh gods, here we go!" The woman gripped her companion's arm as the expectant crowd stirred.

Brock struggled to see. "What's happening?"

"The prisoners have arrived!" said the tall man. "They're being unloaded from the cart."

"They're gagged, blindfolded, and bound," his wife whispered.

"Up the stairs they go," said the man. "Can you see them now?"

Brock nodded as the prisoners were forced to stand beside the guillotines. Two guards removed their blindfolds, then held them steady, displaying them to a half dozen uniformed soldiers standing on a platform raised even higher above the square. "Those are the king's men," said the woman.

One of the soldiers stepped forward to the platform's edge. "Marshal Carson," whispered the woman.

Murmurs rippled through the square as the marshal withdrew his sword and signaled his permission to proceed.

The prisoners were strapped to the guillotines' bascules, their heads placed inside the lunettes. Two hooded executioners appeared, moving in unison to stand beside their instruments of death. They grasped the levers and waited.

A hush fell over the crowd as Marshal Carson raised his sword. It hung in the air for longer than most could hold their breath, then dropped. The executioners pulled the levers. Two angled blades whistled down their tracks, landing with dull thuds. Severed heads dropped into baskets, eliciting loud cheers, screams, gasps, and sobs. The executioners retrieved the heads and raised them by the hair for all to see.

Marshal Erik Carson

Grain and straw pulverized to powder hung like a fine mist glinting in the sunlight outside the livestock pens. The musty smell of it never failed to remind Carson of his childhood. He shielded his eyes from the sun. It was not every day one saw the King of Aranox without the cragens by his side, traipsing through the mud with pigs and goats. The marshal stopped outside the goat pen to lean against its fence rails.

King Axil acknowledged his presence without bothering to look up. "The piglets and the kids were Lewen's favorites, you know." The monarch rubbed the crease of flesh behind the ear of a young goat. "It's done, is it?"

"It is, m'lord."

"You saw with your own eyes?" The monarch tickled the underside of the kid's muzzle, then straightened, waiting for an answer.

"I did, sire."

King Axil spoke lovingly to the kid nuzzling his knees. "I vowed to witness it myself. We should have executed them on castle grounds, after all."

Not this again! "I think you made the right decision, sire. It was important for the people to put this all behind them."

King Axil snorted. "How long do you intend to keep me isolated from the world, cooped up like these poor animals?"

"Apologies, m'lord, but we can ill afford a third attempt on your life. Until we know for certain who wishes you dead—"

"I'm going to die eventually, you know. I'd rather not have cobwebs and spittle hanging from my lips when that day comes. Better to be remembered for having suffered an assassin's blade."

"Not if I can help it, m'lord."

"Ah, finally the truth! It's all about your reputation, is it?" King Axil cinched his robe around his waist before exiting the goat pen.

"It was a proper finish," said Carson with an air of finality.

"It was a good start," said the monarch grimly, sauntering across the bailey.

Carson followed. "A good start? Those who showed your daughter to death's door have been dealt with. All six were slain by Rolft Aerns. The two we just beheaded swore they had no hand in it, but the ledger they carried suggested otherwise. It confirmed what the keepers of The King's Inn and The Raven's Nest told Rolft. They all worked together. Regardless, these last two were responsible for several of Fostead's murders. We're sure of that. Are you not relieved?"

"All were members of the Taker's Guild, were they not?" The king shot the marshal a stern look. "It has grown too large, too bold, and I have been too tolerant of a scourge that preys upon my people—my own flesh and blood among them. No, I am not relieved. We have work to do."

Understood! "We shall cleanse the city of them all, sire."

"This snake slithers all across Baelon, Erik. It makes both kingdoms home now, coming and going as it pleases. Removing its scales from Fostead will not suffice. It knows how to shed its skin. There is but one way to kill a snake. I would have its head. I would destroy The Guild's High Order."

How do I remind a king of what he clearly knows? "We can stop its forays into Aranox, m'lord, and Tegan as well if King Tygre will join our cause, but the Guild of Takers' den—The Hidor—it lies deep within the Lawless Lands. We have no jurisdiction there."

"Juris-what?" The king stopped walking. "Give me your sword."

"What?"

"Give me your sword!"

Carson slowly withdrew his blade, handing its hilt to the monarch.

King Axil dragged its point across the ground between himself and the marshal. "Is this what you refer to? Some silly mark in the dirt?" He erased the line with the toe of his boot, then stepped across the remaining smudge. He was still broad-shouldered and a half head taller than the marshal. "What kind of king would let himself be bound by that?"

Carson was met by Major Stronghart just inside the castle gates. "The guards were uncertain," the major told him. "She's more'n likely a loonster, but I dared not turn her away. Thought you'd want a look, if not a word."

Carson's eyes roved the wagon outside the castle, coming to rest on its two occupants. The driver was a spindly young man dressed in black from head to toe, clean-shaven with rosy cheeks. His passenger—a veiled old woman—sat beside him, huddled beneath a long black shawl that covered her like a collapsed tent.

Carson strode to the driver's side of the wagon. "What brings you to the castle, lad?"

"His business here is the same as elsewhere," the passenger said from beneath her garb. "Leave him be. I've come to visit Mari Dunn."

Carson studied the woman more closely. "She's not entertaining visitors, madam."

"I'm not here to be entertained, child. I'm here to help."

Carson smiled. It had been a long time since anyone had called him that.

"Thank you, madam, but she is under the physician's care. No visitors."

"Physician!" The old woman snorted disdainfully. She nodded curtly in the direction of Major Stronghart and two castle sentries. "How many of you does it take to look us over? Who must I speak with to be let inside?"

Carson stepped closer, placing a hand on the wagon to gain the old woman's attention. "It is I who shall decide whether you enter, madam, and that is all that should concern you."

The woman pulled back her shawl, then lifted her veil to stare at him with piercing gray eyes. "Very well. Madam Dunn has twice now saved King Axil's life, yet she lies dying within your castle. Your physician speeds her death. I should think that would concern you."

So sure of herself! "You know something the palace physician does not, do you?"

The old woman scoffed. "Who seeks your king's death? I know something you do not as well. Take me to Mari Dunn and I shall share it with you."

Are you baiting me? "Why do you take such interest? Who is she to you?"

"I brought her into this world."

Carson took a moment to regroup. "You're Madam Dunn's mother?"

"No, child. Her mother died giving birth. I was at her bedside."

"If that were true…"

"She has a mole on her left behind. A small scar on her right where I marked her. Go on! See for yourself. But be quick about it—you're wasting time!"

Sibil Dunn

Her mother had been moved from the infirmary two suns ago, purportedly to recuperate in more pleasant surroundings. But Sibil knew the truth. The physician had tried everything to no avail. Her mother had not regained consciousness since being grazed by a poisoned arrow. The color was gone from her face. Her hands and feet were cold, the rise and fall of her chest nearly indiscernible. There was little life left in her. She was not "recuperating." She had been moved so that she might die in the comforts of The Nest.

"Don't move unless I ask you to," said Marshal Carson. "Stay still and watch. If you recognize the woman who enters, touch my shoulder."

What? Sibil was too confused to object. She had abandoned her training with Sergeant Cogswell at the marshal's insistence, then hurried after him. She caught her breath as he positioned her in the dimly lit corner of the room closest to where her mother lay. "What woman?" she whispered.

The marshal turned his back on her as the door to the room eased open. Major Stronghart appeared carrying a lantern, followed by a much shorter figure cloaked in black. The two moved slowly to the opposite side of her mother's bed.

Sibil shifted her position to see past the marshal's frame, but the woman's identity—if indeed it was a woman—remained concealed by flickering shadows and a veil.

Major Stronghart raised the lantern to light her mother's face.

"How long has she been like this?" The old woman's cackle was unfamiliar. "Five days, is it?"

"Since the celebration of Six Moons, yes," said Major Stronghart.

The old woman lifted her veil. Sibil shook her head as Marshal Carson turned slightly toward her. *I've never seen her before!* The woman placed a large leather pouch on the bed, pulling its drawstrings open.

"What is that?" asked the marshal. "What are you doing?" He approached the side of the bed opposite the old woman. Holding the lantern higher, Major Stronghart moved his free hand toward the pouch, but the woman dumped its contents onto the bed before he could stop her.

"She's at death's door. If nothing more is done, she shall surely pass before the next sun rises." The crone glared at the marshal. "Are you worried I might make matters worse? Would you have me leave?"

"What do you intend to do?" asked the marshal.

"Did you ask the same of your physician?" The woman sorted through her items. "Was it helpful?" She picked up a small bottle, uncorked and tilted it, moistening the tip of her little finger with its contents. "Can you hear me, Mari? Can you, child? If so, you must let this pass your lips." The old woman worked her finger gently into Mari's mouth. "Let it touch your tongue... that's right! Try to swallow, child. Can you?"

Sibil stood transfixed. Was this a charlatan? Her mother's savior or murderer?

"Remove the dressing from her shoulder," said the old woman. The marshal appeared to weigh his options. "Would you rather see her dead? Do it!"

Major Stronghart adjusted the lantern's position as the marshal peeled back her mother's bandages. Sibil watched the old woman sort several items on the bed, then sprinkle some sort of dust on her mother's exposed wound. "Now these." The woman handed the marshal something else. "Press them firmly onto her skin. Have it wrapped. Do you think your physician can manage that?"

"Will this draw the poison out?" asked the marshal.

"It's far too late for that, but this may counteract it. Time will tell." The old woman stuffed the items remaining on the bed back into her pouch, pulling its drawstrings closed.

"Might I ask what we've administered?" asked the marshal.

"I think you know. Sap, ground bark, leaves... it's all from the same tree."

"Euphoria," whispered the marshal.

Sibil gasped, recalling her dream from the night before Six Moons: her mother on a ceiling made of leaves and branches, purple flowers pouring from her mouth. And an old woman rocking a baby's cradle at the base of a large tree. *"If only you could see what she can see from there."*

Sibil held her breath as the old woman stared through the dark in her direction.

"Ahhh," said the crone with delight. "And who, might I ask, do we have here?"

Sibil entered the palace library on the heels of the old woman, examining her closely—her dusty garb, her hobbling gait, the strands of brittle gray hair visible beneath the back of her black shawl—for anything that might spark a memory. But there was nothing. She had no idea what to expect, no clue as to why the woman wished to speak with her or why the marshal thought this was a good idea. She waited for the old woman to take a seat before lowering herself into an adjacent chair, thankful for the thick upholstered armrests that separated them. She was thankful, too, that Marshal Carson did not abandon her. He shut the library door and leaned casually against a wall of books, far enough away to provide the two women a sense of privacy, but close enough to make his presence felt.

Sibil folded her arms across her chest. She was not going to be the first to speak.

"Men," the old woman said dismissively, glancing back at Marshal Carson. "Give them a task and some are capable enough, but don't ask them to think...someone's bound to get hurt." She took note of Sibil's expression. "You're too young, perhaps, to have discovered that as yet."

Sibil remained silent. "You're Sibil Dunn?" asked the woman. "Mari Dunn's daughter?"

"I am."

"You know what your mother is capable of?"

Sibil hesitated. "They say she sees the future."

"They say. You don't believe it?"

"I'm not sure."

"Seeing shadows is not proof enough something exists, is that it? It needs to bite you, does it, before you will believe it?"

Sibil chose not to answer.

"What do you know about the birth of your mother?"

"My grandmother died giving birth to her."

"True. That's all you know?"

"What else is there?"

"Your grandmother was partial to euphoria. Did you know that?"

"Of course not!" The distribution of euphoria was strictly controlled by the realm. It was not available to the masses, at least not legally. "I don't believe you."

"More shadows, eh? You mustn't be afraid of them, child. Simple facts from the past...they cannot hurt you, only help. Your grandmother became too fond of it. When she bore your mother, there were complications. Nothing unusual. We gave her euphoria to help her bear the pain. We had no way of knowing her blood was rich with it already. Had she not been soaked in it, she might be alive today."

"Why are you telling me this?"

"You and your mother share the same bloodline."

"What's that supposed to mean?"

"A certain amount of euphoria...there's no telling how much...runs through your mother's veins."

Sibil stared at the blood vessels criss-crossing the back of her hands.

"That's right," said the crone. "Have you never tasted it?"

"Of course not!"

"Have you seen nothing of the future yourself, child? No visions that have come to pass? No dreams that have come true?" Sibil tried to repress her recollection of the dream involving an old woman with her mother spewing petals of euphoria from a treetop, but she could not and the old crone's eyebrows rose as though she too was seeing it.

"Mmm. As I thought. Be careful with euphoria, child. It's already made your acquaintance, but that doesn't mean it likes you. You can never be too sure. Small doses when you dare."

Sibil tried to bar the woman from her thoughts by concentrating on her upturned veil. *Foolish! She cannot read my mind, can she?*

The old woman fished a small card from the depths of her cloak and handed it to Sibil. "Stay seated, child. I have business with the human statue there. If ever you're in need, come find us."

In need of what? Find you where? Sibil inspected the card, turning it twice to find it devoid of any writing. There was only what appeared to be a wax seal the size of a thumbprint on one side. It was embossed in the shape of a heart.

"The Wisperal," said the old woman unexpectedly.

How does she know of that?

"Why do they call you that, I wonder?"

"It's nothing but the squires making fun of me."

"Is it?" asked the crone, placing both hands atop her gnarled and knotted cane before shifting her weight forward and rising. "Is it?"

Marshal Erik Carson

Carson escorted the old woman to her wagon just outside the castle, where her young driver had been made to bide his time. He saw her somewhat differently now.

There was only one grove of euphoria in all of Baelon. Its produce was strictly regulated by both realms and dispensed only to physicians.

But the Sisters of Systalene—a mysterious sect of women living in the Lumax mountains—were widely known for their adulation and illicit possession of the substance. He had never given them much thought; they were crazy but harmless, and kept mostly to themselves. They were said to worship life above all else, and so although they had little use for men, they were known to wander untouched amidst the aftermath of bloody battles, administering to the wounded on both sides. For this reason, it was thought, King Axil turned a blind eye to their procurement of euphoria.

Carson placed a hand on the old woman's shoulder, a gentle reminder of her promise to divulge something she knew about the attempts on King Axil's life. Or had that been a simple ruse to gain entrance to the castle?

"The Takers Guild seeks the death of your king," she said bluntly.

Carson flinched. "What proof have you of that?"

"Only the word of a dying man. It isn't much, is it?"

"Please explain."

"Explain why most men can't be trusted, or...?"

"No." This would be a test of his patience. "Please elaborate. What dying man? What did he say?"

"On the day that someone tried to end King Axil's life, my sisters were called to the bedside of a wounded man. He had an arrow tip buried deep inside his chest, the shaft of the arrow broken off beneath his shoulder blade. He could not hide the mark of an assassin on the soles of his feet, nor the fact that he lay dying in the vicinity of the king's attempted murder. He dared not summon his brethren, for fear that they would finish him to secure his silence." The old woman smiled mischievously. "Who else was he to call—the palace physician? My sisters did what they could do; they bathed him, tried to cool his fever, calm his shaking. They gave him sufficient euphoria to ease his pain, but still he spent his last breaths ranting while unconscious, screaming his confession, flailing his arms and legs so wildly that he had to be restrained."

You're either incredibly unreliable or especially trustworthy. "What did he say?"

"Of interest to you? He claimed that he was sent to kill King Axil...commissioned by the Takers Guild. His poisoned arrow found instead a woman. A woman who could see into the future. Soldiers shot him as he fled."

Carson eyed her steadily. The assassin's use of a poisoned arrow was not common knowledge, nor was the fact that one of his soldiers thought he had wounded the assailant.

"And yet you saw no cause to inform the castle?"

"The Sisters do not share confessions, nor do we involve ourselves in feuds or politics. Tell me, does our refusal to play your silly games destroy our credibility? The poison the assassin carried was siplence."

Carson raised an eyebrow. The palace physician had suspected siplence was to blame for Madam Dunn's condition.

"The Systalene cannot see into the future, child. We possess no special powers. But we are devoted to our faith, the love of life and healing. And we know more about the properties of euphoria than those your kingdom pays to manage it. And so we are given passage to places others are denied. People talk, and the Systalene listen. We hear things. How else would I know that the men who tied Princess Lewen to her horse planned to rob the royal retreat at Dewhurst? Or that the same men—members of the Takers Guild—killed both a baron's cook and a bookkeeper the same day as your feast. Or that they planned next to rob this very castle?"

Carson was speechless.

"You may wish to discount the ravings of a dying assassin. You can choose to disbelieve the story of an ancient Systalene. But we hear things, child. This much is true, I assure you."

Regret! Oh, to bring the man with the scar and his associate back to life so that he could further interrogate them! He had not even thought to link them to the king's attempted murder. The Guild had caused the queen and princess's deaths. Perhaps it also sought to kill the king before he could make that connection. It made sense, did it not?

"I should like to see Madam Dunn each day for the next half moon," said the woman. "What must I give to be allowed that privilege?" She flashed a wrinkled smile and teased. "Perhaps you'd like to know who killed your steward?"

She can't know that! Can she? Carson glanced back at the castle sentries, his head beginning to spin. "Whisper that name to me, and you shall be allowed to tend to Madam Dunn for as long as it proves beneficial." He lowered his face to hers, adding, "But on one condition only, Madam..."

Sibil Dunn

The castle chapel boasted ample space for Sunday services, but it could not accommodate all those seeking entrance on this day. Filled to capacity with nobility, knights, army officers, and high-ranking castle staff, its front doors were left open as a symbolic gesture of inclusion to the large crowd gathered outside.

Sibil sat on a small patch of grass, listening below an open window on the building's west side. When she had arrived, few others had been in sight. Now she could not see through the mass of bodies gathered near her. Knees pulled to her chest, eyes closed, she envisioned what was transpiring inside.

Harpists and flautists played light and cheery tunes. Displays of pomp adorned the chapel's interior. A rich array of flowers crowded the choir space. The banner of each house loyal to the king hung from the rafters. On opposite sides of the raised altar sat Marshal Carson and the palace chaplain. Between them, in place of the chaplain's lectern, a vacant throne drew its share of attention. Twenty-three squires on one knee, and with heads bowed toward that empty seat, awaited their reward for almons of sacrifice and training...and for promising a lifetime of devotion to the crown. The knights they served stood solemnly behind them.

When the music stopped, utter silence followed. Sibil pictured King Axil on the altar, his hands raised in the air. She recognized the monarch's voice, though his words were unintelligible. His speech was short and punctuated by the blare of trumpets.

Sibil's pulse quickened.

"Squire Bartholomew Bixby!" It was the king's voice again, louder and emphatic. Sibil pictured the young squire being knighted, then rising, his world changed forever.

"Squire Ansel Dreddit!" It came sooner than Sibil expected. She hastened the pace of the knighting ritual running through her head.

"Squire Timothy Earl!"

"Squire Reginald Everard!"

Sibil bit her lip as she listened in anticipation for the next name to be called.

"Squire Tristan Godfrey!" Mixed emotions welled in her as she imagined Sir Garr tapping Tristan on the shoulder with his sword, both parents of the squire looking on with pride. There were two Sir Godfreys now! How she longed to speak with him!

Murmurs rippled through the well-informed assemblage. It would have been Theos entering knighthood next, if only he had not... Sibil wiped a lone tear from the corner of one eye before it could encourage others. She pictured him watching the ceremony from Baelon above, an irreverent smirk betraying his opinion of those who took themselves too seriously.

"Squire Theos Godfrey!" The king's stentorian voice sent shivers up Sibil's spine. This was unexpected. The crowd turned deathly quiet. Was Sir Kraven administering the posthumous honor, father of the departed standing silent and bereft? She could still hear Sir Godfrey, long ago berating both boys for losing control while training. "*Why do you seek to harm each other? Neither of you will ever be whole without the other! Never forget that!*" And what of Mrs. Godfrey? How heart-wrenching must this be for her? It was unimaginable.

Before too long, the harps and flutes sang out again, and the king's voice ceased to tumble out the chapel windows. The throng surrounding Sibil began to stir and swell as those inside the building slowly made their exit. She rose and shuffled her way through the throng, all the while surveying the heads of those streaming out the chapel doors. She waited, watching until the stream became a trickle, then moved close enough to peer inside. Two dozen figures remained: the king, Marshal Carson, members of the orchestra, newly knighted squires celebrating with friends and family...but no sign of Tristan.

How did I miss him? Sibil rounded the chapel to find Fereliss, Garth, and Yurik loitering outside its rear entrance, presumably awaiting the king's exit. "They earn their title, to be sure," Fereliss told his companions. "But it does not make them better than us." He held his tongue as a seasoned knight hurried past. "Well, better dressed, perhaps," he said begrudgingly, watching the warrior stride away.

"Better paid, without a doubt," said Garth.

"Better groomed as well," said Yurik.

Garth nodded in agreement. "In truth, might they not be better—"

"Enough!" Fereliss shouted.

Garth looked sheepishly at him. "But they—"

Fereliss held a finger up in warning. "Better not!"

Sibil cleared her voice.

"Ah! Miss Dunn!" said a surprised Garth.

"Isn't that a wonder?" asked Yurik, his brow wrinkling as he looked to Fereliss. "He might've waited just a bit and seen to it himself, don't you think?"

"I think his mind is elsewhere still," Fereliss said, rubbing his jaw.

"Whatever are you talking about?" asked Sibil.

"Squire Godfrey," said Fereliss.

"*Sir* Godfrey!" Garth said.

"Ah, yes, *Sir* Godfrey...Tristan, that is. He asked that you be given this." Fereliss reached into the space between his shirt and his sheepskin coat to withdraw an envelope. He offered it to Sibil.

"Wait," said Garth.

Sibil eyed the envelope—plain parchment with some writing on it.

"Are you certain the time is right?" Garth asked. "I thought he said—"

"Of course I am!" Fereliss thrust the envelope forward. "It's meant for you, lass."

Sibil took it cautiously, a lump growing in her throat. She had already glimpsed its outer message:

FOR SIBIL, SHOULD I NOT RETURN.

Sergeant Cogswell sat on a low stool, splicing two pieces of braided rope together. His hair, both crown and beard, appeared longer than usual. It looked as though he had donned a helmet of gray fur.

"You sent for me?" Sibil asked as she approached.

The sergeant-at-arms did not look up. "Is it not noon?"

Sibil raised a hand to her bandaged shoulder. "But I thought..."

"What? That you would not train whilst wounded?" Cogswell pointed at her with the rope. "Do you think that scratch would keep your enemies from striking?"

"Of course not."

"Yet it keeps you from preparing for them?"

Remorse wrinkled Sibil's face.

"Unless you're sick or dying, lass, we meet at noon. Every day. Without fail. When your body is unable, we shall train the mind." He pushed a stool toward her with his foot. Sibil lowered herself onto it. "Tell me, which weapon do you value most? Left with only one, which would you choose?"

"The dagger," Sibil said without hesitation.

"Mmm. I thought as much." Cogswell set the rope aside and began to wipe the blade of a wooden sword with an oiled cloth. "Is that as it should be?"

Sibil sensed a trap. "Surely it is not the sword."

Cogswell laughed loudly. "Surely it is not! Nor will it ever be!"

"What then?"

"I've already told you, lass. Your mind! It should be the weapon you depend on most; the one you keep the sharpest, and the one you are most skilled at using. Yet based on what you've shown me, you have little use for it."

Sibil was speechless.

The sergeant motioned again toward her shoulder. "Tell me why that happened."

Sibil thought back. "Rolft was injured. I tried to help him. I went after his attacker."

"I didn't ask how it happened, lass. I asked why."

"He was too quick for me."

"The little one they called the cat? It's possible, I suppose. He didn't get that name standing still. I was not there, of course, nor have I a witness to rely on."

"You don't believe me?" A hint of anger crept into Sibil's voice. "My word's not good enough?"

Cogswell's steely gray eyes did not waver. "I don't doubt that he was quick. But too quick for you? As I say, it's possible. Yet I have watched thousands on the battlefield and on this training ground, and I tell you, it's unlikely. Think again. Why are you wounded?"

Sibil closed her eyes to help her recall. She frowned. "I was too reckless. My attack, too careless."

"Ahhh. Did you have a plan? Consider your defenses? Were you thinking clearly?"

"No."

"Just rushed in with your heart?"

"Yes."

"Far easier to believe. Do you remember what I told you, the day you first fought here?" Sibil shook her head. "If you learn how and when to harness that speed of yours, you'll be dangerous indeed. You're quicker than you know. If you do not learn to bridle it, your speed may be the death of you." Cogswell pointed to her shoulder. "That might as well have been your heart!"

Sibil nodded slowly.

"So tell me, lass. From this day forth, what weapon will you value most?"

The early morning air was moist. It both chilled and invigorated Sibil as she waited expectantly for Sister Mapel to appear. When the door to The God of Children's House opened to reveal Father Syrus, she smiled with delight. "Good day to you, Father!"

The abbot's brown eyes grew wide. The corners of his mouth rose sharply, disappearing into shiny cheeks. "Good day to you, Miss Dunn! To what do we owe this honor?"

Sibil offered him a bouquet of flowers. His chubby hand grazed hers as he accepted them.

"You've been quite busy, I'm told. Riding with the royal guard and battling giants—or so the stories go. You must tell me all about it—in your own words."

"I really wouldn't know where to start, Father. I'm not even sure I'm free to say."

Father Syrus leaned forward and whispered good-naturedly. "If you cannot tell a servant of the gods, child, who can you tell?"

Sibil could not hide her excitement. "I've been asked to stay at the castle! I think I'm free to tell you that! To live there if I choose!"

"Have you now? I say! That is something. I'll tell you what—the kingdom will be better for it." Father Syrus brought the bouquet of flowers to his nose. "And your mother? There's been improvement, has there?"

"There has. Her eyes have yet to open and her limbs are still at rest, but her color is back, and she's been taking broth. She swallows on her own. What do you make of that, Father?"

"I can't say I know what to make of that, but it's progress, to be sure."

"And her feet, of course. They're much better now, thanks to you and cobbler Nash. Oh! I must bring him flowers as well." Sibil looked disconsolate.

Father Syrus smiled. "Why not bring him these? He would be most pleased, I am sure of it. And if you were to return with mine another day instead—well, that would give me something to look forward to." He handed the bouquet back to Sibil.

Sibil faltered, then suddenly brightened. "Oh! I almost forgot. I've something else for you. Look, Father." She fished the metal amulet from beneath her waistcoat. "Look what I've brought for you!" She proffered it to the abbot.

He chuckled as his fingers wrapped around it. "My, my! This is most unexpected. I'd given up on seeing this again. Where did you find it?"

"It's too long a story, Father, and you wouldn't believe it if I told you."

"Oh, wouldn't I? I may be growing old and fat, but I do still get around. My visits to the parish and the castle keep me well informed. You might be the one surprised at what I've heard these past few days. Here. You need this more than I." Father Syrus handed the amulet back to Sibil. "You've read the inscription, no doubt. 'Protector of Innocence.' Do you really think happenstance brought you to our door? It suits you, child. Wear it in good health. And promise you will not be a stranger."

Sibil crossed the infirmary floor as quickly as she could, jostling for position with the guardsmen.

A stout nurse blocked their way, threatening them with her finger. "Oi!" she shouted. "Marshal Carson'll have your heads!" Garth pulled up in front of her, his arms spread wide to stay his trailing companions.

"The fever's broke," the nurse told them curtly. "But he still needs his rest. A short visit—that's all!" She stepped out of their way. "And then I send for the marshal! Or worse, that witch of his with the euphoria!" They rushed to Rolft's bedside.

"Awake at last!" said Garth excitedly.

"We thought perhaps you'd entered your last sleep," Yurik said.

"How long?" whispered Rolft.

"A quarter moon," said Fereliss, visibly shocked by Rolft's gaunt appearance. "With nothing save broth past your lips. Were it not for all your scars and stitches, we wouldn't know ya!"

"What about the little man who put me here?"

"Even more wee now," said Garth.

"Gone to meet the gods below," said Fereliss. "He and his partner with the scar. Both lost their heads." The edge of his hand simulated a falling blade.

"You watched them die?" whispered Rolft.

"We did."

Rolft smiled wanly. "I've the strength of a child."

"Oh, really? That's not what they say outside these walls," Fereliss said. "You captured both with just your hands, the story goes. Laid down your sword to challenge them! And Thistle, here...or should I say, The Wisperal...she spilled their blood. Folks say she would've killed the wee one had you not stopped her!"

"'Tis true." Rolft chuckled softly until he choked.

"It wasn't like they tell it," said Sibil. "You had the wee man pinned."

"But if your attack had not distracted him..." said Rolft.

"Pfft! He nearly killed me!" said Sibil. "Yours was the bravest act I—"

"Stop! The two of you remind me of my sisters," said Fereliss in disgust. "'You are much prettier than I,' says one. 'Oh, no,' says the other, 'certainly not. You're the more beautiful, to be sure!'"

"No doubt you're prettier than both," Sibil said.

"He is, indeed. I've seen them," said Garth matter-of-factly.

"Sent us on a wild goose chase, and kept them to yourselves, you did!" said Fereliss. "How many times must we suffer this?"

"Never again," said Rolft.

"Same thing you said after the warehouse, if memory serves. This is the last time I let you out of my sight!"

"Swear it," whispered Rolft.

"Me? You swear it!" Fereliss' raised voice drew attention. He lowered it, tilting his head toward those watching from across the room. "How long do you intend to lie there? The nurses tire of your act."

The stout nurse started toward them.

"Here comes trouble," said Yurik.

"Did you want some fresh air?" asked Fereliss, laying a hand beneath Rolft's shoulder. Rolft pushed his palms against the bed and attempted to lift his head.

"What? He'll do no such thing!" said Sibil, slapping Fereliss' arm away and laying a hand on Rolft's chest.

The portly nurse accosted them. "That's it, then! Git out! Git out, I say, before ya kill 'im!" She flailed her arms, shooing the guardsmen from the bed. "He's in no state for this! She's the only one of you with any sense! You can stay, lass. Might do 'im some good. The rest of you, git out! Now!"

Fereliss' expression challenged her, but he submitted to Yurik's tugging on his arm, perhaps imagining the marshal's approach. The nurse followed the three guardsmen to the infirmary's door and saw them out.

Sibil held Rolft's hand. "You're going to mend, are you?"

Rolft managed a smile. "He was just a wee man," he whispered.

Sibil laughed and sniffled. "What can I do for you?"

Rolft licked chapped lips. "Perhaps something with more taste than broth?"

"I'll ask the nurse. What else?"

"Sarah?"

"Reggie spoils her. I visit her and Shadow every day."

"I want for nothing more, lass." Rolft closed his eyes.

Sibil eased away, but Rolft's grip on her hand tightened. "You did well, lass. Princess Lewen would be proud. Tell Sarah I'll be coming soon."

THE END

EPILOGUE

"One must be careful practicing deception. The easiest to deceive will always be oneself." From The GOT's Basic Rules of Taking

Overseer Reynard Rascall

R eynard was adrift, floating on a boat made out of clouds. This was the dream world, to be sure. Everything was jumbled, blurry, nondescript, but moving nonetheless. Indistinct voices mumbling in his ear from far away. *Mumbling... from far away? Impossible!* Invisible hands touching him. It made no sense. A sharp prick in an arm that felt unattached to him...how could that be? Numbness in that limb gave way to a warm tingling.

He remembered now...the dungeon... riding bound and gagged in the soldier's cart... placed on display with Spiro in Fostead's central square... waiting to have his head chopped off!

Had that already happened? Was he in Baelon above? Baelon below? Headless?

Someone slapped him lightly. No, his head was still with him! He tried to open his eyes fully, blinking to remove a crusty seal. This was no dream.

He could see the outline of a man's face. Hooded, light-complexioned, thin eyebrows and a smile to match. "Where am I?" he said, trying to look past the man. *Stone walls of... baleonite? Am I in the castle?*

"How do you feel? All right?"

"Where am I?" Reynard asked again. He was lying down. He could feel it now. A soft pillow beneath his head. A musty smell.

"Can you move your fingers? Your toes?"

Reynard tried to do so. It was awkward.

"Well done!" said the man. "You'll be right in no time!"

"Where's Spiro?"

"You're at The Guild of Takers compound. The GOT. You've heard of it, though never been, I'm told. Is that right?"

"The GOT?" Reynard tried to rub his eyes. Again, awkward.

"Most unusual for an Overseer. Do you know your name?"

"Reynard. Reynard Rascall. Overseer Reynard Rascall. And yes, of course I know of the GOT. Who might you be?"

"I'm Ruler Two of the High Order."

The High Order! What in Baelon is going on? "How did I get here? What's happened? Where's Spiro?"

"What's the last thing you remember?"

"Leaving the palace dungeon. Being carted to town square and put on display. An angry mob throwing food at us. But then rocks, despite the guards' best efforts. One must have hit me... knocked me out."

"Not quite. I must confess to throwing a few stones myself. Just for effect, mind you. My aim was true...none made your acquaintance. An assassin in the crowd blew a dart into your skin. Just enough serum to put you out, but for all the world, it did appear as though you'd suffered injury from the rabble."

"What are you talking about?"

"The soldiers guarding you, Reynard. You should have seen their faces." That wisp of a smile again.

"Imagine their surprise when you lost consciousness!" Ruler Two threw his hands into the air. "The sheer terror that befell them! Were you sick? Were you dying? What were they to think? How would they explain this to their king? That you were killed whilst in their custody? That he would not see you die, after all! That they had deprived him of beheading you? Think on it! Thank the seven gods there was a doctor in the crowd!" Ruler Two patted his own chest. "A traveling physician with his infirmary on wheels! A covered wagon where he could treat your wounds. Perhaps revive you for the king's entertainment! How do you think the guards received that gift from the gods? Were they reluctant to let you out of sight? Of course! But did they have a choice? There was not room in my small wagon for them as well as you, and troubled would I be if they had been exposed to those diseases lurking there, to which I was immune for having slept with them so long. What harm could come from loaning you to me, I asked? How could I do worse than reappear with you in a similar condition to that which they had let befall you? Where was I to go that they could not apprehend me? Nonetheless, I let them guard the horses to my wagon as a show of my good faith.

"Thus, you were dragged into my wagon, stripped, and hidden beneath the floor-boards, while I worked to make another look as much like you as possible. Was he a perfect match? Not really. He was the proper height and build. Long dark hair that needed little trimming. We switched your clothes, of course. Added a scar of cheserak paste. From a distance, he was a good reproduction. Up close, well, you'd be surprised what hopeful minds will see. The guards were told the healing salve I had applied would cause sufficient swelling and discoloration to disfigure you a short time. I encouraged them to get a hood over your face—er, your replacement's face—as soon as possible to avoid unnecessary questions or concerns."

It was a lot to take in. Surreal. "Who was he?" asked Reynard.

"No one important. Someone who valued a thousand kingshead for his family more than life itself."

"Where's Spiro?"

A light tapping sound came from elsewhere in the room.

"Ahhh, the time for me to go has come. I leave you in the best of hands." Ruler Two disappeared.

Reynard relaxed his muscles, too tired to argue. He was able to bring his hands to his face and massage his forehead.

"Overseer Rascall," a raspy voice came from behind.

Reynard did his best to swivel his head in that direction, surprised to find he was in the middle of a room much larger than he had thought it to be. And not alone!

A figure in a hooded robe sat between two others standing tall and motionless. The dark behind them masked their faces.

"Ruler Two adds color and spice to everything," said his host, wheezing. "The truth is much more bland. We plucked you from the king's pocket as though you were his purse. Misdirection, sleight of hand, illusion. Simple, really. You've been sleeping for two days now. It will be one more before the drug wears off completely. In the meantime, you will remain a guest in Takers Tower."

Takers Tower! Home of the magister!

"One of my noms will stay with you. If you need something—anything, food, drink, the company of another—all you need do is ask."

"Where's Spiro?"

"Your friend assisted in your rescue. Leaving him with the guards whilst you were replaced allowed them some semblance of order and control; he was their constant reassurance that all was right with their world. They saw you as a pair, not one, and so your friend's unchanged appearance helped assure them all was right with both of you. Any concerns prompted by the appearance of your stand-in would be resolved by a subsequent view of your friend. We could not save you both."

"He's dead?"

"Beheaded by the king's marshal."

An involuntary urge to vomit assailed Reynard. He gagged. "You're certain?"

"We had watchers in place throughout the day. Your friend was never out of sight. The king removed his head."

Reynard's entire body went limp. "What do you want with me?"

"Nothing. Consider this repayment for your service to The Guild. It has been exemplary. Worthy of reward. You are free to leave at any time...to continue as a member of The Guild or to leave this world behind. The choice is yours. Either way, you will not be judged. Get some rest." The magister rose to his feet with the assistance of two aides. "When your body has fully recovered and your mind is clear, we'll talk again. I have a proposition for you."

ACKNOWLEDGEMENTS

Six Moons, Seven Gods would not have been published without the assistance of several supportive souls, chief among them, my wife. Her continued encouragement and belief helped keep me going, even when the finish line seemed out of reach. My sincere thanks to Erin Young for her writing advice and developmental editing, without which I would still be lost in the Wandering Woods; and to Maxine Meyer, who copy edited this work and made me a better writer in the process.

About the Author, and A Humble Request

Robert A. Walker grew up in Northwestern Massachusetts. After graduating college, he packed his scant belongings in a car with rusted-out floorboards and headed west. He's lived in California ever since, and now resides along the Pacific Ocean with his wife and dogs. When not fabricating stories, he can be found roaming local tennis courts or working on a never-ending list of DIY house projects. Information regarding Robert's current writing projects can be found at rawalkerwriting.com. To be added to his mailing list, please contact fairytalepub@gmail.com.

If you enjoyed this book, please consider leaving a review on Amazon and/or Goodreads at:

http://www.amazon.com/review/create-review?&asin=B0CJ5ZG487

It would be greatly appreciated, and all seven gods will smile down on you!